F
Anthony

Anthony, Piers.

Currant events.

CURRANT EVENTS

TOR BOOKS by PIERS ANTHONY

THE XANTH SERIES
Vale of the Vole
Heaven Cent
Man from Mundania
Demons Don't Dream
Harpy Thyme
Geis of the Gargoyle
Roc and a Hard Place
Yon Ill Wind
Faun & Games
Zombie Lover
Xone of Contention
The Dastard
Swell Foop
Up in a Heaval
Cube Route

THE GEODYSSEY SERIES
Isle of Woman
Shame of Man
Hope of Earth
Muse of Art

COLLECTIONS
Alien Plot
Anthonology

NONFICTION
Bio of an Ogre
How Precious Was That While
Letters to Jenny

But What of Earth?
Ghost
Hasan
Prostho Plus
Race Against Time
Shade of the Tree
Steppe
Triple Detente

with Robert E. Margroff

THE DRAGON'S GOLD SERIES
Dragon's Gold
Serpent's Silver
Chimaera's Copper
Orc's Opal
Mouvar's Magic

The E.S.P. Worm
The Ring

with Frances Hall
Pretender

with Richard Gilliam
Tales from the Great Turtle
(Anthology)

with Alfred Tella
The Willing Spirit

with Clifford A. Pickover
Spider Legs

with James Richey and Alan Riggs
Quest for the Fallen Star

with Julie Brady
Dream a Little Dream

with Jo Anne Taeusch
The Secret of Spring

with Ron Leming
The Gutbucket Quest

PIERS ANTHONY

CURRANT EVENTS

A TOM DOHERTY ASSOCIATES BOOK

NEW YORK

CURRANT EVENTS

Copyright © 2004 by Piers Anthony Jacob

This book is printed on acid-free paper.

A Tor Book
Published by Tom Doherty Associates, LLC
175 Fifth Avenue
New York, NY 10010

www.tor.com

Tor® is a registered trademark of Tom Doherty Associates, LLC.

Library of Congress Cataloging-in-Publication Data

Anthony, Piers.
    Currant events / Piers Anthony.—1st Tor ed.
        p. cm. — (Xanth ; #28)
    ISBN 0-765-30407-4
    EAN 978-0765-30407-0
        1. Xanth (Imaginary place)—Fiction. 2. Endangered species—Fiction. 3. Historiography—Fiction. 4. Historians—Fiction. 5. Dragons—Fiction. I. Title.

    PS3551,B73C87 2004
    813'.54—dc22

                                                                                    2004048039

First Edition: October 2004

Printed in the United States of America

0 9 8 7 6 5 4 3 2 1

Contents

CURRANT
EVENTS

1
CLIO

C lio was tidying up her office, as she did every century or so even if it didn't really need it. Dust did tend to collect, along with dried bugs, apple seeds, and lost wisps of fog. Then she paused, which was easy to do during a dull chore like this. There was a volume on the shelf she didn't remember. That was odd, because she had an excellent memory. She had to, to be a competent Muse of History.

She lifted it up, noting the clean spot of shelf beneath it. She blew off the dust and looked at the title. She couldn't quite make it out, so she opened the volume to the title page. That was written in her handwriting, but was somehow blurred. It might be *CURRENT EVENTS,* but could also be *GETTING EVEN*. Neither one made much sense, as she did not handle either contemporary news or revenge plots. Her specialty was history, past and future. The present bored her.

She turned the pages. They had all been filled out, and definitely in her handwriting, but she couldn't read a word of it. She blinked to clear her vision, but it didn't help; every word was fuzzed. The pages might as well have been blank.

She stood there, bemused. How could she have written a volume of history that she herself couldn't read? It didn't make sense. Was she losing her sight?

Alarmed, she set the volume down and picked up the one next to it. That one was clear enough: *PET PEEVE*, with a picture of a disgruntled bird. That was incomplete, because it hadn't happened yet; she was working on it. So she checked the prior volume: *CUBE ROUTE*, which was complete. That was the story of a girl with gumption, and the text was quite clear.

So it wasn't her eyes, which was a relief. It was the volume. What was wrong with it? And why couldn't she remember writing it? How could she be writing the following volume, and remember its details, while being fuzzy on this one?

Fuzzy: her memory of it was as fuzzy as its print. There was definitely something strange here.

She considered for a good three and a half moments. She seemed to have two or more unenviable choices: principally to let the riddle be, or go to Good Magician Humfrey for advice. Humfrey could surely unravel the enigma, but would take obscene pleasure in her predicament. She hated giving him that satisfaction. But she knew the mystery would bug her until it became a downright nuisance.

She sighed. She would stuff her pride into her nonexistent handbag and go to see the Good Magician.

Humfrey's castle was some distance away from the home of the Muses, so Clio got transportation. She walked down Mount Parnassus and out to a babbling brook and spoke to it. "May I have your attention for a moment?"

The brook ceased babbling and formed a swirling eye. It looked at her, recognized her, and formed a mouth. "So good to see you, Muse," it bubbled.

"I need to pay a call on the Good Magician. Do you suppose I could prevail on you to transport me there swiftly?"

"Gladly, Muse. I owe you favors from way back."

That was true, but she hadn't cared to put it that way. "Then I should be obliged if you would run me there now."

The water humped up into a shape like that of a centaur without a human forepart, standing in the riverbed. "Immediately," it agreed. "If I can make it past the fish."

"The fish?"

"Recently there have been so many fish they clog my channel. It has never been this bad before; normally the water dragons eat them."

"The dragons must be off their feed," she said. That was humor; dragons were never off their feed. Still, it was an oddity.

Clio stepped close to the bank, glanced around to be sure no one was watching, then lifted one leg and swung it over the centaur's back. Skirts were not the most convenient clothing for riding, but they were required for her gender and age. She caught hold of the liquid creature's flowing mane and drew herself fully onto it. "I am ready."

The legs of the water horse went into instant motion. It galloped down the riverbed, following its twisting channel. It had to, because it was unable to run anywhere else. But the running water was so swift that it would soon reach the Good Magician's castle regardless of the indirectness of the route.

She looked down through the horse's translucent substance. Sure enough, the channel was packed with fish so thick it was almost solid. She looked across the landscape around the river channel, and saw rabbits in similar number; in places they were like a gray blanket covering the ground. That was another oddity; were the land dragons similarly off their feed?

She looked in the sky, and saw clouds of crows harassing the other flying creatures. Where were the flying dragons? Normally crows were hardly in evidence, because dragons toasted them on sight. Only in Mundania did they really flourish, normally.

Soon they were in sight of the castle. There was a stream access to the moat that enabled the water horse to reach it. In hardly more time than it took to see it, they were there, splashing to a halt.

The moat monster was snoozing, hardly expecting any intrusion from this direction. It lifted its head and gaped menacingly. Then it recognized the visitors, nodded, and returned to its snooze.

"I thank you kindly," Clio said, dismounting. The water horse had stopped beside a steep bank so that her foot could readily reach it. "Your swiftness was a real pleasure."

The horse nodded, dripping with pleasure. Then it galloped back the way it had come. Running water could never pause long, or it lost its definition.

A sad young woman was walking away from the castle, staring at the ground. "What's the matter?" Clio asked. "I'm Clio; maybe I can help."

"I'm Cayla. I came to ask the Good Magician what my talent is, because I haven't found it yet." She twiddled nervously with a wooden twig she carried.

"That's something you usually just have to find out on your own," Clio said. "It's almost impossible to guess."

"Yes, I've tried guessing," Cayla said. "It doesn't work." She twiddled some more; the twig was taking a beating. In fact there were two twigs getting intertwined.

"So did the Good Magician have the Answer for you?"

Cayla burst into tears. "No! I never got to see him. In fact I flunked the first Challenge."

Clio was morbidly curious. "What was it?"

"It was a big square park set on its end. That is, one corner was toward me as I came to it. I thought the challenge was to get in, but when I got in nothing happened. There was a ball flying around in there, but I had no idea what to do with it. I finally gave up." She blew her nose into a handkerchief, then returned to twiddling the twigs.

A square park, set on its end. "A diamond!" Clio said. "A baseball diamond. You weren't supposed to get 'in,' you needed to get an 'out.' By catching the ball."

Cayla looked at her. "I don't understand."

Clio realized that this would be complicated to explain. "It's only a guess." Then she noticed something. The two twigs were not just intertwined, they were knitted together. "Do you knit?"

"Yes, when I have wool."

"Have you tried knitting other things?"

"Of course not. Why would I do that?"

"Look at those twigs."

"Oh, these are nothing. I'm just frustrated and nervous."

"They are knitted together."

Cayla looked. "Why so they are. But I don't have knitting needles."

"Try something else," Clio said. She looked around and found several bricks. She picked two up. "Try these."

"Bricks? That's crazy!" But the girl took them and put them together.

The bricks twisted and merged. They were getting knitted together. "That's your talent," Clio said. "You can knit wood and bricks. Maybe other things. Maybe anything. You'll have to experiment and find out."

"Oh!" Cayla said, thrilled. "So I don't need the Good Magician after all!"

"You don't," Clio agreed, pleased. This was her first personal interaction with a human person in regular Xanth in some time, and she was glad it had been positive.

"Thank you so much! I was so sad; now I'm so happy." Cayla ran on along the path.

Clio walked toward the drawbridge. This was the obvious way to cross the moat, as she didn't wish to get her feet or skirt wet. But as she approached it, it lifted off the bank, being drawn up by its chains.

"Halt!" she cried. "I wish to use you."

The bridge halted.

She arrived at its resting spot. "Now if you will just drop back down to the bank, I shall be happy to set foot on your sturdy surface," she said.

The bridge started to drop, but a chain snarled and it got hung up. It was stuck a small but inconvenient distance above the ground.

Clio considered it, an unbecoming suspicion hovering at the fringe of her awareness. It wasn't like the Good Magician to have flawed mechanisms. Was it possible that this was not a malfunction? That she was being subjected to a Challenge for entry?

No, of course not; she couldn't believe that of her old friend Humfrey. So it must be a rare glitch in the mechanism.

"Hello the castle!" she called. "You appear to have a problem. The drawbridge is stuck."

There was a little shed associated with the near side of the draw-bridge. Now the bridge tender emerged. "Harold the Handyman here. What can I do for you?"

"I am Clio, the Muse of History. I wish to confer with the Good Magician Humfrey, but am unable to cross the moat. Can you fix the connection?"

"Sure, I'll be glad to lend a hand," Handy said, extending his right hand.

She took it. "Excellent. The lines seem to be snarled, so— EEEEEK!" Her scream was a full five E's, and would have been six, had she not run out of breath.

For the man's left hand had just reached around and goosed her right through her skirt.

"Oh, I'm so sorry," Harold said, hastily retreating. "I forgot to warn you. I have two hands."

"I appreciate that," she said somewhat coldly as she rubbed her indignant bottom.

"I mean, they're different. My right hand helps others, but my wrong hand roves. I can't stop them."

She saw his problem. "Perhaps the Good Magician can help you with that problem."

"Maybe, after I complete my year of service."

"I should think he would fix the problem first, to better enable you to perform your service effectively."

"Not exactly. This *is* my service."

"Tending the drawbridge," she agreed.

"No. Being a Challenge."

She gazed at him. "You are a Challenge?"

"That's right. Any querent has to navigate three Challenges before getting into the castle to query the Good Magician. He doesn't like to be bothered by folk who aren't serious."

"I know that. But I'm not a querent; I'm his friend!"

"You're coming to ask his advice."

The hovering suspicion abruptly landed. She was indeed being subjected to the Challenges. That was as outrageous to her mind as was the goose to her bottom. "Well, I never!"

"My right hand should be able to fix the drawbridge," Handy said. "But my wrong hand will interfere. So I have to deal with my hands before I can deal with the problem."

"And I am expected to fathom how to resolve your problem of hands," Clio said. "As the first of my Challenges."

"You catch on quickly," the man agreed.

She was tempted to think an unkind thought about Humfrey, who was definitely not acting in a friendly manner. The very idea that she should be subjected to this process! He deserved to receive a sour piece of her mind. But unkindness was not in her nature, so she realized in half a moment that this was probably a confusion on Humfrey's part, an error. He used water from the Fountain of Youth to prevent himself from aging beyond a hundred years, and perhaps needed to set the mark a bit younger, to prevent senility. She would suggest that to him, as he surely did not want to be confusing his friends with querents.

But first she had to get in to see him. Well, then, there was no help for it but to tackle the three Challenges, preposterous as the situation was.

She looked at Harold the Handyman. So he had a right hand and a wrong hand. Her challenge was to discover a way to nullify the wrong one, so that he could let the right one function. She doubted that any permanent solution was within her power, as she was a Historian, not a Magician, but perhaps there could be a temporary expedient. One that would enable him to function during the interim of his Service to the good Magician.

"I am neither a Magician nor a Doctor," she said. "So I am unable to offer a cure for your condition. But I may have a way to negate enough of its effect to enable you to perform satisfactorily."

"That would be great," Handy said.

"I believe you should identify your hands. The right one can be called Dexter, and the wrong one can be called Sinister. Put labels on them so that all who encounter you will know them well enough to be able to avoid mischief."

"That sounds great," he said. "Forewarned is foreordained."

"Forearmed," she said.

"Whatever." He fetched some sticky labels and a pen. But when his right hand tried to write on them, his wrong hand jerked the paper out from under the pen.

"Let me see if I can do that," Clio said, smiling. She took pen and paper and neatly printed DEXTER and SINISTER. "Now hold out your hands."

Handy's right hand cooperated, and she fastened its label to the back of it. But the wrong hand jerked away, raising a middle finger. A cloudlet of smoke formed around it, suggesting that this was not a nice gesture. It didn't want to be labeled.

She tried to catch it, but it dodged aside, avoiding her. Then she had a naughty idea. She stood straight, half turning away. "Very well, if I can't label you, I will go elsewhere."

The wrong hand couldn't resist. It dived in for another goose. But as it touched her skirt, she slapped the label against it. Now the hand was marked despite itself.

"You got it!" Handy exclaimed.

"Well, I should hope to be able to outsmart a mere hand." She was privately pleased despite the embarrassing touch. She had, as it were, gotten to the bottom of the problem.

The hand was so ashamed of being tricked that it hid behind the man's back. That allowed the right hand to reach up and unsnarl the lines, and the drawbridge dropped to its proper landing. She had navigated the first Challenge.

At the far end of the bridge was a gate with an oddly folded turnstile. In fact it was shaped like the letter W. Clio paused to examine it. If this was a Challenge, its operation was obscure. It was mounted on a post that allowed it to rotate, so that it should be possible to step into one of the indents and circle through to the other side. What was supposed to be so difficult about that? She was not a suspicious woman, but she distrusted this.

Still, there seemed to be no other way to proceed. She stepped into it, put her hand on an end, and pushed. It turned, briefly enclosing her as she passed through the gate, then releasing her on the other side. No problem at all.

She turned to glance back—and saw another woman right behind her. She looked rather familiar. In fact she looked exactly like Clio herself in the mirror. Where had she come from? She had not been on the bridge.

"Get out of my way, witch," the woman snapped.

Clio stepped out of her way, affronted. "Who, if I may be so bold as to ask, are you?"

"Who do you think I am, idiot? I'm your double, Oilc."

"My double! How can that be?"

"Didn't you just pass through the Double-You? What did you think it was going to do, cut you in half? Have you no wit at all?"

There was something about this woman that annoyed Clio, but she restrained her temper lest there be some misunderstanding. "The Double-You? It doubles you?"

"What else, dullard? Why'd you go through it if you didn't want to be doubled?"

This was evidently another Challenge. How was she supposed to deal with this abrasive copy of herself? Now she realized that the woman's name was her own name, backward. And the woman's character was the opposite of her own, in the ways that showed so far. Clio tried always to be polite, moderate, and helpful, while this creature was unpleasant, aggressive, and sarcastic. Still, maybe she was merely on edge because she had suddenly been created. It was best to give her every reasonable chance.

"What is your purpose here?" Clio asked.

"You need to ask, stupid? You've overstayed your visa. I'll be taking over now."

This set Clio back again. "You'll be what?"

Oilc favored her with a withering stare. "I'd better put you out of your misery." She looked around, and saw a stick of wood lying on the ground nearby. She picked it up and advanced on Clio threateningly, brandishing her improvised club.

Clio stepped back. "What in Xanth are you doing?"

Oilc swung the club at her head. Clio ducked aside just in time. Should she use her talent? No, it was probably blocked here, and if not, the other woman might have the same talent, which would greatly complicate things. So she ran to the side and fetched a stick of her own.

Oilc came at her again, swinging. Clio managed to block the blow with her stick, but it was a physical as well as an emotional shock. How could she be engaging in physical combat? That was not her style at all!

"I really don't understand," she said as she retreated. "Why are you attacking me?"

"You really don't get it, do you, moron," Oilc said as she swung again. "There can't be two of us; people would notice. So one of us has to go. So I'll just eliminate you, and then your life is mine. No one will know the difference, and I'll be able to do whatever I want."

"But you have no positive agenda," Clio protested as she awkwardly fended off the attack. "You would quickly make enemies, and leave my reputation in ruins."

"More fun," Oilc agreed, this time aiming for the knees.

"Who would write the Histories of Xanth?" Clio asked, jerking her knees back.

"Who needs to? They're dull, boring, repetitive, and uninteresting, with egregious puns."

That generated some ire. "Who makes any such claim?"

"The critics, jerk. Who else?"

"Nobody else," Clio said with some asperity.

"Anyway, I won't bother writing anything. It'll be a lot more fun to go around messing people up. They deserve it."

Clio realized that she really had to do something about this double. But how could she get rid of the woman without being unconscionably violent? That just wasn't her nature. Which, it seemed, was why it *was* Oilc's nature, she being opposite in everything but appearance.

Now Clio was backed up against the bank of the moat. One more step and she would fall in, and she rather suspected that this would represent a failure to navigate the Challenge. Whatever was she to do?

Oilc swung again, trying to knock her into the moat. Clio tried to avoid her, but lost her balance and started to fall. She flung her arms out, losing her stick, and happened to catch Oilc by the arm. She hauled on it, trying to recover her balance.

"Let go, imbecile!" Oilc snapped. "I don't even want to touch you, you emotional jellyfish."

Then Clio got a wild idea. She flung both arms around Oilc and hugged her close. "You're my other half," she said. "I love you and want you with me always!"

"Stop it, you mealymouthed disaster!" Oilc cried. "I want no part of you!"

But Clio clung close. She brought her face to the other face and kissed it.

Oilc screamed in sheer anguish. Then suddenly she was gone. Clio was left standing holding nothing, shaking with reaction.

She had done it. She had solved the riddle. She had realized that the only way to be rid of the ugly facet of herself was not to fight it but to take it back into herself and suppress it with her conscience. In this manner she had destroyed Oilc before Oilc destroyed her. She hoped she would never have to go through anything like that again.

She brushed herself off and walked through the main portal into the castle. The entry wasn't straight; it made a right angle turn to the right, then to the left. The wall to the right was carved in the shape of a huge human face.

As she stood there, a panel slid across the passage she had just passed through. She was blocked in; she could not retreat. Well, she hadn't intended to go back that way anyway; her business was forward into the castle.

She looked down the left side passage. It led to a ramp that rose to about head height, then evidently descended beyond. The ceiling rose accordingly, so there was room to walk up and over the ramp to reach whatever was on the other side. It was an odd layout, but maybe there was something beneath that couldn't be moved or altered, so the passage simply had to go over it. Just about anything was possible, here in the Good Magician's castle.

Could this be the next Challenge? The fact that she was closed in here suggested that it was. She had solved one man's problem of wrong-handedness, and abated her doubled alternate self, so this must be some other type of endeavor. Like the drawbridge and the W turnstile, it looked innocuous and probably wasn't.

She would find out. She marched down the hall and started up the ramp. It was steep but not too steep; she could handle it for this short distance.

Suddenly she felt heavy. Very heavy. Something was weighing her down horribly. It wasn't her imagination; her feet were pressing into the ramp and sliding down it as if shoved by a giant hand. She barely kept her footing as she landed back on the flat portion of the floor.

The weight left her. It must have been magic, because there was no evidence of any natural force. This did seem to be the Challenge: to mount to the top of the ramp, when it made her so heavy that she got pushed back down.

She tried it again, bracing herself against the extra weight. And ran right up the ramp as if she were featherlight. In fact her feet left the surface and she floated, drifting back, unable to gain any purchase to push her forward.

Now this was interesting, in an annoying sort of way. The first time she had grown heavy; the second time, light. Both balked her; what she needed was a compromise, her normal weight. How could she keep that?

She tried again, treading carefully up the slope. The heaviness came, increasing until she was unable to drag herself up farther, and had to let herself slide back down. She tried a fourth time immediately, moving slowly, and the higher she went, the lighter she became, until she could no longer maintain contact with the ramp, and drifted back in the slight wash of air coming from its far end.

Well, she had defined the problem. It alternated between heavy and light, and neither suited her purpose. It seemed simple, yet she had no idea how to handle it. Obviously she had to *get* an idea, or she would be stuck here indefinitely.

She walked back down the passage. The huge carved face was still there, gazing at her. The enormous eyes blinked.

Blinked? The face was alive!

"Now I recognize you," she informed it. "You're a sphinx, serving your year of Service."

"Congratulations, Muse," the sphinx replied. "You have solved the first riddle. Do you care for the second?"

"Does it relate to my Challenge?"

"No, it is merely a diversion to entertain you while you remain balked."

"I already know what walks on four legs, then two legs, then three legs," she said with some asperity. She was good at asperity. "A woman, when she's a baby, grown, and old with a cane."

"Unfortunate. I trust you will forgive me if I don't throw myself off a cliff and perish."

"Considering that there's no cliff here, I seem to have no choice but to forgive you."

The sphinx smiled. "So good to encounter a trace of humor. I haven't had a good laugh in centuries."

"Neither have I," she agreed. "Shall we exchange introductions? I am Clio, the Muse of History."

"I am Gravis the Sphinx."

"Gravis. Would that have something to do with gravity?"

"It would."

"In fact, that would be your magic talent: to increase or decrease gravity in a region. That is what is balking my passage."

"Congratulations. You have solved another riddle."

"I am curious: how far does your ability extend? Could it bring a flying bird down from the sky, or raise a fish from the sea, should they happen to traverse the region you affected?"

"It could. In fact I used to make sport of passing birds and fish who did not understand why they could not fly or swim past a given region."

"It is certainly a significant talent."

One eye squinted. "You would not by any chance be seeking to flatter me into allowing you to pass?"

"I would not have the temerity to attempt any such thing." She was not good at temerity.

"That is fortunate, because it would only annoy me."

"I surely would not want to do anything like that."

"That is good to know."

They understood each other. She had of course been trying to flatter him, and he had rebuked her for it.

That left the original problem: how to get past the ramp while the sphinx guarded it. She had no magic to oppose his; she saw no way to counter the unbearable heaviness or lightness of being.

Then she got a notion. Gravis had not had a good laugh in centuries. Maybe she could provide him one.

"I regret I must leave you now," she said, "as I have business within the castle."

"Must we part already? I had thought we would have more time for dialogue."

"Another time, perhaps."

She oriented on the ramp, then lifted up her skirt and charged toward it as fast as she could. Obviously she hoped to run up it at such speed as to get over the hump before the heavy gravity stopped her.

She made it up several strides before the increasing weight caught her. "Oh!" she cried, and toppled back, somersaulting to the base head over heels, her panties surely showing. She landed on the floor with a thump.

"Ho ho ho!" Gravis roared, thrilled by her humiliation. Young women flashed panties deliberately; mature ones concealed them at all costs. He took a breath and laughed twice as hard. The force of his breath made a blast of air down the passage.

Clio clambered to her feet and charged up the ramp again. This time the lightness struck, as it was its turn. In a moment she was floating—and the moving air carried her on up the ramp to the top. It stopped abruptly as the sphinx realized how he had been tricked, but too late; she had passed over the hump.

She recovered her normal weight and touched down on the far side of the ramp, running. She was through. She had navigated the third Challenge. Now to tackle Humfrey.

"So nice to meet you again, Clio." It was a young woman approaching her from the far side of the hall, which debouched into a larger chamber.

"Nice to see you also, Wira." Wira was Humfrey's daughter-in-law, one of the few people he really liked. She was blind, and had seemed useless to her family, so they had put her to sleep. Later Humfrey and the Gorgon's son, Hugo, had awoken her and married her after she had taken a dose of youth water to reduce her age to his. Now she mostly ran the castle, with the help of the Good Magician's designated wives.

"Can you tell me why I was subjected to this querent business?" Clio asked. "I thought I came as a friend."

"I am not sure, but I believe Dara knows."

"She is this month's Designated Wife?"

"Yes, it is her turn. I understand she was after all Humfrey's first wife."

"She was," Clio agreed. "She had half a soul, but gave it up and left him, then regretted it."

"Well, souls are awkward," Dara said, for they were just arriving at the main room. "Can't live with them, can't live without them."

"We mortals can't live without them," Wira agreed. "I will see if he is ready." She departed quietly.

Clio hugged Dara. "It has been a while," Dara said.

"A hundred and fifty-two years since we first met," Clio agreed. "I left after you married Humfrey the first time, and we have encountered each other only passingly since. Did he ever get your name straight?"

"Never. He still calls me Dana. I'm getting used to it."

"Well, he's a slow learner."

They both laughed; it was a private joke. The Good Magician had made it a point to learn everything he could, so he could put it in his Book of Answers. That was just as well, because later he had taken Lethe water and forgotten some things, and now needed the Book to remind him of them.

"What brings you here?" Dara inquired.

"My 28th Volume of the *History of Xanth* is illegible. I evidently wrote it, but now can't read it or remember it."

"Just like Humfrey with his Book!" They laughed again.

"So I came to ask him if he knows of this matter. But I had to go through the querent Challenges, which were a nuisance; I can't say I'm pleased. Do you know why he put me through that?"

"I'm sorry, I don't. I didn't realize it was you until Wira told me. But you know, he has some weird ways. When the Gorgon came and asked him if he would marry her, he made her do a year's Service before he answered."

"I remember. Then she became Wife #5. But there was a reason: he's such a difficult old man that she needed to have that year's experience with him before she could be truly sure she wanted to marry him."

"I don't think 'difficult old man' quite covers it. How about 'irascible ancient gnome'?"

"At present I'm not sure that covers it either. He is going to have to have an excellent reason for treating me this way, or I shall be annoyed."

"You might write him out of Xanth history!"

They laughed again. It was humor; Clio wouldn't actually do that. They both knew she was too nice a person.

"How is it, being his wife for just one month in six?"

"It takes the first week to get used to his grumpiness, and another week to seduce him away from his musty tome, and by the last week his stinky socks are piling up and I'm quite ready to disappear back into demonly oblivion."

"You don't pick up his socks?"

"I'm a demoness! How could I even focus on a dirty job like that? Have you ever smelled one of them?" They laughed again. "Fortunately Sofia Socksorter handles that, in her month. Without her, this castle would melt from the accumulated stench."

"She's a sturdy woman. Of course that's why he married her: to catch up on his old socks."

"She knows. She calls him 'Himself,' because that's what he's full of."

"Does anyone really like him?" Clio asked. It was humor; liking was hardly the point, with the Good Magician.

"Wira does."

"Wira's an angel in human form."

Wira reappeared as if summoned. "Humfrey will see you now, Muse Clio," she said.

"And I shall see *him*," Clio said grimly. But her dialog with Dara Demoness had taken the edge off her irk.

2
DRAGON WORLD

Good Magician Humfrey's study was as small and cramped as ever, dominated by the huge Book of Answers in the center. Humfrey perched on his stool, poring over it.

"Get your nose out of that tome and talk to me, Humfrey," Clio said. "How could you have the temerity to treat me like this?"

He seemed not to hear her. His sunken eyes remained focused on the page before him. Was he adding insult to indignity?

"Father Humfrey," Wira murmured.

He looked up, his countenance shifting from concentration to amelioration. Yes, there was magic in the young woman's presence. Probably the man liked the notion of a daughter who would not leave the premises, and she was a worthy one. His wives could take him or leave him, but Wira was always there, utterly committed to his welfare.

"Muse Clio is here," Wira said, and departed.

"About time," Humfrey grumped.

Her annoyance broiled. "Time for what?"

"For your Service."

"My Service! Listen, you gnarled excuse for a gnome, I have already had more than half a bellyful of your impertinence. I came here as a friend. I am not accustomed to being treated like a querent."

Humfrey gazed at her with something like dawning comprehension. "We are friends; I almost forgot."

"Almost?"

"There is a crisis that only you can handle, so I summoned you here."

"Summoned?"

"Asked," he said, reluctantly qualifying it.

"Neither did you ask. I came here of my own volition."

"That, too," he agreed.

This was weird. "Humfrey, are you well? I suspect you need to drink a cup of Youth Elixir and a gallon of Healing Elixir, then get out into the sunshine for a while. You're letting yourself get too old and isolated. It wasn't always so."

He almost smiled. "I accidentally overdosed on Youth Elixir once, and became a child. I don't care to risk that again."

She had to smile. "I'm sorry I wasn't there for you, but you seemed to cope." She reoriented. "But neither do you need to be a hundred. Why don't you try fifty for a while?"

He shrugged. "I forget: have you asked your Question yet, or are you saving it until after your Service?"

"I have a question, but not for a Service. As I said, I came as a friend."

"I couldn't ask a friend to perform this particular Service."

She got a faint glimmer, like a bright-winged insect hovering just out of range. "Are you trying to hint that there is some remotely serious purpose behind this mischief?"

He nodded. "So I ask you, as a friend, not to question this process. Be a querent. Ask your Question, perform the Service, get your Answer, go your way."

Clio thought of the Gorgon, waiting her year for her Answer. It had seemed outrageous at the time, but had after all made sense. She had to trust in that. Humfrey was definitely not one for practical jokes.

"Very well, then. I have an indecipherable volume on my shelf. I wish to know why I can't read it, since I seem to have written it recently."

Humfrey turned pages on the Book of Answers. "Xanth, History of," he muttered. "Volume?"

"Number twenty-eight. It's the start of the second magic trilogy."

"Obviously." He found the place. "For those events, you will need the Currant."

"Its title may indeed be *Current Events*."

"Currant with an A. A red berry. Find that and your problem will be solved."

"A currant? But that's nonsensical. What has a red berry to do with an obscure history volume?"

"A magical red berry."

"That surely makes a difference."

"But first, your Service. Some background is necessary."

"Background," she agreed, still taken aback by the irrelevance of his Answer.

"The dragons of Xanth are going extinct. It is not clear whether it is environmental degradation, disease, loss of habitat, or some other cause, but the process is far enough along so that we doubt they can recover. We need to restock with fresh blood, as it were, before the loss is complete."

Clio focused. "There does seem to be a dearth of dragons recently. But why would anyone want to save them? They are an endless nuisance." Yet she had noticed the abundant fish, rabbits, and crows. It seemed the dragons weren't off their feed; they were absent.

"They are the backbone of Xanth wildlife. They keep other creatures in check. Without them Xanth would be insufferably safe and dull."

"I find it hard to debate that point. But I know nothing of dragons; I have stayed clear of them all my life. I don't even like them. I really find myself unsuited to such a mission."

"Then recruit assistance."

Clio stopped trying to argue; Humfrey was beyond argument. "You mentioned restocking. That implies a source."

"There is a planet devoted to dragons. Go to Dragon World; it is one of the Moons of Ida. There should be plenty there for this purpose. However, there may be a problem."

"*Another* problem?"

"The dragons may not want to come to Xanth. You will have to persuade a sufficient number."

"Persuade dragons to travel! I would more likely persuade the first one to consume me with ketchup."

"Your talent should suffice."

Clio got another glimmer. It was true that her magic talent was likely to be useful on such a dangerous world. So it was barely possible that she was an adequate choice for such a preposterous mission. "Persuade dragons to emigrate from their world, and immigrate here. How many would be appropriate?"

"Five breeding pairs of each type should suffice."

"Five breeding pairs! Each type!" This was becoming less feasible by the moment, as there were several types of dragons: fire breathers, smokers, steamers; flying, swimming, landbound. That was sixty dragons right there. "Anything else?"

"Yes. Do it within the week."

"Within the week," she agreed. "And is that quite all?"

"Almost. There are a number of varieties, so it will be necessary to move rapidly."

It had been a rhetorical, ironic question, but that nuance had evidently been lost on him. "And if I fail to accomplish this Service within the specified time?"

"That would be unfortunate."

He was impossible. "Yield me this much: a suggestion how to proceed on this unlikely mission."

"I am unable to do that, other than this: fix the concept Dragon World in your mind as you go. That will take you there."

"And when I get to this—this world of dragons—what do I do then? I can't even speak their language."

"Some are telepathic. That should help."

"That should help them zero in on me to chomp."

"True. You may need to think dragon thoughts, so they don't realize you are edible."

This was beyond fantastic. "So I fool them into not recognizing my edible nature. That remains a far cry from persuading any of them to emigrate."

"The compass will guide you to assistance."

"Compass?"

"Extend your left wrist."

Thoroughly bemused, she did so. He touched her wrist with his gnarly fingers. A circular design appeared there, with two little colored arrows in the center and a bright mark on the circle.

She looked at it. "How should I interpret this decoration?"

"The blue arrow points to your destination. The red one indicates your remaining time. Don't be late."

"Late for what?"

But his attention had returned to his page. He had tuned her out.

Wira appeared. "It is time for you to go."

"Time to go! I haven't even assimilated the magnitude of the task!"

"Please. He gets grumpy when kept from his business."

Clio found herself ushered out of the study and down the winding stone stairs. Her head seemed to be spinning. She had decided to trust Humfrey enough to go along with his demand for a Service, but it had turned out to be preposterously impractical. And for what? For the news that she needed a magic red berry to read her own book. If Humfrey had not lost all his wits, surely he had mislaid some of them.

"You look bemused," Dara remarked downstairs.

"Worse. I'm bewildered, befuddled, and benighted. I am one bemused Muse. I need help."

"What kind of help?"

"Help to persuade dragons to move to Xanth."

Dara considered. "Maybe Becka Dragongirl."

It was like a bulb flashing over their heads. "Yes! She should have some idea how to talk to dragons."

"I'll call her." Dara floated to a magic mirror. "Becka, please."

The mirror flickered. In a moment a young woman's face appeared. She had blonde hair and brown eyes. "Hello, Dara. How are things with His Grumpiness?"

"He's pulled another marvel. Clio, the Muse of History, has to persuade dragons to immigrate."

"Wonderful! I was afraid he wouldn't take the problem seriously."

"You knew?" Clio asked.

"I told him about it. Daddy Draco told me the dragons are dying of incompatibility and may soon be gone, and he's feeling none too spry himself. The prey is overrunning Xanth. I'm trying to do my part, but I'm sick of eating crow. I'm so glad the Good Magician decided to do something about it."

"But I don't know anything about dragons!" Clio said.

"Fortunately, I do. Do you want my help?"

"Yes!"

"Then come on over and we'll discuss it." Becka faded out, and the mirror became reflective again.

Clio looked around. "I'm not sure how to—"

"I'll take you," Dara said.

"Thank you." Things were moving quickly, which was just as well.

The demoness put a hand on Clio's arm. There was a dizzy swirl. Then they were in another castle.

Becka stepped into the chamber. "Ah, there you are. I'm so glad to meet you, Muse."

"Call me Clio," Clio said as they shook hands.

"Is there anyone else to notify?" Dara asked.

"How about Che Centaur?" Becka asked. "He's another winged monster, and very persuasive; dragons will listen to him, and all winged monsters are sworn to protect him. He could also carry you while talking to you, which is more than I can do; my dragon mouth isn't good for human talk."

"On my way," Dara said, and vanished.

Clio looked around. There was a mirror on the wall, probably the one Becka had used to communicate with Dara. It was flashing pictures: a black man, a volcano, an evil-looking sorceress, a horrific demon, and a garden. "Oh—this must be Rorrim, the mirror that shows alternate futures."

"Yes. I'm keeping him for Umlaut. But it's hard to interpret his images unless you make a deal with him."

Clio shrugged. "I have already made one deal too many, I suspect."

"Do you know where there are more dragons?" Becka asked.

"It seems here is an entire world devoted to dragons. One of Princess Ida's moons."

"Now that makes sense. But they may not be eager to move."

"That is one of my concerns."

"Still, new hunting grounds should appeal. Game is good in Xanth. Too good, in fact."

Clio did not need to inquire how she knew. "Apart from everything else, there will be a problem traveling to Xanth, as the folk on Ida's moons are mere fragments of souls rather than physical entities. They can't just come here; they would be mere wisps."

"That's true," Becka said. "I hadn't thought of that. Maybe Che will have an answer."

Soon Dara brought the centaur. "How could you carry a person much bigger than you are?" Clio asked, surprised.

"I made myself very light," Che explained. "Greetings, Muse, Becka."

That reminded Clio of something. "You associate with Cynthia Centaur. She was once a human girl, but was transformed by Magician Trent to winged centaur form."

"Which was fortunate for me," Che agreed. "She's a wonderful filly."

"Originally she did not use the lightening magic to make herself light enough to fly, the way you do. Yet the last time I wrote of her, in the episode of the Swell Foop, she was using that magic. How was that possible?"

Che smiled. "Magician Trent transformed her into a roc bird, then back to winged centaur, absentmindedly using the other template. Thereafter she had the lightening magic, though it took her some time to realize it."

"Ah, yes," Clio agreed. "Now I see it. I like to understand things when I write the histories, and that one slipped by me."

"It is understandably confusing," Che agreed. "I'm told you need me to relate to dragons."

"Yes. We need to persuade them to move to Xanth. But we have what may be a more immediate problem: how to transport dragons from a Moon of Ida to Xanth. It seems the Xanth dragons are doomed."

Che considered. He was a handsome young stallion of nineteen, the same age as Becka. He was also very smart. He had to be, because he was the tutor for Sim Bird, the Simurgh's chick, who was destined to know everything in the universe, in due course. "This is true. There is a malady going around that infects dragons without souls. Since those of the moon will have souls, by definition, they will be immune."

"So my father Draco is at risk, and I'm not," Becka said, looking half relieved.

"True. Your human portion provides you with a soul. He may be saved by the infusion of a soul from a souled dragon, however."

"I'll talk him into it."

"Nevertheless, there will have to be new bodies here for the majority of them to occupy. This is not straightforward, because folk existing here are not eager to give up their bodies."

"They can do that?" Becka asked.

"Yes. The process is called morphing. When an existing character is ready to fade away, he or she can morph into an animate blob. Then a theoretical character from Ptero or beyond can animate that blob, giving it the new semblance, and the new character exists. But very few Xanth characters care to undergo this process; all cling to the hope that there may be some great future adventure awaiting them. So it's not a viable procedure for wholesale replacement of dragons."

Clio was starting to feel desperate. "Is there any other way?"

"There should be. Perhaps these bodies can be crafted from organic material, such as swamp peat or topsoil."

Clio liked the way his mind worked. "Is this a thing you might arrange, while we go to that dragon world?"

"I could make the effort," Che agreed. "This would seem to be a problem that needs to be addressed."

"Then perhaps we should leave that to you," Clio said. "While we go to Dragon World."

"Agreed. There is certainly a pressing need for more dragons. I had not before properly appreciated the role of such predators in Xanth."

"Then it is up to me to carry you after all," Becka said. "Come outside where I can change."

They exited Castle MaiDragon, and the girl transformed into a full-sized dragon with bright green scales tinged with purple at the ends. The wings were like those of an insect, with sparkling facets. Overall, a pretty creature.

Clio climbed onto the dragon's back. She would have been reluctant to do so, had she not talked with the girl and seen the transformation. Also, she had written about Becka in prior volumes, so knew she could be trusted.

The dragon flapped her wings, at first slowly, then more rapidly, until they fairly buzzed. She slid forward, then lifted from the ground. Clio clung to the scales of the back as the wind rushed by her body and tore at her dress.

Becka spiraled upward until she cleared the treetops. Then she flew toward Castle Roogna. The ground passed below, with seeming slowness, but Clio knew they were moving rapidly.

There was a cloud ahead. For a moment Clio was afraid it was Fracto, who usually meant trouble, but this turned out to be an innocuous white puffball. It was being harassed by crows. They passed it by fast enough to scatter the crows and stroked on. Then there was another large flying creature, a griffin, with the head and wings of a bird and body of a lion. It veered to intercept them, but Becka let out a warning hiss and the griffin changed its mind. It was not being mobbed by crows, for it was a crow predator. But there were clearly not enough griffins to fill the role of the dragons.

Clio was coming to appreciate working with a dragon girl. Transportation and protection—these were worthwhile.

The castle came into sight. The dragon glided down and landed just beyond the moat. The moat monster's head lifted, spying them.

"Hello, Soufflé," Clio called. "Do you recognize us?"

Soufflé did. He sniffed noses with Becka Dragon, then sank back under the water as Becka reverted to Girl mode.

"I admired the way you backed off those flying predators," Clio said. "You intimidated them."

"I learned that long ago from my friend Bortre. She could intimidate anything, even objects, when she wanted to."

"Friends can be beneficial," Clio agreed, realizing that she had very few friends herself. Her position as the Muse of History tended to isolate her.

"And fun," Becka agreed. "I have another friend called Toney Harper. That's tone-y. He makes evocative music with his harp. When he makes tones of romance, everyone within earshot gets all goo-goo eyes. But the tone of danger brings all manner of danger out of the woodwork. A happy tone makes folk dance; a sad one makes them weep. Toney is great at a party."

"I can imagine." But she couldn't, really; Clio had never been to such a party. She hadn't been out in Xanth proper in some time; she feared she was missing things she might have liked to experience.

They walked toward the drawbridge. Three girls appeared on it, wearing three little crowns. They were the triplet Princesses, eight years old, all of them Sorceresses and full of mischief. Because of their magic power, it could be considerable mischief. Clio knew them rather better than they knew her. What was the best way to handle this?

"Hi, Becka," Melody called. "Who's your friend?" She was the one in the green dress, with greenish hair and blue eyes. She always spoke first.

Becka looked at Clio questioningly. Clio nodded; it was all right to identify her. The information couldn't be concealed from these girls anyway.

They had paused too long. "We already know," Harmony said. She was the one in the brown dress, with brown hair and eyes, and a harmonica.

"It's Clio, the Muse of History," Rhythm concluded. Her dress was red, as was her hair, but her eyes were green. Clio was not sure why Melody hadn't gotten the green eyes, to match the rest of her; the storks might have gotten confused. She carried a little drum.

"Hello, Princesses," Clio said.

The three froze momentarily in place, abashed. But the mood passed in exactly its moment, and they resumed animation.

"Hello, Clio," Melody said.

"We're glad to meet you," Harmony agreed.

"What are you doing here?" Rhythm asked.

"I have to fetch some dragons," Clio said.

"Dragons!" Melody exclaimed.

"Why?" Harmony asked.

"Did they do something wrong?" Rhythm asked.

"Dragons are going extinct," Becka explained. "Because they don't have souls. We need to replace them with souled dragons."

The girls considered half a moment.

"Can we help?" Melody asked.

Clio hadn't considered that, but realized that they might indeed be able to help. Any single princess was a full Sorceress; any two squared their power, and the three together cubed it. That was a lot of magic. "Actually, Che Centaur is arranging for host bodies for them here. That may be a big job. He could surely use your help."

"Che!" Harmony said gladly.

The three vanished, leaving behind only a word from Rhythm: "Bye."

"You handled that neatly," Becka said.

"I was lucky." It was the truth.

They entered the castle. Princess Ida came up to meet them. She resembled Princess Ivy, the triplet's mother, but was immediately identifiable by the little moon orbiting her head. "Dara said you would be coming."

"We need to go to Dragon World," Clio said.

"That is not safe."

"It seems the Good Magician felt I was the appropriate person for it. Becka should be helpful there."

Ida nodded. "That is true. And of course if you get chomped there, you will merely return here. Still, it would be an unpleasant experience. Are you sure this excursion is necessary?"

"I am not at all sure," Clio confessed. "And I'm not partial to dragons to begin with, present company excepted. But it seems this is a thing I must attempt."

"I think the Good Magician has lost it," Becka said. "But this isn't my mission; I'm just helping because I want to save the dragons."

"It is true that the dragon population has been declining," Ida said. "Something needs to be done. Let's hope that this is it."

They went to Ida's office, where they reviewed the mechanism for traveling to the moons. Clio reminded herself to focus on Dragon World, so as to be transported directly there; she didn't want to struggle with the confusing time schemes of planet Ptero.

They lay on couches, and Princess Ida gave them sniffs from a vial. Soon they left their bodies behind and floated up toward Ida's moon Ptero. Clio took Becka's hand and concentrated on Dragon World.

Their souls accelerated toward the looming world. It seemed to be getting larger, but actually they were getting smaller. They zipped down to its surface, for it no longer resembled a tiny moon; it was a giant planet. They came down by Castle Roogna, recognizable because it was the same as the one on Xanth. They flew into it, and into the chamber where Princess Ida stayed, with her pyramidal moon.

They did not pause to greet her; they zoomed right up to the moon, which seemed to expand enormously. Each triangular face of it was a different color: blue, red, green, and gray on the bottom. They descended on the blue section, and flew to the modest house where its Princess Ida resided with her doughnut-shaped moon, more properly known as Torus. On its curving inner surface, on an island in a sea, was yet another Princess Ida, with her moon Cone.

After that, the route fuzzed in her mind. There seemed to be an endless chain of worlds and Idas and worlds. Of course she had written about them before, as she recorded the histories of significant people in Xanth. The most recent one, Cube, had traveled all the way to Zombie

World. But viewing and hearing it in her crystal ball, however much it seemed to put her in the scene, hardly compared to actually being there. Experience was far more intense than observation.

Suddenly, after an endless age, they were homing in on Dragon World. There was no doubt about it, because it was shaped like a dragon. It was serpentine, with six legs, a long tail, and a ferocious head. The dragon's teeth were chomping its own tail, so that the world formed a twisted irregular ring, with the feet in the center, like spokes.

Now she had to depend on her own discretion, which she hardly trusted. Her thought of Dragon World had brought them to it, but where on it were they supposed to land? Where was the destination on this world?

She remembered the compass. She looked at the pattern on her wrist. The blue arrow's position had changed; indeed it was changing as she moved her wrist. It was orienting on its target. All she had to do was go where it pointed. She hoped.

It pointed at the planetary dragon's fearsome head. True, that head was clamping to the tail, so was unlikely to bite a visitor on short notice, but Clio would have preferred some other site.

As they descended, the head expanded horrendously. There was an inordinate number of teeth, each looking larger and sharper than the next, and a great curling lip, and several lake-sized drools of slaver. Were they going to enter that awful mouth?

No, they passed by it and oriented on the snout. This was a prickly horror of hide girt about by tree-sized whiskers. Tiny bugs scuttled across it. No, as they got closer she saw they were neither tiny nor bugs; they were small dragons flying across the surface. No, they were *big* dragons. What a difference distance made!

Fortunately they passed that too, and oriented on one of the great red eyes. That resembled a convex sea of glass, with a monstrous blue crater in the center. No, that was the iris. It expanded to spread from horizon to horizon, with a deep dark black hole in the center, the pupil. They were right in the dragon's sight.

They came to land at last at the edge of that pupil, which turned out to be a vast pool surrounded by a circular blue forest. There was a beach all around the pool with multicolored sands. No dragon denizens were in sight. It was a surprisingly pleasant scene, considering.

"Isn't that the most handsome dragon you ever saw?" Becka asked excitedly. "What fangs! What skin!"

Well, she was a dragon girl. Probably a human face would look no better, seen from a similar vantage. "It will surely do," Clio said.

"Where do we go from here?"

Clio looked at her compass. The blue arrow pointed down along the beach. Then she noticed the red arrow: it was almost touching the bright mark on the circle. It was time!

"We have to hurry," Clio said. "Our deadline is upon us."

"Is it far? I could carry us."

"I don't think so, because otherwise the blue arrow wouldn't have landed us here."

They ran along the beach. There was a copse of trees ahead, with a glade beyond it.

I love you, Drusie. It was a male thought. That was odd, because Clio knew no girl called Drusie.

And I love you, Drew. That was a female thought.

"It's a couple in love," Becka gasped as they ran. "They must be telepathic."

Telepathic! That explained it. They were receiving the thoughts of the lovers.

They reached the copse. In a moment they would see the lovers.

Haaa! It was a physical and mental roar. It was followed almost immediately by a flash of terror. Then an instant of awful pain, and blackness. Clio was revolted; something had just died horribly.

They emerged from the cover of the trees and saw a small dragon chomping on something and licking its bloodstained chops. It heard them and turned to face them. It snarled, about to attack.

Becka assumed her dragon form and snarled back. The dragon, seeing that Becka was larger than it was, turned tail and scooted into the forest on the far side of the glade.

Now there was silence, physical and mental.

Becka resumed human form. "Where to?"

Clio looked at the compass. The blue arrow had faded out. The red one was now just beyond the mark. "We're here," she said. "But it seems, too late."

"Too late for what? There's nothing here."

Clio got a dreadful notion. "That dragon ate them. The ones we were suppose to meet."

"The lovers? That's ghastly!"

"I've got to fix that."

"How? You can't un-eat prey."

"We'll see." Clio exerted her talent. She hated to do it, but it was really necessary.

She and Becka started moving backward. They retreated to the trees. Meanwhile the small dragon charged back, tail first. It turned and saw them, snarling, but Becka was already in dragon form snarling back. Then Becka was in girl form again as they backed into the forest, leaving the dragon chewing on its prey.

They continued on back through the copse and along the beach. There were thoughts of mutual love. Was this far enough? No, not yet. They reached the place where they had landed and stood there talking.

"Isn't that the most handsome dragon you ever saw?" Becka asked excitedly. "What fa—"

"Turn dragon. Carry me to that glade," Clio said, pointing. "Hurry!"

Surprised, Becka turned dragon. Clio leaped on her back. Becka took off. In a few wing-strokes she lifted off the ground and cleared the copse.

The dragon was lurking there, behind a tree, just about to pounce on a pair of little lizards. "Drive it off!" Clio cried.

Becka landed beyond the lizards and growled at the other dragon. Intimidated, it fled.

Meanwhile Clio was jumping off Becka's back and orienting on the lizards. "We're friends!" she cried, realizing as she did so that this was stupid; how could lizards understand human talk?

Friends, the thought came.

Telepathically, obviously. She had understood their love thoughts;

they could understand her spoken thoughts, because they were accompanied by her mind thoughts.

True, the male lizard thought. Then: *But we are not lizards; we are dragons.*

"Dragons!" she echoed, surprised. "But you're so small!"

We are small dragons, of course, he thought, a nuance of annoyance tinting it. *We wouldn't fit our type if we were larger.*

Dear, they are from elsewhere, the female thought. *They don't know about our world.*

"We're from Xanth," Clio said. "We are here to recruit dragons of all types to immigrate to Xanth."

Both dragons laughed, mentally. *And you come to us?* The male asked incredulously.

Instead of to a large leader dragon? the female added.

"I was guided by a—a magic sign. It brought me here, just in time to—" But she halted, not wanting to tell them what had just unhappened.

But they got it from her mind. *Great balls of fire!* The male thought. *It's true!*

Oops. "No need to go into that. The point is—"

She saved our lives, the female thought. *By winding time back. We were crunched as we were kissing.*

Both gazed at her. *In that case, we owe you,* the male said. *We had better go into relationship mode and discuss this.*

"I don't think I understand," Clio said.

You will in the next chapter, the male said.

If you will just step across to it now, the female agreed. *We will be glad to explain.*

"I don't—"

"I think we had better do as they ask," Becka said. "We do need their explanation, if we are to accomplish anything here."

"I suppose so," Clio agreed, halfway flustered.

3
DREW & DRUSIE

C lio stepped into the next chapter. It wasn't hard, as she had been writing chapters for a long time. As with the traveling, it was different actually being *in* one, but she could handle it.

"Wow," Becka said.

Clio looked around. There were two human-sized dragons bestriding a couch. One was blue-scaled and blue-eyed, with translucent wings, the other pink of scale and eye with similar wings. Both were well formed; the blue one was handsome, the pink one pretty.

"Thank you for that thought," the male said, and the pink one blushed red.

"You're welcome," Clio said. "I mean, what happened? I thought you were small."

"We are," the female said. "But with telepathy we can project ourselves to be any size in your mind, for relational convenience. This is similar to visual illusion, just as our translation of our thoughts to sound like your words is similar to sonic illusion. But we can return to the last chapter and be as we were, if you prefer."

"This is fine," Clio said. "Am I correct in assuming that if I tried to touch you, I would find you small?"

"Correct. We don't have touch illusion. Welcome to verify."

"I don't want to be impolite, but this is new to me, and I would like to verify."

"Touch me," the male said.

Clio reached out slowly. When her hand touched his image, she felt a small weight on her palm. "I am Drew Dragon," the male said, and there he was, perched on her hand without reaching beyond it though he was not coiled.

"I am Clio, Muse of History," she said.

Meanwhile Becka reached out to touch the female. "I am Drusie Dragon," the little pink creature said, appearing small.

"I am Becka Dragongirl."

Then the dragons jumped off the hands, spreading their wings momentarily for balance, and reappeared as larger. So did the couch, which was evidently part of the illusion.

"Now we have a situation," Drew said. "We see you do not understand it, as you do not read minds yourselves, so perhaps we should explain it in fair detail, hoping not to bore you."

"We are not bored," Clio said, her amazement slowly fading to surprise. She had not been sure what she expected, but surely nothing like this.

"This is Dragon World," Drew said. "Populated entirely by dragons and their prey. There are five categories, each with five aspects. That makes a total of three thousand one hundred and twenty-five distinct types of dragon."

"How many?" Clio asked, thinking she had misheard.

Drew smiled, which was an interesting expression that could have been mistaken had the smile-thought not clarified it. "This is tricky for little ones to understand, and for visitors. Start with five major categories, such as environment, weapon, size, nature, and mental nature. That's five. Continue with the aspects of each, such as environment: land, water, air, tunneling, or jumping. That's twenty-five. Then with size: giant, large, medium, small, and tiny. That makes a hundred and twenty-five variants."

"Tiny," Becka said. "That's yours."

"Yes. We were consumed by a small dragon, before being rescued by a very interesting process. Then there are the aspects of Nature: friendly, trainable, indifferent, vicious, and committed. That brings it to six hundred and twenty-five. Finally the mental category, whose aspects are telepathic, precognitive, memory, rational, and invisible. That makes three thousand one hundred and twenty-five types in all."

Clio's head seemed to be spinning, but she realized the dragon was making sense. "Five to the fifth power," she said. "It does add up rather quickly."

"You're so smart," Becka said.

"On the contrary, we aren't smart," Drew said. "Our mental aspect is telepathy. But we learned this in dragon school, on pain of getting our tails scorched when we made errors, so we do know it."

"Of course," Clio agreed faintly. "So you are—"

"Tiny, air, telepathic, committed," Drew said. "Then we differ. I am a fire dragon; Drusie is a steamer."

"But then what of the categories?"

"Thereby is our situation," Drusie said. "Types are not supposed to mix. Indeed, all other types are considered predator or prey. So the small dragon gobbled us during our distraction, as was the natural order. We should have been natural enemies, or at least not lovers. But Drew was just so sensible I couldn't help liking him."

"And Drusie was just so cute in pink," Drew said. "I was smitten by her color."

"So it just happened, and we fell in love. But we knew it had to be secret, because we would be ostracized if others knew."

"So we came separately to this secret place," Drew said. "And came together for the first time."

"And expressed our secret love," Drusie said. "And kissed."

"And got gobbled," Becka said. "You didn't know the small dragon was lurking."

"It was mentally invisible," Drew agreed. "So when it hid behind a tree, our minds did not tune in on it."

That clarified one confusing concept for Clio: invisible did not mean physically but mentally, so it was a mental trait. Now she appreciated its advantage.

"And you saved us," Drusie said. "Therefore we are committed to you."

"I realize that is one of the aspects of the category of Nature," Clio said. "But I don't think I quite understand it."

"Some dragons are friendly," Drusie explained. "Of course this is relative. They still need to feed on prey and defend themselves from others. Some can be trained to obey others loyally. Some are indifferent; they don't care about anyone else and will never change. Some are vicious, and will snap at you even if they aren't hungry. We two are committed: if we decide on a course, we stay with it. In this case we realize that we owe our lives to you, so we are committed to repay you in kind. Only when that has been accomplished will we revert to neutrality."

"So we will remain with you until we have saved your lives," Drew concluded.

"You really don't need to do that," Clio protested. "But I could certainly use your help while I am here. I have no idea how to recruit dragons to go to Xanth."

"We do," Drusie said. "But perhaps it would be better if you clarified exactly how and why you saved us, as it could make a difference. It is in your mind, but tangled up in complicated fashion so we really don't understand."

"I hardly understand myself! But the why is that there is a private mystery I wish to solve, and in order to do that I need to do a Service for the Good Magician. That Service is to persuade five pairs of every type of dragon on this planet to emigrate to Xanth. The how relates to my magic talent, which is the windback. When I encounter a difficult situation, I am able to reverse it so that it has not yet happened, and then cause something else to happen. In this case I was looking for you—the Good Magician gave me a magic compass that guided me here—and felt your love for each other, followed immediately by your deaths. So I wound it back and came here faster so that Becka could balk the dragon and save you. It wasn't from humane motive so much as that I knew I needed your help. I doubt my talent will be very useful in recruiting dragons, because I don't like to use it, and do so only in an emergency."

Both dragons nodded. "We see," Drusie said. "At least, enough to clarify your motive. You are a very interesting person, and at some point we would like to learn more of your personal history. But now we must focus on the immediate task."

"Which is how to approach the other dragons," Drew said. "You'll have no problem persuading the two of us to go to Xanth; there we would be allowed to keep company and mate without being censored. It is the other thirty-one thousand and two hundred and fifty dragons that are the challenge."

"That is, five pairs of each kind," Drusie said.

"Yes," Clio agreed, daunted. "I had no idea the number would be so large. It is a challenge to persuade even a few dragons, and this is considerably more than that."

"We will have to go to the leaders of each type," Drew said. "When they are persuaded, they will allow dragons to go. I suspect many will agree to do so, because it is the dream of every creature here to become real by going to Xanth proper. The problem will be getting the leaders to listen, as they tend to be arrogant beasts."

"I suspected that," Clio said wryly.

"But we can help you locate them and communicate," Drusie said. "We shall have to do it separately, so as not to attract attention to our association with each other, but that simply means that one of us will go with each of you."

"But how will we ever get them to listen?" Clio asked. "Rather than try to snap us up as morsels?"

"Dragons love challenges," Drew said. "Mental as well as physical. Are you good at any mental games?"

"Games?"

"Such as riddles or puns?"

"I detest puns."

"Something else, then. Anything to intrigue their sense of competition. Then you can establish stakes: they'll have to listen to your pitch if they lose."

"But suppose they win?"

"Then you will have to forfeit something," Drew said. "But it would be better not to lose."

"Forfeit something," Becka repeated. "Like our lives?"

"Well, you do seem like two delectable morsels."

"Something else," Clio said firmly. But she couldn't think of anything.

"About those puns," Becka said. "You may not like them, but considering your line of work, how is your memory for them?"

"I remember every single awful one. That's why I hate them; I fear my brain will rot."

"So you probably know more than the dragons do. You could win a pun contest."

"I suppose I could," Clio agreed reluctantly. "But it would be like bathing in garbage."

"It wouldn't have to be for long," Becka argued. "Just to get the dragons. Then you could stay away from them forever."

"You can't stay away from puns. They cluster like bad smells. The best you can do is try to ignore them."

"Still—"

"All *right!* I'll do puns, this once. But we still need stakes, for if we lose."

"I have an idea," Becka said. "If we resembled tasty morsels, maybe we could show some flesh."

"Whatever are you talking about?"

"If the dragons would like to eat us, maybe they would also like to see what they might get to eat. So if we agreed to remove an item of apparel for each lost pun, that might be enough. Just so long as we didn't lose completely."

"I can prevent us from losing completely," Clio said. "But as I said, I much prefer not to use my talent."

"If you remember all the puns you've encountered, you should be able to win," Becka said. "So there should be little risk."

"But undressing in public, to be ogled—I can't countenance that. What would the mothers of teenage dragons think?"

Becka nodded; evidently she had encountered some ogling in her young day. "Maybe it's a bad idea. We'll think of another."

But nothing else seemed to work, because the flesh of their bodies was about the only thing that would interest hungry dragons. So finally they came back to that despite Clio's considerable misgivings.

Even then there was a problem. "If some dragons are telepathic, won't they see my puns in my mind, and know the answers?"

"There are protocols," Drusie said. "But maybe the simplest expedient is for us to monitor you in that respect. If any try to peek into your minds, we will know it and warn them off. One telepath can't sneak past another telepath."

Next was the problem of addressing different types of dragons. "We can't possibly talk separately to more than three thousand groups," Clio said. "Even if we did several a day, it would take two years."

"Maybe we could summon category assemblies," Drew said. "That happens when there is reason. Sometimes there is something of interest to all fire breathers, for example."

"Are there water-dwelling fire breathers?" Becka asked.

"Certainly. All types are in all environments. We have the finest assortment of variations known."

"Dear, you are missing her point," Drusie said. "How can land and water dragons be assembled in one place?"

Drew considered. "There are mixed water and land sites. But yes, maybe it should be by environment, for convenience. We could start with the land dragons, and see how it works."

They agreed to start with the land dragons. Drew shut down his mental image, becoming his real size, and flew off to see about it. Drusie, also her real size, perched on Becka's human shoulder. "I will be alert for other dragons," she said, maintaining just that aspect of mental presence; it sounded as though she was speaking to them both. "It will take Drew a while to locate the top land dragon and set it up. Meanwhile you can rest."

"You are sure it is safe?" Clio asked. She found she was tired, though on this world she knew it was only a bit of her soul that formed her body. Much had happened, rapidly.

"Oh, yes, I won't sleep until Drew returns, and I will spot any other mind in the vicinity."

"Then I shall rest," Clio agreed, and sat on the ground with her back against a tree. She had to do what she hated: review the worst puns she knew.

"May I question you about your nature?" Drusie asked Becka. "We have no dragon/human crossbreeds here; I didn't know it was possible."

"Anything is possible in Xanth," Becka said. "My father, Draco Dragon, was diving down to snap up a tasty nymph by a pool, not realizing it was a love spring. They both got doused, and instead of eating her he summoned the stork with her. He was most embarrassed and never talked about it after. I grew up with my mother, then sought my father, and he came to accept me. But such events are rare; I'm the only dragon girl I know."

"Fascinating. I really appreciate the way you scared off that small dragon and saved us from getting crunched."

"It was Clio who made it possible."

"Yes. We both owe both of you. Will we be accepted as a couple in Xanth?"

"I think so. Xanth dragons are not as particular about types; a fire breather can date a smoker and no one thinks anything of it. In fact I date a brassy boy."

"That is so wonderful. If we hadn't had to be secret, we wouldn't have needed to meet far from our homes, and wouldn't have been vulnerable."

"But you'll still need to watch your tails in Xanth. There are many predators besides dragons."

"Tell me about them."

"For example, ogres. They like to crunch bones, twist trees into pretzels, and teach young dragons the meaning of fear. Then there are nickelpedes. They are five times as bad as centipedes, gouging out nickel-sized disks of flesh."

So there was much about Xanth dragons did not know. That should be helpful. Clio drifted into sleep.

She woke when Drew returned. "It is arranged," he said. "The land dragons will gather on the Belly."

"The belly? You said they wouldn't eat us immediately."

"The belly of the beast," Drusie explained. "Our world is in the form of a dragon."

Oh. She should have realized. "Of course. How do we get there?"

"I can fly there, and carry you," Becka said. "If I have guidance."

"I will guide you," Drusie said. "At your cruising rate, there should just be time."

"I will watch out for hostile forces," Drew said. "Do you have a convenient spot for me to perch?"

"My shirt pocket?" Clio asked.

"That's right—you wear clothing. That will do." He flew up to her, landed on her shirt, and disappeared into her breast pocket. In half a moment he poked his head out. "This makes a fine temporary nest. It's well cushioned."

"Thank you," Clio said, slightly embarrassed for no discernible reason.

At that point an elderly human man walked into sight. "I thought you said there were no other humans here," Becka said.

"It's true," Drusie replied. "He must be a stray from some other world."

"We'd better help him," Clio said. She hailed the man. "Hello! I'm Clio."

He saw her. "I am Faxon from the future. Is this contemporary Xanth?"

Clio was taken aback. "That depends on your perspective. Why are you here?"

"Xanth is about to come to a significant crossroads, so I am traveling back in time to see that it is not thrown into a bad alternative."

Clio wasn't sure whether this was legitimate, or the confusion of a man whose brain was suffering atrophy. But she didn't have time right now to figure it all out. "No, this is not Xanth proper. It is a subordinate world. I think you need to travel a bit farther back."

"Thank you." Faxon vanished.

"Was he for real?" Becka asked.

"Yes," Drew said. "I read his mind. He's from about a century hence."

"I hope he doesn't change our past," Clio said a bit nervously. "But meanwhile we have our own job to do."

Becka turned dragon. Drusie flew up and perched on the top of her head. Clio mounted her back, as before.

Becka spread her wings and ran forward, soon taking off. Clio didn't hear Drusie's instructions, but the dragon girl did seem to know where she was going. She circled up over the eye, then flew out over the tip of the tail and up toward the belly. At one point there was a storm; they rose above it and went on. This was after all a planet; it had weather.

It was a fairly long flight, even at dragon speed, but in due course they arrived at the site on the belly. There were many dragons there, ranging in size from giant to tiny; Clio could not distinguish between the smaller giants and the larger large dragons, but presumed the categories were clear to their complements.

"They are," Drew said. "The leader of this assembly is the largest giant land dragon, who is a black smoker, indifferent and rational, which is to say, smart. He will bargain shrewdly, but is very curious to see Xanthly flesh, so will enter the contest. I will translate, as neither of you are telepathic."

"Thank you," Clio said. This was exactly the kind of scene she would have preferred to write about, rather than participate in. But she hardly had a choice.

They came in for a landing. A monster dragon lifted his snoot and sent a warning jet of fire. "Halt! No flyers here." That was Drew's translation; it was a telepathic challenge.

"Cower down, rotten chops," Drew replied similarly from her pocket. "We're here for the pun contest, per the truce." He gave their identification. The guardian dragon nodded, withholding his fire.

Clio got the impression that Drew liked having a pretext to address a giant that way.

"Don't tell," Drew told her privately.

They landed safely, and were immediately surrounded by dragons of every size and type as Clio dismounted and Becka resumed girl form. There were hundreds of them. Technically, six hundred and twenty-five, she realized. All the variants of land dragon. They were all colors, but none of them had functional wings.

Before them was the biggest of them all, a black dragon the size of a youthful mountain. Curls of smoke issued menacingly from his nostrils as he gazed down at them. "This better be good," he said, in Drew's rendition.

"Your turn," Drew told her privately. "Just speak naturally. I'll translate your thoughts, with the appropriate names and titles, and their telepaths will relay it to the others. They won't read anything I don't relay; Drusie is seeing to that with a mental privacy cloud."

Clio appreciated how the two tiny dragons were coordinating. They really were quite helpful.

"Thank you," the two said together. "But get on with it," Drew continued. "Giants aren't known for their patience."

"Greetings from Xanth, Giant Dragon," Clio began somewhat uncertainly. "I have a matter to broach with you—"

"I won't listen to this," the giant interrupted. "Are you going to show some tasty flesh?"

"Only if you win the contest," Clio said. "And if I win, you must listen to my pitch."

He nodded cannily. "First the rules of the game. We take turns showing puns, my turn first. If I win one, I choose what item of your coverage to remove."

He was bargaining. "And if I win one, I am one step toward making my pitch."

"Five steps," he said. "First one to win five, wins. When you lose, we get to eat you and your halfbreed friend."

Clio's knees felt like damp noodles, but she held on. "When you lose five, you listen."

"Granted."

So they were on, ludicrous as the arrangement was.

The black dragon twitched an ear, and a smaller dragon came forward. "Their telepath," Drew explained.

Several long metallic objects appeared in a mental scene. They were projecting from a board. A dragon walked past the board, his tail happening to twitch across it. Suddenly the black spikes sprouted teeth and chomped the tail. The dragon screeched and emitted a cloud of steam as it flew away. The scene faded as a wash of humor spread across the watching dragons.

"Want to see it again?" the black dragon inquired.

Clio recognized the pun; she had encountered a variation a century back. But she didn't want to seem too competent, so she hesitated as if uncertain. "Yes."

The scene played again. This time Clio realized that this was a flying dragon; they were poking fun at one that was not of their type, these all being land dragons. Becka and both tiny dragons were flying dragons, so this was a pointed if oblique teasing.

It was time to answer. "Nail biting," Clio said.

The humor dried up. The dragons had lost one. "One for you, morsel," the black dragon said grudgingly. He fetched a cup of tea and sipped it as another dragon set up a billboard with the score:

DRAGONS 0   MORSELS 1

Now it was Clio's turn. She knew a similar pun. Maybe it would stump them. She thought an image for Drew to animate.

A human man walked into the scene carrying a bucket and a brush. He came to a palm tree with a number of palm fronds that resembled human hands. He dipped his brush and slopped paint on the extremities. That was it.

The dragon struggled. "Painting claws? Skipping palms?"

"Want to see it again?" Clio inquired sweetly, making an obliging gesture with her hands.

The dragon's eye fixed on her hands. "You have fingers instead of claws. That's it: finger painting."

He had it. "One for you," she agreed. Now she would have to take off a piece of clothing. She was wearing a hat, shirt, shoes and socks, and underwear. She was afraid the dragon would ignore the extremities and focus on the middle, which was exactly where she didn't want to be exposed. But she was stuck for it.

But he surprised her. "I like to eat feet. Remove a shoe."

She obliged, not fully relieved. The black dragon gazed at her sock-covered foot and licked his lips. Well, it could have been worse.

It was his turn for a pun. A scene appeared with a demon floating into view. So they did have demons on this world. It was in dragon form, but was floating rather than flying, and slightly translucent. He looked unhappy. He drifted before a dragon. "Demon, you look miserable," the dragon said, or perhaps thought. "I am Feat, unlucky in love," the demon said. "I would kill myself, if I were alive. As it is, I must continue to suffer." He drifted on out of the scene.

Clio considered. Most demons had punnish names, like D. Molish or D. Sire. This one would be D. Feat. But what kind of feat was he accomplishing? He seemed more like a failure. In fact he was almost in agony. Was this a foot pun, because the dragon liked feet?

Then she had it. "The agony of D. Feat!" she exclaimed.

"Curses, foiled again," the black dragon muttered. Now it was 2 to 1 in her favor.

And her turn for a pun. This time she selected a tricky one. The picture was of a bridge over a river, with a woman gazing at it. Then the woman turned away—and the bridge faded out. That was all.

The black dragon pondered. "What is that structure?"

"There are no bridges on this world," Drew explained to her. "I grasp the concept only because I have it from your mind. Dragons fly across rivers, or swing or wade through them, or tunnel under."

"It is a bridge," Clio explained. "We morsels can't always risk our tender flesh in the water, so we make bridges across." She modified the scene to show human people walking across the bridge as the woman on the shore watched. But when the woman looked away, bridge and people disappeared.

The dragon finally admitted he was stumped. "Where's the pun?"

"It's an attention span," Clio said as the billboard chalked up another for her side. It was now 3 to 1.

The dragon audience groaned. Their unfamiliarity with the bridge had distracted them from its related pun.

It was the dragon's turn, and she knew this was going to be a tough one. A scene appeared with a dragon marching onstage. "I have all mental powers," he proclaimed. "I can do anything!"

A smaller dragon appeared. "Then can you copy yourself?"

"Certainly." The dragon huffed and puffed, then spun around so rapidly that he split into two identical dragons. "Now we can both read your mind, you despicable doubter," the second one said as he diminished his spin so he could stand still. "I am a perfect copy of my originator. It's all done through the mind."

"That's amazing," the small dragon said. "What are you?"

But the scene faded out before the copy could answer.

Clio pondered. She had not encountered this one before, perhaps because she had had no truck with dragons. A dragon with mental powers had copied himself, complete with those powers. Where was the pun? He had done it by spinning, but that seemed to be a mechanism, not a pun. Was it a false claim? Was he spinning a tale? Yet for the purpose of the contest, it had to be assumed that what was presented was true.

She watched it again, and finally asked. "Is he telling the truth?"

"Yes. He is really copying himself, complete with mental powers."

It was beyond her. She had to give up. "What's the pun?"

"He's a psi-clone."

Clio groaned. "Oh, I should have gotten that one. A whirling copy of mental powers. What an awful pun."

"Puns are best when they're worst," the black dragon said smugly. The billboard was marked 3 to 2. "Now remove your sock."

Feeling vaguely unclean, she drew off her sock, exposing her tender foot to his hungry gaze. She knew he was crunching that foot, in his imagination. Ugh!

But it was her turn again. This was tougher than she had expected, as the dragon was coming up with some puns that were new to her, but the contest did seem to be fairly run. It was time for her to come up with a tough one of her own.

Her picture formed: a huge barrel, a cask, sitting on the ground. All around it were odd creatures and things: silly-looking demons, weird plants, unlikely animals. Beyond were human people and dragons who approached the region, saw the oddities, held their noses, and turned away, obviously disgusted. Sometimes they accidentally stepped on something, and it stuck to their feet and evidently smelled bad. Nobody could stand the things. Then a crew of people came with nets. They caught the odd things and dumped them in the barrel and jammed the lid on. The scene was clear at last, and now the people were satisfied.

The black dragon viewed the scene several times, mystified. "Those things look like bad puns, but they are cleaned up, so where's the pun?"

"In the barrel," Clio answered. "All of the unruly puns are there, so people can live in peace."

"Puns in a barrel."

"In a cask," she agreed.

Then suddenly he got it. "Puncheon! A cask for unruly puns!"

He had indeed gotten it, just when she thought she had won. Now the billboard was 3 to 3. "Remove your other shoe," he said.

She hated this, but had to do it.

She removed her other shoe, and stood with one foot bare, the other socked. The black dragon licked his lips.

It was his turn. A scene formed, showing a group of centaurs. That surprised her; she had thought that the dragons didn't know about other types of creatures found in Xanth.

"We know about some, when they travel through," Drew explained. "Centaurs are smart, and we learned to respect their archery."

The centaurs formed a circle. One of them stepped into the center. The others were silent, listening while he spoke. Then he stopped out and another went to the center, and was accorded similar respect.

That one was easy. "The centaur of attention," Clio said. The dragon snorted a puff of black smoke, resigned. The billboard showed her ahead, 4 to 3.

Her turn. She showed a young human woman surrounded by demons. They were not making mischief for her in the way demons normally did; instead they were acting like servants, doing her chores for her, bringing her cake and eye scream and other delicacies. Extremely obliging demons.

But just as the dragon's supposedly tough one was easy for her, her tough one was easy for him. "Demons are a girl's best friend!" And the board went to 4 to 4.

Clio had to remove the other sock. One more loss, and she was done. And it was the dragon's turn.

The scene formed: a wooden stake had little legs and was running around, almost jumping, the feet making clip-clop sounds as they landed, approaching a mixed crowd of humans and dragons. "What is the nature of ultimate reality?"

"Get out of here, you crazy stick!" a human exclaimed, and a dragon snorted steam. But the pole was undismayed. "I must have your answer." And it kept after them, until they gave answers, however irrelevant.

Clio pondered. What was the pun? Running something up the flag-pole? But there was no flag. Answering a stick—getting stuck? No. Getting shafted? But the pole wasn't hurting anyone, it was just demanding answers. It was a really funny pole, running around like that.

A running pole. Suddenly she had it. "A gallop poll!"

The black dragon heaved so much smoke he disappeared in the cloud. "And those feet look so delectable," his disgusted voice emerged.

The score was 5 to 4. She had won. Now they had to listen to her pitch. At this fleeting moment, she almost liked puns.

4
DRAGON NET

"Make your pitch," the black dragon said with resignation. "Then get out of here before my hunger overwhelms me."

Clio hastened to oblige. "Xanth is running out of dragons. Ours generally don't have souls, and some ailment is taking them out, so we need new dragons, with souls."

"We are nothing but souls," the black dragon said. "What we lack are bodies."

"We are arranging to make bodies from organic material," Clio said. "So that you can animate them. Then you will have all Xanth to roam. Of course there will be some limits—"

"I have heard enough," he said gruffly.

"But—"

"How many can you take?"

"You're agreeing?"

"Of course. We have way too many dragons here, and are eager for new hunting grounds. Especially in reality. We would all go, if we could."

"We need five pairs of each type. That is, males and females, so they can—"

"We know what they can do. There are six hundred twenty-five types of land dragon. You'll take ten of each, evenly divided in gender?"

"Yes, that is what we want." She could hardly believe it was so easy, after the problem getting him to listen.

"He knew your business," Drew said. "He just wanted to see your tender feet."

"He made me indulge in the pun contest, just to—?" She was overwhelmed by annoyance as she put her socks and shoes back on.

Then the dragons started laughing. After two moments, Clio and Becka were obliged to join in. It had been a good joke, in dragon terms.

"That's six thousand, two hundred fifty dragons," the black dragon continued as the laugh subsided. "How are you going to transport them all to Xanth?"

"Why, when we're done here, we'll just expand back to where we came from, and—" She paused as the dragon shook his head. "And you didn't come from Xanth. You can't do that."

"You're smart, for a human. You had better get some practical advice, while I select the pairs with the privilege of going. Shall we meet again, here, in one day's time?"

"But I have other dragons to contact. The flying, the swimming—"

"Not until you get ours on the way. It will be enough of a traffic jam as it is."

He was right. She didn't know what to do.

"We know," Drusie said. "We'll ask Princess Ida."

"But she's way back in Xanth!"

"*Our* Princess Ida," Drew clarified.

"Oh. Of course. We'll talk to her."

Becka changed to dragon form, a feat that impressed the congregation of dragons. Clio got on, and she took off. She trusted Drew and Drusie to know where they were going.

They lifted above the belly and flew on toward the tail. This was another long flight, but her dialog with Drew and Drusie made it interesting. They had much information about Dragon World, and were very curious about Xanth. But there was one thing that bothered Clio.

"You say the black dragon knew my mission all along," she said. "I had understood that you were guarding my mental privacy."

"I was," Drew said defensively. "No one got it from you."

"Or from Becka," Drusie said. "I guarded her."

"Then how did it get out? Could someone have read your minds?"

"No, we automatically protect our own minds," Drew said.

"From the moment we discovered our commitment to you," Drusie added.

"That small dragon who un-ate you," Becka said. Her thought was relayed as speech by the little dragons. "Could he have done it, just before you started guarding?"

"No, he's not a telepath," Drew said. "He was mentally invisible."

"What about some other dragon in the region?" Clio asked. "Just lying there listening?"

"There could have been," Drew agreed. "We are short-range telepaths, being small. Big ones can range much farther. We weren't guarding our thoughts, and you weren't guarding yours."

"It could have happened then," Drusie agreed. "A big land dragon could have picked up enough from your minds, and relayed it to others as a matter of general interest."

"So by now the whole planet knows our business," Becka said, disgusted.

"Actually it doesn't need to be secret," Clio said. "I was more concerned that dragons might be reading our minds despite your protection. That would make the pun contests dangerous."

"They aren't doing that," Drew assured her.

Reassured, Clio relaxed. She would continue to play the game of puns if that was what the dragons wanted, knowing that they would in the end consider her proposal. Since it was apparent that dragons were eager to become real in Xanth, she knew her mission was bound to be a success. But they would make her go through the motions.

There were flying dragons in the sky, large and small, but none of them approached aggressively. That suggested that they did know her business, and were making a point of not interfering with it. That, too, was reassuring.

Now they were flying along the thinning tail section of the dragon world. Since the world was coiled, this was bringing them back toward the head. Clio was not as alarmed about this as she had been the first time. Now she knew that despite its horrendous shape, it was just a planet, not a living creature.

They were flying above the great eye. It winked.

Clio almost fell off her perch.

"It does that," Drew said. "Our world knows what is going on, and it can read any mind it chooses to. But it never reveals secrets. It just watches. I think it likes you."

"That's nice," Clio said faintly. "But we were *on* that eye. It was solid land and water. How could it wink without disrupting everything, causing earthquakes and storms?"

"Illusion," Drusie said. "The folk down there would not even have been aware of the wink. It was just for us."

"This world grows more interesting by the hour."

"Well, we like it," Drew said. "We wouldn't want to leave it, if only other dragons accepted our relationship."

A small portion of the tail extended beyond the clamping teeth. They flew along this, then glided down to the very tip. Tiny as that seemed from afar, it was like the broad peak of a very tall mountain as they landed. Becka returned to human form, with Drusie in her pocket.

They stood before a modest house. Princess Ida had never been much for show. In fact she was just about the nicest person in Xanth, and her character seemed to be the same on the tiered moons.

The door opened and a dragon peered out. Clio was appalled; had Ida been eaten by a rogue?

"By no means, Clio," the dragon said, utilizing the same thought conversion Drew and Drusie did. "I am Ida."

"But you're a dragon!"

"Well, this *is* Dragon World. We're all dragons here, except for the prey."

Clio realized that it did make sense. After all, there was a tiny moon circling her head: the next derivative world. "I apologize for my confusion. On Xanth, you're human."

"And if you lived here, you'd be a dragon. Do come in, Clio, Becka, Drew, Drusie."

They entered her house, which was more like a big nest inside. There were gemstones galore; dragons did like them. They sat on giant diamonds.

"And what brings you here, from far Xanth?" Ida inquired politely. Obviously she knew, but was observing the forms.

"We are recruiting dragons to replace the ones Xanth is losing," Clio said. "We have recruited more than six thousand land dragons of every type. We are arranging for bodies for them in Xanth. Now we need to transport them safely there."

"Ah, of course. It's a long way, in size. I believe you will need a net."

"A net?" Clio asked blankly.

"A dragon net. I have a number, saved for this purpose." Ida smiled at Clio's evident confusion. "This is not the first time dragons have emigrated to another world. This is after all the source world for dragons; they need a convenient way to reach their destination worlds." She lifted one foot, showing a small net in the shape of a bag. "This should do."

"But some of those dragons are big!" Clio protested. "And there are so many of them. This would barely do for the smallest."

"It stretches," Ida said patiently.

"She knows what she's doing," Drew thought privately.

It wouldn't be polite to doubt her further. Clio took the little net and tucked it into her other breast pocket. "Once the dragons are in the net, how is it transported to Xanth?"

"A Xanth native will have to guide it there in the usual manner," Clio said. "Hold it and will yourself home. You will expand and find yourself there, in my Xanthly study. Do not release the dragons until you are safely beyond the castle, in the neighborhood of their new bodies. Someone will have to assist them in occupying them, because they have never been truly physical before."

"I'll help," Becka said. "And Che Centaur will be there. He's organizing the bodies now; he's very smart."

"That will surely work," Ida agreed. Clio remembered that her talent was the idea, but that she could not originate ideas; once another person who did not know her talent expressed an idea, Ida could agree, and then it was so. Becka evidently did not know, so that was fine.

"But there are more dragons to come," Becka said. "How will I return here for them?"

"Once you have been the route, it is easier to repeat it," Ida said. "Merely return to my Xanth persona and think of Dragon World, and you will soon be here."

That seemed to cover it. "Thank you so much," Clio said, somewhat awkwardly.

"Just remember me in your history of the experience."

"I certainly will! This entire world is so remarkable it will take three chapters. I never liked dragons before, but my outlook is changing entirely."

"Experience does that," Ida agreed.

They left the house, Becka changed, and they took off for the next meeting, which the dragons said was with the water dragons. This turned out to be not far away, as it was in that wet nose of the planetary dragon. They simply flew across from the tip of the tail to the nose.

It loomed hugely: two enormous nostrils filled with what Clio hoped was water. They landed on an island formed of what she hoped was land. Clio dismounted, Becka changed to girl form, and they stood on the tiny atoll. All around was a thickly rippling sea, filled with swimming dragons of all colors and sizes.

A giant head lifted from the water. It was as big as the whole isle. That made Clio nervous, but she reminded herself that the dragons probably weren't really interested in chomping her. They wanted to play the game of puns, then hear her spiel.

Then a long rope-like tongue snaked out, looped around her body, and lifted her in the air. Clio screamed as she was carried toward one monstrous eye. This time she got a good seven E's into it and two K's, her personal record, along with a doubled exclamation point. "EEEEEEEKK!!"

"It's all right," Drew hastily reassured her. "She just wants to get a better look at you."

That spared her the effort of winding back the scene. "But that tongue!"

"It's her weapon. There are five types of weapon: fire, smoke, steam, suction, and the prehensile tongue. But she's not going to chomp you."

"Indeed I am not," the dragoness said mentally. "I know your business, and am interested. But the school would be disappointed if we did not play the game out properly. Present your first pun." And the tongue lowered Clio gently to the ground and released her.

The tongue as a weapon. Clio would have been less impressed if she had not just experienced its competence. The dragon could reach quickly out and snare prey and haul it in to the mouth before it knew what was happening. Fire could toast, smoke could suffocate, steam could cook, but none of them actually brought a fresh morsel to the mouth. Suction would have similar ability. On Xanth the last two categories did not exist.

But she had a pun to present. What would do? She took the first one she remembered; it might not be the best, but it would do. The picture of a human woman appeared, in the air over the water. She was walking, but one leg was shorter than the other, so that she tilted to one side at about a thirty degree angle. "What is her name?" she asked.

"Rumple-tilt-skin," the dragon guessed.

"That's clever, but no."

"Angle."

Sounding like Angel. "Again, no."

"Tilta."

As in Tilda. "Sorry."

"That's three guesses; I lost. What is it?"

"Eileen."

There was a moment of silence. Then the sounding dragons laughed, blowing water and steam into the air. "I Lean!" the dragoness said. "Very nice." A scoreboard appeared, with one water ball in the column marked MORSELS. She was certainly a good sport.

It was the dragon's turn. A field of vines appeared, with large yellow blossoms. They looked innocent, but then a small dragon swam in a canal and reached out to sniff a flower. It closed on the dragon's snout, and compressed it to a tiny portion of its former size. The dragon fled with its miniature snout. Then a flying dragon came to land in the field, and several blossoms closed on it, squeezing its feet so hard that they became mere stubs. "What are they?" the dragon asked.

This was new to Clio. She had encountered carnivorous plants, but not carnivorous flowers. Though these flowers weren't actually eating creatures, just squeezing them awfully. Regardless, there did not seem to be anything funny about it. Where was the pun?

The flowers resembled those of the dreaded gourds. Was this a gourd reference? But gourds used their fruits to trap people, not their flowers.

"I'm afraid I don't get it," she confessed.

"Squash blossoms." A water ball appeared on the dragon's side of the scoreboard.

Clio knocked her head with the heel of her hand. That was obvious! How could she have missed it? But that was the nature of puns: they were obvious in retrospect, seldom in foresight.

Her turn. She remembered a thoroughly nasty teacher she had once encountered. The picture showed a human man of ugly middle age, standing before a class. "Now this is an ass," he said, and showed a picture of the midsection of a human female as seen from the rear. The girls in the class looked shocked. The man laughed. "Haven't you dolls seen one of these before? Look in the mirror, you &&&&s!"

That was too much. Three girls fainted, and the rest walked out of the class. Even the boys looked dismayed. "You'll never pass this %%%% course!" he yelled after them.

The class continued, with the teacher presenting crude subjects and cussing out anyone who tried to object. "Who is the teacher?" Clio asked at last.

The dragoness considered. "I'm not sure what was considered indecent about such a fresh meaty rump," she remarked. "I would have snapped it up in half an instant." She pondered. "But I suppose the point is he was abusing the sensitivities of his students. I could see they didn't like him. No dragon would do that; it's much better just to chomp them, sparing them humiliation."

Clio realized that this dragon was not a bad person; she merely had a dragon perspective. "Yes, he's an abusive instructor who swears at his students. That is the point, not the, uh, rump."

"Bad teacher," the dragon said. "Abusive instructor. Profane professor." Then a lightbulb flashed over their heads. "Professor Profanity! Prof. Anity. Profanity."

Clio realized she should have kept her mouth shut. "That's it. Another for you." The board showed 2 to 1 in favor of the dragon.

Now the dragon made a picture. It was of an aerial view of a section of the planet. These were not flying dragons, but with telepathy they surely had garnered such images from their cousins the flying dragons. The land was thickly forested, interspersed by clearings. Then an odd thing happened: the clearings started moving. That was technically unlikely, because a clearing was a region where trees did not grow. How could trees ungrow like that, and suddenly regrow as the clearing moved on?

Yet it seemed to be so. The clearings converged on one region until they were thickly clustered. The day brightened, then faded, and the fields moved back toward their original places. They had gathered for just one day.

And she had it: "Field day! The fields made a field trip for it."

The board showed 2 to 2. She was even again.

She cast about for another pun to use, but her mind was stubbornly blank. All she could think of was a dirty one, and she didn't want that. But since she couldn't remember a clean one, she had to use it.

The picture formed, this time showing the sea around them, complete with swimming dragons. A ship sailed into view, causing the dragons in the picture to stare because they had never seen one before. She rather liked that touch. But they surely knew of ships from other travelers. That was important.

The ship expanded to take up the whole scene. The view focused on the highest deck at the stern. There were small flying dragons coming in and depositing their digestive wastes on it, splattering the clean wood. They were dropping their turds and flying on. That was all.

The dragoness peered at the image. "Why would any dragon do a thing like that to such a rare vessel? It's disgusting?"

"It's a disgusting pun," Clio said. "What's going on?"

"I don't even care to guess! Get rid of it."

The scene faded. "You are giving up?"

"On this one."

"It's the poop deck."

There was a mental shout of laughter from a number of the younger male dragons. Their mothers hastily shushed them. The score went to 3 to 1 in favor of the morsels.

The dragon formed a picture of a tree. It looked like a fig tree, but instead of figs its fruits were little globes of air. A dragon came by and ate several, and licked its lips as if they were tasty, but they didn't seem to be very filling. That was all.

Clio gazed at it, but didn't get it. It was amazing how many puns were new to her; apparently they flowed from some inexhaustible font of base humor, so that no matter how many she remembered, there were always more she hadn't encountered. Eating globes of air instead of figs? In fact they seemed on closer inspection to be entirely imaginary. So what was the point?

"I give up," she said. "It makes no sense to me."

"Figments." The score went to 3 to 2, still her favor.

Fig mints. Imaginary figs, unfilling because they had no substance. How could she have missed that? She was disgusted with herself.

Her turn again. Her picture showed an old human woman walking with difficulty, evidently lame. Then a huge yellow citrus fruit walked up on little legs, and used little arms to help the woman make progress. She thanked the fruit as she reached her home. That was all.

"A grapefruit," the dragon said.

"Actually it's a smaller variant."

"A lemon. But that's a bad thing."

"Oh, the fruit is sour, but not bad in that sense."

Then the dragon got it. "Lemonade! Lemon aide."

She had it. The score was 3 to 3.

The dragon formed a picture of a very nice looking little plant. A human person walked past, and it reached out a vine to stroke the person's leg. The person burst out laughing and skittered away. Then a dragon walked by, and the plant touched it similarly, making it puff smoke and depart in good humor. The plant treated several passersby that way, between times folding its foliage about it in a most aesthetic form. That was it.

Clio pondered. This was yet another new one. These pun contests were more formidable than she had anticipated. A planted joy? That didn't work. Sweet revenge? No, the plant wasn't hurting anyone; in fact they seemed to like being touched. They were tickled to be touched. But tickle-touch wasn't a pun. Tickled pink? But they weren't changing color. Was it that it was a nice plant? Nice tickle? No pun there.

She couldn't get it, and had to give up. "Cuticle," the dragon said. "We call it the Kew-Tickle flower."

Clio groaned. Cute tickle! She had been so close. Now the score was 4 to 3 in the dragon's favor. She couldn't afford to lose another.

At least her memory was returning. She remembered a credulous bovine that might do. She formed her picture: A bull was grazing in a field when a fox approached. "Hey, there's much better pasture behind that tree," the fox said. "There is? Thanks!" The bull hurried around the tree.

But instead of pasture there was a snoozing ogre. The bull banged into the ogre before he could halt. The ogre woke, annoyed, took hold of him, and twisted him into the form of a pretzel before throwing him back where he came from. It was a most uncomfortable occasion, and it took the poor bull an hour to untangle his legs and get back to his feet.

Then the fox came again. "Say, there's a really sexy cow behind that other tree." "There is? Thanks!" The bull went around the tree, but instead of a cow there was a snoozing fire dragon. The bull stumbled into the dragon, who woke and toasted his rear so hotly the bull had to leap into the nearest pond to douse his smoldering fur.

Then the fox came again. "There's a bare icade behind that third tree."

"There is? What's an icade?"

"Go there and see. She's quite a sight."

So the bull charged around the tree—and ran straight into a temporary wooden wall made of planks that surrounded a sleeping bear. He crashed to the ground, getting splinters in his hide, and the bear woke and angrily swiped at him. "What's this?" he demanded of the fox, who was smirking. "It doesn't look like a bare icade."

"Oh, you must have misheard," the fox said. "I said it's a bear icade."

The scene faded. The dragon pondered. "That's a stupid bull."

"Extremely. He never learns. The fox keeps fooling him."

"A fox and bull story?"

"You're thinking of cock and bull."

The dragon sighed. "So I am. I get fables confused." She was unable to fathom the pun.

"He's Gulli Bull," Clio said.

"Gullible!" the dragon cried. "I should have had that!"

Clio knew exactly how she felt. Now they were tied 4 to 4. She still had to win another pun.

A picture formed. It was set in the fabled land of Mundania, where folk were pretty dull because they lacked magic. It showed a building where all manner of ugly things were available for those who had the funny stuff they called money. A woman came to buy a flattened snake that was clenching its tail in its mouth, like Dragon World only much smaller. She put it around her upper torso to hold her bosom up. It was a co-bra. A man bought a big cucumber labeled Dill—and turned into a pickle. Another man bought a machine with a screen whose brand name was Post—and started decaying into dirt. It was a com-post. In short, everything there was dirty or unpleasant.

Clio had written about Mundanes often enough; they stumbled into Xanth fairly regularly. She didn't remember any shopping place of quite this nature, but it seemed possible, because one never could tell about Mundanes. What was the pun? "Dirty money?" she asked.

"Nice guess," the dragon said smugly.

The point did seem to be the people or the store rather than the money. Then suddenly she had it: "Gross-ery store!"

"Ah, well," the dragon said, not unduly dismayed. "We shall draw lots to determine which of us have the privilege of becoming real in Xanth. You said five couples of each type?"

Clio hadn't said, but didn't argue. "Correct."

"We will have them ready this time tomorrow."

It was time to move on. Becka changed form, and they took off. "You handled that well," Drew remarked. "Making them think you didn't know they knew."

"I really wasn't sure they knew. Those were some tough puns."

"Only three more contests to go."

They flew to the tip of a wing, where the air dragons ran her through another barrage of puns, then agreed to assemble their volunteers on the morrow. After that it was the inside of a front claw, theoretically used by the Dragon World for digging, for the tunneling dragons. They all had stout forelimbs and dull colors, but were smart enough. Finally it was the jumping dragons, on the top of the head.

These were especially interesting, because they had an ability no Xanth dragon had: they did not jump physically, but magically. They moved by teleporting short distances. So if a dragon wanted to take one step forward, it vanished where it was, and reappeared almost instantly one pace ahead. The fact that most of its bulk was occupying the same space as before did not seem to matter; it had made its move. If it had farther to go, it teleported in a series of jumps, looking like a staccato picture. This meant that these dragons could not be barred from any place by physical barriers; they teleported right through them, sometimes pausing part way through without apparent discomfort. Clio was hard put not to stare as the big leader dragon approached her in several rapid little jumps.

"They are good hunters," Drew remarked. "And good guards. But bad enemies."

Clio was sure that was the case. Fortunately she had not come here as any enemy, and her dealing with these dragons was similar to the others. Soon they too had agreed to assemble a suitable number for transport the following day.

They returned to spend the night with Dragon Princess Ida, who was a marvelous host. She served human food for Clio and Becka, who was in human form, and small dragon roasts for Drew and Drusie. She was intrigued by Becka, and the two got along well. Meanwhile Clio reviewed the day with Drew.

"Those dragons don't seem to be so bad, now," Clio said in her mind. This illusory dialog was quite convenient.

"Drusie and I are reforming our impression of humans, because of our association with you."

"All the same, I'll be glad to return home tomorrow."

"And we'll be nervous. But we should be safe as long as we stay with you and Becka."

"That may be a problem. You want to be together, naturally, but Becka and I are working together only temporarily. We will soon separate."

"That's a problem." The dragons consulted, and concluded that they would have to stay with Clio. Fortunately her shirt had two pockets. Once they had saved her life, they would go on to Becka and save hers, acquitting their commitment.

Next day they went to the land dragon site. The dragons were there, two by two and in collections of five couples, covering the landscape. Six thousand, two hundred fifty dragons. How could they ever fit into the tiny dragon net?

"Just toss it over them," Drew suggested.

Feeling foolish, she flung the net out toward the assembled dragons. It spread like exploding sunbeams and extended to cover the whole vast array. It settled down on the dragons, scintillating.

And the dragons shrank beneath it. They did not seem to be in any discomfort; they simply became smaller as the net drifted down and drew in its edges. Soon it lay on the ground, its original size.

She went to pick it up. It was full of exquisitely tiny dragons, the largest no bigger than motes of dust. "It seems it's large enough," she said. "I hope all those dragons are not uncomfortable in there."

"They aren't," Drusie said. "To them, the net seems big."

They were alone on the plain that was the belly of the beast. "I think it is time to return to Xanth," Becka said. "Do we travel separately, or together?"

"I would feel more secure together. We can hold hands."

"Done." They took hands, then willed themselves home.

They expanded in much the manner the net had. Dragon World seemed to shrink. As it became the size of a Ping-Pong ball one eye fixed on them and winked again. Then it shrank into mote size, and disappeared.

Now they saw the huge Princess Ida around whose head this world orbited. She wasn't exactly human, but Clio couldn't quite decide what species she was before she shrank into oblivion and her world came into view.

They expanded past a succession of worlds and Idas at an accelerating rate. Clio had to close her eyes lest she become dizzy. Then, seemingly suddenly, they were back in Xanth, floating toward their two resting bodies. They plunged in.

Clio felt as if she were suffocating. She was surrounded by ponderous flesh! Then she took control and made herself breathe. She opened her eyes, and saw Becka recovering also.

"It is good to have you back," Princess Ida said. "Did you achieve your object?"

Clio looked down at her hand. There was the dragon net bag. "I believe we did. But it's only partly done; we'll have four more trips to make."

"Where are Drew and Drusie?" Becka asked.

Oops. Clio had forgotten them. She glanced at her pocket, and found it empty. "We lost them!" she exclaimed, horrified.

"Oh, no!"

"We're not lost," Drew's faint voice came. "We merely lack substance at the moment."

Oh, of course. They needed physical bodies too.

"There are others with you?" Ida inquired.

"We have two dragons in our pockets," Clio said. "And more than six thousand in the net."

"In soul form," Ida said.

"Yes. Your analog on Dragon World gave me this net to contain them. We must take them to Castle MaiDragon where Che Centaur is assembling the raw material for bodies. Then we will return for our second trip."

"I will be expecting you."

They left Castle Roogna. Then Becka changed to dragon form, Clio mounted, and they flew to the Castle MaiDragon. Becka hurried, so it didn't take long.

Che Centaur was there amidst piles of substance. "This should animate in the correct forms, once the souls take over and guide it," he said. "Do you have them?"

"A few," Clio said. "But let's try it first on two special cases."

"Sure."

"Drew and Drusie, can you take hold of the substance you need?"

"We'll see."

After about a moment and a half, two little forms rose out of the nearest mass of substance. They spread their wings and flew up to perch on Clio's and Becka's shoulders.

"Che, meet Drew and Drusie," Clio said. "Drew and Drusie, this is Che Centaur, who gathered your substance."

"Much thanks," Drew's thought came. "It is excellent."

"It's so nice to be real at last," Drusie said.

"Let's do the rest," Becka said. "We'd better stand back."

Clio lifted the dragon net and opened it. She saw nothing, but soon shapes started rising from the substance, forming into dragons. Before long there were six thousand, two hundred fifty of them.

"Tell them to spread out across Xanth," Clio said. "And to avoid humans and human settlements. Che Centaur will answer any questions they have. Don't eat him!" Because they were after all dragons.

"And to avoid hostile puns," Becka added.

We shall, a dragon thought came. *Thank you, kind Muse.*

The dragons started spreading out. Meanwhile Clio and Becka got ready to go for the second batch. "Where do you want to be, Drew and Drusie?" she asked.

"With you, of course. We haven't saved your lives yet."

Clio laughed. "Then ride in our pockets, as before. We have much still to do today." She picked up the limp dragon net as Becka changed back to dragon form. She had a real feeling of accomplishment.

5
THREE CURSES

All the dragons had been delivered, and Becka and Che Centaur were orienting the last batch, with the help of the three little princesses. "I believe I'll go home now for a rest," Clio said. "It has been a long day."

"And we shall go with you, of course," Drew said. Drusie flew across from Becka and took Clio's other shirt pocket.

Clio looked around. She did not want to bother Becka or Che, who were busy. How was she to get home quickly? It was a long walk from here.

Princess Melody appeared. "You need a ride?"

Her sister Harmony faded in. "We can help."

"Just use the search engine," Rhythm said, there for only long enough to speak. Then all three were gone.

"A what?" Clio asked belatedly.

Something that looked like a little Mundane choo-choo train chugged up on invisible tracks, blowing puffs of smoke. That was evidently the locomotive the princesses had summoned. It eased to a stop before her, leaking steam from around the wheels. The word GOO was printed on its side. Clio hoped it wasn't gooey.

Melody appeared again. "Feed it coal-ins," she said.

"Not semi-coal-ins," Harmony added.

"And tell it to fetch you home," Rhythm concluded.

Then the three of them morphed into three chunks of black coal shaped like dots and commas.

Clio picked up two dots and tossed them into the coal-in car behind the engine. "Home, please," she said, and stepped onto the next car, which had a suitable seat.

The engine digested the coals, bleeped twice, and started its wheel turning. At first it was slow, but soon it was faster, and after that it was very fast. It steamed across the terrain, making a blur of the scenery.

Then Mount Parnassus loomed ahead. Next thing, the train stopped at the home of the Muses, letting out more steam. Somehow it had gotten halfway up the mountain and past the various obstructions without noticing them.

Clio got off. "Thank you, Goo," she said.

The engine puffed a sweet smelling ball of smoke in acknowledgment, and chugged off. No doubt someone else had some coal-ins for it.

"This is a big mountain," Drew said. "Why do you live here?"

"That is a long story," Clio said, lying down on her bed. "I doubt you would be interested."

"But we are," Drusie said. "We need to know all about you, so we can save your life."

Clio wasn't sure of their logic, but knew the little dragons meant well. "It begins when I was delivered, a hundred eighty-four years ago. I can review it in my mind, and you can skip the dull parts."

"And animate the bright parts," Drew agreed.

"But you don't look that old," Drusie said.

"Well, I'm not, really. It depends how you measure it."

"We'll measure it sympathetically," Drew said.

Clio relaxed on the bed, and thought about her origin.

King Ebnez took office in the Xanth Year 909, after the Ghost king had been exorcized by the people who wanted more life at the court. With the considerable assistance of his wife Mnem, whose talent was perfect memory, he signaled the storks for eight daughters in eight years. Their names were Calliope, who learned to recite epic poetry, Euterpe, who preferred lyric poetry, Melpomene, who liked tragedy, Terpsichore, who was strong on song and dance, Erato, who liked love poetry, Polyhymenia, who preferred sacred poetry, Urania, who became an astronomer, and Thalia, who liked comedy. Between them they kept the king and queen so busy that finally they were sent to a very private place, Castle Roogna, which had been lost for centuries. A nice woman, Rose of Roogna, was there, in hiding from her own family situation, and she was very helpful, so they were satisfied to be in this anonymous exile.

As it happened, there was a curse drifting around, and the king and queen were wary of it. It was that they could have as many as eight daughters happily, but the ninth would be cursed. So they decided not to signal the stork for any more. Besides, it was now the year 917 and the LastWave was invading from Mundania. It was all the king could do to handle that. So there was no time for another baby.

But then something went wrong, despite the king and queen's very loving relationship. No one was ever quite certain what, but apparently a signal went out to the stork, and a ninth baby was delivered. This was disaster, as they were completely unprepared, and there was also that curse. What were they to do? The stork was insistent: it was not about to take the baby back. They had to accept it.

King Ebnez' Magician talent was to adapt magical inanimate things to other purposes. So he made a daring plan: he would try to adapt the magic curse, which was presumed to be inanimate, to something else. That way it would be safe to accept the baby.

Thus it was that Mnem received her ninth daughter, Clio, who was destined to have an affinity for history. She had a sweet face, but her body was bony. And that was the first evidence of the curse: she was destined to have a body without nice feminine curves, so no man would want to marry her. They learned this from a magic mirror that knew something of curses, having been cracked up by one.

The king touched her and concentrated. "I will mitigate this curse," he said. "She may never have curves of her own, but she will find some." That was the best he could do; the original curse was exceedingly strong, and he had not had time to plan a really apt diversion.

But the curse was not done. It turned out that this girl would have danger every day of her life, enough to harm or even kill her. So the king concentrated again: "She may face daily danger, but will have the means to nullify it." He didn't know what the means might be, just that Clio would have some sort of magic to handle it.

Still the curse attacked, with the worst strike yet: she would die young. Once more the king concentrated. "She may die young, but she will be young a long time."

The curse was finally done; it had no more malign energy. The king collapsed in a royal swoon, having used all his strength to counter it. But at least he had saved his daughter, somehow. As a further precaution, he sent her to join her sisters at Castle Roogna, where no one would find them, since the castle remained lost.

Clio was the youngest sister, by three years. The others were pretty girls; Clio's prettiness halted at her neckline. She could run and jump and play, having no weakness or physical deformity; she just didn't look very good, with her string-bean torso and knobby limbs. Others averted their eyes from her, and it was clear that when she grew into a woman, men would avoid her. It was not true that men were interested in only one thing; they were interested in at least two curves above the waist, and two below it. She had none. But there was a remedy; she just had to find it. Meanwhile Rose assigned a nursemaid for her who made her look good in comparison: Agora Ogre, whose body was so ugly it added another crack to the mirror, and whose face, like that of all ogresses, looked like an overcooked bowl of mush that someone had sat on. Agora was unusual for an ogre in one respect: she was afraid to go out into the open. That was fine, because it meant she stayed inside all day, watching out for her little charge.

So at a young age Princess Clio went into the orchard, where the king had adapted many trees to bear wonderful new fruits, and searched. The king assigned Agora's brother to watch over her, because at least once a day some bad threat came. He was Medi Ogre, who was dull even for an ogre but alert and loyal. When harpies dive-bombed her in the orchard, the ogre raised his hamfists and bashed them out of the air. When poisonous snakes came at her, Medi tromped them. When she reached for live cherries or a pineapple, the ogre flicked them with his hamfingers and detonated them before they could hurt her. So she was all right, though what she would do when Medi's term of royal Service was done she didn't know.

Clio was attracted to an unusual tree. It was one of ancient King Roogna's failures. He had tried to make its trunk grow the shape of the body of a nymph, but the bark had been too tight and squeezed the tree until it expired. The top had fallen off, and there was just the remnant of the trunk remaining, suitable for birds to perch on. "I want it," she told Medi. So the ogre obligingly ripped the bark up and off the trunk and gave it to her.

Clio got inside it, and something remarkable happened. It closed in on her body and fit snugly, with branches covering her arms and legs too. The bark was not rough; it was soft and smooth and flexible, like the body of the nymph it was supposed to be, and made her look, well, shapely. This was all the more remarkable for a four-year-old. She walked back into the castle wearing it, and her sisters were astonished. "Where did you get the nice body?" Thalia asked.

"From the orchard," she replied.

Soon all her sisters were admiring it. Then the eldest, Calliope, who was fourteen, caught on. "You found your curves!"

Indeed it was so. The failed nymph bark had become a successful girl bark. One aspect of the curse had been mitigated.

But there remained the other two aspects, and these worried the others. Every day there was some direct threat to her welfare, and sooner or later one was bound to get to her and kill her, completing the third aspect. Probably sooner, making her die young.

But there was hope. Every person in Xanth, except for the brutish Mundanes of the LastWave, had a magic talent, of greater or lesser power. Clio's talent had not yet been discovered. Maybe it would save her. She was supposed to have the means to handle danger, after all.

One day when she was six Agora Ogre was busy with laundry and Medi Ogre was asleep, so Clio sneaked out on her own. Naturally she got into trouble. A flying dragon spied her and swooped down to snap her up. She hadn't even seen the danger until she was being carried out of the orchard, the cruel teeth drawing blood from her body. She knew she was doomed, and that it was her own fault. She wanted more than anything for this never to have happened.

Suddenly the dragon reversed course. It flew backward and down into the garden, and released her, and the pain of the bite eased. The dragon didn't stop there; it continued flying backward, back into the air, tail first. Clio herself was walking backward. She relaxed, safe after all.

Then she resumed walking forward, and the dragon came at her again. But this time she knew the danger. She dodged behind a tree just as the dragon snapped, and it missed and went on, a surprised look on its snout.

Clio ran inside to tell her sisters what had happened. They didn't believe her, of course, and she couldn't make them understand. She tried to demonstrate, by making them reverse course, but when they resumed forward motion, they didn't know that there had ever been any reversal. It was her secret, not because she wanted to keep it but because its very nature was hidden. Soon she realized that this was both her magic talent and the mitigation of the curse: with the windback, as she called it, she could reverse any bad thing that happened to her, and act to prevent it happening again. It wasn't a perfect answer to the dangers she faced, but coupled with sensible alertness, it very nearly nulled the curse.

There remained the third aspect: dying young. So she would be young a long time—how was that possible? She saw her sisters growing up and becoming young women, some of them beautiful, some pretty, some so-so, and realized that in time they would inevitably become mature women, and then old: twenty-eight or -nine. Surely the same fate awaited her—except that the curse would kill her before she ever got old. How was the amelioration ever to work?

Her sisters did mature, and became marriageable, one by one, at yearly intervals. But they did not marry, because they were all princesses, and would not marry beneath their station—and there were no princes. So they were stuck, and not particularly pleased. They remained anonymous at Castle Roogna.

When Clio was thirteen something happened elsewhere that made a difference: a rather small ugly baby boy was delivered to a family of tic farmers. The father was teaching the elder boy how to run the farm, and the mother was teaching the girls how to be suitably bossy, so there was no one to supervise the youngest child, whose name was Humfrey. So when he was two, Clio got the job of babysitting him. She didn't have to do it, being a princess, but it got her out of the castle, and she was pretty sure she could handle it because of her secret talent. If he got into mischief or had an accident, she could unwind it and make it right before it went wrong. She was fifteen, and did want to get out on her own. Naturally she did not tell the boy's family where she lived, because the privacy of the secret castle was important.

It worked out well. She seemed to have a magic touch, for there was never any trouble the family knew about, since they did not know how many scrapes she unwound and fixed. Little Humfrey turned out to be very smart, with an insatiable thirst for knowledge. Soon he figured out her talent, and figured out something else: when she used it, she probably aged faster. That was to say, that others did not remember, because they never really lived through the woundback episodes. But she did remember, because she lived through them coming and going. So if she got into five minutes worth of trouble, and wound it back five minutes, that was ten minutes of her life. It wouldn't have mattered much, except that she knew she was cursed to die young. That meant that using her talent would bring her life toward its end more rapidly. She didn't like that.

But Humfrey learned unusual things, even as a very young child, and one of them was that there had once been, and might still be, folk on Mount Parnassus called the Muses who were ageless. Maybe she should go and seek their secret. If she didn't age, she would remain young for a long time, abating the third aspect of her curse.

Thrilled with that notion, she kissed the four-year-old boy, much to his disgust, and at the age of seventeen set out to find Parnassus. She knew its general location, and since she didn't want to tell her sisters, who would interfere, she would have to go there alone, on foot. Well, she would do so.

She set out, wearing her nymph-shape bark, which had grown with her and now provided her with enviable curves above and below the waist. She removed it only rarely, as she preferred the curves to her natural state. She pretended to be offended when men stared at her body, but she wasn't; it was nice being attractive.

Little Humfrey had calculated that Mount Parnassus lay to the south, so that's the way she went. There were no safe enchanted paths, though there were some unsafe ones; the safe ones would come later. So she carried a long wood staff that she really didn't know how to use, and poked at anything she wasn't sure about. What she really needed was a traveling companion, preferably a strong male. But that wasn't completely safe for other reasons. Unless she could find a safely married man to travel with, though she understood they weren't always ideal either. Her sisters had done babysitting for some families, and had some disquieting reports. Still, her ability to wind back problem events reassured her, though she would avoid using it if she possibly could. What use to save her life, if it only hastened the end of her life?

She passed a big pantree. This one had pans growing above, and panties inside, and underpants on the ground beneath it. She got the pun: pants under it. Fortunately she didn't need any underwear; she had a spare pair of panties.

Beyond it was another tree that blocked her best path. Its branches spread out to either side, effectively balking her. "How do I get past you?" she asked rhetorically.

"I'm a Poe tree," it replied, surprising her. "You recite poetry."

Oh. She pondered, and did her best to come up with something suitable.

"I think that I shall never see, a monster lovely as a tree," she said. "And unless you let me by, a monster may catch me on the fly."

"That's doggerel," the tree protested. "I was thinking of high classical, or at least something about a raven."

"You didn't specify what kind of poetry."

"I suppose I didn't," the tree agreed grudgingly. It moved its branches aside, letting her by. "But you may deserve to be caught by a monster."

"I have already met monsters, thank you."

"Nevermore," quoth the Poe tree.

She went on beyond it, deciding not to inquire how it was a tree could talk the human language. The land was more open here, and she could walk without difficulty. She saw a box with a pair of boxing gloves on top. Curious, she approached it—and the gloves rose up on thick stems and menaced her. "What in Xanth are you?" she asked, taken aback.

"I'm a boxer, of course. I punch out enemies."

"I'm not an enemy, I hope."

The box considered. "I suppose not. You sound like a girl."

"I *am* a girl."

"That explains it." The gloves settled back on the box.

Clio went on. She was evidently in one of the oddities regions of Xanth, where things were neither friendly nor hostile, just odd. Well, that was better than being pursued by monsters.

She saw a large cake resting on a rock sculpted in the form of a voluptuous woman. By it was a sign saying EAT ME, and in smaller print, CHEESE CAKE. Clio distrusted this, but she really liked cheese-cake, and it reminded her how hungry she was getting, so she decided to try it. She broke off a small piece and tasted it. It was delicious.

Then she sneezed, and sneezed again and again, helplessly. The remaining cake flew out of her mouth; she couldn't help herself. It was awful.

Finally the fit passed. Her eyes were watering. The sneezing fit had come without warning, and just at the wrong time. She had lost her cake.

Then as her eyes cleared she saw the small print more accurately. It said SNEEZE CAKE. She should have known.

Not far beyond was another sculptured rock bearing another cake. This rock was in the form of a marvelously muscular man, and its sign said EAT ME—BEEF CAKE. She passed it by without pausing; she was no longer hungry.

She spent the night on the back of a tree the shape of a frog: a tree frog. It was comfortable, and the sides were steep enough so that nasty creatures on the ground would have trouble getting at her as she slept. That left only the flying bugs to worry about. Actually there weren't many, because the tree frog's tongue snapped out and hauled any that ventured close in to its mouth. But in the morning it decided to change its location, and jumped. She fell to the ground, hurting her leg. She had to windback so she could slide gracefully off just before the jump.

She found pie trees and fresh streams, so was able to eat and drink as she continued south. Whenever a monster spied her and attacked, she wound time back so she could avoid it. She didn't like doing that, but when it was a choice between shortening her life or dying immediately, it seemed warranted.

In due course she reached Mount Parnassus. This was a huge double-peaked mountain extending far into the sky. She had no idea where the Muses might be, so simply would have to climb to the top and hope she found them along the way.

The north peak was closer, so she started up that. There were a number of paths that separated, ran parallel, and joined, so it was easy to find her way; she simply took whatever branch was headed uphill at the moment.

Then something huge appeared. It was the largest serpent she had ever seen. Its head was half the size of her body, with a jaw that could surely open a mouth capable of swallowing her whole. She stared at it half a moment, horrified, then tried to turn to run away—and could not, for the giant eye had caught her gaze and held her immobile.

"Wh-what—?" she asked, her mouth unable to get more words out.

"I am the Python," the serpent hissed. "I am the passion and neme-sis of all the female gender. I roused desire in the first woman, and made her ashamed of her ardor, yet she could not deny it. I will possess the last woman to ever exist. Bow down before me, you helpless crea-ture, for I am about to do you the favor of consuming you." He slithered forward, holding her gaze.

Clio finally acted. She wound the scene back until the snake was out of sight, then quickly dodged to another path and hurried along it, away from the horror. It wasn't just the thought of being swallowed whole, it was the dreadful compulsion of the reptile's speech. He had stirred a feeling in her that she had never had before, an urge to be possessed in some unknown manner. She had to get away from that!

Then the Python appeared before her. How had that happened? She should have left it behind.

"I know your location and nature, innocent girl," he hissed. "You can't escape me." His terrible gaze transfixed her again; she could not move. "No woman can escape me, for I am desire itself. Come to me, my delicious morsel."

Clio wound the scene back again, and fled. This time she ran down the slope, to make better speed. But soon the Python appeared before her once more. "I love to play with you, morsel," he hissed. "But I wonder how you manage to slip my noose? Ah—you possess an unusual magic talent!"

And the serpent was telepathic! That explained how she was hearing him talk, and why she was feeling those awful yet alluring feelings. He had read her talent in her mind, and learned what she had done.

She could not continue winding back and being caught again. She had to find a way to escape him permanently. What could that be?

"There is no way," the Python hissed. "You are destined to be mine, for you are a mere female. All females are mine."

A new emotion entered the fray: annoyance. The reptile was belittling her nature, and she wasn't at all sure he was telling the truth. That prompted her to try again. This time she wound the scene well back, almost to their prior encounter. Then she dodged to the side and ran north, along a level path around the slope of the mountain. By the time the snake realized she hadn't gone where she had gone before, she would be too far ahead to catch. She hoped.

She came to a wine-red pool. Around it sat a number of buxom bare girls. They stared at her, startled. They were long of leg, small of waist, full of bosom, cute of face, and had wild long hair flaring from their heads and bouncing on their shoulders. Every one of them looked like man's desire.

Then they leaped up. "The maenads feed today!" one cried, and started toward her.

Clio did not like the sound of this. Normally pretty girls were nothing to fear, but these ones had pointed teeth, and the wildness of their hair extended to their blazing eyes. That made her nervous, so she wound the scene back and took another path. But she heard a slithering sound, and realized that the Python was coming down this trail. She was caught between the bloodthirsty maenads and the hungry snake.

Then she realized that she might be able to make something of this. Instead of doing another windback, she turned and ran back toward the wild women in real time. She knew the Python was following, and gaining on her; he could slither with remarkable swiftness. But she had a plan.

She rounded a turn. There were the maenads, charging toward her. She ran right into them, dodged, and past them, surprising them. She ran on toward their colored pond.

Meanwhile the Python was the next to come upon the maenads. "So the snake intrudes!" a maenad screamed. "Get him!"

Clio risked a look back. The maenads were swarming over the reptile, clawing at him with their bare hands. He in turn was writhing and snapping. It seemed to be a fair battle.

Meanwhile, Clio was left alone, and for once she hadn't had to use the windback. She kneeled by the pond and scooped up a palmful of its water. She sipped it.

Water? This was wine! It was delicious, but very strong. It went right to her head, making her feel wild.

A maenad appeared, coming from the other direction. "Who are you?" she demanded, baring her teeth in what was definitely not a smile.

"Just a visitor. I was thirsty, so I paused here to—"

The maenad screamed and pounced. She actually leaped through the air, her hair flaring dangerously, and caught hold of Clio, bringing those teeth down for a bite of her shoulder. The pain was awful.

Clio wound back the scene, meanwhile thinking fast. She did not want to speak falsely, but it was clearly unsafe to tell the truth to a maenad, who regarded all other creatures as prey. It would be better to divert the bloodthirsty girl.

So when she resumed normal activity, she answered, "Did you know there's a fight with the Python?"

The maenad was horrified. "And I missed it? Where?"

Clio pointed. "Down that path. You won't miss it."

The maenad set off at a run that made all her flesh ripple. It was remarkable how young and sweet she looked, yet how vicious she was. Soon she disappeared around a turn. Clio trusted that she was not too late for the fight.

She was alone again, but surely not for long. Other maenads might be appearing, and she couldn't divert them all. She also couldn't drink much more of this wine; it made her feel too much like a maenad.

A bulb flashed. Maybe she could *be* a maenad, just long enough to find her bearings.

She removed her clothing, keeping only the snug nymph bark that gave her shape. She looked at her reflection in the pool as it stilled. Yes, she looked a lot like a maenad, except that her teeth were not pointed and her hair wasn't as wild. So she fluffed out her tresses, and would try to keep her mouth closed. She wadded up her clothing to make it seem like a tattered chunk of something dead and carried it in her hand. Then she walked on up the mountain, following the most direct path. More than one maenad saw her, but took her for one of them, especially when she chewed on her chunk of tatter.

When she was well clear of both maenads and Python, she unwadded her clothing and donned it again. It was badly rumpled, but that couldn't be helped. No one was seeing her anyway; the height of the mountain seemed to lack both people and wildlife.

At last, tired, she reached the top. There at the apex grew a mighty tree with rich green leaves. She was so hungry that she plucked a leaf and chewed it, and it did help; it made her feel remarkably healthy. Maybe there was Healing Elixir in it.

But there was nothing else here, so she walked on down the south slope of the north peak toward the north slope of the south peak. She moved faster, in part because the downslope was easier, and in part because of the renewed vigor the leaf had given her. Before nightfall not only was she off the north peak, she was well up the south peak. Just as dusk was sneaking in, wrapping around the mountain, she reached the top.

There was another tree, just as grand at the other, with a great variety of colors and leaves, as if it were of multiple species. And perched on one of its mighty branches was the biggest, brightest bird she had ever seen. It was the size of a roc bird, though she had never before been close to one of those, but its colors were different. It had feathers like iridescent veneers of light and shadow, and its head was crested like fire. Its wings did not seem quite solid, though they surely were; they were like scintillating veils of mist over a mountain.

A GREETING, SOLITARY GIRL. It was an ineffably powerful thought, as from the mother of all creatures.

Clio jumped. "What?"

YOU DO NOT KNOW ME. It was not a question.

Clio stared. "The bird!" she exclaimed, astonished. "You're the bird!"

I AM THE BIRD OF BIRDS, THE SIMURGH. I HAVE SEEN THE UNIVERSE FADE AND REVIVE THREE TIMES. I GUARD THIS TREE OF SEEDS AGAINST MOLESTATION.

"I—I'm sorry. I'm Clio. I don't want to molest anything. I was just looking for the Muses, because—"

NOW I SEE. And it was obvious that the bird was peering right into her mind. THERE IS MUCH YOU HAVE TO LEARN.

"I didn't mean to intrude. I don't know anything about the Tree of Seeds. I'll go now."

NOT YET, good girl. YOU HAVE EATEN OF THE TREE OF LIFE.

Did that mean she was in trouble? "Is that the other big tree? I did eat a leaf, because—"

YOU WERE HUNGRY. YOU DID NOT KNOW. The Simurgh flicked a wing, marvelously, and a seed sailed toward Clio. EAT.

She caught the seed. It was a big one. She didn't recognize its type, but it looked and smelled good, so she took a bite. It was delicious and filling. "Thank you. I—"

YOU ARE NOW IMMORTAL AND SAFE, AS LONG AS YOU REMAIN IN THESE ENVIRONS.

"Immortal! But I'm doomed to die young!"

YOUR CURSES ARE ABATED HERE. YOU WILL NEVER AGE OR BE EXPOSED TO DAILY DANGER. YOU HAVE ACHIEVED

YOUR AMBITION, WITH ONE CAVEAT. WHEN YOU LEAVE MOUNT PARNASSUS, YOU WILL RESUME NORMAL AGING AND DANGER.

Amazed, Clio grasped at that straw. "Then I want to stay here! But what can I do to earn this reward?" For she had no intention of taking something for nothing.

THE MUSES ARE GONE. THEY WENT TO MUNDANIA SOME TIME AGO. THEIR RESIDENCE IS VACANT.

Clio tried to cushion her disappointment. Had her journey been wasted? But perhaps not, if she already had the secret of remaining young. Still—

WE HAVE BEEN LOOKING FOR REPLACEMENTS, BUT SETS OF NINE SUITABLE SISTERS SELDOM PASS THIS WAY.

"Replacements? I don't under—"

YOU HAVE EIGHT SISTERS. WILL THEY SERVE?

Clio tried to digest this. "You mean, to live where the Muses did? To maintain the premises."

TO BE THE MUSES.

This was beyond understanding. "We can't—we don't—"

THEY, TOO, WILL BE ALLOWED TO EAT OF THE TREE OF LIFE, SO AS TO BECOME IMMORTAL. NONE OF YOU WILL AGE; YOU WILL REMAIN YOUNG ETERNALLY.

"They'd like that! But how can any of us possibly fill such elite roles? We don't know anything about the roles of the Muses."

YOU WILL LEARN. IT SEEMS YOU WERE FATED FOR THIS. YOUR INTERESTS ALIGN. SO DO YOUR NAMES. YOU WERE CLEARLY GUIDED. GO BRING YOUR SISTERS HERE.

"But my sisters want to find good men, princes, to marry. They don't want to be in isolation all their lives."

THEY ARE WELCOME TO GO OUT TO SEEK PRINCES, AND TO BRING THEM HERE TO STAY, PROVIDED THEY FULFILL THEIR ROLES AS MUSES. YOU, TOO, MAY SEEK A PRINCE OR MAGICIAN TO MARRY.

Clio laughed uncomfortably. "Somehow I doubt any would be interested, since I would not deceive him about my curves."

THAT WILL BE YOUR CHOICE. BRING YOUR SISTERS.

"But—"

The Simurgh's beak might have shown impatience, had she not been an eternally patient bird. EAT OF THIS SEED, AND TAKE IT WITH YOU FOR THEM. Another seed flicked toward her.

Clio caught it. Still she tried to protest. "I don't think they could get past the Python and the maenads. When I left them, they were fighting each other, but some may survive, and they're vicious."

THEY ARE IMMORTAL. THEY KNOW THEY CAN'T DIE, SO THEY FEEL FREE TO FIGHT.

Oh. That did make sense. "But suppose the Python swallows a maenad?"

SHE WILL PASS THROUGH HIS DIGESTIVE SYSTEM AND EMERGE UNSCATHED, IN DUE COURSE.

Clio had to smile. "But I suppose she would not much like the experience."

There was an echoing smile in the Simurgh's thought. TRUE. YOUR SISTERS WILL TRAVEL SAFELY. NOW EAT OF THE SEED.

She had forgotten it for the moment. She nibbled on it. Suddenly she was filled with positive belief. "I'll do it," she agreed.

IT IS THE SEED OF CERTAINTY. REST HERE THIS NIGHT.

Suddenly that seemed the most sensible thing to do. She lay on the ground where she was and slept. That hinted how tired she was, because princesses never roughed it in such manner. Walking the way she had was bad enough; this was downright crude. Suppose some man came by in the night and gazed lasciviously at her exposed ankles?

In the morning she woke, well refreshed. She discovered a downy feather the size of a pillow under her head, and a flexible feather the size of a quilt covering her. She had had a most comfortable bed, and her ankles were not exposed.

She got up and stretched. The Simurgh remained perched on her limb, evidently asleep. There was no point in bothering her; Clio had a job to do. She turned and looked for a suitable path down the mountain.

I WILL TAKE YOU, GOOD GIRL.

Then a taloned foot reached down and enclosed her gently. Clio hadn't even realized that the bird had taken wing; her flight was quite silent. Suddenly they were gliding down the mountain slope, then up into the sky, then across the variegated landscape of Xanth.

Before she really got her bearings, they were at Castle Roogna, landing by the orchard. The Simurgh set her down and disappeared, literally: there was no sign of the bird. But Clio didn't hesitate; she walked purposefully to the castle, entered, and called out: "Sisters! I'm back, and I have somewhere for us all to go."

In a moment they clustered around her. Rather than try to explain, she held up the big seed. "Try this first."

They tried it, as it was fragrant and tasty. Then they too were certain. "We will go," they agreed. "This is what we have been waiting for."

They gathered their things and bid farewell to Rose, who was sorry to see them go but recognized the need. Then they went outside.

An invisible curving cage formed about them. It lifted, carrying them into the sky. Once they were fully airborne, the rest of the bird appeared; they were within the loose enclosure of her talons.

"Sisters, meet the Simurgh," Clio said. "Simurgh, these are my eight sisters. We are all certain we want to join you on Mount Parnassus, and assume the roles of the nine Muses."

"And so it was," Clio concluded, opening her eyes and seeing the tiny dragons. "We became the Muses in the year 937, and have been so for the past hundred and sixty-seven years. The Simurgh was right: we learned, and I think we have performed adequately. We seldom leave the mountain, though I did attend Humfrey's first wedding and have seen him on occasion since then. I have written many histories of Xanth, and now am on a quest to discover why one volume has become opaque to me. I have to find a red berry. I will age normally as long as I am away from the mountain, and face daily danger, but it just has to be risked. If I get too old, I will die, but I hope to wrap this up expeditiously and remain young enough to live."

"We will assist you," Drew said. "Those maenads seem like fun. So does the Python."

"I will introduce you to them. They no longer chase me, lest I write them out of history."

The two tiny dragons chuckled. "You have power now," Drew said. "That helps. But we'll help too."

"We can do a lot, when we put our little minds to it," Drusie agreed. "We'll find the red berry. This should be easy."

Clio suspected that they were mistaken, but she didn't argue. It would be nice if it did turn out to be easy.

6
SHERLOCK

S o how do we start?" Drew asked.

"Well, I'm not sure. I had rather expected more direction from the Good Magician than I received."

"You are being polite," Drusie said, reading the situation in her mind. "I'd have steamed his little toe."

Clio stroked the little pink dragon's back with one finger. "I appreciate the support, but there's surely a reason for his attitude."

"Take us there," Drew said. "I'll toast his big toe until he gives you more information."

Clio suppressed a wicked temptation. "That would not be expedient. I believe it is best simply to muddle through on my own."

"The trouble with you is that you're too nice a person."

"Would that it were so. Then maybe I could find a compatible man and marry."

"You can do that?" Drusie asked.

"Marry? Of course. Except that who would want to marry a Muse and be confined forever to Mount Parnassus?"

"We'll work on it," Drew said.

They meant well. "Thank you."

"What's that on your wrist?" Drusie asked.

Clio looked. There on her left wrist was the magic compass Humfrey had given her. She had thought that would fade out, now that her Service was done. "That's the device I used to locate you, so that you could help me on Dragon World. The blue arrow shows the way I should go, and the red one shows how much time I have to get there."

"That must show you where to go next," Drew said. "You don't seem to have long."

Surprised, Clio actually read the dials. "True. I'd better see what it wants me to see."

They set off. Clio knew the fastest paths down the mountain, and no one bothered her. Soon they were walking across the regular terrain of Xanth.

It turned out to be a longish walk, with the red arrow constantly getting nearer to zero hour. Clio hurried, but realized she might be a bit late.

Naturally, since she was in a hurry, she encountered another person. But maybe this would help. "Hello. I'm Clio. My talent is to wind time back when I need to."

The girl jumped. "Oh, I'm sorry—I didn't see you. I'm Deirdre. My talent is oversight. I see everything from above, but nothing in front of me."

"Do you see anything unusual in the direction I'm going?"

"Well, there's an ogre with a garden. That's unusual."

It was, but Clio doubted that was where she was headed. "Thank you." She hurried on.

"Another girl ahead," Drew said.

Sure enough, there she was, right in the path. Clio couldn't escape another introduction. "I'm Clio, and I'm in a hurry."

"I'm Michele, and it's not my fault."

Clio paused. "What's not your fault?"

"That you're in a hurry. My talent is shifting blame or credit."

That was interesting, and Clio would have liked to learn more of it, but she simply couldn't wait. "It's working; my hurry has nothing to do with you." She rushed on, leaving Michele somewhat nonplussed.

Just as the red arrow touched the mark, they came into sight of an ogre. He was twice the height of a human man, and solid in proportion. "Me bash, you crash!" he said in the typical dull rhyme that was all most folk ever heard of ogre talk. He struck something, and it went flying into the distance.

The blue arrow followed the flying object.

Clio sighed. She had another windback to do.

She wound back the scene. The flying thing reappeared, came up against the ogre's hamfist, and touched the ground. "!hsarc uoy, hsab eM"

She wound it back a bit more, then looked. It was a human man getting bashed. "Stop that ogre!" she cried.

Both dragons darted forward, flying low. One jetted a small blue flame, toasting the ogre's right big toe. The other pink-steamed his left little toe.

"He go, me toe!" the ogre said, aware of some slight discomfort. But that was enough to distract him from the man he had been about to bash. He squatted, swatting at his feet. The dragons zipped away and rejoined Clio.

Clio caught the man's arm. "Get out of here," she said. "We'll distract the ogre."

The man stumbled away, obviously uncertain what was happening. Clio stood before the squatting ogre, whose huge ugly face was now about her own head height. "What do you think you're doing?" she demanded imperiously. She could invoke the Voice of Authority when she needed to.

"Me Bash, he dash," he said.

"I saw that." Though now it hadn't happened.

"He means his name is Bash," Drew said from her pocket. Because this was a mental effect, he was inaudible to the ogre. "He hurried to save his garden from molestation."

"Garden! Molestation!" Since when did ogres care about either? Yet this was obviously the gardening ogre Deirdre had mentioned.

"Since Bash started farming puns," Drusie said. "He's got a garden of them, and the man messed it up. So Bash got rid of him. He has a case."

"He doesn't grow them all," Drew said. "Some he collects. He really cares about it."

What a reversal! But it seemed this was a situation she needed to rectify. It did not seem to have anything to do with a red berry, but maybe that was in another part of the garden. "Hello, Bash. I am Clio. Perhaps I can help. What damage did the man do to your garden?"

The ogre pointed a hamfinger to what looked like the wreck of a Mundane car. Steam was rising from it.

"It's a car-burr-ator," Drew said. "It's supposed to freeze cars, whatever they are. Now it makes them overheat."

"I will fix it," Clio said. "What else?"

Bash pointed to an apelike creature.

"You certainly look charming, fair lady," the ape called. "You must be a king's daughter."

Of course she was a king's daughter, but that was a long time ago. "What is wrong with this?" she asked Drew.

"That's a harang-u-tan," the dragon explained as he did more mind reading. "He's supposed to hurl insults. Now he wafts compliments."

Which ruined the pun. "I will fix that too," Clio told the ogre. "What else?"

He pointed to several big white letter F's lying in a pile. "Those are tasteless white F's," Drew explained. "They used to be tasty brown E's."

"That too," Clio said with a sigh.

There turned out to be a number of spoiled puns in the garden. There were retro specs that could see the past; now the glasses looked into the future. There was a grain of sand that was actually a peep show, showing a distant person whatever it saw; Clio had heard of those, and knew they were popular with young men who liked to scatter them around girls' private living quarters. Now it was reversed, showing the person who was trying to use it. There was an impro vise that was supposed to hold anything on the spot; now it repelled things. This garden had become a disaster.

Clio did what she didn't like, and wound the scene back farther yet, until the visiting man was entirely gone from the scene. That should fix the problem.

"Now we need to intercept the man and find out what he did to that garden," she told the dragons. "But he came from the other side, and I'll have to run by the ogre to get to him. That hardly seems feasible."

"I'll fly ahead and intercept him," Drew said. "I'll tell him to wait where he is and meet you when you arrive."

"Thank you." The dragons really were helping.

Drew flew ahead so rapidly he looked like a small blue bird. Clio walked at her normal sedate pace. In a generous moment she passed the garden, which now had a car motor with frost on it, a pile of warm brown E's, and a talking ape. "Who do you think you are, you crazy damsel?" he demanded. "Can't you see this is private property? If my master Bash Ogre finds you, he'll squeeze you into pulp juice."

Yes, the garden was back in form. She ignored the haranguing ape, avoided stepping over the peep show sand, and walked on. Soon she encountered the ogre. "Who you?" Bash demanded truculently.

"I am Clio, the Muse of History. I believe you'll find everything in order in your garden."

"Me see." He tromped on to investigate.

"Why didn't he squeeze you into pulp?" Drusie asked.

"He didn't think of it. I distracted him by reminding him of the garden. Ogres are proud of their stupidity, with good reason; they can't entertain two thoughts at the same time. Actually they are not bad folk, once you understand them. They don't even speak in dull rhyme among themselves; it is only the ignorant who hear them that way, expecting no better."

"But you heard him in rhyme."

"I didn't want to socialize with him, so I kept it basic. Another time may be different."

"At least you have handled your danger for today," Drusie said.

"I don't believe so. The ogre was never a threat to me. That's why I was so bold in bracing him."

"So your danger is still to come?"

"Yes, I believe so."

"Then when it's done you'll be able to relax."

"No. Actually there is no maximum limit; I can encounter more than one danger in a day. Just never less than one. So I must be on constant guard."

"That's one mean curse," the dragon said.

Clio nodded. "I am accustomed to it. But it is another reason I'm generally not keen on leaving Mount Parnassus."

They came to the man, who was standing still with the tiny dragon perched on his shoulder. Drew had given her time to talk with the ogre without encountering the man at the same time, thus avoiding another bashing sequence.

He looked up and saw her. "Hello, Muse; I am honored to meet you."

"I told him all about you," Drew said proudly. "And how you just saved him from getting bashed by Bash Ogre."

Clio sighed inwardly. She would have to caution the dragons about saying too much to strangers. She preferred to introduce herself, and to keep personal information to herself unless making it known was warranted.

"Oops, sorry," Drew said contritely.

"I am glad to meet you," Clio said somewhat insincerely to the man. "There was a problem, so I abated it."

"The telepathic dragon says that you wound time backward so as to spare me mischief. To what do I owe this considerable favor?"

"I am not sure." Now she really looked at him for the first time, and saw that he was an unprepossessing middle-aged man of dark countenance. "You look familiar; have you been a significant character before?"

"Oh, yes. I am Sherlock, of the Black Wave. I made one of your volumes when I traveled with Dug Mundane twelve years ago, helping him play his game while I searched for a suitable region for the Wave to settle. That turned out to be around Lake OgreChobee. We normally get along well with ogres; I find it hard to believe that I affronted one, or will do so."

Sherlock. Yes, he was a decent man from Mundania who would now be about forty-five. He should have settled down and married long since, instead of wandering out here in nowhere. "I remember you now. I agree; you are not likely to give offense to anyone. Yet it seems you did to that ogre, by changing aspects of his garden."

"I wouldn't know how to change a garden." Sherlock paused, considering. "But I can't say I'm surprised. Weird things have been happening around me. That's why my people no longer wanted me around. No one wants me around for long."

"We must explore this," Clio said. "Because I was guided to you. I do not know why, but of course the things set in motion by the Good Magician are often devious."

"I agree. Maybe he made a mistake this time. I'm really a person of no account, and I wouldn't want to cause you any mischief, Muse. I appreciate the good work you are doing. So I think I should just be on my way before anything else happens."

Clio glanced at her wrist. The blue arrow still pointed to the man. "No, we have business together, and it behooves us to discover what it is."

"No offense, but I find that hard to believe. You are an important person and are surely wasting your time with me."

Clio smiled. "Let's find out." She looked around, and saw a couch potato. She sat in it, and it was comfortable. "Join me, please."

Sherwood shrugged and sat beside her. But as he did, the cool soft couch suddenly became burning hot. Both of them leaped out. The thing was now a hot potato.

"That must be your danger," Drusie said.

"I doubt it; I didn't need to wind back to get out of it."

"It's happening again," Sherlock said, dismayed, as he brushed off his hot backside. "Really, you don't want to associate with me any longer, Muse."

"I believe I do," Clio said firmly, though her own backside was none too comfortable. Had it not been insulated by the curvy nymph bark, she could have been burned. "It is quite possible that whatever mischief is besieging you is the reason I was sent to meet you. We merely have to establish what it is."

"Maybe so," he agreed. "I'd certainly like to know what's wrong with me."

They found separate stones to sit on. "Please describe exactly what effects you have noted."

"That's hard to do, because they're all different and they don't make any sense I can see."

"Start at the beginning. When was the first untoward incident?"

"I'm not even sure about that. In retrospect things I took for coincidence seem not to have been. Maybe it was the beans."

"Beans?"

"I harvested some garden-variety beans from the garden and brought them in for the communal pot. We elder Black Wave folk don't have magic, though our children do, so we have to do things the mundane way. But when we started eating the beans, we all went into violent coughing fits. They were coughee beans."

"Why in Xanth would you harvest that kind of bean? Didn't you recognize them?"

"I do recognize them. What I picked were ordinary beans, not magical ones. I'm sure of it. But somehow they turned out to be the wrong kind. Some thought I did it on purpose, and others thought I was incompetent. I wasn't allowed to harvest beans anymore."

Clio glanced at the couch-sized hot potato, which seemed to be cooling. "I am sure that was a couch potato when I sat in it. It changed when you touched it. So I can believe that the beans changed."

"Thank you. But how? I couldn't do such magic if I wanted to. I don't think there's an evil Magician following me around; why would he bother?"

"That is a good question." She considered. "I have two friends, one of whom you met: Drew Dragon. They are telepathic. They can check to see if there are any other minds nearby, and what their intentions are. Dragons?"

"On it," Drusie said.

"Meanwhile," Clio continued, "what else has happened in your vicinity?"

"Another day I harvested onions. But when I brought them in, they turned out to be credit onions."

"I am not familiar with that kind."

"It's not edible. It's active only on weekdays, nine to five. You have to open an account, and there's a penalty for early withdrawal. So we couldn't even get rid of them. After that I wasn't allowed to harvest anything. No one believed I hadn't done it on purpose. I don't even know what a credit onion is, just that it's supposed to pay interest. How do you pay interest? You're either interested in something or you aren't."

"I believe they have ways in Mundania, where a person may pretend interest in order to flatter another. This certainly looks like magic. What else happened?"

"We had two grand trees by the entrance to our settlement, that made anyone who touched them feel good. One was the loyal tree; the other was the royal tree. I was feeling rejected, so I went out and touched them both. After that they were a disloyal tree and a peasant tree. That was when I was asked to leave the settlement."

"Did that solve the problem?"

"Perhaps it did, for them. Not for me. I had not gone far before I encountered a man and a woman, twins. The man's talent was to manipulate bodies, while the woman manipulated minds. But after they met me, he found he couldn't handle demons, and she couldn't affect the minds of nymphs or ogres. They were most annoyed, and refused to have anything more to do with me."

"Perhaps that was just as well," Clio said. "Those talents could be dangerous if they lacked limits."

"Maybe so. They were planning to conquer Xanth, but now are afraid they won't be able to do it. I really didn't mean to interfere, but somehow I must have."

"We have found no hostile minds within range," Drusie reported. "Just several human girls having a picnic. We think they're harmless."

"We had better be sure," Clio said. "Who are they and what are their talents?"

"They are the sisters Lon Leigh, who stops loneliness for others, and Luv Leigh, who makes anything lovely. Their friends are Re Joyce, who gives folk joy—"

"She's very pretty, for a human," Drew said.

"And Inertia, who makes things stay at rest, or stay in motion. That's an odd talent."

"But not one that would account for the mischief Sherlock has encountered," Clio concluded. "The others seem innocuous also. There are no others nearby?"

"There's a child and an animal," Drew said. "Do they count?"

"They may. Describe them."

"One is a six-year-old Mundane girl named Stephanie. She had— they took knives and cut her throat—"

"They do that in Mundania," Clio said. "It's called surgery."

"To take something out. But they weren't supposed to, and she kept on bleeding. Then she found herself here without her family. She was very confused. But then a horse named Angel found her, and gave her a ride, and she's feeling better now. They're both lost, and looking for their homes."

Clio felt a chill. "They won't find them. They live in Xanth now."

Sherlock glanced at her, and did not comment. He understood. The two dragons read her mind, and understood.

They heard footfalls. The horse was coming this way. They paused in their dialogue, sitting on their stones.

The horse appeared, a mare, walking carefully along the path. A chubby child with pigtails was on her back. The horse saw the people and stopped, sending a glance at Clio, as if asking directions.

"She knows the child is as lost as she is," Drusie said. "She needs to know where both of them should go."

There would be time enough for them to learn the truth. "Continue the way you are going," Clio said. "You will intersect an enchanted path. You will be safe on that, and there will be rest stops with all you need, including places to eat, wash, and sleep. Continue until you reach Castle Roogna. Three little princesses there will help you."

Angel Horse nodded and walked on. In Xanth, animals could under-stand a lot more than they could in Mundania. They would get there in a few days, and the princesses would be glad to help them.

Now they got back to business. "So we have ascertained that there are no hostile influences in the neighborhood," Clio said. "That means it must be something associated with you. Have you any idea what it might be?"

He laughed. "Not unless I'm haunted."

"Have you considered magic?"

"You mean, magic I do? Remember, I'm from Mundania."

"There is something you may not be aware of, as it isn't widely known. Mundanes who remain in Xanth for a sufficient time can develop magic talents of their own. It can take a decade or so, but it happens. Often they don't realize it because they are so sure they lack magic that they never look for it. So, like the centaurs of Centaur Isle, they live in ignorance of their true abilities."

He stared at her. "You're telling me I may have a magic talent?"

"I believe it likely. This would account for the effects you have been experiencing."

"I find this hard to believe."

"I appreciate that. If you wish, we can experiment to see if we can identify its nature."

"Well, I wouldn't want to take your time."

"I believe that for the moment you are my business, Sherlock. So I need to take the time to ascertain the situation."

"In that case, thank you, and I'll try to cooperate to make it as efficient as possible. I know you have other things to do."

She knew he wasn't being facetious; he was a nice man, and she found herself liking him. "Now these effects have been significant changes in the natures of things you have touched, like beans or onions as well as the potato. And of course there were the problems in the ogre's garden."

"Ogre's garden? Oh, yes, the little dragon told me."

"I did," Drew agreed.

"Things were changing, even becoming the opposites of what they had been." Clio paused as a bulb flashed over her head. "Opposites: that suggests reversal. Could there be reverse wood? Do you carry a chip of that?"

"Like this?" Sherlock asked, a chip of wood appearing in his hand. Then he stared at it. "How did that happen?"

"I believe you conjured it," Clio said. "That may be your magic. Can you do it again, intentionally?"

"I'm sure I can't. Maybe it just dropped into my hand from above."

There was nothing but sky above them. "Try, Sherlock."

He concentrated—and a bolt of wood appeared in his hand, so big and solid it dropped to the ground before him.

Drew had been perching on the man's shoulder. He dropped too, and lay on the ground, looking changed.

"Drew!" Drusie exclaimed, flying to him. Then she too dropped.

"Drew! Drusie! Are you all right?" Clio asked. They didn't answer. Then she saw that they looked like lizards.

"It *is* reverse wood," she said. "It nullified them. Quick, abolish it!"

The wood disappeared. Sherlock stared again. "I didn't know I could do that."

The two tiny dragons recovered. "That was awful," Drew said. "Suddenly I was a dumb animal."

"So was I," Drusie said. "If that's reverse wood, I want nothing to do with it."

"That was a lot of reverse wood," Clio said. "I don't believe I've ever seen so large a chunk; normally it's tiny chips." She looked at Sherlock. "I believe we have discovered your magic talent: conjuring reverse wood."

"I am amazed."

"It will surely be a useful talent, as you learn to bring it under control. Since we have established that you can abolish it as well as summon it, control should be easy."

"I'll practice," Sherlock agreed, looking dazed.

"Certainly you will not want to be aggravating ogres in the future; that's dangerous." Clio considered. "However, you should also be able to use your talent in self-defense. A chip of reverse wood might make an ogre weak, so that he could not bash you."

"I suppose that would help, but I would prefer to stay clear of ogres regardless."

Clio smiled. "Of course. Perhaps you have some private place in mind, where you can practice undisturbed."

Sherlock shrugged. "I'll find one. This is all so amazing!" He stood, and looked around.

"He's confused," Drew reported. "He has no idea where to go."

Clio glanced at her compass. It was still pointing to Sherlock. She sighed. "Perhaps I can help you further," she said. "Would you like to travel with us for a time?"

"I don't want to be a—"

"I'm sure you can make yourself useful, as you did when traveling with Dug Mundane."

"But you have better things to do!"

"Sherlock, there is an indication that I am not through with you. So it behooves me to follow my own course, which seems at the moment to be to make a continuing effort to help you find yours. Please travel with us, at least for today."

He shrugged. "I will, then."

"He's much relieved," Drew reported. "He believes that you know many more answers than he does."

Clio hoped so. "Then let's move on and find a place to spend the night, as the day is getting late." She wasn't entirely easy about camping with a man, even one she knew to be decent, but this was where her compass led her. Apparently only when she resolved his problem would she be free to resume her quest for the Currant.

They followed the path in the direction Clio had indicated for the girl and horse, and in due course reached the enchanted path. They followed it to the camping area. The girl and horse weren't there; apparently they had elected to continue traveling, now that they had a safe path and a place to go.

Sherlock did make himself useful, while Clio relaxed. He fetched wood for a fire, and foraged for suitable pies and water. Soon they had heated pot pies, which were of course in the shape of little pots.

"Well, now." It was a voice from nowhere.

"A demon!" Drusie said. "That must be your danger."

"Hello, Metria," Sherlock said.

"No danger," Clio said to the dragon. "I know her."

"Bleep, you recognized me," Metria said. A swirl of smoke formed and condensed into the shapely demoness. "I had hoped to be isolation."

"Hoped to be what?"

"Closeted, inmost, intimate, privy, undefined—"

"Incognito?"

"Whatever," she agreed crossly. "How did you recognize me?"

"How could I fail to know such an adorable creature?"

The demoness looked less cross. "Our paths must have crossed before."

"On occasion," Sherlock agreed.

"Who's your friend?"

"Clio, the Muse of History."

Metria looked, and puffed into fragments in her surprise. "So it is! Something interesting must be happening."

"It may be," Clio agreed wryly.

"I make it a point to get into every new history volume, with as big a part as I can swing."

"I had suspected that." Indeed, it explained a lot. Clio hadn't been aware of that effort, but Metria had appeared in many recent volumes, once as the lead character.

"You aren't going to write me out of this volume, are you?"

"I seem to be in this volume myself. It's not my business to write folk in or out, merely to record what happens."

"Things are happening all over, all the time. You select which ones are worthy of writing about. That gives you horrible power."

Clio was taken aback. "I don't see it that way, though some people do joke that I might write them out of a volume."

"It's no jolly."

Clio tried to resist, but couldn't. "It's no what?"

"Wisecrack, caper, absurdity, fooling, banter—"

"Joke, you idiot! I just used the word."

"Whatever," the demoness agreed, frowning. "You do have that power. So what do I have to do to be sure you don't abolish me from the scene?"

Clio considered. "Maybe you can help. We're trying to clarify Sherlock's magic talent."

"He conjures reverse wood."

"You knew that?" Sherlock asked. "Why didn't you pop in and tell me before I got bashed by an ogre?"

"You got bashed? That's one incident I missed."

"Clio unwound it. But I'm bound to run into more trouble if I don't get a handle on it. It's gotten me banished from the Black Wave."

"But to answer your question: reverse wood is dangerous, so I stayed clear until you got more interesting. You never can tell what it will do."

"So I've been discovering."

"It might make me always get the right word the first time, or it might make me helpful instead of mischievous. I couldn't risk it."

"I suppose that makes sense."

"So why are you so interested, Muse?"

"The Good Magician told me I needed to obtain a certain red berry, a currant, in order to fathom the mystery of an unreadable volume of history. He gave me a compass to find my way. The compass led me to Sherlock."

"Just in time to save me from the ogre," Sherwood said. "But I have no idea how to help with a red berry."

"I know where there are red berries," Metria said.

"I suspect it's not any red berry, it is one particular berry," Clio said. "I also suspect it will not readily be found, and that Sherlock has some relevance to my search."

"And maybe if I help, I'll be relevant too."

Clio saw that the demoness really did want to be wanted. "Perhaps."

"Then let's get on it." Metria oriented on the man. "Would a demonic kiss inspire your imagination?"

"I don't think—"

"Or maybe a glimpse of something sinfully nice?" The demoness's dress shrank, exposing curves above and below. She of course knew exactly what interested men.

"I doubt this is relevant," Clio said. Metria was entirely too eager to flaunt her ample charms.

"I'm not clear how your flesh can help," Sherlock said. A chip of wood appeared in his hand.

"Oh, all right, I'll cover it up."

Metria's dress disappeared entirely, exposing her overloaded bra and panties. Sherlock's eyeballs locked into place and his jaw dropped. He had freaked out.

"Metria!" Clio snapped. "That's not appreciated."

"Oops. I meant to cover. It went the wrong way. I'll try again." Then her underwear vanished. "Oops!"

Sherlock's eyeballs started sweating. His eyes couldn't close, so they were in danger of melting.

Clio caught on. "He's holding a chip of reverse wood. It's reversing what you're trying to do."

"Oh! Then I'll go bare nude naked unclothed." The full dress was back, decorously high and long.

Clio snapped her fingers. Sherlock resumed animation, blinking. "Yes, that's good," he agreed.

"He doesn't know about his freakout," Drew reported.

"A blue dragonfly!" Metria said, spying him. "How cute!"

"I'm not a dragonfly, I'm a telepathic dragon," Drew told her indignantly. "Do you want me to toast your toe?"

"Apology," the demoness said insincerely. "I haven't met many telepathic dragons."

"We're colonizing Xanth, to replace the soulless dragons it lost."

"Ah, now I see. But you do seem rather small to terrorize other creatures."

"Drusie and I are just part of the migration. There are big dragons too."

"Fascinating. And you have souls?"

"We're from Princess Ida's moons. We were all soul; now we have bodies too."

Clio noted something odd. "Wasn't that a flat chip you conjured, Sherlock?"

"Why yes. I wasn't even aware of doing it."

"Then why is it now a sphere?"

Startled, he glanced down. "I don't know."

"You worked it with your hands," Metria said. "It must be softwood."

"No, it's hardwood," he said. "Feel it." He held out the chip.

The demoness reached for it—and puffed into smoke. "Ouch! It reversed me," her voice came out of the roiling cloud.

"I'm sorry." Sherlock withdrew the chip.

"You *are* dangerous," she said, the roils forming into spinning legs, arms, torso, and finally head. "How can I seduce you if I can't touch you?" Her clothing formed with the assembled body.

"Only fully clothed and in your right mind," he suggested with a smile.

"Both are against my element."

"Against your what?"

"Composition, animus, persuasion, character, bias—"

"Nature?"

"Whatever. You'll just have to get rid of that reverse wood."

He glanced at the little wood sphere. "Clio thinks it may protect me from danger. She may be correct."

Clio suppressed her smile. He meant the danger of being seduced by a demoness.

Metria caught on. "Seduction isn't a danger, it's a delight."

"Whatever," Sherlock agreed, frowning.

"We will take your word that the ball of wood is hard," Clio said. "But it does seem to have changed its shape. Did you abolish the chip and conjure a sphere?"

"I don't think so. I just worked it with my fingers, like this." He stroked his fingers over the ball, and it deformed into a flattened form.

They all stared. Now there was no doubt: he had worked hard wood as if it were soft clay.

"A second talent?" Clio asked. "This isn't usual." It was an understatement; no person in Xanth had two talents.

7
GETAWAY GOLEM

We are confused," Drew Dragon said, projecting his seeming voice to all of them. "What is this about talents?"

"In Xanth," Clio said, "Every creature is said to be magic, or to have a magic talent. Thus human beings are not magic, but they have magic talents. Each has just one talent, and each person's talent is different, with certain notable exceptions. The curse fiends, or curse friends as they call themselves, all have the same talent of cursing, though there may be variations of curses there. The winged centaurs all have the talent of flying, as their wings could not sustain them naturally, but there are variations in the magic mechanisms of their flight. But we know of no exceptions to the single-talent rule." She glanced at Sherlock. "Which is why I am inclined to doubt that this is the present case."

"But he conjured reverse wood," Metria said. "Now he's molding it with his hands. So he's a conjurer and a hand sculptor. That's two."

"There has to be another explanation," Clio said firmly. "We simply have to find it."

"You realize, of course," Metria said, "That this is far too interesting to allow me to depart."

"Of course," Clio said wearily. It was just about impossible to get rid of the demoness when one wanted to. But she did have redeeming qualities, carefully hidden.

"Could the wood be soft when he first conjures it?" Metria asked.

"It isn't," Sherlock said. He set down the squashed sphere and conjured a new chip of wood. "Can you handle it, Muse?"

"Call me Clio. Yes, I believe I can, as long as I'm not trying to perform magic." She took the chip. It was indeed hardwood, inflexible, and it had the tingle of magic. It was reverse wood, all right. She handed it back. "Now mold it."

He took it back and ran his fingers over it. The wood bent and twisted. In a moment he had fashioned a little donut shape. He handed that back to her. It was quite hard.

"What's the verdict?" Metria asked.

"This figure is perfectly firm," Clio said. "You may touch it if you wish."

The demoness laughed, her flesh bouncing in ways a normal woman could barely aspire to. "Even if I didn't trust you, Clio, I would take your word, since I don't dare touch it. Why doesn't it reverse you?"

"Perhaps it does," Clio said. "Let me try my magic, cautiously."

She held the wood torus and tried to wind back just a few seconds. Instead the scene around her speeded up. Metria flitted to the side, Sherlock snatched the wood from her, and she stopped her magic.

"So nothing happened," Metria said, seeming disappointed.

Clio was guarded. "Perhaps. Tell me exactly what did happen."

"You told Sherlock to take it back, he did, and that's all."

"What happened before then?"

"I asked why it didn't reverse you, you said you'd try it. I moved to the side to get a better view. All routine."

Clio nodded. "I was trying to wind back time. Instead I wound it forward. I *was* reversed."

"It did not seem so to us," Sherlock said.

"Well, it wouldn't. Others don't know about the windbacks either, except the dragons, who can read it in my mind."

Metria glanced at Drew. "So?"

"It is true," Drew said. "We saw things happening routinely, but in her mind it was a blur, speeded up."

"She fast-forwarded into the future," Drusie said. "The rest of us didn't realize."

"And the effect stopped when she no longer carried the reverse wood ring," Metria said. "So it works on her too, when she does magic. The rest of us *are* magic, so it nullifies us anytime."

"Was that a danger?" Drew asked.

Clio smiled. "No, merely a harmless reversal. But I shall have to be most careful, lest I encounter a situation where a reversal *would* be dangerous."

"All of which means I had better go my own way, so as not to represent mischief to you," Sherlock said. "Regretful as I am to do it, because you have helped me gain far more understanding than I had before."

"I don't think so," Clio said. "My compass still points to you. Whatever I need from you has not yet been accomplished."

"I would give it to you immediately, if I knew what it was."

"Maybe your clothing," Metria suggested.

"She wants to get him undressed," Drew said. "Then she'll undress and tempt him."

"At the very least, she hopes to embarrass him awfully," Drusie said. "She loves mischief."

"Tattle tails," the demoness said, looking at their tails. Both dragons laughed, appreciating the pun.

Sherlock tried to blush, but was too old and dark to manage it. "If anything I wear is what she needs, I'll give it to her."

Clio wanted to demur, but couldn't be sure that wasn't it. "Try one item at a time. Put it away from you, and if the compass follows it, then we'll know."

Obligingly, Sherlock removed his shirt, set it on the stone, and walked away from it. The blue arrow followed him. He took it back and tried his shoes. They weren't it either. He went behind a tree and tossed out his trousers. They weren't it. Then his underpants. Not them.

Then he was stuck behind the trunk, because he would have to go naked below the waist to recover them. "Ah, if you ladies would depart for a moment—"

"Not a chance," Metria said, her dress dissolving. "I'll fetch them for you." She scooped up his pants and underpants.

"Just toss them behind the tree," Sherlock said.

"No, I'll carry them around to you." She walked toward the tree, deliberately jiggling in places that no normal woman could manage.

"Metria!" Clio said, appalled, knowing that her objection wouldn't stop the demoness. She had the man where she wanted him, defenseless.

Sherlock tossed something from his hiding place. It landed at Metria's feet. She tossed the clothing behind the tree, reformed her full dress, and retreated.

Some distance away, she halted. "Now why did I do that? It was the opposite of what I intended."

Both dragons laughed again.

Then Metria caught on. "Reverse wood! That chip at my feet didn't null me, just reversed my action. Instead of humiliating you, I helped you."

"Which I sincerely appreciate," Sherlock agreed, stepping out from behind the tree, fully clothed.

Clio smiled. The man had outsmarted the demoness. He was learning how to use his talent.

But that reminded her of the blue arrow. "So it's not your clothing. So it must be you yourself. And we still have not solved the riddle of your two talents."

"That reverse wood has gotten to me," Metria said. "I'm going to be genuinely helpful. Could they be two aspects of the same talent? Such as handling reverse wood?"

"That has promise," Clio agreed. "But is it just reverse wood? If he is able to shape other wood, that would make it a separate talent."

Metria disappeared with a visible pop, and reappeared half a moment later with a loud image. "Here's a chip of regular wood." She flipped it to Sherlock.

"Thank you." He worked it with his fingers, but it did not change. "This appears to be immune to my effort."

"Try other materials," Clio suggested. "Just in case. We'll have a better idea once we define your talent."

Sherlock tried stone and bone and a piece of metal that Metria fetched. None of them changed their shape.

"So he handles reverse wood," Metria said. "By conjuring it or shaping it. Not really two talents, just one larger talent."

"That seems to be the case," Sherlock agreed. Another piece of wood appeared in his hand, and he began molding it into the shape of a human figurine.

"Do you have artistic or sculptural talent?" Clio asked, interested.

"Some," he agreed. "Not magic; I merely like to carve wood or shape other substances, like clay, into things I can trade for food or whatever. I'm not great at it, but usually others can recognize my forms."

"You're sculpting me!" Metria exclaimed. "Look at that shape!"

It was true: the wood was assuming a voluptuous form. "Sorry," Sherlock said, and squeezed it so that it became mannish instead. "I didn't mean to embarrass you."

The demoness paused. "Does he mean that?" she asked the little dragons.

"Yes," Drew said.

"After the way I tried to embarrass him?"

"Yes. He's a decent guy."

"Darn! My half soul is getting to me. I can't make trouble for him now."

"Souls can be awkward for demons," Clio agreed. She remembered when Metria had gotten hers, by marrying a mortal, whom she now kept out of the way in perpetual bliss. Demonesses could do that to mortal men if they chose.

"How do they do that?" Drusie asked.

"Actually D. Mentia is doing it at the moment," Metria said. "She's a little crazy."

"You let another demoness be with your husband?"

"She's my alter ego. It's all right; she's pretending to be me."

Both dragons looked confused, so Clio stepped in with a more coherent explanation. "Demoness Metria was trodden on by a sphinx, centuries ago. She survived, but it fragmented her into three alternate selves, the third of which is a child. The adults can operate independently, so Mentia is distracting her husband while Metria is free to stir up mischief elsewhere."

"Can't her husband tell the difference?" Drew asked.

"Surely he can, because Mentia gets her words right. But it seems he has the sense not to complain. Some men prefer their wives a little crazy."

"Xanth is strange in ways we did not expect," Drusie said. "Should I try to be crazy, Drew?"

Drew considered. "You're already perfect."

"I could be perfectly crazy."

"That seems good." They both laughed, exchanging a mental kiss.

"Love is good," Sherlock said a little wistfully.

"You never found love?" Clio asked. She wrote the histories, but wasn't much aware of what folk did when they were offstage. There were simply too many people and creatures in Xanth, all doing different things simultaneously.

"I never did," he agreed. "And surely won't, since my youth has passed me by."

There wasn't anything positive Clio could think of to say to that, as it was probably true.

Meanwhile, his nimble fingers continued to work, shaping the small wood figure. He was really quite good; even the tiny face was fully formed, seeming about to speak.

"So you're making a little man," the demoness said. "Make sure he has a—" She glanced around. "Are there any children here? How old are you little dragons?"

"We're adult," Drew said. "Why?"

"It's the dreaded Adult Conspiracy to Keep Interesting Things from Children. They have to be eighteen before they can use bad words or know how to summon the stork."

"That's ridiculous!" Drusie said.

"Of course it is. What's your point?"

"Why shouldn't children know such things?"

Metria dissolved into smoke, and reformed as Woe Betide, her little child aspect. "Gee, I don't know."

"It's to prevent children from summoning babies until they know how to care for them," Clio explained.

"Never mind," Sherlock said. "My golem has one. See." He held up the golem.

"Eeee!" Woe Betide screamed, freaking out. She fractured into flying shards of glass, which glinted prettily in the sunlight, then dissolved into smoke. The smoke swirled and condensed back into Metria. "How *could* you, you pervert!"

"Sorry. I forgot you had changed. Will Woe Betide survive?"

"It will take her some time to unfreak. Finish your bleeping figurine."

Sherlock smiled. "If poor little Woe heard that word, she'd freak out again."

"No she wouldn't; she wouldn't recognize it. She's a nice girl."

"Don't little human girls ever see little human boys without clothing?" Drew asked.

"They sometimes do, but they freak out," Metria said grimly. "You saw."

"And they never tell," Clio said, remembering her childhood.

"It's done," Sherlock announced, holding up the figure. It was a perfect little wooden man.

"Get him some clothes," Metria said.

"Why? He's intended to be a work of minor art as he is."

"Because children are coming."

"How do you know that?"

"D. Vore's turn is ending; my turn is starting."

"Demon Prince Vore is Princess Nada Naga's husband," Clio explained to the dragons. "Their daughter DeMonica keeps company with Metria's son Demon Ted. The demon adults take turns babysitting, because the human spouses can't keep up with them."

"We don't need babysitting!" DeMonica protested, appearing at Metria's left. She was a rather pretty girl with three oink tails.

"After all, we're eight years old," Demon Ted agreed, appearing at her right. He was a handsome boy with an unruly shock of hair.

"The same age as the three Princesses," Monica said.

"An excellent age," Clio agreed. "And are the princesses allowed to go unsupervised?"

"Well, they're not half demons."

"And you are," Metria said. "And you will still have adult regime."

"Adult what, mom?" Ted asked.

"Fosterage, auspices, countenance, administration, influence—"

"Supervision?" Monica asked.

"Whatever," Metria agreed crossly.

"Awww," they said together, then broke out laughing. The funny thing was that Metria joined them. It was clear that she liked both children, and was trying to be a good parent. That was her half soul operating again. Actually it was now a quarter soul, since Ted had taken half, but it seemed to be up to the job.

"What's that?" Monica asked, turning to Sherlock.

"A figurine," he said, quickly wrapping his hand around its middle section. "We need some clothing for it."

"We'll conjure some," Ted said.

Clio had a reservation about that, but let it be; it was better to let the children experiment.

A small pair of trousers appeared in Ted's hand, and a matching shirt. "Here."

"Thank you." Sherlock took the shirt and put it on the figure. The shirt promptly puffed into smoke and floated away. "Oops."

"You dope," Monica said witheringly. "You conjured it out of demon substance. That doesn't last away from a demon."

"Did not," Ted retorted. "I made it from some cloth I found."

"*What* cloth?"

"Your skirt."

She looked down. There was an irregular patch missing from her skirt. "You beast!" she cried. She conjured a thorny club and smashed it down on his head before the adults could stop her. It landed with a horrendous hollow thunk.

"Oooh, I'm done for!" Ted moaned, whirling around and dropping to the ground. "The harpy has done me in."

"Serves you right for calling me a harpy, you goblin."

"You'll be sorry when Mother sees me dead." Ted dissolved into a glob of goo.

Clio applauded politely. "Very nice show, children," she said. "You must have rehearsed it."

"They did," Metria said complacently.

"Gee, did it fool you?" Ted asked, reforming and getting up.

"At first."

"What gave it away?"

"That hollow thunk," Sherlock said. "That's a slapstick. It makes a loud noise and doesn't hurt at all. We use them in our whiteface comedy shows."

"That's where we got the idea," Monica confessed. There was no longer a hole in her skirt.

"Meanwhile you need clothing for the anatomically correct figurine," Metria said. "Nothing made magically will do, because the wood will reverse it."

"I'm make some from reverse wood." He looked around. "I need a place to conceal him while I work on it."

"Wedge him in a crevice of the rock, so his lower half doesn't show."

"That seems good." Sherlock moved the figure toward a ragged crack.

"But won't it hurt him?" Monica asked. "He looks so—so alive."

"Alive? He is merely wood." Sherlock set the figurine firmly into the crevice.

"Hey, watch it!" the figure cried. "My poor tender feet!" He scrambled out of the crevice.

The others stared, astonished. Monica screamed as she caught a good glimpse of the torso. "Freeeak!"

"Get over it, doll!" the figure said, and ran to the edge of the rock, jumped off, and fled across the ground.

Clio rushed to catch Monica before she fell. She had freaked out; her eyes were fully round and staring.

"I'll catch him," Ted said, running after the figure.

"Not on your own," Metria said, following him. "You can't touch reverse wood."

"I'll make that clothing," Sherlock said, recovering his poise. More wood appeared in his hand. "Is she all right?"

Clio snapped her fingers before the girl's face. Monica's eyes focused. "What happened?"

"You saw something that freaked you out," Clio said. "It's gone now."

Monica nodded. "I'll never tell."

"That's best," Clio agreed. Because demons had different standards she couldn't be sure the girl had really freaked out, but it was best to maintain the pretense. She had played the scene correctly.

"Yow!" It was Ted's voice from the forest.

"I told you you couldn't touch reverse wood," Metria's voice answered. "Now leave it alone."

"Yeah, poop-for-brains," the figure's voice came. "You can't touch me. Nyaa! Nyaa!"

Monica smiled. "Ted doesn't like being teased."

"Surely not," Clio agreed. "But I don't think it's wise to have reverse wood running around like that. There's no telling the mischief that could generate."

"Like maybe an explosion?" Monica asked hopefully.

"Can you control it?" Clio asked Sherlock.

"How?"

"Perhaps you could conjure it back to your hand."

"That's right. It's my talent. Conjuring reverse wood." He glanced toward the taunting sounds.

The figure appeared in his hand. "Hey!" it cried. "Let go of me, you hamhanded cretin!"

"You can't get away," Sherlock said. "Because I can bring you back." He set the figure down as Clio hastily turned Monica away.

"I'll get away! Get away from me." The figure took off again.

"I think what you have there is a rebellious golem," Clio said.

"Getaway Golem," Sherlock agreed.

"Getaway!" Monica said. "The perfect name."

Sherlock considered. "I suppose I should abolish him. He's obviously nothing but trouble."

"You must not do that," Clio said, alarmed. "He has become an animate, feeling creature, however obnoxious. He needs control and training, not destruction."

"But he is uncivilized."

"Then we must civilize him."

"You tell him, wench," the golem said as he jumped off the stone.

The golem reappeared in Sherlock's hand. "You must not address the Muse of History in that manner."

"Yeah, blackface? Who'll stop me?"

"I will. She has just interceded to prevent me from mashing you back to anonymity. You ought to show her some respect." He set the figure back on the rock.

"Yeah?" The golem looked at Clio. "Respect this, wench." He turned around and bent over, displaying his tiny bare bottom. Both children stifled titters.

Clio was somewhat taken aback, and not just by the bottom, which also was anatomically correct. The golem had a very difficult attitude.

"You see the thanks you get for helping him," Sherlock said. "I think this is a bad job."

"You know, he's like the inanimate, when King Dor makes it talk," Metria said. "It's pretty shallow, always making smart-bottom remarks and threatening to peek up girls' skirts and blab the colors of their panties. But Queen Irene makes it behave by threatening to stomp it."

"That she does," Sherlock agreed. "This golem was very recently inanimate, so must be similar. It has to be taught respect."

"Go fry your middle-aged face," Getaway said, heading for the edge of the rock.

"Like this," Sherlock continued evenly. He conjured the figure back to his hand. "You will be polite, or I will squeeze."

"Go soak your fat—oooh, that smarts!" For Sherlock was slowly squeezing.

"The correct expression is 'Yes, Sherlock, I will be polite from now on.' Do you think you can manage that?"

"The bleep I can! Ouch!" For at that point the squeeze resumed, as the two children blanched at the bad word.

"This is not a type of discipline of which I wholly approve," Clio said uneasily.

"He insulted you, yet you still plead his case? You're a nicer person than I am."

"She's nicer than anyone," Drusie Dragon said.

The golem looked at her in Sherlock's pocket. "Go steam your tail, snake-snoot."

"Did you ever have a child?" Metria asked Clio.

"No, of course not. I never married. Still, certain standards seem warranted."

Metria turned to the two children. "What do you think?"

"He's worse than we are," Ted said.

"He shouldn't say such words," Monica said.

"And he's got Xanth's worst attitude," Metria said.

"So stomp him," Ted said. "Mother would stomp *me* if I ever said such a word, if I even knew it."

"But of course we don't know what it means," Monica said contritely. "And wouldn't want to know." A little fake halo appeared over her head.

"I'll tell you what it means, you hypocritical brat," Getaway said. "It means—ooomph!" For the squeeze was on again.

Metria put her face close to Getaway's face. "Get this, you little piece of bleep. If you don't shape up in a hurry, we'll all gang up on Clio to make her let Sherlock squeeze you into pulp. We're trying to do something here, and you're getting in the way."

Getaway opened his mouth. Sherlock squeezed. "Uh, all right. I'll try to manage to be polite. For now. But you gotta do something for me, too."

"The bleep we do!" Metria snapped. Then, conscious of the flinching children, she modified it. "Like what?"

"Like making me a gal golem so we can—" he paused, as a squeeze threatened. "Make nice together."

"Out of naughty pine," Ted said, giggling.

"And they'll sing 'Love is a many splintered thing,'" Monica said, adding her giggle.

"That seems fair," Clio said, relieved to have a positive inducement. "People do need companions of their own kind."

"But not right away," Metria said. "Make him behave for a month first. Once he's civilized, then it will be time to break in another. If he messes up, deal's off."

"And make him help find the red berry," Ted said. The dragons had evidently caught the children up on that.

"And if he helps a lot," Monica said, "You'll even make her pretty, with a shape like Metria's."

"I can do that," Sherlock agreed. Indeed, he had recently done it. He faced the golem. "How about it? Is it a deal?"

"Let me see that shape again."

Metria's shape suddenly became phenomenally voluptuous. "Like this." Her décolletage slipped slowly down.

The golem's eyes locked into place. "Now that's interesting," Clio said. "He's freaking out."

"Wonderful!" Metria said, delighted. "It means I can disable him without touching him." Her dress became more concealing.

"Will I be able to do that when I grow up?" Monica asked jealously.

"Certainly," Metria agreed. "It's a girl thing."

"Aw, I'll never fall for that, no matter how old I get," Ted said.

Metria and Monica exchanged a glance and a smile.

"Deal," Getaway said as he caught his breath.

"Good enough," Clio said. "Now put on your clothing." Because in the interstices Sherlock had managed to make a pair of shorts.

Getaway put them on, and seemed to need nothing more. He was, after all, made of wood. That made him presentable.

"Now we were trying to ascertain Sherlock's talent," Clio said. "We have observed that he can conjure reverse wood, and shape it despite its hardness. I think we have just experienced another aspect: animation."

"Are you talking about me, you per—" Getaway paused, reconsidering. "You perceptive creature?"

"Nice recovery," Metria murmured.

"I am," Clio agreed. "You were a mere wood figurine. Then you animated as a golem. Sherlock must have done this."

"I didn't mean to," Sherlock said. "It just happened."

"Can you animate something else?" Metria asked.

"I can try." Another chip of wood appeared in his hand. "What would you like?"

"Not another golem, yet! How about a plant?"

Sherlock molded the chip into a small plant with roots, stem, and several leaves. He set it in the ground.

The plant straightened out, its leaves orienting on the sunlight. It was alive.

Or was it? "Dragons, can you read the minds of plants? I am curious whether that plant is alive or merely animate."

"Animate," Drew said. "It has no living mind."

"Neither does the golem," Drusie added.

That answered her question. Sherlock was not creating life, merely animated things. She was relieved; life was in its way sacred. Still, it was a considerable talent, though limited to reverse wood. Perhaps reverse wood had special properties most folk couldn't know of, because they were distracted by its problematical effect on their magic.

"It seems you can animate the constructions you make," Clio said. "But they are indeed golems, not living things."

"I am not inclined to animate any more very soon."

She smiled. "I appreciate that."

"Time for us to go home," Metria said. Her interest diminished when things got dull by her definition. "On my mark, children. Three, two, one—"

"Mark!" the children exclaimed together as the three of them vanished.

"Which leaves us," Clio said. "It is late, and we must sleep. There are two shelters; we can each use one."

"I agree."

"What about me?" Getaway asked.

"Do you need to sleep?"

"No."

"Then you can explore the premises during the night, and notify one of us or the dragons if you see anything that could cause us trouble. The campsite is enchanted, so should be safe, but it's best to be careful."

"How do I tell the dragons? Do they understand person talk?"

"Why, they're telepathic," Clio said. "Just think to them."

"He can't," Drew said. "He has no living mind."

"But he sassed Drusie when she said Clio is nice," Sherlock said.

"I saw her snoot poke out of your pocket," Getaway said. "She has a mind?"

"Go roast your bottom, woodhead," Drusie said.

The golem did not react. He couldn't hear her, since she was mind speaking, not physically speaking.

"Tell me," Sherlock said.

"Got it, master."

"There's no need to call me that." But the golem was already gone.

"At least he's polite now," Clio said.

"Good evening," Sherlock said, and stepped into his shelter.

"And a good night to you." She stepped into hers.

And froze. It was overrun by nickelpedes.

"Now that's a danger," Drew said.

"All too true," she agreed.

"Get out of your shelter!" Sherlock called.

She was already on her way out. "You saw nickelpedes too?" But she knew he did, because the dragons had relayed the images. "How could this happen? This campsite is supposed to be enchanted against monsters."

"There must be a leak." Sherlock raised his voice. "Getaway! See if you can find out where the nickelpedes are getting in."

"I already found it," the golem said, reappearing. "There's a piece of reverse wood on the perimeter. It nulled the spell. I thought you put it there."

"I did not. Move it clear."

Getaway paused. "Now I don't want to be impolite by calling anyone an imbecile, but you do realize that would trap the monsters inside
the camp?"

Sherlock laughed. "I'm glad you didn't call anyone that. You're
right; leave it there for now and I'll try to herd them out."

"I can do that."

"Then do it."

Getaway ran into the nearest shelter. "Come play with me, monsters!" he cried. "I want to hug you."

There was an instant scuttling as the insects scrambled out of the
golem's way. They knew what reverse wood was, and wanted no part of
it. They must have skirted the piece across the boundary very carefully.

Clio stepped back as several came toward her. But Getaway was on
it, running to intercept them. It was weird to see such fearsome little
monsters being afraid. He herded them toward the same gap they had
used to enter.

It took a while, but in due course all the nickelpedes were gone and
the stick was off the perimeter. They were secure from suffering nickel-
sized gouges from their flesh.

"So have I helped?" Getaway asked.

"You certainly have," Clio agreed. "You have made an excellent
start." She had doubted that the golem would be much help, but now
was reconsidering.

"That's good." Getaway was off again, making his rounds.

"But did the danger count?" Drew asked. "You never wound back."

"I don't have to wind back if I don't need to. In this case Getaway
handled it. Had he not been here, I might have had to do it myself. Certainly the danger was real. Nickelpedes are really nasty creatures."

"Now I think I understand. When a danger comes that you can't
handle, it will be our turn—mine and Drusie's—to save you."

"Perhaps so."

It was safe now. Even so, it took Clio a while to get to sleep. She
didn't like being so long out in the world, because every hour added to

her age, and she did not know just how young she was slated to die. On the other hand, it was nice having such an adventure. She had almost forgotten how un-dull mortal existence was.

And Sherlock was turning out to be a good companion. It was probably his facility with reverse wood that had caused the compass to point him out, but it was nice having company for a while. She would be sorry when they parted company.

8
DEMON WAVE

Clio woke refreshed. She had had a good night despite the events of the prior day. There was something about living in reality she liked, despite the inevitable aging it forced on her.

"Welcome to a new day," Drew thought.

She had a sudden notion. "Did you have something to do with my sleeping well?"

"Yes. I projected a pleasant, calming ambience. Was I wrong?"

She stroked his little head. "No, dear. But didn't that prevent you from sleeping?"

"No, it's easy. We use it to enhance our own sleep."

"Bit by bit, I become more satisfied with your company."

He sent an image of himself turning bright pink with pleasure. She had to laugh, because it made him look like Drusie.

But there was a problem. Her dress was rumpled, because she had slept in it, having nothing else. That was a detail she had not anticipated; she had been long away from real life. She would have to wash it. But how? She was not alone, and there was only the neighboring pond.

Well, she would handle it. She nerved herself and stepped out of the shelter.

Sherlock was up and busy. He had a fire going and had breakfast pies and milkweed pods lined up. Getaway Golem sat on a stone, watching.

"You are a fine housekeeper," she told Sherlock, smiling.

"I'm used to doing for myself, and Getaway helped," he said. "It's nice to have human company, however briefly."

She glanced at her compass. It still pointed to him. "I do not wish to inconvenience you, but it seems I still am not through with you. Do you mind keeping company longer?"

"Not at all. I had assumed I was a burden to you."

"No burden, Sherlock!" She hesitated. "However, there is a bit of awkwardness. I need to wash, and wash my clothing."

He understood immediately. "The near end of the pond is within the enchanted region, and is pleasantly warm. I will absent myself for a suitable time."

"No need of that," she said. But there was need; she did not care to expose herself to any man. It wasn't modest, for one thing, and there was a worse problem.

"Suppose I sit by the fire, facing away from the pond," he suggested. "The dragons will guarantee that I don't peek, much as I might be tempted to."

That was a neat solution. He had assured her privacy while complimenting her feminine appeal, without being crude. There were things to like about this man. "That will do."

She walked to the pond as Sherlock sat facing away from it. "Why don't you want him to see you wash?" Drew asked in a private communication as she removed her shoes and socks.

"Because it is not proper for unrelated men and women to see each other's bare bodies. It's a social error."

"He's not watching."

"Thank you." She nerved herself again, and pulled off her dress. She dropped it into the warm water and stood for a moment in her underwear. That needed washing too, so she removed it and added it to the dress. Even her hat was soiled, so that too was added.

"Does Getaway count?" Drew asked from the bank.

"He's looking?"

"He's staring. But I can't see into his mind; it's all reverse wood."

She made a decision. "Let him watch. He's a golem, not a true human person. Golems and dragons don't count." But she waded deeper into the water, so that her body was concealed from the shoulders down.

Now she remembered the nymph bark she wore. It was so comfortable that she tended to forget she had it on, but it got soiled too. She held her breath, ducked below the surface, and pulled its shell off over her head. She let it float beside her as she rubbed herself off.

"You seem to be a healthy person of your species," Drew said. He flew in to land on the bark. "Is this an item of clothing?"

"In a manner," she agreed. "I am endowed with no curves, so I wear this nymph bark to provide them. It's a foolish affectation."

"Curves are good," Drew agreed, circling around to admire his sinuous body.

"I'm glad you understand."

"Without those curves, you look almost like a human child, very young. Much younger than Sherlock."

"Appearances are deceptive. Chronologically I am much older. In fact, I am about quadruple his age. But physically I remain teenage, because of the effect of the leaf of immortality within the Mount Parnassus environs. Though my body is mature, the lack of curves makes me look younger yet."

"He thinks you are beautiful."

She clutched the wet dress to her bare front. "You said he wasn't peeking!"

"He isn't. When he first saw you yesterday, he was amazed by how young and pretty you looked, even in your clothing. Then he chided himself, because he thought the Muses are not supposed to be seen that way."

"He was being a gentleman." But she felt foolishly flattered, despite knowing it was really the nymph bark he had observed. She had thought Sherlock had never noticed her apparent physical age.

"He's sure you notice his age, though. He knows he's in the least appealing segment of his life, neither young enough to be handsome nor old enough to be wise. He regrets that."

Clio felt guilty as she scrubbed her clothing. She had demanded that

Sherlock not peek at her, yet she was in effect peeking at him. But she couldn't help herself. "He ought to know that men don't have to be handsome or young. Intelligence and decency suffice."

"It seems not in the Black Wave. Especially not after the weird things started happening around him."

"His developing magic," she agreed. "But we are solving that. It's really a very strong talent, with its several facets. Once that is clarified, he should be able to return to his home and find a suitable woman."

She was done washing, but now there was another problem. Her clothing needed to be hung out to dry, and she couldn't wear it then. The nymph bark she could wear wet; moisture kept it limber. But that was hardly fitting apparel by itself. What was she to do?

"Would illusion help?" Drew asked.

"In what manner?"

"I could clothe you in illusion. That is, the appearance of illusion; it would be effective only for the minds within my range."

"The appearance of illusion," she repeated. "At some time we must discern the distinction between apparent illusion and real illusion."

"Real illusion is independent of the observer," he explained patiently. "Any creature or thing that can see or hear or feel will see, hear, or feel it, and all visitors will see the same thing. Apparent illusion is a perception of only those minds in which it is planted; others won't be aware of it. I will have to maintain it, but that's easy to do, just as I maintain the semblance of spoken words for you."

"That's right—the golem can't hear you speak." Then another thought occurred. "So will the golem see the illusory clothing?"

"No. He'll see you bare."

"I am not comfortable with that."

"If you wear the nymph bark, he will see that. It may be magic, but it's not illusory."

"And he will think it is my real bare shape?"

"Is that bad?"

She pondered briefly further. "I suppose not. It is human eyes I prefer not to be seen by, either in my nymphly state or truly bare."

"That is easy."

"Then that is the way it shall be," she said, ducking down to slide back into the nymph bark. She felt guilty for pretending to have curves she lacked, but the taunts of her childhood remained, and she preferred to continue faking it. It wasn't as if she were trying to tempt men into folly, in the manner of a demoness; she just wanted to make a good passing impression.

"Sometimes we tiny dragons use our fake illusion to make ourselves seem larger," Drew said. "Just to avoid trouble."

"Close enough," she agreed, appreciating his understanding. "I think every creature has a certain amount of foolish vanity. Now, if you please, clothe me in the semblance of the illusion of clothing."

"Done." And as she gathered her washed clothing and waded out of the pond, she looked down and saw that she seemed to be wearing a wooden barrel around her midsection.

"Uh," she murmured.

"I'm not very good at clothing," Drew said. "We don't use it ourselves."

"Perhaps something more like cloth wrapped around my body."

"Like this?" The barrel became the windings of a mummy.

She considered. The dragon was really doing his best, and it was in any event a temporary expedient. "This will do."

She spread her clean dress and underwear out across several may-pull branches. "Yes you may," she said, and the branches caught the clothing and pulled it flat so that it would dry without creasing.

"I seed her panties!" the adjacent tree rustled. "I seed her bra!"

Clio ignored it. Seed-her trees were more aromatic than grammatical.

She walked across to rejoin Sherlock, who had waited to eat until she was ready. "Thank you for your patience."

"What a shape!" Getaway said, staring at her.

"If you want a lady golem with a similar shape," Sherlock murmured, "best not to comment openly on the Muse's appearance."

"But she's bare!"

Sherlock looked at Clio, then at the golem. "You do not see her windings?"

"My apparel is illusory," Clio explained. "While my clothing dries. That is, it is the semblance of illusion; only full minds can see it."

Sherlock smiled. "Were I of a cruder nature, I might remark that I envy the golem."

"It's a good thing you aren't crude." Indeed he was not; she liked the way he handled potentially awkward matters.

"Nevertheless, you make a rather fetching mummy."

"Thank you." She couldn't help it; she liked being complimented, even for what wasn't really hers.

They had their breakfast, and discussed prospects. The compass still pointed to Sherlock. "I must seek the red berry."

"The currant," he agreed.

"I would appreciate it if you would accompany me, at least until my business with you has been accomplished."

"I shall be glad to. I like your company."

"And I yours." She saw a motion as she spoke, and glanced again at her wrist. "The blue arrow has changed direction."

"Then our business together must be finished. You are free to resume your quest."

"I don't think so. The arrow changed only when we agreed to travel together. That suggests that this *is* our business with each other."

"Traveling," he agreed. "Perhaps there is some way I can assist you in your quest."

"That must be the case. I regret imposing on your time."

Sherlock laughed. "My time is nothing. You have done me the considerable favor of identifying my magic talent, which had seemed to be more like a curse. I am more than glad to repay the favor in any way I can."

"You are more than gracious."

"Some time we must settle who is truly gracious."

She smiled. "Sometime."

"Sickening," Getaway said. Then, as Sherlock looked sharply at him: "I mean, sometime." He moved to place Clio between him and Sherlock.

The arrow pointed to the east, off the enchanted path. That was unfortunate, but it was not her policy to rail at inconvenience.

"We can help," Drusie said. "We can identify hostile or dangerous minds before they get close enough to hurt you."

"That pipsqueak dragon is talking," Getaway said, peering around Clio at Sherlock. "I can tell by the way she looks at you."

"She was offering to help us travel."

"I'll help too, you know. We have a deal." He was plainly jealous.

"We will appreciate that too," Clio said. "You were extremely helpful last night, cleaning out those nickelpedes. Your qualities will surely be useful again."

Getaway looked at Sherlock again. "Is she making fun of me?"

"No. She is too nice a person to do that. She's complimenting you."

"That's weird."

"When you behave in a civilized manner, others treat you like a civilized person," Sherlock said. "In time you'll get used to it, foreign as it may be to your nature."

The golem frowned. "Are *you* making fun of me?"

"To a degree. I'm not as nice a person as the Muse is."

"Okay. I understand you better." The golem kept his distance from the man.

Soon Clio's clothing was dry. She donned it, and the windings disappeared.

"You still have a good shape," Getaway said. He had stayed close to her, probably concerned that Sherlock might yet squeeze him into some other form.

Clio realized that the golem was trying to cultivate her favor. He wasn't very good at it, but the effort was worth encouraging. "That brush is pretty thick. Suppose I carry you?"

"I can make it on my own!" Then he reconsidered. "But sure. I can see better from your height."

Clio bent down and closed her fingers gently around the golem's little body. She picked him up and set him on her shoulder. "Height can help," she agreed.

They set off, following the direction indicated by that arrow. It wavered some, but pointed generally east, into the thickest of the brush. It was awful. They had to wedge through dense vegetation, and it wasn't friendly. First there was a patch of flowers that turned out to be snapdragons, snapping at their feet. Drew made it back off by presenting himself as a dragondrop. The flowers did not want to be dragged and dropped, so they stopped snapping.

Then they came to a mass of blue hats. Sherlock was about to push through them, but Clio stopped him. "Those are blue bonnets! If you touch them you'll get Bluebonnet plague."

He halted immediately. "I didn't recognize them. Are you sure your blue arrow points this way?"

She checked her wrist. "Yes, right that way. But we certainly don't want to go through those."

"I can help," Getaway said. "Those flowers are magic, right? Hold me toward them. If they touch me, they'll reverse. Then they won't hurt you."

"That's a wonderful idea, Getaway," she said, lifting him off her shoulder. She advanced on the bonnets.

They refused to be cowed. One swayed forward to touch the golem—and turned into a red shoe. It had been reversed. The others, seeing that, leaned back, letting the party pass.

"See? I helped."

"You certainly did, Getaway," she agreed, and kissed him on the top of his head.

"Yuck! I mean, thank you."

She smiled. He really was trying.

They forged through the thicket, freely reversing threats, and came to a large stone arch. The clearest way through seemed to be under it, but again Clio was wary. "That's an arch enemy. Anyone who passes under it will become so nasty he'll make nothing but enemies."

"Let me at it," Getaway said.

She held him out to the arch. He touched it. Nothing changed. "Try it now," he said.

She walked under the arch—and suddenly felt like being friends with all of Xanth. It had indeed been reversed.

Beyond it was what seemed to be an inlet of the sea, though this was well inland. Along the shore grew plants with leaves like nets. But when she stepped close, they became more like sharp swords and stabbed at her. "Bay-o-nets!" she exclaimed, belatedly recognizing them.

"I've got it," Getaway said. She held him forth again, and he reversed the swords so that they became plowshares.

"I don't mean to be critical," Sherlock said. "But it seems to me that your compass could have selected an easier route."

Clio was curious about that too. Her route had been easier before; why had it abruptly turned difficult? But like the Good Magician's cryptic Answers, there was probably a reason.

Next they came to a small village hidden in the jungle. The people there appeared normal, but were very quiet. The blue arrow pointed right through it, so that's where they went: down the central street.

But it might help to ask directions, or at least inquire where they were. Clio approached a man sitting on a chair on his front porch. "_____." she said.

And paused, confused. No sound had come out, at least nothing she could hear. She looked at Sherlock. "_____?" she asked.

"_____!" he replied. He did seem to be saying something, but she couldn't hear it.

She looked at Drew, in her front pocket. "_____?"

There's no sound, he thought. *Everything is silent. We can't even make the illusion of sound.*

That was it! They could neither make nor hear any sounds. That was what was so odd about this village and its people. There was a blanket of silence covering it.

No, Drusie thought. *There is sound. We just can't hear it.*

That was it, of course. They were actually talking, but were unable to receive the words. The villagers, evidently accustomed to this, weren't trying to talk. Instead they were making gestures with their hands.

Sign language! They were communicating visually. Unfortunately she didn't know that language.

But Sherlock did. He was exchanging signs with the man on the porch. *This is the deaf village,* Drusie translated. *They have lived and worked here all their lives, and get along well.*

"But we're not deaf," Clio protested silently. "Why can't we hear?"

Because this is a silent zone. Other creatures don't like it; it makes them nervous. But the deaf folk are used to silence, so have no trouble. That's why they settled here. Hardly anyone bothers them, and no one ridicules them.

Clio appreciated why that would be so. "Tell them that we are just passing through, but are glad to have met them," she said without effect; it was her focused thoughts that counted.

They know. They are preparing a banquet for us. They want to catch up on all the news of Xanth.

For half an instant Clio thought to demur, as this would delay them for hours. Then the friendliness of the arch friend they had passed under asserted itself. What did time matter when among friends? "Tell them thanks. We'll do our best."

It was a good meal, and with the help of Sherlock and the dragons, who could read the minds of the villagers, they shared all the news of Xanth they could fit in. In the end they accepted a house for the night, unable to turn down such warm hospitality.

Unfortunately, the villagers had assumed they were a couple. The confusion wasn't evident until they entered the house and found a single bedroom with a single large bed.

Sherlock wasn't concerned. He got a pillow and blanket and made himself comfortable on the floor of the main room, leaving the bedroom to her. Almost she wished he had wanted to share the bed with her; they were both, after all, well into the Adult Conspiracy age. But he treated her deferentially, as the Muse of History, and suppose they considered stork summoning, as men and women in such circumstances tended to do? She would have to reveal the artificiality of her curves, and that would surely turn him off. So any attempt to broaden their relationship would destroy it.

He would have liked to share the bed with you, Drew thought. *But he's afraid that even the faintest suggestion of such a thing would so affront you that you would hate him.*

What an irony! She had never actually been with a man, and realized that she would like to if she got the chance, if only to discover what it was like. There was no chance on Mount Parnassus; she and her sisters were socially isolated there. An occasion like this, a temporary liaison with no expectation beyond—this was the time to do it, if ever.

She felt a sudden resolve. She would do it. She would go and invite him to share. And if he indicated doubt, she would show him the truth: that she was not curvy. She would remove the nymph bark.

And he would be appalled. There was nothing about her body that would appeal to a man, even a middle-aged one. She had nullified the curse of curvelessness in appearance, but not in reality. Better to at least *seem* desirable, than to reveal the truth. It was a deception, and it made her ashamed, but she was stuck with it.

"Drew," she murmured. "I think it best if you and Drusie no longer tell Sherlock and me our private thoughts about each other. I think we need our privacy in that respect."

As you wish.

Clio was doing what she felt right, and what she had the courage to do. She hated it. She had never cried herself to sleep before. This was the first time.

In the morning they bade farewell to the villagers and resumed their trek, following the blue arrow. Beyond the village the sound gradually returned, and so did the problems. Sherlock encountered sturdy footwear sitting by a sign saying TAKE ME. "Those look like steel-toed boots," he said. "They could really help protect my feet in this nasty jungle."

Clio was wary of such seeming gifts; with the exception of the deaf village, this trek had been almost constantly awful. Even the village had led her to a realization that made her feel worse than she had in decades. But she did not speak; it was his choice.

Sherlock reached for the boots—and they became metal toads that jumped up and kicked him. "Ouch!" he cried, grabbing his ankle. "Steel toads! And I fell for it."

"I can unwind that," Clio said.

"No, I deserve to suffer for my error. Save your power for true need."

She let it be, though it did look as if he would have a nasty bruise.

The way ahead slowly cleared, forming a rough path. There were dangerous plants, but they were back from the path, and no bad animals were near. They were suspicious of this, but the blue arrow still pointed the way, so they followed it.

They came to what might be a far-flung branch of the Gap Chasm. It was a serious depression, too broad to jump over, with a narrow winding path down the side. The blue arrow pointed to this path. Clio had severe misgivings, but what could they do? The arrow was their guide.

They followed the path down, Sherlock leading with Drusie, Clio following with Drew and Getaway. The path was almost too narrow to support them, but not quite. Portions were slippery. They followed it slowly, not taking any chances. As a result, it was the better part of an hour before they reached the base of the crevice. Clio was relieved to stand on level ground again.

A horrendous face appeared. "Abandon hope!" it intoned dramatically.

"You're a demon," Sherlock said.

"Demon Zaster, not at your service," the thing agreed.

Clio groaned inwardly. That would be D. Zaster, or disaster in the punnish nomenclature of demons. They generally took names that reflected their interests or nature, so this was not a good sign.

"We're just passing through," Sherlock said. "We'll soon be out of your way."

"I think not," Zaster said. "We have use for you."

"How come this one's not sexy like Metria?" Getaway asked at her ear.

"Female demons like to be sexy," she replied. "Male demons like to be ugly."

"What use?" Sherlock asked.

"I will be candid," Zaster said, "though I hardly need to be. We want your souls."

"You can't have those!" Clio protested. "It's not possible."

"So you say. You're just trying to fool us. The only thing you dull humans have that demons don't have is souls. You think that makes you better than us. So we're just going to take yours, and then we'll be better than you."

"I think we had better get out of here," Sherlock said.

"I agree." It wasn't possible for the demons to take their souls, but she hardly cared to let them make the attempt.

They turned back to the steep path. But now four more demons appeared, barring their retreat. Each looked worse than the others.

"Meet my henchmen," Zaster said. "The Demons Stroy, Viate, Mise, and Mean."

Clio ticked them off in her mind: Destroy, Deviate, Demise, and Demean. This was not good.

"Maybe the other direction," Sherlock whispered.

They turned—and there was another demon, this one female. "Demoness Lirious," she said with a dangerous smile.

"What's a nice girl like you doing with a bunch like this?" Sherlock asked her.

Lirious laughed so hard she fogged. "I'm not nice, and I'm not a girl," the fog said. Then it reshaped into a form that would have done an ogress proud. "This one's mine," she said to the other demons.

"I doubt it," Sherlock said, a chip of wood appearing in his hand.

The figure fogged again, becoming twice as shapely as before. "Doubt you may," she said. "But meanwhile I will play with you." Her clothing melted away, revealing purple bra and panty, each fuller than the other. "We've been watching you for an hour, letting you walk into our trap."

Sherlock was silent. Clio looked at him, and confirmed the worst: he had freaked out, dropping his chip of reverse wood. That was the liability of being a man.

"This must be the Danger of the Day," Drew said.

"It certainly seems to be," Clio agreed grimly. "Some are worse than others."

"We'll toast and steam them."

"I fear that won't be effective."

"We'll see."

They launched themselves from their pockets. Drew flew down at Zaster's feet, jetting fire. But the fire passed right through the demon's material without effect.

"What's this?" Zaster asked, amused. "A firefly?"

"A dragon!" Drew said, though Clio knew the demon couldn't hear him. He flew up and fired a blast at Zaster's left eye. But that too passed through harmlessly.

The demon whipped his hand around and caught the dragon. "I think we'll have dragonfly soup today." Drew was caught, his wings pinned back. He tried to bite the demon's fingers, but his jaws snapped on nothing. The demon's flesh was solid only where he wanted it to be.

Meanwhile Drusie was having no better luck with Lirious. She steamed first a toe, then the nose. The demoness's mouth became long, like that of a wolf, and snapped the little dragon out of the air. Drusie too was caught.

Clio had been afraid that the little dragons were overmatched in this case, and that had been confirmed. They had been bold but insufficient.

"Well, we seem to have the situation in hand," Zaster said, glancing at Drew in his hand. "Now for the finale."

There was no direct escape. Clio realized that she would have to use the windback. But she dreaded it, because they had taken an hour to get here, and she would have to wind back that time to get them back to the brink of the canyon. That would add an hour to her age, and might not help much, as the demons had surely not lied about watching the party descend. The demons had been there, invisible, ready to grab them the moment the party tried to turn back. Also, where else could they go? The blue arrow had led them here.

She had to try to find out why. Maybe the demons would explain, if she inquired. Bad characters often loved to brag to their victims; it was part of their badness. "How do you expect to take our souls?"

"We'll make you give them to us," Zaster said, still holding Drew helpless.

"And how do you propose to do that?"

"First we'll ask you nastily. Then if you don't do it, we'll torture you until you do. If you hold out until you die, we'll grab for your souls when they try to flee your bodies. Something should work."

This was looking worse. Humans did sometimes lose or yield their souls, though it was seldom if ever pleasant for them. "Why do you want souls, when other demons don't?"

"Other demons are soft. We're from a more recent Demon Wave of colonization, and still fresh and mean. They have accepted the local order; we know better. They think they can get half souls only by marrying mortals; we figure to get whole souls without tying ourselves down like that."

Clio hadn't realized that there were demon waves of colonization, but that was because she hadn't been paying attention. She had recorded only the human waves. That would have to be rectified, at such time as she returned to writing Xanth histories. *If* she returned; this just might be where she met her early death.

"But souls are only burdens to demons," she said. "They make demons behave halfway decently. They hate that. You really don't want souls."

"So you say," he repeated. "But we figure that's because other demons have taken souls on human terms. We'll take them on our terms, and not suffer any of the bad effects."

There was no reasoning with him. But there had to be some way out of this, otherwise the blue arrow should not have brought them here. What could it possibly be?

"Enough dawdling," Zaster said. "Time to ask you for your soul." He stepped close to her and put his ugly face almost against hers. "Give it to me, you helpless mortal creep." True to his threat, he was asking her nastily.

What could she say? "No."

"Good. Now we get to torture you." He stepped back, appraising her with a disconcerting squint. "You're a shapely one, so we'll make female use of you first."

"You mustn't," she said, alarmed.

"Ah, but we must. Unwilling mortal women can be a lot of fun. Promise you'll kick and scream."

"No." But somehow that defiance seemed less than ideal.

"Yes," he said zestfully. He noticed the dragon in his hand, and threw it away. "I will go first."

Clio tried to flee, but the four other demons jumped to grab her arms and legs. Their hands were brutally hard. They held her upright, facing their leader.

Zaster reached out and grabbed her shirt. He ripped it off, exposing her bra. "Yes, nice, because it's mortal."

Actually the fullness of her bra was provided mostly by the nymph bark, but the demon hadn't inspected her closely enough to catch on. He was already going for the skirt. He ripped it off, exposing her panties. They were clean, but the way he stared at them made them seem dirty. Unfortunately he didn't freak out; demons weren't as vulnerable that way as mortal human men.

"Now for the real goodies," Zaster said, one hand reaching for each piece of underclothing.

Clio couldn't help herself: she struggled and screamed. Neither was effective, but the demon was pleased. "Good, but I think you can do better. Kick harder and scream louder, please."

She shut her mouth and stood still. But when his brutish hands grabbed at both pieces, pinching her flesh right through the material and bark, she kicked valiantly and screamed louder.

"Excellent. I think you are ready for action now."

She was at the end of her tolerance. She would have to start the windback, even if it did have to go back an hour or more. If it shortened her life or killed her—well, she'd rather die that way, than this way.

A small voice rose from the ground. "I'm trying to be polite. How long do I have to do it?"

It was the golem, who had been flipped off her shoulder when the shirt came loose. He was dusting himself off.

Zaster looked down. "What in heaven are you?" Bad demons swore by invoking their worst concepts.

"I am Getaway Golem, sir."

"Well, get away, golem, before I squish you under my foot, like this." Zaster's horny callused foot stomped down as the golem skittered aside.

Getaway turned to Clio. "Do I have to stay polite?"

Something clicked in her comprehension. "These demons have shown themselves to be unworthy of politeness," she said carefully. "You may treat them in whatever way you wish, and we shall not hold it against you."

A grin spread across his face that was almost bigger than he was. "Really?"

"Really," she agreed. "In fact it might be amusing to see to what extent you are able to annoy them."

"Great!"

Zaster allowed a twisted smile to meander across his face. "If the dialog with the midget is quite finished, we shall resume our more important business." He reached again for Clio's underwear.

"Is that so, spittoon puss?" Getaway inquired, allowing his effort of politeness to fade.

Zaster's hand paused. "How's that again, splinter?"

"I guess I did get your name wrong. Your puss looks more like a used chamber pot."

Demons were difficult to insult, but this seemed to be getting there. "*What* kind of pot?"

"Outhouse, offal, refuse, crap, poop, whatever fits. It's the first time I've seen a blivet that talks like a demon." Getaway paused. "You do know what a blivet is, stink-mouth?"

For half a moment the demon froze, his eyes bulging remarkably. It seemed he was familiar with the term.

"I'm sure I don't know that word," Clio said politely. "Perhaps Demon Zaster is also unfamiliar with it. In that case it would be unkind to clarify it for him."

The golem grinned, understanding her perfectly. "Get this, peanut-brain. It's a five-pound container overflowing with ten pounds of stinky—"

This time he paused but did not dodge as the demon's foot stomped down on him. The foot landed—and vaporized. It had been reversed.

"Owww!" Zaster exclaimed, hopping about on his other foot as the first one drifted away in acrid smoke. His leg now ended at the ankle.

"Serves you right, gimpy," Getaway said. "Next time try to stomp more effectively. I don't like messing with amateurs. You should be able to do it without losing half your mind."

The foot reformed. Zaster jumped, coming down on the golem with both feet.

Both feet went up in smoke. "Now you've lost the other half of your mind, pinhead. I know by the stench."

Zaster dived for the golem, grabbing him with both hands. And of course the hands puffed away.

"And there goes your personality. What are you going to use to snatch at panties now, idiot?"

This demon really was rather stupid. "Get the midget!" he shouted to his henchdemons.

They promptly let go of Clio and dived for the golem. Getaway dodged right into the first, so that the demon's descending head smacked into the wood body—and vaporized. Then he ran around in a circle, spreading chaos whenever he touched a demon. "Nyaa! Nyaa!" he cried. "Can't get me, you boobs! Whatsa matter with you? Got butterfingers?"

But the demons were done for. They were floating away as disorganized roils of smoke. They would surely reconstitute in time, but they would not be bothering the human party again.

"One remains," Clio murmured as she chafed her wrists. She might have bruises, but she was glad to be free and unmolested.

"Got it." Getaway charged across to where Lirious stood. "Hey, ogress-face, whyn't you put some flesh in that underwear? You don't want folk to call you stringbean, do you?"

The demoness oriented on him. Evidently she had been so busy fascinating Sherlock that she hadn't picked up on the action elsewhere. She removed the dragon from her mouth and spoke. "What in Xanth are you?"

"Getaway Golem, here to spank your anemic bottom, prune head. Whatcha going to do about it?"

Demonesses were not notably easier to insult than demons, but the golem did seem to have a knack for it. "Listen, you pipsqueak wood chip, I don't have to take that from you."

"Yeah? Then get out of my way, hag." He charged toward her nearest foot.

Lirious threw the dragon at him. Drusie spread her dented wings and zoomed clear. Clio had been concerned that she had been damaged, but it seemed the demoness had not gotten around to chewing.

Getaway ran right into the foot. It, too, puffed into smoke. "Why you little beast!" the demoness cried. "Reverse wood!"

"Well, at least you're not quite as stupid as your malefolk. Now get out of here while you still can, you imitation piece of meat."

Lirious considered, then vanished. She had evidently concluded that the advice was good.

Sherlock, freed at last from the spectacle of overstuffed panties, revived. "What happened?"

"You freaked out," Drusie told him. "Getaway saved you." She projected more details of the recent action.

Sherlock nodded. "Thank you, Getaway. I'm glad I made you."

"Just remember I helped, a month hence."

"I will." Sherlock turned to look at Clio—and freaked out again. Because she remained in bra and panties, filled by the nymph bark.

"Clothe me in fake illusion!" she told Drew.

Sherlock, recovered, addressed Clio. "Are you all right?"

"I am, thanks to Getaway. He certainly came through this time. He saved us all. But I remain mystified why the compass directed us here." She glanced down at it.

The blue arrow now pointed back the way they had come. That suggested that their business here was finished. But what had they accomplished that would help her find the Currant?

Getaway ran to rejoin her—and the blue arrow swung back the other way.

A lightbulb flashed over her head. "The compass is reversing! That's why it pointed the wrong way—Getaway was close to it, affecting it."

The golem stopped. "Did I do something wrong?"

"No, dear. Not intentionally. It's just that I forgot that your nature would affect the other magic I have. We were going not where we should, but where we shouldn't. I'm afraid you will have to ride with Sherlock henceforth."

Getaway looked at the man. "Remember, I saved you."

"I remember. Though I suspect there are details I missed." He stooped to pick up the golem.

"There are," Clio agreed. "But Getaway did prove himself most admirably."

"It's a relief to know that this was a mistake," Sherlock said. "Let's get back on the correct path."

Clio was more than happy to agree.

9
ELF ELM

It was late in the day, but they didn't wait; they forged back up the steep path, determined to get clear of the demon region. Darkness came, filling in the chasm below them, creeping up behind as if to catch them and draw them back. They were tired, but they hurried.

They reached the brink as night closed about them. They were safe, or at least out. It would have been better to get farther away, but Clio was dead tired. "I must rest," she said.

"We all must rest," Sherlock said. "The dragons were battered too."

"Yet it is dangerous to remain here. There are many predators of the night."

"I'll put reverse wood around us in a circle."

Then Clio saw the blue arrow changing direction. The clock arrow was nearing its mark. She glanced at Sherlock, and saw Getaway sitting on his shoulder. So the golem wasn't influencing it. So why was it shifting?

"I wonder—could the compass be directing us to a safe harbor, as it were? Because we need it?"

"Whatever that is would have to be close," Sherlock said. "Both fatigue and darkness prevent anything more."

"I'm not tired. I'll look," Getaway said.

"We would appreciate that," Clio said.

The golem set off in the direction the compass pointed. Almost immediately there was an angry screech. "Get away from me, you despicable thing!"

"That sounds like an unfriendly girl," Sherlock said.

"Which may mean she's normally friendly," Clio said. She saw that the compass's red arrow was now at the mark. This was it, whatever it was.

"Hello!" Sherlock called into the darkness.

"Who the bleep are you?" the voice demanded irritably.

"Getaway, get away from her," Sherlock called.

There was a pause, then a small girl appeared. "Oh! I don't know what came over me. I'm normally the friendliest elf of the Elm."

An elf! That was why she was small; it was normal grown size for an elf. She wore a green tunic and was proportioned like an adult.

"We are tired travelers, in need of a safe haven for the night," Clio called. "We have a golem made of reverse wood; that's why your nature suddenly reversed."

"What a relief!" The elf approached. "I am Nissa. I live in the local Elf Elm, which is very close by."

An elf elm! "Could we spend the night at its base?" Clio asked. "That should certainly be safe."

"Why of course! We are always glad to have company."

"Please show us the way." Clio tried to stand, but sank right back down. She was too tired to get to her feet.

"Let me help you," Sherlock said. But he stumbled and had to clutch at a tree trunk. He was too tired too.

"I'd better carry you," Nissa said.

"But you can't possibly—" Then Clio remembered a quality of elves. The closer they were to their elms, the stronger they were. So maybe Nissa could. "Thank you."

The elf put her little hands on Clio and heaved her up across her shoulders. At first the burden seemed to be too much for her but with every step she gained strength, and soon had no trouble at all.

The trunk of the Elf Elm loomed, rising into the darkness. Nissa set Clio down and went back for Sherlock. "Don't get near the golem," Clio called weakly after her.

"No danger of that," Getaway said from nearby.

"That's good. You would nullify her nature and her strength."

"I reverse everything. I'm not much good, unless there's a demon to beat up."

"That's not true, Getaway. You have been nullifying threats all along on this journey."

"Threats you wouldn't have faced if I hadn't reversed your compass."

"True. Let's call it even on that score. You have been doing well in the matter of politeness, and it seems there is a time when it is expedient to be impolite."

"It was fun insulting those demons."

"It was indeed. If I ever encounter similar creatures, I hope you are on hand to protect me again."

The golem hesitated. "Was that a compliment?"

"Yes."

"Well. I like it."

"There are rewards for good behavior."

"Maybe I'll stay polite even after I get what I want."

She smiled. "No need to go to extremes." Then, seeing his confusion, she explained. "That is humor. Of course you should stay polite even if there is no obvious reward."

"Does that really make sense?"

"It does if you want to have friends."

He was silent, digesting that difficult concept.

Nissa returned, carrying Sherlock. Clio would have been amazed to see a seeming child carrying a man four times her height, had she not known the nature of elves.

"Thank you," Clio said as Nissa laid the man down beneath the elm. "We shall surely be safe here."

"Oh, I wasn't going to leave you out here," Nissa protested. "You must be my guests for the night."

"Well, we are, in our fashion," Clio said. "You have brought us to a safe haven, and we shall surely be much recovered by morning. I think the elm has a beneficial effect, though we are not elves; I'm feeling better already."

"It does," Nissa agreed. "It took us elves generations to become fully attuned to the benefits of the elms, so now we are dependent on them, but others get some strength and health too. Injured or sick animals come to rest beneath the elms, and they are helped. We have a rule: no fighting by the elm, so even natural enemies can sleep in peace here."

"That's beautiful."

"Now you must join me in my cubby, you and your cute little pet dragons. It's much more comfortable."

"But we are too large," Clio protested. "We couldn't possibly share your chamber."

"I have an accommodation spell."

"Oh. In that case, thank you; it will surely be very nice."

"What's an accommodation spell?" Getaway asked.

"You'll see. Stay close so you are included."

Nissa brought out something that wasn't quite visible. She gestured, and suddenly shrank to a quarter her former height. The tree trunk shrank too, to half its prior diameter. Or rather, they had grown to twice their former sizes. Now the golem stood as tall as the elf.

"It reversed!" Sherlock exclaimed. "We forgot the reverse wood effect."

That was true. "Oh, my," Clio said. "Getaway, I shall have to ask you to step out of the range of the spell. It is intended to equalize human and elf size, but went the wrong way."

"I understand," Getaway said glumly. He walked away.

The spell, freed of his influence, reverted to its normal effect. Now Nissa was their size, a seemingly normal human person. Or rather, they were her size; the tree trunk loomed four times as thick as it had a moment before. They were half their regular height, and the elf was twice hers, instead of half.

"The golem," Nissa said, looking shaken. "I forgot."

"So did we. It seems we must exclude him."

"I'll get by," Getaway called.

"Don't go away," Clio called back. "This is merely a complication, not a conclusion. I don't think anything can hurt you. We'll pick you up again in the morning."

"Okay." The voice sounded wistful. That made Clio feel guilty, but she saw no other way to handle this.

"Follow me," Nissa said. She approached the trunk, and now Clio saw that there was a winding set of steps spiraling up it. Perhaps the magic of the spell made them visible.

They followed the elf up, several times around the tree, until they reached the tall foliage. It looked somewhat drooping, but that was probably an effect of the darkness. They entered its canopy, and came to a green bower whose walls were leaves and branches. It was quite pleasant.

"We have plenty of room," Nissa said. "Make yourselves comfortable. I'll fetch something to eat."

Clio started to protest, but reconsidered before the words got out. She was hungry, and surely Sherlock was too; they hadn't eaten anything since midday.

Nissa brought a bowl of fresh fruits, and several milkweed pods. All of these seemed much larger than normal, but that was the effect of the accommodation spell. They were very good and filling.

"I don't wish to pry into what may not be my business," Sherlock said as they ate, "but I am curious where the other elves are. Doesn't an elm normally have a full complement?"

"Oh, you noticed," Nissa said. "I didn't want to bother you with our problems. It's not the courteous thing to do."

So there was a problem. "We would like to know," Clio said. "Possibly we could help."

"It's the dreaded malady, the Dusty Elm disease," she said sadly. "It spreads mysteriously from tree to tree, and we haven't found out how to stop it. It's slow, but in time it kills the tree. So the other elves have had to move to other elms, as this elm can no longer support them, and I am the last one left. Soon I'll have to go too, and I hate that, because I love this tree; it's my home. I'm so lonely!"

It was coming clear why Nissa was so friendly. But was this problem relevant to the mission? Clio glanced at her compass. It pointed to the elf girl.

"Do you have any notion of the actual agent of destruction?" Sherlock asked.

"Very little. I've seen bugs chewing on the bark, and the tree wasn't sick before they came. But I don't see why a little chewing should make the whole tree ill."

"I can," Clio said. "The bugs could carry something with them that causes far more damage than they do. I suspect we need to get rid of the bugs, and then deal with whatever it is they brought."

"That would be nice," Nissa said wistfully.

"Let me think about it. Maybe there's an answer."

"Then there's Paul."

"Who?" Clio asked.

"The lumberjack."

"The what?" Sherlock asked.

"He's a giant with an ax and a big blue ox. He chops down trees and hauls them away. Now that this elm has lost most of its elves, Paul has his eye on it. I'm not formidable enough alone to stop him. It would require several elves, because he's so big and strong. He's going to come any day with his big ax and start chopping."

"But who would chop down an elf elm?"

"Paul would. Because it's a big tree." Nissa paused. "But I don't want to bore you with my troubles. Maybe if the tree can be cured, the other elves will return in time to stop Paul. Then it will be all right."

Clio exchanged a glance with Sherlock. It was not all right. But at the moment the threat was distant, and they were not sure what they could do about it anyway.

They talked about other things. Nissa was eager for news about the rest of Xanth, for she had never traveled far from her tree. She listened avidly as they described different features of Xanth, such as Castle Roogna and the Gap Chasm, and the dragons described Dragon World. "Oh, I wish I could see them myself! But I can't, because I would become too weak to exist, that far from my elm. The other elves had to travel from elm to elm, barely making it."

That was a sad fate: wanting to see the sights, but unable to travel far.

Finally they settled down to sleep. The dragons, assured that no one would be in any danger during the night, took over an old bird's nest near the dome of the chamber. Sherlock found a leafy alcove on one side, while Clio took another.

"Oh, I thought you were a couple," Nissa said privately, embarrassed.

"A couple of travelers," Clio said. "Actually five, counting the dragons and the golem. We'll all go our own ways in due course."

"That's too bad."

"Too bad?"

"You all seem like such nice folk. Even the golem; he means well. He can't help being what he is. And the man is really nice, for a human. But I suppose you're too young for him."

"I'm older than I look, and less lovely."

"I don't understand."

Clio removed her clothing, then her nymph bark, as it was more comfortable to sleep without it. "Underneath, I'm shapeless, as you can see."

"That's why he's not interested?"

"That's why he wouldn't be interested."

"And I'll bet he thinks you wouldn't be interested in a middle-aged man."

"That's not true!" But her protest lacked conviction. Age was immaterial to her, but it was quite possible that Sherlock did think that.

"I'd be interested, if he were an elf."

"Accommodation spells go only so far."

"Actually they can enable a lot. Elves have used them to summon storks with humans. But long-term relationships don't work well."

"I can appreciate that." Clio remembered how Bluebell Elf had done that with Jordan the human barbarian; she had written up that history, though it had happened before her time. Their descendant Rapunzel Elf had married Grundy Golem, and they had a daughter named Surprise.

"Well, good night."

"Good night."

Nissa went to her own sleeping nook. But Clio's thoughts were disturbed, and not for the first time. She knew she should simply cross over and ask Sherlock whether curves mattered a lot to him. He noticed them, and freaked out at the sight of curvaceous panties, but every man did that; it was a reflex. He might be more sensible when considering an actual relationship, however temporary. She should ask—but somehow didn't dare.

And why didn't he ask her whether age mattered? If he were interested, wouldn't he ask? Unless he suffered the same severe hesitation she did. It could be an awful irony, yet there it was.

She sighed, and slept less well than she might have.

In the morning Nissa had more fruit and milk. Then Sherlock spoke. "I have been pondering something."

"Yes?" Clio asked, her pulse quickening.

"The elm illness. Could it be reversed?"

Why had she thought he had any other question on his mind? "How could it be reversed?"

"With reverse wood. It might stop the bugs from eating the bark, and stop whatever else is going on, if it is by any chance magical."

"Now that's an idea," she agreed. "Can we test it?"

"We could try touching the bugs with chips of reverse wood."

"You couldn't get at them," Nissa said. "They hide under the bark, and they're in crevices or way out on limbs you couldn't reach."

"What about Getaway?" Clio asked. "He's small."

Sherlock nodded. "I'll ask him."

"But he can't enter the accommodation spell."

"We'd have to clear out and let him investigate alone."

It seemed good. "Let's do it."

They went down the winding stair and reached the ground. Then Nissa terminated the accommodation spell, and suddenly they were back to human size and Nissa was elf size.

"Getaway!" Sherlock called.

"I am here, master."

"We may have a job that only you can do. Can you check the elf elm for magic bugs or magic disease?"

"But if I touch the tree, won't it reverse it?"

"Only its magic aspects—and those are in trouble because of an illness. We wonder if it is possible for you to cure it, by reversing the malady."

"I'll check." The golem walked to the big tree and touched its bark. Nothing happened. He walked around the base, stroking a little hand along it. "There's one." He put his whole hand flat against it. In a moment a beetle appeared, visibly disturbed, and flew away.

"Its taste for elm bark must have become distaste," Sherlock said, smiling.

"There's more," Getaway said. "Something magical and ugly. It's sort of spread out."

"The disease!" Nissa said.

"More like fungus," the golem decided. "It gets in there and sucks out the life of the wood. It's fading now, because I'm reversing it. But it would take a long time to clear it from this whole tree."

Clio was excited. "But you *could* clear it?"

"Oh, sure, if I had a month or two."

"Maybe you should take that month."

"And lose my reward for being polite for a month? Or are you planning to stay too?"

"What reward do you want?" Nissa asked. "If it is in my power— oh, please please, save my elm if you possibly can!"

"If you feel up to doing this," Clio said carefully, "Maybe we could return to see to your reward." She glanced at Sherlock.

"And suppose you get tangled up somewhere, and don't make it back?"

"Perhaps we can do better," Sherlock said. "If you will commit to curing this tree, I'll craft Knotty for you."

"I'm working!" Getaway said eagerly, and practically hugged what he could of the huge trunk.

"Knotty?" Clio asked.

"She is to be made of naughty pine."

"There's a naughty pine tree not far from here," Nissa said. "We don't go near it, because it is very indiscreet. Anyone who touches it says embarrassingly naughty things."

"Excellent. But I must conjure this myself, as it must be reverse wood pine."

"Reverse wood comes in different types?" Clio asked, surprised.

"Yes." A knotty reddish piece of wood appeared in his hand. "I did not know this until now."

"I think it was unknown until now."

He began shaping the wood. Two knots became breasts, and a third the head.

"That's amazing," Nissa said.

"Well, I thought the knots should form the important parts."

"I mean the way you bend the wood around. And it's reverse wood?"

Sherlock extended the forming figure toward a nearby common scents plant. When the wood touched, the plant transformed into a small crescent-shaped bug.

"That's a luna-tick!" Nissa exclaimed. "It makes folk act crazy." Then she caught on. "From common scents to crazy. It was reversed."

Sherlock continued molding the figure, then paused, unsatisfied. Clio could appreciate why: it was exaggerated and lopsided. "I need a model, to get the proportions right. Um, Clio—?"

"I'd rather not," she said, conscious that her proportions weren't genuine.

"I'll model, if I'll do," Nissa said.

"Will she do?" Sherlock asked Getaway.

The golem looked at the elf. "Well, she's not a demoness, but she'll do."

"I certainly am not a demoness," Nissa agreed forcefully. "Why would anyone want exaggerated fake curves like that?"

Clio tried not to wince.

"Why, indeed," Sherlock agreed. He resumed his sculpting, looking closely at the elf girl. The proportions of the figure became less pronounced and more realistic. For Clio's taste she was becoming more attractive.

Soon the figure was finished. It had reddish brown skin and long wild hair. In fact it resembled a maenad. "Is this satisfactory?" Sherlock asked Getaway, holding it forth.

The golem considered. "Will she have clothing?"

"If you wish."

"I wish. As much as I have, anyway."

Sherlock conjured another small chip and fashioned it into a panty. He put that carefully on the figure.

"That's perfect! She doesn't need any more clothing." Clio might have differed, but it was the golem's choice. He clearly had typical male taste. He might be made of reverse wood, but his nature wasn't reversed.

"I don't think Knotty is a nice name for a girl," Nissa said.

She had a point. "She's for Getaway," Clio said. "How about Comealong? That's complementary."

"I don't want her complimenting people," Getaway protested. "I want her wild, like me."

"ComplEmentary," Clio clarified. "That means she is your counterpart; together you're perfect."

"Perfect!" Getaway echoed, understanding.

"Then here she is," Sherlock said. "But she'll have to be polite too." He set the figure down.

"I'll make her polite!"

Comealong animated. "You'll what, sawdust brain?" Then she took off running.

Getaway ran after her. In a moment the two were hidden in the surrounding brush.

"I don't think he knows how to handle women," Nissa said with at least half a smile.

"And she has yet to be tamed," Clio agreed.

"Maybe if someone gave him some advice," Nissa said. "I think she likes him."

"She should," Clio said. "They are the only two reverse wood golems in Xanth."

"I can conjure them back," Sherlock said. "But they would just run again. I think they need to work it out themselves."

"But will they return to save my tree?" Nissa asked.

Clio saw the elf was seriously worried. "I think we need to help get this situation under control, if we can. But I'm not sure what we can do."

"Maybe we can help," Drew said. "We can track the golems for you, so you'll know how to advise them."

"But you can't get into their minds," Sherlock said.

"We don't need to. We'll just show you what they're up to, so you can do something."

Sherlock rolled one eye. "I suppose it is our responsibility."

"Go ahead," Clio agreed. "We'll figure out something."

Drusie left Sherlock's pocket and flew rapidly after the golems. Drew remained in Clio's pocket. "She will observe the golems and send the scene to me," Drew explained. "I will show it to you."

"Thank you," Clio said, wishing she could figure out exactly what use this was likely to be.

In two and a half moments the scene appeared: Comealong was running fleetly through a field, Getaway in hot pursuit. "I see it!" Nissa exclaimed. "A vision!"

"Drew is putting it in your mind as well as in ours," Clio explained. "It's the semblance of illusion, re-creating a real scene."

"How can you do it at such a distance?" Sherlock asked.

"Drusie and I have a close mental connection. She's compressing the picture and sending it on a tight beam. I'm decompressing it for you. It's one way in which two telepaths are better than one."

"I am truly impressed," Nissa said.

"They are impressive dragons," Clio said.

Comealong ran up a mountain. It looked cold up there; in fact there was an ice man with a pole. The golem paused. "What are you doing?" she asked.

"I'm ice fishing," the ice man replied as his line pulled in an ice cube.

"Oh." She ran on by him. Too close; her body touched his, and suddenly he was a fireman with a ball of fire on his line. He had been reversed. He looked disgruntled; his countenance was smoky.

Getaway charged by, touching the fire, and it reversed again, becoming the ice man.

Comealong ran down the other side of the mountain. There was a beautiful woman brushing her radiant hair before a mirror. The golem paused again, assessing the woman, frowning in the manner women did when considering competition. This creature was as competitive as it was possible to be. "Who are you?"

"I am Iri Sistible. My talent is to attract men."

"So why are you alone?"

"I don't want a man who is merely hostage to my talent. I want one who is immune. Then when I win him, I'll know it's true love."

"Good luck," Comealong said, and brushed by her.

The woman became a hag whose talent was clearly to repulse men. She did not look entirely pleased by her conversion, though surely only true love would keep a man near her.

Getaway arrived. "Ugh!" he said, and tried to avoid her.

But Iri was not a fool. Maybe she had seen what happened to the ice man. She reached out and touched him. And became as she had been.

"Wow!" he said. "On second thought—"

"Your girl is escaping," she reminded him.

"Oh. Yes." He ran on.

Meanwhile Comealong came to several mermaids lolling in a spring. They were robustly healthy and lovely, as that species tended to be, but these were even more so.

"What's going on here?" the golem asked.

"We live in this healing spring," one replied, flinging her lustrous tresses about. "It gives us healing powers."

"Interesting." Comealong touched the water.

The mermaids suddenly looked sickly, and the healthy foliage surrounding the spring wilted. "Oh, we are undone!" one cried. But the golem was gone.

Getaway arrived. He touched the water, and all was restored. "Oh thank you!" a third maid exclaimed, her bare bosom heaving prettily. "However can we thank you?"

The golem hesitated, eying her healthy front. Mermaids put on excellent fronts, though they tailed off behind.

"Remind him he can't touch her without reversing her," Clio murmured.

"We can't get into the golems' minds," Drew reminded her. "Because they don't have minds."

That was true; they were animated solely by magic. "What about the mermaids?"

The mermaid's expression changed. "But your touch will destroy us," she said sadly. "So you must go on."

"Oh, right," Getaway agreed, prying his eyes away. He ran on.

The scene oriented on Comealong, who was approaching a ridge with two peaks. "What are you?" she asked.

"We are two tors," they answered. "We can privately educate you."

"Ha!" She ran between them.

The tors turned ugly as Getaway arrived. Daunted, he paused. "What are you up to?"

"We are tor mentors," they replied. "We will make you miserable."

But he ran between them, and they reversed again, becoming amiable tutors.

"There would be serious repercussions if he didn't cancel her mischief," Clio said. "We can't let this continue; it's dangerous. Let me talk to him again."

"I'll connect you to the nearest dryad."

Getaway was passing a tree Comealong had overlooked. A bare girl appeared before him. "Let me give you some advice," she said.

He paused. "Who are you? You don't look reversed."

"I am Meggie, the nymph of this tree."

"But that's a maple tree, not an oak!"

"Yes, I am much sweeter than those tough oak dryads."

"What's this advice?"

"You'll never catch her if all you do is chase her. She has to want to be caught. Only then will she let you."

"But how can I make her want to be caught?"

"Tell her you love her."

"That's ridiculous."

"Try it anyway. You need to enlist her help in curing that Elf Elm."

The golem didn't question how an isolated nymph knew about that. He ran on. "Comealong! I want to tell you something."

She paused, about to touch a bell in the shape of a door. Normally it would ring when a person opened it: a doorbell. Clio wasn't sure how it would reverse. "Tell me what?"

He came close. "Something really important."

"Well, out with it," she said, about to run again.

Getaway hugged her. "I love you!"

"Stop mauling me, you pervert!"

Getaway hesitated. "You must be kidding."

She delivered a wooden stare. Then slowly her expression softened. "Yes. I was reversed. But you need to understand who's governing this relationship."

"I am!"

She drew away and turned around, flashing her tiny panties at him. Getaway freaked out and fell down.

Comealong pinned him to the ground and kissed him. "Who?"

"You are," he said dazedly.

"I'm glad we got that settled. Now what's going on?"

"We're curing an elf elm."

She nodded. "Then let's get to it."

They returned to the elm.

"I think we're done here," Clio said as the picture faded. "Thank you, dragons."

"Oh, thank you so much!" Nissa said. "This is so wonderful!"

"A return for your hospitality," Sherlock said.

But as they were about to go, there was a shuddering of the ground. Something huge was tromping near.

"What could that be?" Clio asked alarmed. She glanced at the compass; the blue arrow was wavering uncertainly, and the red arrow was about to hit its mark. The deadline was short, for whatever it was.

"The Danger of the Day," Drew said.

"A huge horrible giant," Drusie agreed.

And Clio had an appointment with it. The compass knew.

"Oh, I know that tromp!" Nissa said. "That's Paul!"

"Who?" Sherlock asked.

"The big lumberjack! He's coming to chop my tree."

"We shall have to stop that," Clio said.

"When the tree is better, and the other elves return, they'll protect it," Nissa said. "But right now it's defenseless. Oh, woe!"

Now the ground shuddered worse, and the giant came into sight. He was the size of an invisible giant, but visible, with a burly body and a huge ax. Behind him came a beast the size of a sphinx, solid blue. That was his ox, ready to haul away the trunk.

"Stop!" Clio cried, running out in front of the giant.

He didn't hear her. His giant boot came down, about to crush her.

She wound it back and tried again. "Stop!" she cried from the side.

He still didn't hear her. He tromped up to the tree and brought his ax off his shoulder. Nissa screamed, but he didn't hear her either.

"I have an idea," Sherlock said.

"Make it quick," Clio snapped. It was not her nature to be sharp, but she was desperate.

"Dragons," he said. He sent a thought to them that so surprised them they forgot to relay it to her. "Do you think that would work?"

"We'll try it," Drew said.

"Try what?" Clio asked, trying to focus. But that monstrous ax mesmerized her. It would require only about ten brutal chops to fell the tree.

Paul lifted the ax high behind his shoulder. He was about to chop. Nissa screamed again.

Then the tree fuzzed and became the big blue ox. Paul blinked. "Babe!" he boomed. "Don't stand in my way when I'm harvesting." But the ox didn't move.

Paul looked around. There to the side was the great Elf Elm. "Oh. I guess I got turned around. Well, sure as I'm the greatest logger ever, I'm gonna take it down." He marched toward the tree, hefting the ax menacingly

The tree backed away from him.

Paul stared. "Since when do trees move?" he demanded. He strode after it.

The tree retreated faster.

"Hey, you can't do that," he said. "No tree escapes Paul Bunyan." He broke into a lumbering run.

The tree moved through the forest, staying just ahead of the giant logger. Soon they were out of sight.

Clio blinked. There was the Elf Elm, exactly where it had always been. "What's going on?"

"The dragons switched the images," Sherlock explained. "They made the tree look like the ox, and the ox look like the tree."

Nissa laughed. "So now he's chasing his ox across the landscape, and Babe knows better than to pause."

Clio was amazed. "That was an effective idea, Sherlock." She looked around. "Where are the dragons?"

"They are staying with Paul and Babe, to maintain the illusion. They'll keep those two moving until nightfall. With luck, Paul will forget about this particular tree until the elves have time to return to protect it."

"That's marvelous," Clio said. "How long will it take for the elves to return?"

"Some should come tomorrow," Nissa said. "They check back every few days, just in case. They'll alert the others."

"Then it should be all right." Clio considered. "But we had better wait here until they do, just to be sure."

"That's great," Nissa said.

"And of course we need to be where the dragons can find us," Sherlock said. "And if the logger returns too soon, they'll be able to lead him astray again. He doesn't seem to be too bright."

Clio laughed. "I was fooled too." But she was well satisfied with the day.

10
DREAM MAN

They were on the proper route; the blue arrow pointed back the way they had come, which Clio knew was correct because it was opposite to the way it had pointed when reversed. Just the four of them: Clio, Sherlock, and the two little dragons.

"I realize that we needed a place to stay for a time and recover," Sherlock said. "But that turned out to be a bit more of an adventure than I might have expected, and we did manage to do a nice elf a favor. Do you think your compass intended all that?"

"I confess to being in doubt myself," Clio said. "Had I known about the threats to the Elf Elm I would have been glad to help; the elves are generally good people. But I don't see the compass as being a caring device. I'm not sure now that it even cared about our being tired or uncomfortable. I think it simply points to where I'm supposed to go. The benefit to the Elf Elm was probably incidental."

"That was my thought. Did the timer function?"

"Yes. It indicated short deadlines when we met Nissa, and when Paul Bunyan came."

"So it seems we were there to save the tree. I am glad we were able to do that, but I don't see how that forwarded your mission."

"There must have been some way."

"The golems," Drew said. "They had a bad effect on your compass. Did you need to get rid of them?"

"I wouldn't do that!" Clio protested.

Sherlock smiled. "You wouldn't do it in an unkind manner, but it seems it was done. They were given a useful assignment that separated them from us. When that elm is cured, there will surely be others to cure. They are likely to be busy for some time, and well appreciated by the elves."

Clio nodded. "Indeed, that is my idea of an ideal separation."

"So the compass pointed the way to separating from the golems," Drew said. "So that you could resume your quest."

"That seems to be the case. I may have underestimated its sophistication." Then she remembered something. "We were where we weren't supposed to be, because of the day's reversal of the compass. So maybe it simply reoriented from there, taking us to the closest safe harbor. Then it saw about the golems."

"And with respect to me," Sherlock said. "Does it show a time?"

"It never showed a time for you."

"Still, perhaps my time has passed. Maybe I, too, should be assigned elsewhere, so as not to get in the way after my usefulness to your mission is done."

The blue arrow suddenly swung to point to him. But the time arrow faded out. "It seems to suggest that you remain relevant, but without a time limit."

"Then I will remain until it is time for me to go." He paused, then added, "I admit to being relieved."

"So am I. You have been very useful." That didn't seem quite adequate, but she wasn't sure what else to say. Meanwhile the arrow swung back to point ahead; it had deviated only to confirm the need for Sherlock's presence.

"It is pleasant being useful."

"Yet your association with me exposes you to my daily dangers."

"Which I am glad to help abate, if I am able."

They were near the Region of Madness, where magic was especially strong. Clio hoped they would avoid it, as strange things could happen there. Sometimes those strange things wandered on out into Xanth proper.

"There is something strange ahead," Drew said.

Exactly what she dreaded. "But the compass points that way. Is it dangerous?"

"I think not to us. But we need to be careful."

"To be sure."

"I can flip a reverse wood chip at it if I need to," Sherlock said. "I am finding this talent to be increasingly useful."

"Maybe that would work," Drew said dubiously.

Clio wondered what would make a telepathic dragon doubtful, but she stifled the wonder; better to find out for herself.

"It's a dragon!" Drusie exclaimed.

"Why so it is," Drew agreed, amazed. "But so different I didn't recognize it."

Then the creature appeared, coming toward them along the trail. It was huge and sinuous, and it had three heads. It spied them and paused, the heads side by side, snorting small jets of fire.

"That's not from Dragon World," Clio said, surprised.

"And I think not from Xanth," Sherlock said.

"That's why we were confused," Drew said. "It's a foreign dragon."

"Can you communicate with it?" Clio asked. "I'd rather not have trouble."

"We're trying," Drew said. "But it thinks in a foreign tongue."

"Try harder," Sherlock said dryly as the three heads seemed to share a decision. The huge dragon might be getting ready to launch itself at them.

Drew scrambled from Clio's pocket and flew to the big dragon. He hovered before the middle head.

"He's trying harder," Drusie explained.

But it wasn't enough. The dragon launched, spreading its wings and leaping toward them. They didn't have time to get out of the way.

There was her danger. She wound it back, having no choice. "Trust me," she said to Sherlock as Drew flew toward the monster dragon. "Flee!"

They turned and fled just before the dragon launched. Caught by surprise, it landed where they had just been. It blew three more jets of fire and gathered itself for another flying leap.

"We'd better get off the path," Sherlock said. "The forest will slow it so I can organize some wood chips."

So that he could reverse the dragon's attack. That made sense. She saw a narrow avenue between the trees of a dense grove. "Here!"

They swerved into the avenue. The dragon landed again, right behind them, and slid on past, caught by surprise again. That gave them another bit of respite. It would take it a moment or a moment and a half to get back on their track.

They ran around a trunk and almost collided with a big hairy baby. It was an ogret—a baby ogre. It was playing an ogre game of smashing stones into pebbles barehanded.

They stopped. The ogret might be harmless, by ogre standards, but its parents would not be. They needed to pass it amicably. "Hello, ogret," Clio said. "What's your name?"

"Adora-ble Bash-ful," the baby answered shyly, squeezing a pebble to dust in its distraction.

"That's nice. We're going on now." They sidled around the ogret and went on.

Just in time, for Bash-ful's parents were returning; the forest floor was shaking with their heavy tread.

The dragon arrived. "Me see drag—ee!" the ogret cried, delighted.

The tromping sounds got abruptly louder and faster. Mature ogres took on young dragons, but this was a baby ogre and an adult dragon. There were sounds of hissing fire and scales being bashed. "That will slow it somewhat," Clio gasped as her feet caught up with her pulses.

The way opened out, leading to what looked like a schoolyard. There was a sign: BOARDING SCHOOL. In smaller print, it said LEARN EVERYTHING ABOUT BOARDS. Well, that did make sense.

But as they entered the yard, a board came flying out and bounced on the ground. "The board is bored of boarding the board!" an angry voice yelled.

"Let's not go there," Sherlock said.

Clio was glad to agree. They dodged to the side again, just as the dragon appeared at the edge of the yard. Somehow it had gotten around the angry ogre family.

They almost ran into a tower. "Help!" a girl called from a window at its top. She wore a robe and a small crown.

Sherlock looked up at her. "I'm not sure how we can do that. Why are you confined?"

"I'm a princess in distress," she said. "I got bored with boarding school and tried to run away, so the motherboard gave me detention and the fatherboard put me in here. I must stay here until I draw a blank."

"We should help her," Clio said. "But I confess I draw a blank on how to do so." Then, hearing herself: "No pun intended."

"But maybe a pun *is* intended," he said. He faced the princess. "Try drawing a blank."

"If I knew how to do that, I'd already be out, silly," she said.

"A blank is a circle of metal that looks like a coin," he explained. "Draw a picture of one. Just draw a circle on the wall."

"Like this?" she asked.

Suddenly the buxom princess appeared on the ground outside the castle. "It worked!" she exclaimed. "I'm out. Oh, thank you, black knight." She flung her arms around Sherlock and kissed him resoundingly, her robe trying to fall open.

For some obscure reason that disturbed Clio. "You should return to boarding school," she said. "You don't want to be late for class."

"Oh, that's right!" the princess said. "I might get spanked by the disciplinary board." She ran toward the school, drawing her robe back together.

"They probably enjoy spanking her," Sherlock remarked.

"I don't understand."

"Fortunately. It's a Mundane thing. We had better move on."

But the way ahead was blocked by a wicked thicket. When they turned to seek another way, the dragon was there. But it no longer seemed as threatening. "Drew has made progress," Drusie said. "The dragon is willing to listen now."

"That's a relief," Clio said.

"The language is weird, but the thoughts are beginning to take shape. This dragon is from—from Asia. Is there such a place you know of?"

"Yes," Sherlock said. "It's part of Mundania."

"But they don't have dragons in Mundania!" Clio protested.

"They do in Asia. In their mythology, at any rate."

"That's it," Drusie said. "Drew's getting it now. There were many dragons, but as time passed the humans expanded and became more skeptical and squeezed them out, and the dragons had to move. But there was hardly any place left to go. This one fled down into a long narrow region, the kam—kam—"

"Kamcatka," Sherlock said. "It's a big peninsula on the eastern side of Russia, in the north Pacific."

"A peninsula!" Clio exclaimed. "That became an entry to Xanth. It happens."

"Yes, I have heard of a number of cases. There's something magical about peninsulas."

"How did you learn of this?"

"We have a good communication system in the Black Wave. It's called Black Mail."

Clio winced. "So this is a Mundane oriental dragon. It must be feeling somewhat lost in Xanth."

"Yes," Drew said. "The last human folk it encountered attacked it with stones and spells, so it thought you would too. I explained that you're not a normal human, you're nice. But it still would like to encounter something familiar."

Clio winced again. From a dragon's perspective, few humans were nice. "I appreciate that. Maybe it should go to Castle MaiDragon, where Becka and Che can surely find it a compatible hunting ground."

"But it's lost. How will it find its way?"

That was a problem. "Perhaps we can find it a guide." She had no idea how, but it seemed better to seek a guide than to hold too long a dialog with this huge alien dragon.

"Let's go back to the regular path," Sherlock said. "Maybe we'll find someone there."

They returned to the path. The three-headed dragon was now behaving well; Drew's contact with it had been effective.

"Wait out of sight," Clio told the dragon. "We'll need to explain things first, to any prospective guide."

The dragon settled down behind a beerbarrel tree. They went onto the path.

An oddly garbed man was walking down it. He looked confused.

"He's another stray from Kamcatka!" Drew said. "In a manner."

"There must be an interface," Clio said. "They can form randomly, and sometimes whole Waves pass through before they close." Then she picked up on his qualification. "In a manner?"

"Maybe he can explain it."

"Hello," Clio said to the man as they met on the path.

He looked at her blankly.

"He doesn't speak our language," Drew said.

"But every human speaks the same language in Xanth. It's part of the magic."

"He doesn't know that. He's not a normal man."

Clio brushed aside the uncomfortable oddity. "It doesn't matter. Tell him he can speak and understand our language."

Drew did. The man looked surprised. "I can?"

Clio smiled. "Yes. I am Clio, and this is Sherlock. Who are you?"

"I am Mikhail. I am seeking my true love. But I got lost, and can't seem to find her."

"Who is she?"

"I don't know."

"Then how can she be your true love?"

"By definition. I am her dream man."

Clio paused to take stock. She was beginning to understand Drew's qualification. "I fear I am a bit slow today. She knows you, while you do not know her?"

"Yes. But I am sure she is a very nice person, and that I am ideal for her."

"Let's hope so. Perhaps we should start at the beginning. When did she come to know you?"

"Several months ago. She wished to have a man, but there were none in her village that were suitable, so she dreamed up one who would be perfect for her. As it happened, I fit the description, so her dream governed me. I must be with her! But something happened, and I was unable to locate her. So now I am looking, for she surely misses me."

Clio looked at Sherlock. "Can you make sense of this?"

"I think so. It is the habit of lonely folk to dream of ideal companions. I have done it myself. Usually nothing comes of it. Nothing did for me. But with the right magic, who knows? This woman must have had a talent for dreaming, and her dream man became real. I should think that originally he would have gone to her, but—well, he came to Xanth instead."

There was an ugly nuance that she elected not to explore. "And she did not? That would explain why he can't find her."

"Perhaps. But since there's very little magic in Mundania, maybe it could happen only in Xanth."

"Only if she's in Xanth too."

"We have to assume that she is."

There was still something obscure about this. "Well, we need a guide for the dragon. Is there a chance that Mikhail will do?"

"Well, it would be easier for the dragon to travel in the company of a man. The man could ask directions."

"Men don't ask directions."

Sherlock smiled. "Then he needs to find his woman soon, so she can ask directions."

"I am very tired," Mikhail said. "I must sleep now."

"Can you wait a moment? There is a dragon I'd like to introduce you to. We have an understanding; I think you will be able to sleep safely in its company."

"A dragon," Mikhail repeated warily. "It is hard for any person to be safe in such company."

"Nevertheless, I believe we should see." She took him by the hand and led him along the path.

There was the dragon, curled near the tree. "That's a Russian dragon!" Mikhail exclaimed. "Why didn't you say so?"

"You can get along with it?"

"Well, I don't know that, but at least it's familiar. Everything else has been uncomfortably strange."

"Introduce them," Clio told Drew. "Let them converse a bit. I will go consult with Sherlock."

Drew stayed with the man and dragon, connecting them telepathically. Clio returned to Sherlock. "You said we should assume that Mikhail's dream woman is also in Xanth. What is your rationale?"

"I think he blundered into Xanth," Sherlock said. "Yet he still feels her desire for him. So she must be here too. It may be like the dragon's telepathy. I don't think she could reach him from Mundania."

"This seems like tortured logic to me. How could—"

She broke off, for another person was coming along the path. This was a young woman. She was petite and well formed, with black hair to her waist. Like the dragon and man, she appeared dazed.

"Hello," Clio said. "I am Clio."

"I am Noi. I am lost."

"Where is your home?"

"In Thailand."

"Tie Land?" Sherlock asked. "Where they grow ties, and are fit to be tied?"

Noi looked at him blankly.

"I was there once. There's a small village in the center called Knottingham, named after Granny Knott," he said. "The favorite dinner there is bowtie pasta."

"I am sorry, I do not know of this place," the woman said.

"I think that's Thailand, Mundania," Clio said. "How did you come here, Noi?"

"I was riding a motorcycle, but something happened. I don't know how I came to this strange land."

Things were coming magically together. "Did you dream of a man?"

Noi looked sharply at her. "How do you know this?"

"As you said, this is a strange land. Strange things happen. We just met a man who said he was the dream of a woman."

Her eyes grew large. "Is his name Mikhail?"

"Yes."

"I dreamed he would come from a romantically far land to take me away. But I never thought he really would. You say he is here?"

"Yes. We just talked with him. He said he was tired, so we introduced him to a dragon—"

"A dragon!"

"We have come to know this dragon, and it knows that this man is not to be eaten. We think they can travel together, with the man handling the humans they encounter, and the dragon protecting him from monsters. Such things happen, in Xanth."

"This land is Xanth?"

"Yes. It's a land of magic and puns, and many nonhuman creatures who may be as smart as humans. You will surely like it when you get to know it."

"Maybe if I could find my dream man, it would be easier."

"Readily done. We'll introduce you now." Clio led the way to where the dragon waited.

"I hope it happens," Noi said. Evidently she had suffered disappointments before.

The dragon was there, but not the man. Clio suppressed a horrible suspicion. "Where is Mikhail?"

"He's gone," Drew said, flitting to her pocket. He spoke only to her.

She answered him silently; she had learned to communicate in mock illusion. "But the dragon was not supposed to—"

"It didn't. Mikhail lay down to sleep, and faded out."

"Faded out!"

"As if he no longer existed. We have been looking for him, in case he just teleported somewhere else, but then I should be able to find his mind."

"His mind faded too?"

"Yes. He's completely gone."

Clio turned to Noi. "It seems there is a confusion. Mikhail was here, then he disappeared. The dragon did not harm him. I don't understand it."

"I think I do," Noi said. "He is my dream man. He doesn't exist when I'm not dreaming him."

Clio took stock. "Let's discuss this with Sherlock. Perhaps he will have some useful idea how to handle this." She was coming to depend more on the Black Wave man, as he was generally sensible.

They returned to Sherlock. "Noi's dream man does not seem to exist when she isn't asleep. What can we do?"

"This is new to me. We had better discuss this with the dragons. Four minds are better than two."

Clio introduced the little dragons to Noi, and explained about their telepathy. The dragons made contact with her mind, reassuring her. Then they settled down to a serious discussion.

"So you dreamed Mikhail, and he came to exist," Sherlock said. "He knows he is your dream man, and wants to be with you. But it seems this is possible only when you are asleep."

"That is my understanding," Noi agreed. "I had not realized that he existed at all, outside my mind."

"He does now," Clio said.

"Maybe we should talk to Mikhail again," Sherlock said. "If Noi sleeps, will he reappear?"

"I should think so," Clio said.

"With magic, many things are possible. We just have to find something."

Clio doubted that this would be easy to do, but had no better idea. "Do you think you could sleep now?" she asked Noi.

"I don't know how to will myself to sleep."

"I believe I saw a clothing tree nearby," Clio said. "It may have shirts."

Noi looked at her blankly, but Sherlock understood. "It does; I saw it. I'll fetch one." He walked back along the path.

"We have an entire realm of dreams," Clio said. "It can be entered via a gourd with a peephole. It might be possible for you to meet him there, in the gourd."

"But I want to meet him in life," Noi protested. "I have lived so long without my dream man, I don't want to be without him any longer."

"Life does get lonely, without a man," Clio agreed.

Sherlock returned, carrying a shirt. "Try this on," he told Noi. "It's a sleep-shirt."

The woman shrugged and pulled the shirt on over her head and clothing. It came all the way down to her knees. "It's a good shirt, but I don't see how—"

Sherlock caught her as she fell asleep on her feet. He laid her down carefully on a mossy bank.

"She doesn't understand about the way magic works here," Clio said. "She assumed that the shirt was merely to wear when sleeping, not that made a person sleep."

"Mikhail is back," Drew said. "He thinks he merely slept for a while."

"Tell him to come here," Clio said. "Maybe if he actually sees her, it will be all right."

Soon Mikhail appeared. "Your little dragon said—" He paused. "Who is she?"

"Do you like her?" Clio asked.

"She's a sleeping beauty. I find her strangely attractive, though I've never seen her before."

"She is the woman who dreamed you."

Mikhail stared. "She's the one? I have found her at last? This is wonderful!"

"But there's a complication."

"I must wake her and tell her I am here."

"I'm not sure that is feasible."

Mikhail got down on his knees, leaned forward, and kissed Noi on the lips. She continued sleeping.

"She's in a sleep-shirt," Sherlock said.

"She won't readily wake."

"Then she must remove it," Mikhail said.

"We can do that," Sherlock said.

"I don't think—" Clio said.

Sherlock lifted Noi up, and Mikhail gently worked the shirt off her. Then Sherlock laid her down again, and Mikhail kissed her again.

She woke immediately—and Mikhail faded out. "I was afraid of that," Clio said.

"What happened?" Noi asked. "Did I sleep? I apologize for—"

"The sleep shirt put you to sleep," Clio explained.

Noi looked down at herself. "But I don't seem to be wearing it."

"We took it off you," Sherlock said. "So you could wake. But—" He looked somewhat helplessly at Clio.

"Mikhail was here," Clio said. "He said you were a sleeping beauty. I tried to caution him, but he did not listen."

"He is like that," Noi agreed. "Impetuous in love."

"He kissed you. But when you woke, he faded. We had hoped for better."

Noi nodded. "That is the way it would be." A tear trickled from the corner of one eye.

"There may be a way," Sherlock said. "But it is risky."

"A way for me to be with him? I will take the risk."

"I have what we call reverse wood. It reverses things. If I gave him a chip, it would reverse him. But not necessarily in the way we wish. It might make him real instead of dream—or it might abolish him even as a dream. We can't be sure."

Noi considered. "I don't want to destroy him. I don't want to risk hurting him. Better to let him go to some other woman. Perhaps she will treat him well." Another tear trickled.

"I think we should let him decide that," Clio said. "Will you let him do that?"

"I would not go against his wish. But oh, if he should perish because of me—I would rather perish instead."

"He may feel the same. It's a gamble, but perhaps the only way to resolve the dilemma. I think we should explain it to him."

Noi considered again, then nodded. "Let it be as he wills it."

Sherlock gave her the sleep-shirt, and she donned it again. In less than a moment she was asleep. Clio had to agree with Mikhail: she was very pretty in repose, with her black hair spread out to frame her face.

Mikhail reappeared. "I seem to have gotten confused. I was about to wake my love, but I'm not sure I did."

"You kissed her," Sherlock said. "She woke—and you faded out. You are her dream man; she has to be asleep to dream you. Now you have a grave decision to make."

"I will gladly kiss her again!"

Noi was right: he was romantically impulsive. That was a nice trait in a man.

Sherlock smiled. "Not that, exactly. The problem is that you are out of phase with her; you are here only when she sleeps. If we could reverse that, you could be with her when she is awake. We may be able to do that. But there is a risk."

"I'll take any risk, to be with her."

"The risk is that the reversal might destroy you. We can't be sure."

Mikhail gazed at Noi. "She dreamed me to be her ideal. But she is *my* ideal. I must be with her, or seek oblivion."

Clio was extremely nervous about this, but kept quiet. Their ploy would either work, or not.

A chip appeared in Sherlock's hand. "Take this chip of reverse wood. It will magically reverse you. For good or ill."

Without hesitation, Mikhail took it.

Nothing happened.

"Not all reversals are immediately apparent," Sherlock said. "Let me get her shirt off so you can kiss her again."

"I'll help!"

They tackled the job as before, while Clio wondered. How could the chip have no effect? Was it real reverse wood?

Noi was now without the shirt. Mikhail kissed her. She woke.

Mikhail remained.

"Mikhail!" Noi exclaimed, sitting up. They kissed again.

Sherlock glanced at Clio, nodding. It had worked.

Before they could celebrate, an awful smell coalesced around them. It was like rotten fruit, only worse.

Noi paused in her kissing. "That smells like ripe duran."

"Duran?" Clio asked, trying not to gag. "Is it poisonous?"

"No, it's a fruit that tastes better than it smells."

Then a little girl appeared, walking along the path. She held a piece of fruit, from which she was nibbling. As she approached, the smell intensified. Noi was right: the awful smell was from the fruit.

Clio happened to have a little bag in her pocket that had a secure seal. She rushed to intercept the girl. "Please—let me put that away for you," she gasped. She almost snatched the piece of fruit and jammed it in the bag, closing it tight.

The smell alleviated, now that its source was gone. She was able to breathe again. She inhaled enough to speak in a normal manner. "Hello. I am Clio. Who are you?"

"Malinee. I'm lost."

Another lost soul! And surely from the Asia section of Mundania, by the look of her. "Where do you live?"

"Thailand."

"That's where I live," Noi said.

"Is it by chance a peninsula?" Sherlock asked.

"Oh, yes. Why?"

"Peninsulas can be avenues." He didn't clarify further, and the girl did not inquire. "I'm not sure we can get you back to Thailand, but would you like to travel with a dragon?"

"A dragon!" Malinee said, delighted. She spied the dragon, who was waiting down the path, and ran to give its center neck a hug. It was evidently her type of dragon.

Sherlock turned to Mikhail and Noi. "How would the two of you like to take a long walk around the peninsula of Xanth, conducting a dragon to where the folk will be able to help it get settled? Taking Malinee along?"

"Why not?" Mikhail asked. "Suddenly everything is wonderful."

"Like a honeymoon," Noi agreed blissfully.

Clio gave them general directions, and the group started off, Malinee riding the dragon. They would surely get there safely.

"That worked out rather well," Sherlock said.

"It was as though the four of them were meant for each other," Clio agreed. "But you know—"

"That none of them will be able to return to their Mundane peninsulas," he said. "I thought it best not to discuss that aspect." He meant that some who died in Mundania came thereafter to Xanth.

"Actually some people find Xanth alive."

"And some don't. But with the fickleness of peninsular connections, they can't expect to return regardless. So it seems best for them to make their homes in Xanth. In time they should develop magic talents, as I did."

"As you did," she agreed. "It has been quite useful."

"Now we are four again. But I wonder: was this another part of your quest? I can't see that you gained or lost anything from the interaction, apart from the satisfaction of helping three people and a dragon find their places."

Clio considered. "I am of course glad to have helped them. I'm sure they'll all become good citizens of Xanth, in their fashions, including the dragon."

"The dragon should be something of a novelty, even among dragons. Three heads!"

"It has been a season for placing dragons," she said, glancing down at Drew in her pocket. "But it is true: this does not seem to have been guided by the compass."

"Is it pointing anywhere now?"

She glanced at her wrist. The blue arrow was pointing toward the pocket where she had put the bag. "Oh—I forgot to return the fruit to Malinee."

"I doubt she cares. She's got a dragon now."

"But what am I to do with this? The smell is atrocious, and it's unlikely to improve with time."

"Try leaving it somewhere."

She set the bag somewhat gingerly at the base of a tree. But as she walked away from it, the blue arrow on her wrist swung around to orient on it.

"That's what I thought," Sherlock said. "This was a compass episode. For the duran."

"But what would I ever want with such a vile smelling thing?"

"I don't know. But I suspect we'll find out, in due course."

"In due course," she agreed weakly.

11
BAD DREAMS

There was no suitable campsite, but day was ending, so they stopped by a river and Sherlock conjured a number of reverse wood chips to make a protective ring around them. Then he foraged for blankets and pies, while Clio consulted with the dragons. There were dangerous creatures in the vicinity, but none that wouldn't be stopped by the reverse wood.

She got busy with brush and a fragment of firewood she found, and it made a fire to heat the pies. They ate and settled down for the night, guarded by the dragons' extended awareness.

"This is our first night together alone in the open," she said. "I find it awkward."

"I will sleep elsewhere, if you wish. I do not wish to embarrass you."

"Please. I think I need to speak with a certain candor. The compass led me to you, and keeps me with you. I am beginning to wonder whether we are intended to associate longer."

"Perhaps as long as it takes to complete your mission, so you can return to Mount Parnassus."

This was twice as difficult as she had imagined. "Would it bother you if it turned out to be longer than that?"

He paused before answering. "No."

"I don't mean to presume. But you are a nice man, and I like your company."

"Thank you."

"Would you by any chance be amenable to residing on Mount Parnassus?"

"You mean to stay with you?"

"Yes."

He thought about it. "I would want to be useful. I'm not sure that there is much use for reverse wood there."

"Surely uses could be found."

"You, as I understand it, are eternal. I am already middle-aged, and would fade out before too long on your scale."

"Not if you ate a leaf from the Tree of Life. You would become eternal too."

He gazed at her in the gloom. "I fear a misunderstanding. May I be blunt?"

"By all means."

"I thought your interest in me was as a person who can be useful as a traveling companion. Is it more?"

"Yes."

"I have liabilities that make me doubt. I am unprepossessing."

"As I come to know you, I find qualities that impress me."

"I am middle-aged."

"I am older."

"I am black."

"I don't understand."

"That is perhaps an appealing thing about you. Neither did you understand my remark about the disciplinary board enjoying spanking the princess."

"That's true. Do you care to explain?"

"The princess was a buxom lass. There are men who might like to touch her bottom under the pretext of discipline. Spanking has a special reputation when it applies to big girls."

"I still don't understand."

"Because you have never been exposed to the baser human instincts. That's an engaging quality."

Clio was frustrated by her inability to decipher this. She shifted to the other confusion. "What is this about your being black? All members of the Black Wave are."

"I was an adult when we migrated from Mundania to Xanth. My appreciation of particular aspects of human nature was fairly well set. You might say I remain Mundane in a certain fundamental manner, despite my recent development of a magic talent. It affects my outlook."

"What outlook is this?"

"As a general rule, in Mundania, white folk are not interested in black folk unless there is something specific to be obtained from them. Such as money, or entertainment, or brute labor on less pleasant chores. So it seems to me that you would not be interested in me as anything other than a temporary assistant."

"Because of your color?" she asked incredulously.

"Yes."

"I truly don't understand."

"You are saying that my liabilities are no bar to a more personal relationship?

"What liabilities?"

Sherlock shrugged. "I think you are serious. But my mundane background doubts."

Almost, she understood. "I have my own liability."

He smiled. "Not that I know of."

Now at last she had the courage. "My curves aren't real."

"It's dark now, but they certainly look real by daylight."

"I was cursed to have no curves of my own, but to find some. I found a nymph bark that provides me a shape I otherwise lack."

"I don't understand."

She laughed. "It's nice that this time it is you who is baffled. I'll show you."

"I can't see you in this light."

"Perhaps that helps." She nerved herself before she could change her mind again, took off her clothing, then stripped the bark. Now she was naked. She was being bolder than she ever had been in her life, but now seemed to be the time. "Give me your hand."

"I don't understand," he repeated.

She found his hand in the dark and brought it to her torso. "This is my body. As you can surely feel, it has no curves."

"That can't be you!"

"It is me. Establish it."

"May I?"

"Yes."

He sat up and used both hands, running them over her bare body. "I don't believe it."

"It is nevertheless true. I will leave the bark off in the morning, if you wish to verify it by daylight."

He abruptly withdrew. "No need."

She had turned him off, as she had feared. "I apologize for misrepresenting myself. It was foolish vanity."

"Please don't."

She was silent. She had done what she had to do, and paid the price she had to pay. She put the bark back on, and her clothing. Then she settled miserably to sleep.

Sherlock said nothing in the morning. He went about his business as usual, fetching in pies for breakfast. They ate, and organized for the day's walk. The blue arrow pointed on along the trail, and the red arrow was back, with little time remaining. They were close to another contact.

It wasn't long before they found it. Five walking skeletons appeared, coming toward them. Their hollow eyes spied the two, and they rattled their bones menacingly.

"Marrow Bones and Gracile Ossein are nice folk," Clio murmured. "Somehow I don't think these ones are." In fact, this seemed to be her Danger of the Day.

The skeletons charged, grinning with their skull faces, reaching out with their bone fingers. Sherlock stepped in front of Clio, a chip of wood appearing in his hand. He flipped it at the nearest skeleton. It touched, and the skeleton transformed into a mild-looking man. The man looked surprised.

The other skeletons closed in. Sherlock flipped more chips, and they became inoffensive men and women.

"Who are you?" Clio demanded.

"We're actors in dreams," one man said. "I think we need to find the casting agency for good dreams."

"Dreams! What are you doing out here in Xanth, by daylight?"

"We don't know. We were going to a casting call, but lost our way."

"Bad dreams!" Sherlock said. "You're from the gourd!"

"Yes. But we don't want to act in that kind anymore."

"You'll have to find a daymare," Clio said. "They know where the good dreams are made."

"We'll find one," the man agreed, and led the group on down the trail. One of their hands brushed Clio's hand, and passed through it; he was a man of no substance. That made sense, as the creatures of the dream realm normally had no reality in the physical realm.

"How did they get out?" Sherlock asked.

Clio glanced at the compass. The red arrow was on its mark. "I think that's for us to discover. There must be a hole in the dream framework."

"There must be. I've never heard of this happening before."

"Things do go wrong on occasion." She was privately glad that they were able to talk about things. She had been afraid that after her revelation of the night Sherlock would find some pretext to depart, and she could hardly blame him. Yet she had had to tell him the truth some time.

"Is this something your compass suggests you need to deal with?"

"It did point us toward the skeletons, and the time was when they appeared. I suppose it could be coincidence."

"I doubt it. The compass seems to have its own mind."

She smiled with understanding. "It does."

"What does it say now?"

She looked. "Another short deadline, down the path."

"Should we flee it?"

"No. I have to complete my mission as soon as possible."

"There is a time limit?"

"There may be."

"Something is coming," Drew said.

Then a ghost appeared. It was a wild frightening one, drifting above the path, its sheet flapping. It spied them with its vacant eye-holes and floated menacingly toward them.

"I have a weird notion," Sherlock said. "Is it possible that we aren't supposed to nullify the bad dreams? All they can do is scare us, and frankly, I'm not scared."

"But they could do mischief to others. I think we'd better nullify them."

"As you wish." He flipped a chip at the ghost, which became a flat soft children's bedsheet, decorated with cute animals, and drifted away.

"You mentioned a time limit," Sherlock said as they proceeded on along the trail. "Is this something I should know about?"

"Yes, probably. It's—"

"More coming," Drew said.

Then a swarm of ugly things appeared. They were indescribable, but had aspects of squashed caterpillars with messy tentacles and drooling mouths. "Get a load of this!" one exclaimed. "An old black man and a sexy slut! Charge!"

"Oh, my," Clio said. "Those are ghastlies. They're dirty and horrible to touch, and their mouths are worse."

"There are too many to catch with chips," Sherlock said.

"Just get out of their way, lest—" She was too late; they were already swarming over the two of them.

"Lest?" he asked as he shook them off.

"Lest they defecate on us."

Indeed, they were already dripping with stink. "Ugh!"

The ghastlies tumbled on down the path, looking for others to besmirch.

"This is getting out of hand," Clio said.

"Out of something, anyway." He tried to brush off some of the guano, but it just smeared worse. Clio was no better off; she feared her hair would never be the same. Even the two little dragons had been soiled.

"We've got to find a way to plug that leak," Clio said.

"I agree. But first I'd like to get clean."

"Yes! There's a stream nearby; we'll wash there."

They slogged down to the stream. "We'll have to strip."

"I know it," she agreed. "It isn't as though we have physical secrets from each other."

They pulled off their clothing, and Clio also removed the nymph bark, which had gotten grimed too. They splashed water on themselves, washing off the clinging filth. The two dragons dived under the surface and came up again, shaking their wings; they weren't any happier about the foulness. Sherlock helped her with her hair, which she had to let down and immerse in the water, slowly rinsing it.

"I wonder," he said.

"Yes?"

"If those were more escapees from the dream realm, how could their refuse be solid?"

"That's an excellent question. It shouldn't be. It should be more apparent than real."

The remaining gook disappeared. "We figured it out, and it went," Sherlock said. "It was all in our minds."

She tried to laugh. "I never realized my mind could be so dirty."

"We were fooled too," Drew said, chagrined.

Sherlock looked around. "Uh-oh."

"More horrors?" she asked, alarmed.

"Not exactly. It's that I think we lost our clothes."

She checked. Everything was gone. "The stream must have carried them away while we were distracted. We weren't really dirty; we merely thought we were. But the water is real, and it acted as water does. We'll have to hurry to recover them."

"I'll do it." He waded downstream, only to pause before getting far. "Uh-oh," he repeated.

"I hate that expression! What is it?"

"There's a waterfall. Our clothes are gone."

"How can there be a waterfall? This is level land."

But there was. The water tumbled far down into a crevice and vanished. There was no hope of recovering their things.

"We can look for them," Drew said.

"They would be too heavy for you to carry."

"So the ghastlies may not have had substance," Sherlock said. "And their mess wasn't real. But it fooled us into making mischief for ourselves."

"We'll have to find clothing trees," she said. "Fortunately they are fairly common in this region."

"Will any have another nymph bark?"

She had lost that too! "I'm afraid not. You will have to bear with me as I am."

"This I am satisfied to do."

For how long, she wondered. Still, she was glad she had told him about the nymph bark, because it had prepared him for the disappointment of her real body.

They found a pant bush with a number of pants on it, each decorated with bounding catlike animals. They were even marked HIS and HERS. She had never quite figured out how such labels came to be; surely plants weren't literate. They picked and donned pants as appropriate.

There was an urgent grunting sound, as of some hot animal breathing hard, followed by a higher pitched series of gasps. Both of them looked around, but there was nothing in view. The sounds were coming from very close, however. In fact—

"It's from the pants!" she exclaimed, hastily getting out of hers. "They're panting!"

"We missed the pun," he said ruefully, getting out of his. "Pant-hers, pant-his. Like rutting felines."

"As if we haven't been humiliated enough."

He paused. "Have we?"

"Have we what?"

"Have we really been humiliated?"

"We're standing here naked!"

He shrugged. "I see another clothing plant. Maybe this one will be legitimate."

It was. In due course they were respectably clothed again, with the two little dragons in their pockets. Sherlock looked good; she wished the same could be said for herself.

"The matter of the time limit," he said. "You were about to tell me."

"So I was. It's that I am cursed to die young. Because I live on Mount Parnassus and have eaten of the Tree of Life, I'm immortal, so have remained physically young. But when I leave Parnassus I resume aging, and use of the windback adds further to my age, so I could die if I don't get promptly back home."

"I had not realized that you made such a sacrifice to accomplish your mission."

"I don't regard it as a sacrifice, just a risk. So I do want to return home as soon as is expedient."

"And you asked me to return with you."

"Yes. But I had to tell you about—" She glanced down at herself. "My liability."

"I appreciate that. It gives me the chance to get to know you without being distracted by your curves."

"To be sure." He was of course being polite.

"Something may be coming," Drew said. "It seems metal."

They returned to the path. Just in time to encounter the next gourd escapees. These were brass men and women wearing brass hats, brassards, and brassieres, as appropriate. They saw the two travelers and scattered brass tacks in front of them to step on.

"Brassies," Clio said. "They do much of the construction in the gourd realm. They're not usually used directly in bad dreams."

They stood aside and let the brassies pass, ignoring the tacks. There was no point in reversing folk who weren't up to any mischief.

"However," Sherlock said, "there are bound to be many others that will freak out ordinary folk. We need some way to locate that leak."

"Maybe the blue arrow will point to it. But getting there could take some time. I want to handle it faster."

"Short of getting a magic carpet or something to ride, I'm not sure how."

"Something to ride," she agreed. "Let me see if I can reach Mare Imbrium."

"The daymare? These are nightmare things."

"But she knows their ropes, and has her body back."

Clio focused on Imbri. In a moment the mare appeared.

A dreamlet formed, containing a black-clad young woman. "Hello, Muse," she said.

"She speaks the way we do!" Drew exclaimed.

"In the mind," Drusie agreed.

"Imbri, meet my friends Drew, Drusie, and of course you know Sherlock. Folks, this is Mare Imbrium, once a night mare, then a day mare, now a tree nymph."

"You have a soul," Drew said to Imbri, surprised. "I thought dream creatures didn't."

"I have half a soul," Imbri's dreamlet figure said. "It's a long story. You dragons have souls too; I thought dragons didn't."

"We're from Dragon World," Drusie explained. "It's one of the Moons of Ida."

"Now I understand. I've been to the moons, though not that one."

"We're pretty far up the line," Drew said.

The dreamlet image returned to Clio. "Why did you summon me, Muse?"

"There seems to be a leak in the dream realm. Bad dream figures are roaming Xanth. We need to locate that leak and seal it before there's any real damage."

"That explains the disappearance of some of the gourd workers. I received a report. Some dreams had to be abridged because the actors or craftsmen didn't show up."

"We saw skeletons, a ghost, brassies, and a mess of ghastlies," Sherlock said. "We had to wash."

The dreamlet girl seemed to stifle a giggle. "I'm sure. So you do need to find that leak and stuff it."

"Can you help us?" Clio asked.

Imbri considered. "It must be a bad gourd. Sometimes they rot. They're supposed to be fail-safe, but every so often a glitch gets into the works."

"Those glitches must be as bad as the ghastlies," Drew said.

"They're not as ugly or dirty, but they're just as much trouble," Imbri agreed. "The Night Stallion tries to keep them under control, but they keep getting into things."

"That's their nature," Clio said. "So can you locate the bad gourd for us?"

The dreamlet shook her head. "We'll have to check every gourd until we find it. There are hundreds of them."

Clio winced. "I would prefer to do this expeditiously."

Sherlock, who now understood her situation, stepped in. "If this is on your schedule, the compass should point the way. We'll simply need to be able to move rapidly."

"I'll carry one," Imbri said. "I can be solid now. But the regular night and day mares can't carry people of substance. For that we need a physical mare. But regular horses don't roam Xanth. Ah—I know. Juana. She'll do it."

"Juana?" Clio asked. "I don't believe I know of her."

"She wanted to be a day mare, and she had marvelous dreams, but her territory was Mundania. She was unfairly banned, and is out of a job. So she's neither dream nor Xanth, but in between. She'll surely be happy to help." The dreamlet figure put her hands to her mouth, forming a funnel, and called "Mare Juana!"

There was a stirring, and a sweetish odor as another mare arrived. A dreamlet formed over her head, with a somewhat dazed maiden clad in brown, matching her real color. "You have a job for me?"

"We need to track down a leaky gourd," Imbri said. "Will you carry a human person?"

The maiden was plainly disappointed. "Not dream work?"

"Not dream work," Imbri agreed.

"Oh, well, I suppose it's better than nothing. Who must I carry?"

"I believe that's me," Sherlock said.

The dreamlet maiden gazed at him. "Oh! A Magician! Why didn't you say so?"

"I'm no Magician," Sherlock protested. "In fact I only recently discovered I could do magic, and that's sort of scattered."

The maiden flushed. "My error. I apologize. Usually I'm sharper than that."

"You can recognize Magicians, when they're not doing magic?"

"Usually. But maybe not reliably, it seems. There's something about them, I don't know what, but I smell it."

"I hope you'll still carry me, though I'm much less than you thought."

"Oh, I will, certainly. Get on my back."

"I lack experience riding. Can we get a saddle?"

"A saddle!" Juana exclaimed, affronted. "Never!"

"Sorry. I just don't want to fall off the moment you move."

"Oh, don't worry about that; you won't fall."

Sherlock glanced helplessly at Clio. "She's correct," Clio said. "If a mare wants you to stay on, you'll stay on. Similarly if she wants you off, you'll be off, regardless of your skill as a rider. Neither night nor day mares can be held against their will."

"All right," he said, looking as if it was not even partly right. He stood beside Juana and jumped, trying to get on her back. Suddenly he was there, looking surprised. "How did I do that?"

"She did it," Clio said. "She has some dream qualities." She faced Imbri. "And you'll carry me?"

"Yes. Jump on."

Clio jumped, and found herself similarly mounted. She knew about the magic, but it was impressive anyway.

"Where to?" the dreamlet maiden asked.

Clio looked at the compass. "That way," she said, pointing down the trail. "I don't know how far."

"We'll simply gallop to the first gourd along this route. If that's not it, we'll go to on the next. The direction helps a lot; there shouldn't be too many."

"That's good," Clio said, relieved.

Both mares took off at an instant gallop. Neither Clio nor Sherlock had any trouble remaining mounted; it was as though each had spent a lifetime riding horses. Magic had its benefits.

In a moment both mares halted. It seemed they knew where the gourds were; all they needed the direction for was to select the particular gourds to be checked. Sure enough, there was a vine with a hand-some gourd beside the path.

Clio got down and approached the gourd. It was green and looked healthy, but that was not necessarily proof that it didn't leak. How could she be sure of it, one way or the other?

Sherlock joined her. "I assume that if it is in good operating order, its peephole will usher people in to its wonders. I'll take a look. Just don't depart and leave me here."

"It's my mission," she said firmly. "I'll look. Give me about five minutes, then haul me out."

"As you wish, of course."

She lay down before the gourd, propped her chin on her fist, and stared into the peephole at its end.

She stood in a desolate black and white scene. The sky was overcast and dismal; the grass was so bedraggled that it was uncertain whether it had ever rated better days. There was a rickety picket fence with several broken slats. Beyond it was a dull yard with two dormant or dead trees. But mainly there was the haunted house.

For that was all it could be. The wooden slats were warped, with paint flaking off. The steps to the front veranda looked unsafe. The windows were cobwebbed and cracked. The roof looked leaky. The door looked forbidding. No one with any sense would enter this house.

But of course there was no other way to proceed. This was the first stage of a bad dream. It forced the visitor to do what he least wanted to: enter the structure.

"This is interesting. I've never seen a home like this before."

"Drew! You're with me!"

"I am with your mind, sharing your vision. Am I intruding? Do you wish to enjoy it alone?"

"No, I'm glad to have you here." She glanced down and saw his head poking out of her pocket. "You are a comfort, dragon. I'll be sorry when you finish your business with me and depart."

"We'll be sorry too. You are giving us a wonderful tour of your world."

She refocused on her mission of the moment. So far so good; this seemed to be a healthy gourd. But she had to be sure. She swung open the decrepit gate and walked down the walk and up the steps to the front door. She pressed the doorbell.

Ouch! There was a thorn in it. She had forgotten about that. She stuck her thumb in her mouth to suck out the pain, then tried the doorknob. And got shocked. She had forgotten about that too; it had been a decade or so since she had covered this setting in a history tome. "Mice!" she swore.

"This is a bad word?"

"It's as bad as a lady of delicacy is allowed to use."

"What would an indelicate person say?"

"**$$$$!!**" The wood of the door developed a scorch mark, and chips of burned paint dropped to the floor. "I mention it purely in an advisory sense, of course." But she felt better.

"I will remember that word," Drew said. "And never use it in your presence."

"Thank you."

She used her foot to push the door open. A chill draft washed out, smelling faintly of something too-long dead. She stepped into the dark hall. A ghost swept up. "Booo!" it cried.

"Hello, Booo. I met your friend outside, and turned him into a child's blanket."

The ghost's mouth opened in horror. It faded out.

"That was cruel of you. The ghost was only doing its job, after all."

"I regret my intemperance already," she said with satisfaction.

She found herself moving. The hall floor was a level escalator that was carrying her on into the center of the house. She tried to see where it was going, but the shadows were too thick.

Then suddenly she was falling. The escalator had dumped her into a hole. In fact it was an oubliette, seemingly bottomless. She fell for a long time before remembering she was supposed to scream. She screamed. Only then did she land in a squishy puddle. Her feet slipped out, and she sat down on the squish. She reached down to discover by feel what it was.

And recoiled. It was a bed of snakes! "%%%%!!"

The snakes recoiled, hurt. She felt guilty. They, too, were only doing their job.

"How did you learn such dangerous words?" Drew asked.

"I recorded them in prior volumes of the history of Xanth. I tried to erase them from my mind, but it seems I didn't succeed. I am appalled at myself."

She worked her way to her feet—and suddenly was blinking in daylight. Sherlock had put his hand between her eye and the peephole, interrupting the connection and reverting her to the physical realm.

"Five minutes, you said," he reminded her. "I suppose I could have waited a bit longer, if you preferred."

"Thank you, no. I have ascertained that this gourd is in normal working mode. Do you know what I was experiencing?"

"Yes, Drusie showed us the pictures Drew had from your mind. The horror house."

"All quite in order. So we can proceed to the next one."

They remounted and rode to the next gourd, passing assorted stray spooks along the way. They stopped at the gourd.

"My turn," Sherlock said. "The burden need not be yours alone."

She was touched. "There is no need. I'm sure you aren't required to do what I can do myself."

"I might as well help, however." He lay down, propped up his head, and looked into the peephole. He froze.

A picture appeared above him, as Drusie relayed what was in his mind. It was inside the city of the brassies, Brassilia. Shining brass was everywhere. Ahead were straight long golden streets, perfectly squared off, with cubic buildings along them. There were no windows or doors, just blank brass surfaces.

There was a brass button on a pedestal. "Leave that alone," Clio warned, but Sherlock didn't hear her. He pushed the button.

A klaxon alarm sounded. Suddenly the city was in motion. The buildings slid on tracks from one block to another, rapidly.

A gleaming brass wall was sliding toward him. Sherlock looked behind him, but saw only another wall, too high and slick to scale. He ducked down into a cubic hole in the ground and let the wall slide over him. It was the outside of a brass structure. Soon it set down brass pegs and anchored itself.

Sherlock climbed back out of the hole. He was in a huge hollow building. It was filled with pedestals on which stood brass statues of men, women, and children. That was all, except for another brass button nearby. "Don't touch it," Clio said, but he did.

The statues came to life. They were the brassies, in stasis until summoned to action. They spied Sherlock and closed in around him. "Who are you?" a brassy man demanded, brandishing a brass club. "What are you doing here?"

"Well, nothing," Sherlock said. "I was just looking."

"Looking for what?" a brassie woman asked. The females had the feminine spelling. "Company? I can be very soft when I want to be." Indeed she looked soft in all the right places.

"Sorry, my interest is elsewhere." Sherlock made as if to leave, but they grabbed him with brass tongs.

Clio put her hand between the man's eye and the gourd peephole, breaking the connection. Sherlock blinked, recovering his orientation. "That was an experience," he said.

"Brassies aren't necessarily friendly," Clio said. "But I think this gourd, also, is in proper working order."

They went on to the next gourd. Clio took this one, staring into its peephole.

She was in a world of paper. A flat yellow paper circle pinned to a paper blue wall was the sun, and clouds fashioned of white crepe paper floated beneath it. Across the cardboard landscape were houses of cards. Even the ponds were paper.

That wasn't all. The animals were paper too, origami constructs moving among the pasteboard plant life. Folded paper bugs crawled through the green paper streamers of grass. Paper birds flew down, scratching for pleated worms.

Despite her prior knowledge of this region, Clio was fascinated. She walked around, studying it.

But a cardboard man spied her. "Intruder!" he cried, his voice like a rattling paper horn. "Destroy her!"

Oops. She turned to go, but a paper tiger sprang out of the brush to cut her off. She turned again, and was peppered by paper balls fired from paper tanks.

Then she was looking at a brown hand. Sherlock had blocked off the peephole. "No sense in letting you get attacked," he said. "You have already verified it."

"This gourd, too, is functional," she agreed.

They continued to the next gourd. Before Sherlock could address it, a fierce harpy squeezed out of it. She collided with his face, except that her body passed right through his head. "Watch where you're going, blackhead!" she screeched. She whirled in the air and dive-bombed him from the other side.

Sherlock flipped a chip at her. The harpy became a gentle lovebird. "Oh, what a dear man!" she said in a dulcet tone, and kissed him on the forehead. Her lips passed through him, but did no harm.

"This must be the gourd," Clio said as the lovebird flew away. She got down to inspect it more closely. Sure enough, it was rotten at the core. "What's the most effective way to fix it?"

"Reverse wood?" Sherlock asked.

"Just destroy it," Mare Imbri's dreamlet image said. "Animals eat gourds all the time, and they never function well after that."

Sherlock lifted his foot and stomped down on the gourd with his shoe. It squished flat, squirting goo to the sides. A splotch of orange goo flew out and landed on Clio's wrist next to the compass. She was about to wipe it off when she saw that the blue arrow was pointing right toward it.

Could it be? She fetched another bag from her pocket and scooped the goo into it. She moved the bag around—and the blue arrow followed it.

She had found what she had come for, weird as it might be. A pulped fragment of a defective hypnogourd.

12
COUNTER XANTH

Where to now?" Sherlock inquired as they came to a crossing of trails.

Clio looked at the compass. "East."

They took the eastward trail. Soon they saw a giant snake going the other direction. Sherlock readied a chip, but Clio cautioned him. "This is an enchanted path; anything on it should be friendly."

Indeed, when the snake saw them, it shifted, developing a head. "A greeting, travelers. I am Ana Conda Naga, touring Xanth for fun and romance."

"Hello, Ana," Clio said. "I am Clio, and my friend is Sherlock. We're following an assigned direction."

Ana eyed Sherlock. "Are you a couple?"

"Just friends," Sherlock said.

Ana shifted to full human form. She had no clothing, being unable to wear it with her other forms. Some shape shifters had clothing included; some didn't. She had exactly the kind of curves Clio had lost. "Would you be interested in a passing dalliance?"

He laughed. "What would a healthy young creature like you want with an aging black man?"

"Variety. Older folk have more character, and they expect less."

"I'm flattered. But I think my heart is committed elsewhere."

"She must be quite something."

"She is."

Ana shifted back to naga form. "Then I'll be on my way." She returned to full serpent form and slithered rapidly onward.

Clio felt a pang. She had understood Sherlock was emotionally uncommitted. But maybe he had just said that to avoid embarrassment with the naga wench. Still, Ana Conda had been right on target about character and expectations.

They went on. They passed an open area where piles of fluffy stuff were scattered. Sherlock checked it. "Wool, just lying around. Someone must have lost it."

"No, I've seen this before. Someone was daydreaming, and this collected."

"Daydreaming?"

"Woolgathering."

"Oh. My thinking seems woolly today." He was a good sport about missing the pun.

They passed the wool and came to a pleasant region with a cave opening by a river. "Why this is Com Passion's cave," Clio said. "I recognize it. I must have business with her."

"Maybe she has what you seek."

"A currant? Then why wasn't I led to her directly?"

"You seek a current? In a river? I thought we had had more than enough of that."

"Currant with an A. It's a red berry. The Good Magician told me to find it. I have no idea why it should help me."

He nodded. "Ah, now I remember; you told me when the Demoness Metria was distracting me, and it slipped my mind."

Clio smiled. "The demoness has that effect, deliberately."

"I know it, yet can't prevent it. My intellect knows better, but not my eyes."

"That comes with the state of being male." But she was heartened; it meant he might be freaked out by certain sights, but was not completely governed by them. "Just as my intellect can't seem to explain the reason for the currant."

"It certainly isn't obvious to me. But if that's what you need, that's what you need, and I'll help you find it if I can. Let's talk to Com Passion."

"You are remarkably patient." She didn't add that he surely wanted to return to the woman he was committed to. She was almost sure he had said he had no prospects, but maybe he loved a woman who didn't love him.

Confound it! She had to know. So she didn't go into the cave. "Sherlock—it may not be my business, but my feminine curiosity is tormenting me. You told the naga lady that your heart was committed elsewhere. But I had understood that—"

He held up a hand, smiling. "You must have told the dragons to stay out of my mind."

"I did. It seemed inappropriate to spy on your private thoughts."

"I appreciate that. Complications remain, but the one I meant was you."

"Oh!" Surprise and relief prevented her from saying more at the moment.

"We could have told you," Drew said, "if you had let us. He really likes you."

"I regret embarrassing you," Sherlock said. "Maybe I shouldn't have said it."

"But my lost curves—how—?"

"As the naga said, older folk have more character. I like yours. You are the nicest and most mature woman I have encountered. Curves are for the eyes; character is for the heart. But since I have no right to presume, I assure you that I will not act in any untoward manner. One advantage of age is that we have better emotional discipline."

That was true, yet she was thrilled. "Next time you get the urge to presume, please do so."

He shook his head. "You are kind."

"I am serious."

He paused, then seemed to make a decision. "Now is not the time. But when the occasion seems appropriate, then you may repeat what you said, and maybe we can come to a better understanding."

"I agree." At that time he would surely set her straight about the distinction between intellectual admiration and physical attraction. "Now we must brace the friendly machine." Without giving herself any more time to consider, she marched into the cave. Sherlock followed.

A screen lighted with pink script. *Greetings, travelers.*

"And hello to you, Com Passion," Clio said. "I think you know me. My companion is Sherlock of the Black Wave. We also have two small telepathic dragons from the moons of Ida, Drew and Drusie."

Dragons! What a delight. Terian, come see.

A lovely young woman appeared. "This is Mouse Terian, Com Passion's mouse," Clio murmured to Sherlock.

"Glad to meet you," Sherlock said politely.

Terian stepped into him and kissed him on the cheek. That effectively silenced him. Then she looked at the little dragon in his pocket. "Hello, Drusie."

"You're a mouse!" Drusie exclaimed. "It's in your mind."

"Yes, I really am a mouse. But I assume human form when meeting humans. I regret I don't have a dragon form."

That can be arranged, the screen scripted. Com Passion, like her friend Com Pewter, had the power to change reality within her cave.

"No need," Drusie said. "We can project as mouse forms if we need to." She glanced across at Drew. "But we don't need to." She projected an impression of jealousy for Terian's beauty. It was humor, as neither dragon nor mouse cared much for the nuances of human appearance.

And what brings you here, Muse of History?

"A compass lent me by the Good Magician. It pointed me here without explaining why."

I don't know why either. But perhaps it was to do me a favor.

"Perhaps," Clio agreed warily. The sapient machines could be extremely demanding.

Panion, appear.

A miniature version of Passion appeared, looking shy.

This is my daughter-system, Passion explained. *She is getting complicated enough to set up her own site, but Com Pewter and I haven't found a suitable one in Xanth. Since you are going to Counter Xanth, that may be a better place. Take Panion along.*

"Counter Xanth!" Clio repeated, surprised. "How do you know that?"

It's on the Outernet.

"I'm really not sure—"

Muse agrees.

"I'm sure it's all right," Clio agreed. She knew her reality had been summarily changed, but it did seem all right. The compass had led her here, after all.

She picked up the tiny machine and put her in her other pocket, along with the bagged piece of gourd and the durian fruit.

Muse gets immediately on her way.

And thus they were on their way to Counter Xanth. Com Passion had been somewhat overbearing, but it seemed that this was what the blue arrow intended, for now it pointed a new direction.

"What is Counter Xanth?" Sherlock asked.

"That's complicated to explain. It's an alternate magic land that is now being settled. Things are reversed there."

"Ah—like reverse wood. That interests me."

"Not like reverse wood. You'll have to see it to understand, I think."

"I'll be glad to."

A bell sounded, startling them both. Then Clio realized it was from her pocket. She brought out the little machine. "Was that you, Panion?"

YES, the screen printed in neat little slanted capitals. *WHAT IS REVERSE WOOD?*

"You don't know that? Didn't Passion share her database with you?"

SHE SAID I SHOULD LEARN THINGS ON MY OWN, SO AS NOT TO BE A PERFECT COPY OF HER.

That seemed sensible. So Clio explained reverse wood for the little machine's little database. And realized that this was a child machine, subject to the Adult Conspiracy. That meant she would not be able to discuss serious things with Sherlock while Panion was with them. She sighed inwardly.

They met a girl walking the opposite way. "Don't get close to me," the girl said.

Clio was taken aback. "My dear, we are not going to do you any mischief."

"It's not that. It's because my name as Ann Gina, after my curse. If I touch anyone I make throats sore, and if I get really close, I make hearts hurt. So stay away from me."

"We'll be glad to. Thank you for warning us. But don't you get lonely?"

Ann burst into tears. "Yes!"

"Maybe I can help," Sherlock said. "Take this." He proffered a chip of reverse wood. "It should enable you to make throats feel better, and hearts too."

"Really? I don't understand."

"It's reverse wood. I can't guarantee it will do that, but it seems worth the experiment. Touch me."

A bell sounded. Clio brought Panion out. *WHAT'S GOING ON?*

"You don't need to print all the time, dear."

What's going on?

"Sherlock is using reverse wood to cure Ann Gina."

Tentatively, Ann touched Sherlock. "I feel fine," he said. "I suspect if I had a sore throat, it would be better now. In fact I think my middle-aged heart is beating more strongly."

"Oh!" Ann exclaimed. "Thank you so much!" She kissed him on the cheek and went running on down the path. "I must tell my sister, Anna Sthesia!"

"Let me guess," Sherlock said. "She makes folk numb."

"You are getting popular with the girls," Clio remarked teasingly.

"I admit it's fun. Too bad I'm not a generation younger."

"I think your age is fine."

He glanced sidelong at her. "Are you bringing up the matter of presumption?"

A bell rang. Clio brought Panion out again.

What does presumption mean?

Clio defined the word as well as she could, then added to Sherlock: "No. Not while we have underage company."

What aren't you saying? Panion demanded.

"Nothing, dear," Clio said with a smile. But then she had to explain the Adult Conspiracy.

That's horrible, Panion scripted.

"But it is nevertheless the way of it in Xanth, and in much of Mundania too," Clio said. "You must age to maturity before you are allowed to know certain things."

I hate that.

"Children do. Then they grow up and join the Conspiracy themselves."

I'll never do that.

Clio just smiled. She had encountered that before. Children inevitably aged, despite their best intentions, and joined the enemy.

"Drusie and I can't get into Panion's mind either," Drew remarked. "It's frustrating."

"Well, she's a machine."

"Even machines are bound by the Adult Conspiracy?"

"So it seems. Perhaps they are humoring us, as the demons and centaurs do. Passion surely would have told her about this aspect of Xanthly culture, had she wanted her to know."

The day was warm, and they were walking swiftly so as to get somewhere by nightfall. They came to a small river with several stepping stones. "I'm tempted to take a dip, just to cool off," Sherlock said.

"So am I. We have dipped before, in less positive circumstances."

But before they could do anything about it, a head appeared in the water. "Hello, humans!"

"We didn't realize anyone was swimming here," Sherlock said, removing his hand from a button.

"Well, it's not as if I could do anything else." A tail flipped out of the water behind the head.

"A mermaid!"

"Yeta Mermaid," she agreed, drawing her foresection out of the water to show exactly those curves Clio lacked. She had dark short hair, but the rest of her was plainly female.

"I am Sherlock, and this is Clio. We also have two small dragons and a baby computer along."

"Dragons! I don't want to mess with them."

"Small, I said." Sherlock took Drusie from his pocket and presented her to the mermaid. "Meet Drusie Dragon."

Yeta laughed. "Oh, you meant *tiny!* And pink. How cute."

Drusie jetted some steam in her direction, not far enough to burn her. "We are telepathic."

"Oh, I'm going to kiss you!" The mermaid moved forward with a stroke of her tail and kissed Drusie on the snout. "Sorry about that; I'm just so impulsive and dramatic, and I love anything weird or crazy. Not that you are, of course."

"Of course," Drusie agreed. It was clear that the mermaid liked the little dragon precisely because she seemed weird or crazy.

"Still want to dip?" Clio asked Sherlock teasingly.

"With a dramatic mermaid? I know better."

"Well, some say a mermaid has all the good parts of a woman and none of the bad parts."

"I want the bad parts too."

"I heard that!" Yeta called, laughing. "Come on in, you and the dragons. The river's big enough."

"She looks young," Sherlock said.

She did, but Clio really wanted to cool off. So she did something that in some quarters might be considered unethical. "How old are you, Yeta?"

"Fifty-four!"

Clio turned to Sherlock. "See? She's old enough."

"How many decades did she add to her real age?" Sherlock asked Drusie. "Four?"

"Don't answer that!" Clio said. "We won't question anyone's word."

Yeta laughed again, as she did so readily. "I love acting on the spur of the moment. Don't you?"

"Yes," Clio said. She set Panion upright on the bank so she could see what went on, took off her clothes, and jumped into the water. It was delightfully cold. In a moment Sherlock joined her, compromising only by leaving his undershorts on. The dragons dived in too. They had a fine splashing contest and got thoroughly cool.

But soon they had to move on. "Bye!" Yeta called as they resumed their walk. "It's been fun!"

And, indeed, it had been fun. "I'm glad we did that," Clio said. "I haven't done anything like it in ages. I mean, not for fun. Ghastly poop washing doesn't count."

"Neither have I," Sherlock said, laughing. "Though I do have wet undershorts."

Clio tried to think of a smart remark, but couldn't. The mermaid surely was underage, and a completely naked man was banned by the Conspiracy.

The bell sounded. *Why was it fun?*

By the time they explained that, they were well along the way, and it was time to camp. They foraged for wood and food, made a fire, and settled down to enjoy the evening repast.

"What's that?" Clio asked as she saw something amidst the pies and fruit.

"Why that's bread. There's a breadfruit tree nearby."

"That's pun-kin bread! With pun-kin seeds on top."

"So?"

"So anyone who eats that will emit egregious puns all evening."

The bell sounded. *What's a pun?*

"Oh, my, has your education been neglected!" Clio exclaimed.

Sherlock took a bite of the bread. "Did I ever tell you about my two aunts? Auntie Biotic always made me feel well when I was ill, and Auntie Septic made me very clean."

"You ate the pun-kin bread," Clio said. "Now you're emitting puns."

He laughed. "Actually I nullified it with a chip." He showed the chip of reverse wood. "I feel quite serious."

"You were teasing me."

"Or Panion. Puns are best appreciated in action."

She leaned across and kissed him on the cheek. Then she realized what she had done. "Oh, my! I'm getting impulsive."

"Like the mermaid. It's contagious."

"It must be." Then she got to work explaining the nature of puns to Panion, who had trouble getting it.

As she settled down to sleep, with Panion set in a makeshift crib, the dragons searching out bugs to toast, and Sherlock at a decorous distance, Clio realized that she had enjoyed herself more this day than in any prior time she could remember. For the first time in decades she felt truly alive, though all this living in real time was inevitably bringing her closer to that dreaded fate of youthful death. Maybe it was that she truly wanted to experience the passions of life before she lost her life, so was being very free. Or maybe she just liked the company.

In the morning they resumed travel, refreshed. Soon they reached the Gap Chasm. "This would seem to be a challenge," Sherlock remarked.

"We'll cross the invisible bridge."

"Of course."

She knew where it was, having written about it many times. Still, it was awesome stepping out over the immense abyss that was the Gap with no seeming support. She suffered the ridiculous notion that someone might be down there, peering up under her skirt. She knew it was ridiculous, because what man would have an interest in doing that, now that her curves were gone? Still, she felt exposed, and was relieved when a small cloud passed beneath them, obscuring the ground below.

They reached the far side. "Now we bear right, down the cliff."

"But there's no path!"

"There's an invisible path, or rather, one covered over by illusion." She demonstrated, feeling carefully with her feet. Soon she was walking knee-deep in apparent rock.

"We see it too!" Drew exclaimed. "That's nice illusion."

I can change it, Panion scripted. And the illusion vanished, showing the ledge-path as it really was.

So the baby machine did have the same ability the adult machines had. But this was not the place. "Put it back," Clio said firmly. "This is supposed to be concealed."

Awww. But the illusion reappeared.

"Why hide a path into the chasm?" Sherlock asked.

"Because it's really a path elsewhere, and we don't want just anybody using it. You'll see."

They moved on down into deeper illusion, until it closed over their heads like a canopy. They came to the face of a building set into the stone cliff. Clio raised a knuckle and knocked on the door.

It opened. A rather homely young woman stood there. "Who—" Her eyes widened. "Can it be?"

"Clio, the Muse of History," Clio agreed. "With Sherlock of the Black Wave. I believe we have business with you, Cube."

"Then come in. You couldn't have found us by accident."

"It does seem unlikely."

There were three others in the stone building. Cube introduced them: "Ryver, my fiancé. Cory, and Tessa." Then, to her companions: "This is the Muse of History, and Sherlock."

"Welcome," Ryver said. He was an uncommonly handsome young man. It would have been hard to imagine what he saw in Cube, had Clio not known their story.

"I am actually traveling with three others," Clio said, "two small dragons and a baby machine: Drew, Drusie, and Panion, the daughter of Pewter and Passion." She showed Panion, whose screen turned pink. "She can change reality in her vicinity, but I have asked her not to do that here. The dragons are telepathic, so will seem to speak to you by touching your minds."

"Hello, folk," Drew said, poking his snout out of Clio's pocket.

"Oh, how cute!" Cube said. "May I hold you?"

What was it about girls and dragons?

Drew consented to be held in the girl's hands. "You summon nickelpedes?"

"Yes. Here's one." A nickelpede appeared before him. "But you know, we have a dragon of our own here, a big one. Well, not exactly here at the moment, but Drek Dragon is part of our operation." She glanced at Clio. "You are going on to Counter Xanth?"

"It seems we are," Clio agreed.

"Then Cory and Tessa will take you there. You know about sidestepping?"

"I do." That was a special interdimensional mode of passage that only the two women could manage. Cory was a tall woman, taller than any of the rest of them, while Tessa was shorter than the others. How they had come to be close friends was another story, safely sealed in another volume of history.

"So nice to meet you, Drew, you handsome blue-eyed rascal," Cube said, giving him back to Clio. "Be sure to meet Drek; he doesn't see many other dragons. There's been a mysterious shortage."

"Not anymore," Clio said. "Xanth is being restocked."

The two women took their hands and brought them into the stone. Sherlock stared.

"It is sidestepping," Tessa explained. "We step sidewise into a parallel realm, which forms a kind of shortcut to where we are going. It is safe, but do stay in the aisle."

They formed a small procession, with Cory leading and Tessa at the end. There wasn't anything to see; it was just rock all around, though it didn't get in their way.

Then they came to an open region that was somehow different. Clio was silent, letting Sherlock discover it for himself. "Where's the Gap Chasm?"

"This is it," Clio said, gesturing at the huge mountain range behind them. "Reversed."

He stared, appreciating it. "As tall as the Gap is deep! Now I understand what you meant about a different kind of reversal. I love it."

"That's just the beginning," Cory said. "Ah, here come Drek and Kay." Two centaurs were galloping toward them.

"That's not her name," Drew said to Clio.

"But that's the name we'll use for her."

"Drek is not a centaur," Drusie said. "He's a dragon."

"But he was able to save a reversal, in this case an exchange of forms," Clio said. "Sometimes Kay becomes a dragon."

"This realm feels like home," Sherlock said. "There's just something about it."

The centaur arrived. "Hello," Kay said. "It is nice to have settlers." She had large white wings, brown flanks and tail, and copious fair hair and face.

"These aren't regular settlers," Tessa said. "This is Clio, the Muse of History, and her companion Sherlock of the Black Wave. They have special business here."

"Will this be within established parameters?" Kay asked.

"That seems unlikely," Clio said.

"Then we had better come along," Tessa said. "Is it likely to be far?"

"I don't know, but fear it could be."

"Then you will need to ride. I can carry one." She turned to the other centaur. "Drek, you'll have to revert."

Drek nodded and started away.

"If you have to go somewhere to do it," Sherlock said, "maybe I can save you the trouble. Would reverse wood do it?"

Drek considered, then returned. Sherlock touched him with a chip, and suddenly the centaur became a sizable dragon. He had a large head with a long green snout, myriad teeth, big eyes, and small ears. Taken as a whole, he was not a handsome creature. But he was large enough to carry several people.

They discussed it, and decided to have Clio ride on Kay, while Sherlock, Drusie, Cory, and Tessa rode on Drek. Drew and Panion remained with Clio.

"You have a guide to what you seek?" Kay asked.

"I have a compass with a blue arrow that points my way." Clio looked at it. "That way."

"Through the Gap Range," the centaur agreed.

"Oh, I forgot! We can't just cross the invisible bridge again. How will we ever get over such towering mountains?"

Kay laughed. "We sidestep. Actually Cory and Tessa have made a number of permanent aisles for us to use; they found they can do that here. See, the invisible tunnel is marked."

Clio saw: a line had been drawn on the sheer face of the rising cliff, showing an entrance. It seemed to be straight stone there, but the cen-

taur blithely trotted into it without impact. They were in a tunnel illuminated every so often by blobs of glowing fungus.

"Oh, Karia, that's marvelous!" Clio said.

The centaur's hooves lost contact with the floor. She drifted in the
dark air. She wasn't flying; her wings remained furled. She was just
aimlessly floating.

"We seem to have a problem," Drew remarked.

"Oh, I forgot another thing," Clio said, chagrined. "I called her by
her real name, and she got carried away. That's her curse of a talent."
She slapped the centaur on the flank. "Kay! Snap to!"

The hooves dropped to the floor. "Oh, did I do it again? I'm sorry."

"My fault," Clio said. "I know your name, and I used it. I'll try not
to do that again."

"That's best," the centaur agreed. "Nobody knows my name here,
other than my friends, and they don't use it."

"I will think of you only as Kay."

The bell sounded. Clio brought Panion out. *I can fix it,* the little
screen said in illuminated script.

"But would the fix remain after you left her vicinity?"

No.

"Then I think it best to leave well enough alone."

They moved on through the mountain, the dragon following. "You
have a relationship with Drek?" Drew asked Kay.

"Yes. I know, I'm a centaur, he's a dragon, and not even a handsome
one. But in this land we are able to change forms, as you saw, if we
manage it carefully, so we can match when we want to. He was
eschewed by other dragons because his breath is not the traditional fire,
steam, or smoke; it smells of perfume when he's happy, and like a
sewer stench when he's upset. Dragons ridicule that. But he's a decent
person with a fine mind. What more can a filly ask of a male?"

"Nothing more," Clio said, appreciating what she herself saw in
Sherlock.

"I can see it," Drew agreed. "My love for Drusie is miscegenous,
and would not have been allowed on Dragon World."

"Miscegenation," Kay agreed. "We are annoyed by that term."

The bell sounded. *Term?*

"Miscegenation means marriage between races," Clio explained. "Some folk object to it. It's largely meaningless in Xanth, where a number of major species are crossbreeds, like the mermaids, harpies, and werewolves."

"And centaurs," Kay said. "Even there, there can be a problem. The centaurs of Centaur Isle object to winged centaurs as unwarranted crossbreeds with magic. They consider magic to be obscene in centaurs."

Term?

"Obscene," Clio said. "Morally offensive, indecent. A word often favored by narrow-minded folk."

Kay laughed again. "Which describes the residents of Centaur Isle."

"And Mundania," Clio said. "Do you know they don't believe in magic?"

"Which is surely why it's such a dreary dull place."

They emerged from the sidestep tunnel. Counter Xanth spread out to the south, with lakes where mountains were in Xanth proper, and hills where lakes were. It still managed to look much like Xanth, but with an eerie difference.

"Puns!" Clio exclaimed, remembering. "There are no puns here."

"Yes, that is a considerable relief," Kay agreed. "This is really a fine land, as long as we avoid the worst reversal zones, which I am doing. When your arrow points us into one, we'll have to sidestep to avoid the consequences. We're not as familiar with the southern region, but are extending our knowledge daily."

Clio looked back. Drek was emerging from the invisible tunnel. "Drusie tells me Sherlock was impressed," Drew said.

"It's an impressive land," Kay said. "Would you like to fly? I can orient more clearly on your destination from above. Drek can follow; I won't go out of his sight."

"Yes, let's fly," Clio said. "I haven't flown a centaur before."

Kay flicked Clio and herself with her tail to make them light, galloped, gaining speed, spread her great white wings, and took off. Clio was exhilarated; there was just something about sailing up from the ground, seeing the landscape pass beneath. Counter Xanth was even more impressive when seen from above.

"Now where do we go?"

Clio checked the compass. "That way," she said, pointing. "South."

"South it is." The centaur winged swiftly onward.

Clio glanced back and down, and saw the dragon moving with excellent speed, keeping up. Probably Kay could fly faster, but was taking care to remain in Drek's view. They were coordinating nicely.

"And there," Clio said in due course, pointing again. They were approaching a large conical depression.

"That's Mount Pin-a-Fore!"

"That's no mountain," Clio said. "And it sounds like a pun. How can that be?"

"It's merely my humor. That's where Mount Pinatuba would be in Xanth, so it's a funnel instead of a cone, and surely female instead of male, so I dub her Pin-a-Fore. I doubt she would find it amusing."

"A female volcano," Clio said. "Inverted. That does make sense. That does seem to be my destination."

"We must be cautious. She can be unpredictable and ill-tempered."

"Just like a female," Drew said. Their words were being relayed by the dragons, so that it seemed that they were in a single group, despite being in two groups.

They laughed.

The bell rang. *What was that?*

"Drew Dragon said something funny," Clio said. "That being unpredictable and ill-tempered is just like a female."

That's not funny.

"It is if you know it's not so."

I don't understand.

"That may simply be something you will have to learn from experience."

That sounds like the Adult Conspiracy.

"Perhaps it is, dear," Clio said, smiling somewhat wistfully. But apart from the humor, she wondered whether she was about to encounter her danger for the day. She hardly relished winding back a volcanic eruption.

I don't like the Adult Conspiracy. Mother runs a site called Mate-Rix for true-love matchups, and they are always alluding to things I'm not allowed to understand.

They landed on the steep slope of the funnel. The compass pointed down toward the center, where a pool of lava bubbled like a boiling pot of stew. As they gazed at it, a fountain of fire developed, lovely but dangerous. "I am not completely comfortable with this," Kay said. "Let's wait until the others catch up."

Soon enough they did. Sherlock and the two women dismounted and stood gazing at the base of the funnel. "A lady volcano," Sherlock said. "What would she want with us? I'm sure she'd much rather associate with Pinatuba."

"Which is of course impossible," Kay said. "Volcanoes can't travel, and if they could, what would they do with each other? Share magma?"

The fire fountain intensified. Pinafore was evidently listening, and not thrilled with their remarks.

Clio had a sudden idea. She glanced up to see if a bulb flashed over her head, but there was none. That sort of thing, too, was absent from this land. "We understand the heartache of having no one of the opposite gender to associate with. Pinafore must be lonely. But maybe we can do something about that."

The fire fountain smoothed out, becoming less threatening.

Sherlock nodded. "How so?"

"Pinafore would surely like to be in touch with Pinatuba, but can never meet him physically. However, she might have a rewarding correspondence with him. Perhaps we can arrange that."

"I suppose we could carry messages back and forth," Sherlock said without enthusiasm.

"I was thinking of the magic of electronics. Panion needs a situation; she could be the magic net interface with Xanth. She could receive and send messages on the Outernet that would travel much faster than walking people could handle them."

The bell rang. *Yes I could.*

"Let's see if Pinafore is interested." Clio faced the lava pool. "Would you be willing to keep this little machine safe, if she relayed messages between you and the handsome hot-coned Mount Pinatuba in Xanth?"

The lava pool became so calm it was almost reflective.

"I take that as a Yes," Clio said. "Let's set it up now." She looked around. "We need a good safe place for Panion to stay. Normally her kind resides in caves, but there doesn't seem to be—"

She broke off, for there was a lava tube cave. She set Panion just inside it. Immediately it developed curtains with cuddly figures on them, and several scattered toys on the floor. It looked like a child's playroom, by no coincidence.

"Now about the messages," Clio continued. "Can you understand what Pinafore says?"

Yes.

"And can she understand the messages you receive?"

An illusion appeared at the mouth of the little cave: a big screen facing the pool. *Hello, Pinafore. Show us a sparkle.*

A new fountain developed in the pool. This one made a shower of bright fire sparkles.

Kay nodded. "I think she's got it."

This was working better than Clio had hoped. "And can you transmit messages between here and Xanth?"

The illusion collapsed into a pile of glass and plastic rubble. *No.*

Oops. "Why not?"

I lack the conversion code.

"I don't understand."

"But we do," Cory said. "Counter Xanth is crafted from contraterrene matter, opposite to regular matter. Xanth and Counter Xanth can never actually touch each other; they would disappear in energy. Sidestepping enables us to travel between them, but messages between them would disappear similarly. They need a conversion code so they can make it safely across."

Clio's head felt overloaded, but she took it on faith that this made sense. "How can the conversion code be obtained?"

Daddy has it.

"Com Pewter has it," Clio repeated. "If we ask him for it, will he give it to us?"

No.

"Then what—?"

He'll send it to me. Then we'll have the connection.

It was beginning to make sense. "So if we travel back to Xanth, and ask him, he'll send it, and Pewter and Pinafore will be in electronic touch."

No.

Clio had patience. "There is another detail?"

You must explain to Mount Pinatuba, and set up a terminal there.

Ah. "And will Pewter have a terminal to use?"

My brother Com Pound is with him. He's sort of violent.

"Likes to hit things," Sherlock murmured with a straight face. "He should get along well with Pinatuba."

"Then that's what we'll do," Clio said, relieved that this had turned out nice instead of ugly. That was never a certainty when dealing with volcanoes.

She glanced at the compass. Sure enough, it pointed back the way they had come. They had completed another stage of her quest.

"We must give you a tour of Counter Xanth," Kay said. "You will want to experience some of the reversals." It did seem time to relax a bit.

13
UNDERSTANDING

K ay and Drek took them back to the northern side of
the Gap Range, where they had more of the landscape
zeroed in. Then they gave the tour. They had sidestep
paths throughout, and Cory and Tessa were on hand to get them out of
any reversals that were unkind. It was clear that these folk liked showing off their new land, and they were good at it.

"We have protected you from the first reversal most folk encounter,"
Tessa said. "Now you can experience it, briefly."

"All we've seen is the inversion of the terrain," Sherlock remarked.

"Speak your companion's name."

"Oilc." Then he looked startled.

"What's that, Kcolrehs?" Clio asked. And was startled herself.
"What did I say?"

"You said his name backward," Tessa said. "Try our names."

"Asset," Clio said. "Yroc."

"Eisurd," Drew said.

"Werd," Drusie said. Both dragons laughed.

"We're saying them backward," Sherlock said. "Without meaning
to. It just comes out that way."

"In this section," Cory agreed. "Other sections have other reversals.
Do you wish to experience them?"

"Oh, yes!" Sherlock said with surprising pleasure.

Clio remembered now: she had written about this not all that long ago. It was different, experiencing it. "Yes, as long as they are harmless or can be reverted to normal."

"That's why we are with you," Tessa said. "Yak and Kerd can handle them, but you could have problems. This way."

"Yak" and "Kerd" carried them to several other sections. Along the way they saw six-legged cows, four-winged birds, and twin-hulled fish, the natural creatures of this land. There were sparkling clouds of insects that didn't sting. Then the reversals: in one section Clio and Sherlock, normally thin, became fat, and not with nice curves. They reverted to normal the moment Cory and Tessa guided them back into a sidestep aisle. In another they both became dull to the point of utter stupidity, the opposite of their usual natures. Then something odd happened.

"I'm a—I've got a—" Clio said, appalled.

"And I have two—" Sherlock said. Indeed, he had become a middle-aged woman with a prominent bosom.

"You reversed genders," Cory said, ushering them back into the aisle.

"That was awful!" Clio said.

"Yet for those dissatisfied with their genders, this would be ideal," Tessa said. "It's painless and permanent, if they don't enter an aisle."

In another section, Sherlock turned white and Clio verified with a mirror that she had become a member of the Black Wave. Their clothing changed color too.

In another, Sherlock became a thin young man, while Cory and Tessa became thick old women. Young and old ages had reversed. Clio didn't change. She realized that perhaps she had become as young as she looked; since she was essentially ageless, it didn't show.

In yet another, Cory and Tessa exchanged heights. Clio and Sherlock hardly changed; they were average and remained so. Thus being in the center range was a safeguard.

Then Sherlock turned supremely handsome without changing his age or color. And Clio had genuine curves.

"You may stay the night here, if you wish," Cory said. "It is getting late."

"Kay and Drek are already bringing food for supper," Tessa said. "And a tent with bedding."

Clio started to protest, but couldn't get the words out. To spend the night in this condition—it was wickedly tempting. Where else was it even possible?

"Why not?" Sherlock asked rhetorically.

They had a nice meal of wholesome fruits and juices, with no boot rear or other puns. No pies either; they did not grow on trees. It was odd but satisfying.

Drew and Drusie elected to go with Drek to see dragon things, knowing they were unlikely to have another chance. Both of them found this land fascinating.

"It is safe here," Kay said. "We'll pick you up in the morning." She and the others departed.

Thus suddenly, Clio and Sherlock were alone. "You know this isn't coincidence," Clio said.

"They set it up," he agreed. "They regard us as a couple, and they assumed we would want to take full advantage of this setting."

"Why did you agree to this?"

"Because I relate singularly well to this land, and want to experience more of it. Also, we have a serious matter to discuss, and this gives us privacy we can't otherwise have."

He certainly had a point. "I thought you might find a pretext to depart, once you saw me curveless."

"Let's prepare for bed, and talk before we sleep."

Was he avoiding the issue? They took turns washing in the nearby stream and changing to the night clothing their hosts had thoughtfully provided. It was totally dark as they settled down within the tent, lying beside each other.

"Did you peek as I washed?" she asked.

"I did," he admitted. "I couldn't help myself. You are absolutely lovely."

"So did I. You are such a handsome man, at the moment."

"It is true that I admired your curves from the outset," Sherlock said. "I am after all a man; this is what men do. But that was never the main barrier between us."

"My supposed curves were a barrier?"

"Yes, because what would such a beautiful woman want with an old and thoroughly ordinary man? My foolish days are behind me; I learned realism about women the unkind way."

"And never married."

"I can't blame them. I never had much to recommend me."

"You were a good and decent man!"

"What is your point?"

This set her back. Obviously the woman of the Black Wave had been more interested in handsome, powerful, or otherwise impressive men. Sherlock had been unimpressive. She had seen it before; young women could be foolish.

"But I am not young, regardless of my appearance, with or without curves," she said. "I do value decency. And you have other admirable qualities I have come to know. I would like to have a closer relationship with you."

"Perhaps."

Now she was nettled. "Is it some failing in me? I confess I have no direct personal experience with men. If I have made blunders, perhaps that is to be expected. If I have offended you, I deeply regret it. I hope you will tell me where I went wrong."

He reached out and took her hand in the darkness. "You have not gone wrong, Clio. I think I love you."

She had hoped for candor, and for a positive outcome, but this was more than anticipated. "You—think?"

"I have learned caution in all things. Things and people are not necessarily what they appear to be, or may have hidden aspects. I myself am a constantly changing mystery, and not merely because of my surprising affinity for reverse wood. I know better than to speak with any certainty of my own emotion. But it seems to answer the description of love."

She kept a tight rein on her own emotion. "Isn't love impulsive and heedless of consequences?"

"Young love is," he agreed. "But I am not young. I have made many mistakes in my life, and on occasion learned things I would rather not have known. I would truly regret making a mistake in love."

He was making absolute sense. She hated it. "Can't you be romantic and impulsive this one night?"

His answer was oblique. "You are cursed to encounter danger every day of your life, while you are out in Xanth."

"Yes, of course. You have seen it."

"I have. What threat did you face today?"

She paused, reviewing the day. "None that I know of. That's odd."

"It means you have yet to face it."

"But we are assured of safety here," she said doubtfully.

"Physical safety."

"Yes. What other kind is there?"

"Emotional. I suspect the danger you face is passion. Perhaps it is that you wish to make a commitment that will destroy you."

She was horrified. "To you? Sherlock, I can't believe that you would ever seek to hurt me!"

"Never intentionally. That is why we are having this discussion."

"I don't understand."

"You are a princess and a Muse. You must marry a prince. How could you do so if you soiled yourself with me?"

Her horror doubled. "You're not a prince!"

"I am not a prince," he agreed. "And will never be."

For a moment that was rather longer than it should be, she was in chaos. Then she recovered. "Not so. When ordinary girls marry princes, they become princesses. It happened to Electra and to Jenny Elf. It works the other way, too; Princess Melody will marry Anomie in the future and make him a prince. If I marry you, you'll be a prince."

Now he paused. "I had not thought of it that way. Still, you are the Muse of History, while I am nobody. I am not worthy of you."

"I don't care about that!"

"But I do, and consideration of your curse seems to confirm it. You dare not waste yourself on me. That is the threat you face today, and I must protect you from it."

"But you say you love me!"

"Yes. I am doing my utmost not to hurt you."

"I can't accept this."

"Then I will clarify the matter. I know that before I can be anything other than a passing companion to you, I must prove myself worthy of you. I doubt I will ever be able to do that, but I don't know the future. Should I commit to you without that worthiness, you would inevitably tire of me and regret your mistake."

"That is more brutally clear than I like."

"But sensible. I would like nothing better than union with you. But I must bring more than decency or even love to it. Otherwise I would be tying you down."

"I can't stand this!"

"You are being emotional. You are cursed to die young, unless you remain continually on Mount Parnassus. You want to experience life and love while you have the chance, knowing that your window of opportunity is brief. You have fixed on me as a prospect, but I believe you are being overwhelmed by the desire for romance rather than by sensible consideration."

"That's not so!"

"Then say you love me."

Clio opened her mouth—and burst into tears. She couldn't say it. He had fathomed her feeling and found its weakness. Her passion was driven by something other than true love.

"Oh, Sherlock," she said at last. "I'm so sorry."

She felt his wan smile in the darkness. "So am I."

So they slept, holding hands but doing no more. They had achieved understanding, but it was awful. His present handsomeness and her beauty were wasted on each other.

In the morning they woke, cleaned, dressed, and this time openly admired each other. It was all they could do, each knowing the other wished for so much more. Clio had never been flirtatious, but now she tried, and Sherlock responded. They were like lovers who hadn't quite caught on. Unfortunately they *had* caught on, and the understanding was brutal. The fault was in her, for the words she couldn't quite say. *Damn* his honesty, and hers.

In due course the others arrived. *Tell nothing,* Clio thought silently to Drew. She knew Sherlock was warning Drusie similarly. The truth could not be concealed from the little dragons, but it did not have to be shared with anyone else.

Cory and Tessa opened a sidestepping aisle, and Karia and Drek carried them along it, back to the central mountain range and the tunnel to Xanth proper. Clio thanked the centaur and dragon for their kindness.

Back at the Gap Chasm house, Cube took one look at them and winced. "Oh, I'm sorry."

We didn't tell, Drew thought.

Cube immediately carried on with other matters, saying no more. Cleo realized that it was simply woman's intuition. Women could have very sharp awareness of the feelings of others. Neither Clio nor Sherlock were romantically experienced; they probably emitted unconscious signals. They would have to watch that.

They thanked Cory and Tessa, and Cube and Ryver, and went back up to the invisible bridge. But they did not go over it; their next connection would be with Com Pewter, to set up the connection between realms. Pewter resided north of the Gap.

They followed the enchanted path generally north. "Walking seems slow, after the rides we had," Sherlock remarked.

"I agree," she said, laughing. It felt good to laugh; it eased the pain of her personal failure. "We have become spoiled."

"Let's be spoiled. Can we find rides? I'm willing to trade reverse wood chips, if anyone wants them."

"We can look for steeds," Drew said.

"Do that," Clio said.

The two little dragons flitted from their pockets and disappeared into the sky.

"Now that we are alone," Sherlock said, "May I presume?"

"I don't understand."

"Our relationship may not have a future, but it does have the present. I want to kiss you."

She was taken aback. "Oh. I thought—"

"You tend to think too much. So do I." He took her into his arms and kissed her.

She clung to him, kissing him back. Half a welter of impressions clustered around them, ranging from fond to naughty, before they broke for breath. "Oh, Sherlock," she gasped. "I've never been kissed before! I mean, not like that. I'm floating."

"I can't say I have been either," he said. "But it's very nice."

"Let's do it again."

"We really shouldn't, considering our lack of commitment. It isn't proper."

"Oh, fudge!" She hugged him and kissed him again.

After one or more timeless moments—she was unable to focus on counting—they broke again. "Oh, Clio," he said. "I wish we could do this forever."

"Despite my lack of curves?"

"And despite my lack of handsomeness."

"We don't seem to need those things," she said. "Yet last night, when we had them—"

"We wasted them. I've regretted it ever since."

It had been only a few hours, but she knew what he meant. "Me too. If we get another opportunity, let's not waste it. As you say, we do have the present."

"I agree." They kissed again, and though it was the third one in succession, the feeling didn't fade. If anything, it was stronger.

"We are adults," she said. "We can do anything we want, and we don't have to commit to anything beyond the present."

"That makes it feasible," he agreed.

"So why didn't we think of that last night?"

"I think I will never understand that."

"I think I do. We were looking at the future."

"And it blotted out the present," he agreed. "So we lost our recent past."

"Let's see if we can recover some of it."

They were about to go into another clinch, but the dragons returned. "We found a roc bird," Drew said as he came to Clio's pocket.

"A roc!" Clio exclaimed, putting herself straight. She had gotten pleasantly mussed, a condition the dragons surely noticed but refrained from remarking on.

"A small one," Drusie said. "He'll be here in an instant."

And in an instant, the sky darkened as a huge bird glided down. "This is Pebbl Roc," Drew said.

Pebbl landed on the path before them. He was big for a bird, but very small for a roc, standing about their own height. He squawked.

"He says he is pleased to meet the Muse of History, and wants to know how he can help," Drew translated.

Clio realized that a bird could fit a lot of dialog into a single squawk. "Well, I'm not sure. We were looking for rides to Com Pewter's cave." She didn't need to add that this miniature roc was too small to carry them anywhere.

Pebbl squawked again. "He says he'll scout the area," Drew said. "He can cover much more territory than we can, and he knows the local folk. He'll locate suitable steeds for you."

"Thank you," Clio said.

The little roc spread his wings and took off. There was a blast of air as he powered upward. Even a little roc was a lot of bird.

"So what did we miss?" Drew asked.

"You dragons need to learn to be more sneaky," Sherlock said with a smile. "Then you wouldn't have to ask."

"Oh, we did miss something!" Drusie said, disappointed.

"It was just some kissing," Clio said. "Like this." She embraced Sherlock and kissed him again.

"Oh, that's so romantic," Drusie said. "I wish we had seen it."

"Well, maybe there'll be another time," Sherlock said.

There was a galloping sound. "Ah—one is coming," Drew said. "A centaur."

"I like riding on centaurs," Clio said, remembering Kay.

The centaur hove into view, her hair swirling around her bare human top as she braked to a halt. "Hello. I'm Chele. A little roc bird told me I was needed here."

"It is true that we have a distance to travel, and could use some assistance," Clio said. "I am Clio, and this is Sherlock. We are going to Com Pewter's cave."

"I'll be glad to carry one of you to it, but I won't go inside. Pewter is notorious for changing things in there."

Clio nodded. "No need for you to do that. We shall merely speak with him briefly, then head for Mount Pinatuba, south of the Gap Chasm."

"Oh, that sounds exciting. But I don't know the way to the volcano."

"We do. We can direct you, if you care to make that much of a journey."

"I do. I understand Pinatuba is quite impressive."

"He is."

There was another sound of galloping hooves. "That's a unicorn," Drew said.

"A unicorn! We hardly ever see one of those in Xanth."

"Paucity of virgins," Sherlock murmured.

The unicorn came into sight. It was a filly with a bluish coat and blue horn. She eyed them warily before approaching.

"I am Clio, unfortunately virginal," Clio said.

"I am too," Sherlock said.

"I'm not, not that it matters," Chele said. Centaurs were quite open about natural functions. "I've had three foals."

"Fortunately you don't need a ride," Sherlock said.

The unicorn came near, avoiding Chele. "There's something different about her," Drew said.

Then the unicorn abruptly became a human girl. She had dirty blond hair to her waist and dark blue eyes the same color as the unicorn's horn. Clio's jaw dropped. "You're a crossbreed!"

"I am Danielle Girl/Unicorn," she agreed. "A little roc bird told me I was needed here."

"We would like rides to Com Pewter's cave," Clio said. "Then south to Pinatuba, the volcano."

"We don't have much to trade for such assistance," Sherlock said. "Just some chips of reverse wood."

Danielle jumped away so quickly that her blue panties showed. They matched her eyes. "I don't want to be reversed!"

"No need," Clio said. "He just meant that—" She paused, for Sherlock was standing motionless. Oh—the surprise glimpse of panties had freaked him out. She snapped her fingers to bring him to. "He just meant that if you have any likely need, such as if you travel into monster country, you could carry a chip in a bag and use it to reverse some obnoxious creature."

Danielle reconsidered. "Yes, I could use something like that. Sometimes men who aren't—well, they try to—such a chip could be handy."

They worked it out, putting reverse wood chips into two small bags so that they could not be touched by accident, and giving them to the filly and girl. Then Sherlock mounted Chele and Clio mounted the unicorn, and they galloped northward toward Com Pewter's cave.

Then Clio saw something running along the ground ahead of them. There were two of them, looking like leapfrogging bunnies, except that they had no legs or heads or tails. They were just open objects, hollow from above, moving rapidly. One would leap ahead, passing the other. But when it landed the other leaped and passed it back. It was weird.

"What are those?" Sherlock asked.

"Oh, they're just running shoes," Chele said. "There are several pairs in this area. They're harmless. They come out for exercise."

"A pun!" Clio said, laughing weakly. "We're back in Xanth!"

"How could you have been anywhere else?" Drew asked. "I am speaking for Danielle, who can't talk at the moment."

"We just visited Counter Xanth," Clio explained. "That's like Xanth, only everything is reversed, and there are no puns. We were there only a day and night, but somehow I got accustomed to the change."

"It sounds rather dull," Chele said.

"It really isn't. It's just different."

They came to a large chain across the path in the center it had one very active link that glowed and danced about as if trying to go somewhere else. "I don't recognize that," Chele said. "We'll have to move it out of the way."

"Don't touch it," Clio said, jumping to the ground. "It might be my Danger of the Day."

"But there shouldn't be any dangers on the enchanted path."

"I am cursed to encounter danger regardless," Clio said. "That curse might override the positive enchantment."

"Maybe I can nullify it with a chip," Sherlock said, also dismounting.

"First let me find out what it is," Clio said.

"Don't risk—" he said, alarmed.

But she was already touching the active link.

Suddenly she was in Mundania; she recognized it by the dull houses and listless vegetation. What had happened? Whatever it was had put her into danger, because she had little idea how to survive in this alien land. Worse, she had carried Drew Dragon into danger too; he was now a frightened lizard in her pocket.

She tried to wind it back, but there was no magic. She was stuck. She had thought she could provoke the danger, identify it, then unwind it and avoid or nullify it. She had truly fouled up.

Then she saw a familiar figure: a very old centaur. "Bsopmef!" she cried. And paused, amazed; it had come out all wrong. Then she remembered: she couldn't even speak intelligibly in Mundania.

But the centaur heard her and glanced her way. Then he walked across. "You must have touched the hyperlink," he said. "It instantly transports folk to another location."

"Arnolde!" she repeated, and this time it came out right, because she was in his aisle of magic. She felt Drew recover his dragon identity. "I'm so glad to see you!"

"I shouldn't have left the chain there," he said apologetically. "I expected to be right back, and to move it before anyone blundered into it, but my errand proved to be more complicated than I expected."

So it was not intended to be a danger, except that her curse had made it so. At least now she could unwind it, because of his magic ambience. Or could she? She might unwind only to her passage through Mundania, and stall out in that dearth of magic. She was still in trouble.

She would have to figure out another way. "I am Clio, the Muse of History. I did touch the hyperlink. I should have known better. But perhaps I can accompany you back to Xanth, when you return."

"I shall be happy to take you back, Muse," he said.

"What is your errand here, and how did it complicate?"

"Demon Earth came to me in a vision, and asked me to speak to David Baldwin on his behalf. It seems the Demon has an interest in a certain young Mundane woman—"

"Jaylin," Clio said, remembering. "She visited Xanth and helped with the Swell Foop. But she has a boyfriend."

"David Baldwin," he agreed. "It seems that the Demoness Fornax has a connection with Jaylin, and Demon Earth thought he might develop a similar connection with David. That way he could have a certain relationship by proxy, since Jaylin is not interested in any further association with a Demon."

"And David isn't interested either," she said, seeing the problem.

"Yes. As you know, my talent is to have an aisle of magic in Mundania. I had assumed it was some concentration of magic within me, but it seems it is facilitated by natural energy of the Demon Earth. His magic is gravity, and it seems I draw on that, translating its energy to magic. He promises to greatly enhance it, if I am successful in persuading David to cooperate. I am no longer young, and would like to have that enhancement."

Indeed, Arnolde was no longer young; he was 135 years old, prevented from fading out only by magic and some Fountain of Youth Elixir the Good Magician had provided. She appreciated his interest.

"Perhaps I can help," she said. "Rather, my friend Drew can help."

"Glad to," Drew said. "How?"

"Telepathically convey my identity and sincerity as I talk to David."

"Talking isn't sufficient," Arnolde said. "I just tried. David doesn't like the idea of a Demon snooping on his romantic life."

"That is understandable, but I fear he doesn't have a choice. Take us to him."

"This way," Arnolde said. He led the way to a nearby house. Mundanes were in the area, but they paid no attention. "I have a disinterest spell," the centaur explained. "Otherwise I would attract unwelcome attention."

"The Demon Earth is watching," Drew said to Clio.

She glanced around and spied a cloud forming. It did not look natural, and it certainly wasn't Fracto. "Tell him I'm helping Arnolde make his plea, but he must agree to my condition."

The cloud hovered, not necessarily agreeing.

Arnolde knocked on the door. David Baldwin answered. He was a handsome young man of twenty. "I'm sorry, Arnolde, but as I said before—" Then he saw Clio. "Hello."

"Hello, David. I am Clio, the Muse of History. This is Drew Dragon, who is telepathic. He will connect our minds so that you will know that you can trust what I say."

David looked surprised and dubious. Then he nodded as Drew connected. "I know it, Clio."

"When Jaylin went to Xanth, she interacted with demons, and there are some residual effects. The Demoness Fornax retains a certain association; you may have noticed."

"Yes, it sure changed Jaylin! But I like her this way."

"Demoness Fornax has no interest in Jaylin's long-term welfare, or yours. She merely seeks an avenue to increase her status at the expense of other demons. You dare not deal with her alone."

"Well, I'm not."

"When you are with Jaylin, you may also be with the Demoness. Working through Jaylin, she has resources to put you into heaven—"

"I have had some of that, with Jaylin."

"Or hell. At her whim."

David paused reflectively. "I hadn't thought of it that way. You're right; she could. What Jaylin has told me of the Demons scares me."

"You need a Demon with similar powers on your side, to neutralize the Demoness."

He nodded. "I do. As long as he doesn't foul me up."

"Demon Earth promises merely to observe, and to act only to neutralize the ploys of the demoness." She glanced at the sky. "Doesn't he?"

The cloud dissipated. "Yes," Drew said.

David nodded. "Okay, I agree."

"Thank you," Clio said. "We'll return to Xanth now."

"I feel stronger," Arnolde said. "The Demon is lending me more energy."

"Demons do keep their deals," Clio said.

Arnolde invoked the return hyperlink he carried, and suddenly they were back in Xanth. There were introductions, with Chele Centaur looking startled and shy, for Arnolde was a legend among centaurs. Then Arnolde removed the chain, and they resumed their journey. Clio had navigated another danger, and perhaps done some good in the process.

They moved well, thanks to their galloping steeds, and by midday reached Com Pewter's cave. There was an invisible giant there, about to herd them into the cave, but the little dragons flew up to get within telepathic range of his unseen head and informed him that they were there on important business. "Okay," he boomed, and tromped away.

They dismounted and entered the cave while Chele and Danielle, in human form, conversed amicably outside. The unicorn girl did not touch the centaur, but otherwise had no special problem with her. It seemed it was male nonvirgins that were her main problem.

A troll came to greet them. "Pewter is not available at the moment," he said. "Please go away."

"Why hello, Tristan," Clio said. "I am Clio, the Muse of History, here on business. Whatever is the matter?"

"Clio!" the troll said, recognizing her. "Maybe you can help. There's a terrible problem. Look."

They looked. There was snow and ice on the machine's screen, which said CRASH FAULT in frigid print against a cold blue background.

"Why Pewter's frozen!" Clio said, astonished. "What happened?"

"I don't know. The ice just suddenly appeared and he stopped communicating. I've been trying to help him recover, but he's completely nonresponsive."

"I have heard of this sort of thing," Sherlock said. "I think he got a virus or a bug. Tell us exactly what occurred, step by step."

"Well, he was on the Outernet, and he found a Data Base. The pictures showed folk in military uniforms running around, Facts and Figures. The Facts were in trousers, the Figures in dresses."

"Male and female," Sherlock said.

"He picked up something there. Then his screen started going crazy, letters started falling out of his printed words and piling up at the bottom of the screen, and I knew he was in trouble. I tried to go for his icons, because that's where he keeps his virus antidote, but whenever I reached for one, it danced away and I couldn't catch it. Then he froze up really cold, as you see."

Sherlock nodded. "He's got a bug all right. A clever one, that knew to elude his defenses. We have to get it out."

"Yes, but how?"

Sherlock looked around. "How do you clean up the cave?"

"You mean when Passion and Terian come? I sweep it out and wash off the surfaces."

"I was thinking more like a vacuum cleaner."

"Oh, yes, I use that too."

"Fetch it."

Tristan went into the back of the cave. "I hope whatever you have in mind is viable," Clio said.

"It should be. Drusie, have you located the bug?"

"Yes. It is hiding deep in the works."

"Keep tracking it."

Tristan returned with the vacuum cleaner. "I am not clear what good this will do in this instance."

"We'll need to lift Pewter up so Clio can vacuum beneath."

This was more curious by the minute. But she played along. Sherlock and the troll carefully heaved the machine up, and she turned on the vacuum and sucked the dust out from Pewter's bottom. There was a fair amount.

"Drusie?" Sherlock inquired.

"He's hanging on so as not to get sucked up," she said. "He's very smart, for a bug."

"Now reverse the vacuum," Sherlock told Clio. He and Tristan were still holding Pewter up in the air.

"But that will—" Then she grasped his strategy. She changed the switch, and suddenly instead of sucking it was blowing warm air out.

There was a flutter and something was blown out the other side. Drusie launched herself from Sherlock's pocket and snapped it out of the air. One crunch of her jaws, and it was gone. She had gotten the bug, which had been caught by surprise by the sudden reversal of air.

They set Pewter down. Then Clio played the jet of warm air across his screen until the snow and ice melted. Pewter was no longer frozen.

The print clarified. **THAT WAS AWFUL.**

"We got the bug out," Tristan said. "The Muse of History and her friend Sherlock are here to see you. They saved you from freezing."

The print organized itself, swept up the loose letters remaining at the bottom of the screen, and Pewter reverted to normal. **WHAT IS YOUR BUSINESS HERE, MUSE?**

It was perhaps too much to expect gratitude from the machine. "I need to establish contact with Counter Xanth. I understand you have the conversion code to send to your daughter Com Panion."

WHAT'S IN IT FOR ME?

"A compatible placement for your son Com Pound," she answered evenly.

That set the machine back. **WHERE?**

"With Mount Pinatuba, facilitating his communication with Mount Pinafore in Counter Xanth. It is surely a significant post."

Grudgingly, Pewter acknowledged that. **FETCH POUND.**

Tristan took the vacuum away and returned with another small machine. "Hello, Pound," Clio said.

An image of a hammer appeared on the little screen. It pounded at the baseline, denting it. HELLO.

GIVE POUND THE CODE. A disk was extruded from a slot beneath Pewter's screen.

Tristan took the disk and put it in a slot under Pound's screen. There was a brief whirring sound. Then he removed the disk. Pound had the conversion code.

"Thank you, Pewter," Clio said. She picked the little machine up; he was conveniently pocket-size, like his sister.

MUSE GOES IMMEDIATELY ON HER WAY.

Thus they left the cave and mounted their steeds. "I might have reversed the order, with a touch of wood," Sherlock said.

"There was no point; we needed to be on our way anyway."

They galloped south, toward the invisible bridge, but time had passed and night was closing before they reached it. "We must camp," Clio said. "If we are keeping you too long, Chele and Danielle, you will be free to depart."

"There is no problem," Chele said. "We'll camp too, and get you there tomorrow."

Clio had privately hoped the two would go elsewhere for the night, and return in the morning, so that she could be alone with Sherlock. But perhaps it was just as well this way. "Thank you."

They found a campsite, and camped. Soon they had a nice fire and a number of pies. Actually it was pleasant to be in company; Chele and Danielle in girl form had questions and comments, and were polite. Clio and Sherlock shared a tent; no one questioned that. The little dragons participated, and so did Pound, who was as curious as his sister about new vocabulary. But it was not the occasion to make up for lost chances.

Still, it was pleasant lying in the darkness, holding Sherlock's hand, as they had done the night before. There was a good deal more to a relationship than kissing or stork summoning—or, indeed, permanence.

In the morning Clio emerged to discover Danielle in girl form working in the adjacent lot with an odd garden tool. "What is that?" she asked.

"I found this grove of small pantrees," Danielle explained. "Their panties are very fresh, but they are likely to run if you don't harvest them carefully. So I'm using one of these panty hoes. Even so it's tricky."

"Panty bushes," Clio said. "I should harvest one myself." She took another one of the hoes, which were leaning against a fence. She hoed out a panty, which was modestly covered by foliage.

But just as she got it clear, a nasty boy jumped out of the brush. "Boo!" he yelled, startling her so that she dropped the panty.

Immediately the panty set down its feet and ran away. The boy chased after it.

"Oh, it ran," Danielle said. "That panty raider did that on purpose."

"Never mind; I'll hoe out another," Clio said.

But her hoe had fallen apart. It seemed that panty hoes were no good after a run. She had to get another.

Soon, armed with fresh new panties that hadn't run, they returned to the camp. Sherlock and Chele had pies heating. "Look what we got!" Danielle said, as they both lifted their skirts to flash their panties.

Chele smiled as Sherlock freaked out. "There's nothing like new panties to make a man pant."

Clio went up to Sherlock and kissed him. He recovered, blinking. "Did you do something naughty?"

"We harvested new panties. We couldn't waste them, could we?"

"I suppose not. But some time I may touch them with reverse wood and make you freak out instead."

"That should be fun."

After breakfast they resumed traveling. They crossed the invisible bridge, Danielle changing to girl form for the occasion, and a wind came up and whipped her skirt about. A bird flying below them glanced up, then went into a diving fall. Fortunately it recovered before losing too much altitude. Clio continued to be amazed by the power of a really fresh panty, but was sure the unicorn girl's youth and fullness had something to do with it. Clio's own panty wouldn't perform like that, she was sure.

At last they reached Mount Pinatuba. It sent a warning column of smoke up as they approached. How it did that when its cone was full of water Clio wasn't sure, but she decided to keep a safe distance clear.

"Pinatuba," she called. "I have something for you."

The smoke thinned. The volcano was listening.

"Contact with your inverted parallel on Counter Xanth," she continued. "Pinafore, the lady volcano. She would like to establish a correspondence. Provide Com Pound here with a safe cave, and he will relay your messages to her, and give you her responses. Are you interested?"

Of course he was. Soon Pound was ensconced in a nice volcanic cave and relaying messages.

As they were turning to go, something flew out of the cave and landed at Clio's feet. The blue arrow pointed right at it, so she picked it up. It was a bit of light volcanic rock, labeled TUFF STUFF.

It seemed that this was what she had come for: a fragment of tuff. She put it in another pocket.

14
CONSPIRACY

Well, my mission here seems to be done," Clio said. "I thank you, centaur and unicorn, for your assistance."

"It was fun," Danielle said. "And I made a new friend." She changed to unicorn form.

"We'll be running along now," Chele said. She was speaking literally; the centaur and the unicorn galloped off into the sunset.

"Where to now?" Sherlock inquired.

Clio looked at the compass. "North, and the arrow of time isn't in a hurry."

"One might think that the northern errands could be handled together, and the southern ones, so as to eliminate the need to travel."

"Only a sensible person would think that."

He smiled, and they started walking north. But soon the way became confused; the trail might be enchanted, but it wasn't clear. Brush had overgrown part of it, and there were several paths trying to find their way through it.

"We are in danger of wandering off the safe path, if we guess," Sherlock said.

Clio looked at the compass, but it simply pointed north, not deigning to notice the confusion immediately ahead.

"Big stupid man coming," Drew reported.

"From behind," Drusie added.

They turned to look back. An ogre came toward them, shaking the ground with his heavy tromping. Sherlock readied a chip.

"This is an enchanted path," Clio reminded him. "It should be a friendly ogre."

"I am nervous about ogres, since learning of the drubbing I received from one, that you wound back. But I'll bear with it."

"Thank you. I will wind it back again if necessary."

"We can't tell if it's friendly," Drew said. "Its mind is too dull."

"Ogres are justly proud of their stupidity," Sherlock said, repeating the stupidly well-known adage.

The ogre spied them and tromped to a halt. It was twice their height and solid in proportion. It peered somewhat blearily down at them, huge hamfists at its sides.

"Hello, Ogre," Clio said. "We are Clio and Sherlock."

"Which which?" he demanded, confused.

"I am Clio; he is Sherlock."

"Opaque Ogre me, no rhyme be."

Clio appreciated the problem. She knew of no words that rhymed with either "opaque" or "ogre." "We accept that. Considering that ogre dull rhymes are more perceived than real, shall we dispense with them and converse normally?"

The ogre peered around as if fearful of being overheard. "Do you think it is safe?"

"We promise not to tell."

"Very well then. Did you have reason for waiting for me, instead of hiding until I passed?"

"Stupid reason," she said with a smile. "We can't find the proper path."

"That I can clarify. My talent is to clarify or confuse things, depending on how they start."

"We have talents too, but they don't seem to apply here. Are you saying that you can see the correct path?"

"No. I'm saying that if I encounter cloudy water, I can make it clear water. If I see a clear way, it becomes confused. I passed this way this morning; I must have changed it inadvertently. I should be able to change it back now."

"That would be appreciated."

He faced forward and marched. The way cleared as bushes hastily got out of his way and paths wriggled to avoid getting tromped when out of position. Suddenly there was no trouble finding the correct route.

They followed Opaque north. Then he halted. "I believe we are through the confusion," he said. "The way ahead must be clear—so I will have a problem with it. Perhaps you should go ahead."

"And leave you to stumble through alone, after your courtesy clearing it for us?" Clio asked. "There must be an alternative."

"Reverse wood is risky," Sherlock murmured. "It might reverse his strength."

"Do you have far to go?" Clio asked the ogre.

"Not far. My sister Clarificant is home; she usually accompanies me to cancel my effect."

That explained how he normally got around. "Suppose you close your eyes and follow us? We could lead you there."

"That would be very kind of you."

So Opaque closed his eyes and followed them, able to hear their footsteps between his tromps. Soon they came to the ogre's den, where an ogress waited. "Oh, you're safe!" she exclaimed, sounding relieved.

"These nice humans assisted me," Opaque explained.

"We cooperated," Clio said.

"Come in," the ogress said. "I have a pot of meaty skulls boiling with fresh bones."

"Thank you, no," Clio said quickly. "We must be on our way."

They moved on. "Ogres are just like people," Sherlock remarked. "When you get to know them."

"They *are* people. Just not quite like us."

They came to a convenient shelter, and settled for the night. But before darkness quite closed, a gaggle of girls arrived. "Hi, old folk," one called. "We are Parsley, Sage, Rosemary, and Thyme. We'll be your cheerful company tonight."

"Welcome," Clio said somewhat grimly. It seemed they were fated not to be alone.

There was just one shelter, so they spent the night half buried in giggling girls. Sherlock did not seem nearly as annoyed as Clio would have liked. In the morning the girls had a tittering bare wash-up; Sherlock tried not to look, but they kept running around attracting his attention. Clio had to unfreak him more than once. The girls seemed innocent, but Clio wasn't sure that they had to be quite so open, boisterous, or active about their ablutions. There seemed to be a certain flirtation to it.

But when it came to making a pot of porridge for breakfast, the girls were helpful. It was surprising how tasty their assorted spices made what would otherwise have been rather dull. They would surely all make good housewives, in due course.

"So how was it, buried in spice girls?" she asked Sherlock once they were traveling again.

"They were fun, but I knew they would never have stayed the night in the same shelter if you hadn't been there."

"Me! You were the focus of their attentions."

"Precisely. They regarded me as safe only because you were there. It's a game, to see how much you can show with impunity."

Clio considered, and realized that he was probably correct. The girls could play because nothing could happen while an older woman was there. It was not a game Clio herself could play, without her curves. That bothered her more than she cared to admit.

"Monster ahead," Drew reported.

"Of what description?" Sherlock asked, a chip appearing in his hand.

"Similar to Tristan Troll."

"The trollway!" Clio exclaimed. "We are coming to it."

Sure enough, in a moment they came to a troll standing guard by a wide paved avenue. A sign said STOP. PAY TROLL.

"Why should we pay a troll anything?" Sherlock asked. "We're just passing through."

"You're not familiar with the trollway? You have a nice experience coming. It will take us rapidly as far north as the arrow leads."

So Sherlock dickered with the troll, and gave him a bag with a chip of reverse wood. Then they went to a bench beside the wide road and waited.

"The trollway traverses the full length of Xanth," she explained. "It is a much faster mode of travel."

"I am satisfied with slow travel, while with you."

She was touched. "Oh, Sherlock!" She leaned over and kissed him. She loved being with him, but she still couldn't say those key words "I love you." While it might be an exaggeration to say that broke her heart, it nevertheless dented it somewhat.

A vehicle appeared, rolling along the trollway from the south. It had metal wheels. A melody sounded as it came to a halt beside their bench. It was a tuneful trolley.

A door opened in its side. They entered, climbing steps to reach the passenger compartment. When they were in, the troll driver cranked a handle, the door closed, and the trolley got moving again.

There were four other people riding, two men and two women. Clio and Sherlock took seats near the front.

Clio began to feel odd. It was as if something were touching her body, yet nothing was. She thought she felt a hand on her ankle, then one on her shoulder. When it squeezed her right thigh she jumped up "Oh!"

"Stop it, Feelup!" one of the women snapped. And the invisible touches stopped.

"What's going on?" Clio asked, facing back.

The woman got up and came to her. "My brother's talent is to feel things remotely. He's not supposed to do it to people. Especially women. But he still tries to sneak it in." She glared at the man who had sat beside her. He stared down, not meeting her gaze.

"Groping is known in Mundania, too," Sherlock murmured tolerantly. Then he jumped. "Hey! I got goosed!" It seemed he felt less tolerant.

"Feelup!" the woman said severely. "I apologize for my brother's misbehavior. He just wears his feelings beyond his sleeves."

"That's all right," Clio said, though it wasn't. She didn't like getting remotely groped by strange men.

"My talent is related, only it touches inside rather than outside a person's body. I am Digit Alice, and I do healing massages."

"Interesting," Clio said, though she was hoping the woman would go away. She sat down again.

"I can heal a broken heart," Alice said proudly. "Let me show you." She came to stand behind Clio.

Clio was about to protest, but Alice put her hands against her back and began to massage it. The touch was surprisingly therapeutic; the good feeling went right through her muscles and bones and touched her heart. The dent in it eased, then disappeared; her heart felt whole again. "Oh, thank you," she said.

"It was the least I could do." Alice returned to her seat.

The trolley squealed to a halt. "Demon Construction," the driver said with resignation. "We'll have to wait."

"I wonder," Sherlock said. "Mind if I take a look around?"

The troll shrugged. "We aren't going anywhere."

Clio followed Sherlock out, wondering what he was up to. She saw signs of the demon's work all across the trollway, but no one was actually working. In fact no one was there.

"I've seen this sort of thing in Mundania," Sherlock said. "They rush out to block off the access to the most important highway they can get at, then do nothing for six months. It is calculated to inconvenience the greatest number of people with the least effort. This demon must have studied the technique. But maybe we can clear the way."

He walked to a line of orange cones that crossed the road. He took hold of one—and the others all jumped on him. He was buried in cones. Then they all reversed and flung themselves away from him. He got up, brushing himself off. "I walked into that one. I took them for pylons. Instead they're pile-ons. So I reversed them."

Beyond the cones was a sleeping bull lying in a pile of ashes. "Bulldozer," Sherlock said. "Scraping the ash-fault level. When he's working."

Then a dragon appeared. They backed nervously away, but this dragon was rolling end over end as it fired out steam. It rolled over the ashes, leaving them flat. "And a steamroller," Sherlock said.

It was clear beyond that. They returned to the trolley, and reported to the driver. "We can get through now."

The troll nodded, and started the vehicle moving again. Suddenly a person as wide as four men dashed up. "Hey, you can't do that!" But he was too late; they were already through the section and beyond.

"That was the four-man," the troll said, seeming privately satisfied. "He hates to let a trolley through before its time."

The trolley rolled on. They gazed out the windows, but the scenery soon became dull.

"I'm bored," the other man at the rear announced. "Let's pass the time by telling each other something about ourselves."

Clio was bored too, now that she wasn't getting groped. She discovered that the seats would turn in place, so she could face back to talk with the others. "I'm amenable. I am Clio, and my talent is the windback. I can wind back recent events, but I seldom do it because others don't realize it has happened."

"That's terrific," Alice said. "Does that mean that if the troll falls asleep and crashes us into a tree, you could unhappen it?"

"Yes. But I would prefer that he not do that."

Everyone laughed. A crack appeared in a window. The troll looked back, glowering. "You broke the ice. Stop that or I'll put you off the trolley."

So the windows were made of panes of ice. Clio wound it back until the crack disappeared, then stopped her statement at "Yes." That thawed the ice without breaking it, and the window merely sweated a little. No one except the dragons realized that it had happened. Actually they seemed to be asleep.

"I am Sherlock," Sherlock said. "My talent is working with reverse wood. That has a negative effect on the magic of other folk, so I don't invoke it often."

"Could you reverse my brother's talent?" Alice asked.

"I doubt it. Reverse wood doesn't necessarily reverse in the way one expects. I think it best not to gamble."

"I am Ken," the other man said. "I have the talent of telling the opposite of the future. Therefore I seldom try to use it, as my predictions never come true."

"Nevertheless, I am curious," Clio said. "What's my unfuture?"

Ken looked at her, his gaze uncomfortably penetrating. "I see the promise of great happiness, followed by disaster."

"But if that's the opposite, then I may be threatened with great sadness, followed by success."

"You may," Ken agreed. "But it's like reverse wood: my visions aren't always wrong in the way you expect. Don't trust it."

That was a fair warning, but she was relieved. It suggested that however difficult things might become, they would work out in the end.

"I am Crystal," the other woman said. "My talent is that of seeing ourselves as others see us."

"Don't you mean seeing yourself as others see you?" Clio asked.

"No, though that is part of it. Touch my hand."

Clio reached out to take Crystal's hand. Suddenly she became aware of herself in a new and not wholly comfortable way. Feelup saw her as a largely sexless object not worth feeling, considering his sister's rebuke. Ken saw her as a pretty face without a body. Alice saw her as a somewhat pushy person who was unlikely to rate either disaster or success. Crystal herself saw her as probably a fraud who claimed a powerful talent that could never actually be demonstrated to others: how convenient. And Sherlock saw her as a significant, wonderful creature he wished he could somehow be worthy of associating with. He did love her, not caring at all about her lack of curves, but knew he didn't deserve her.

"Oh!" she said, letting go of the hand.

"Now you know," Crystal said. "It can be cruel."

Much more than that! "Thank you for the demonstration," Clio said faintly.

"You are welcome." There was a polite hint of a sneer in the tone. The woman knew she had set her back.

Then Crystal's face went blank for a moment, turned awed, and finally appalled. "Is something wrong?" Ken asked.

"No." But it was obviously a lie.

Then Clio had a notion. *Drew!*

"I just couldn't resist," the little dragon said to her alone. "She was so arrogant in her ignorance, I just had to tell her the truth."

What truth?

"That your talent is real, and you are the Muse of History."

Well, it was the truth, and maybe deserved. But after that the conversation lagged, and she was glad when their stop came.

Clio and Sherlock got off, while the others rode the trolley on north. The day was late; they had ridden longer than it had seemed. "We are at a truck stop," Sherlock said.

That was apparent. There were a number of trucks on the trollway, ranging from little to monstrous, and every one of them squealed to a stop at the STOP: PAY TROLL station before going on. They looked mundane. What were mundane vehicles doing here in the middle of Xanth? Then she realized that this probably represented a shortcut for the Mundanes, which they used without understanding its nature. All Mundanes cared about was getting their dull work done so they could eat, sleep, and relax. The trolls didn't care, as long as they were paid. Trolls were a lot like Mundanes, actually.

"Perhaps we should stay the night here," Sherlock suggested, "and brace Xanth in the morning."

"That appeals," Clio agreed. She was still shaken by the revelation of how others saw her; she had had no idea there were so many negatives. She knew that their reactions were really normal, because they didn't know her, but still it wasn't a pleasant experience.

Sherlock negotiated with the troll in charge of the truck stop for a room for the night. It turned out that only one was available, the one no one else wanted, because it was on the sewer side: where the garbage and refuse of the passing travelers were piled. There was a smell. But Clio just wanted a place where she could be alone to sort out her feelings, and urged him to take it.

The room itself was pleasant, with a toilet and a type of a magic mirror that showed a series of entertaining pictures. There was a magic machine that provided milkweed pods and fairly fresh pies. Satisfied, they lay on the big soft bed and watched. The trolls were surprisingly sophisticated in their accommodations.

"Sherlock, we're alone," she said. "The dragons don't count, in this respect."

"We're alone," he agreed. "And it's dark."

They kissed, and kissed again, needing no more than the sense of touch. It was wonderful. They removed their clothing and embraced. This time they were really going to do it; she was determined not to balk, and knew he felt the same.

Then something awful happened. There was a horrible roaring and squealing sound, and the wall crashed in, crushing them.

She unwound it instantly. As it played backward she saw that it was a huge lighted truck. Then the wall reverted to solid and the sound faded; it had been there before, getting louder, but they had not noticed. When she had wound it far enough back to provide sufficient time, she stopped it.

They were hugging each other on the bed, bare in the darkness. She jerked her head away from his. "Sherlock! Grab your clothes and get out of here immediately. I'll follow."

He didn't question her. He rolled off the bed, feeling for his clothing, and she did the same, but neither could find anything in the confusion. There was a small light by the door; they stumbled toward it, opened it, and ran outside.

The sound was louder here, and increasing. They ran to the sewer, tumbling in as the truck crashed into the room. Everything exploded, but they were safe; it had missed them.

In little more than an instant, trolls were everywhere, organizing the recovery and cleanup. "The driver got caught by a trollway hypnosis spell," one said, not seeming to notice their stinking nakedness. "Lost con-troll. It happens. We'll get you another room." Trolls weren't much for emotion or concern for lives.

Soon they were in another room; it seemed these could be found when necessary. They washed thoroughly and went to bed again. But the mood had been shattered.

"My Danger of the Day," Clio said ruefully. "I had forgotten about that, and I shouldn't have."

"I gather we were actually caught by it, and you wound it back?"

"I did. Sherlock, the dangers are getting worse. Yesterday I almost couldn't get back from Mundania. Today I almost got crushed. I'm afraid my end is approaching. I need to complete my mission soon, or I won't survive the effort."

"There can't be much more," he said. "I'll help all I can."

"Your help has been wonderful. But you can't fight my curse. This time it almost took you out too."

"I can't think of anyone I'd rather expire with."

He had such a positive outlook. "I think you should reconsider your concern," she said. "I'm sure in time I'll be able to say the words you want. I think I just need to complete my mission first."

"Perhaps so."

"I'm too overwrought to sleep."

He took her hand, and his touch had a marvelously pacifying effect. She would have wondered about that if she hadn't been so tired.

Holding hands, they slept.

Next day they left the truck stop and followed the blue arrow to the edge of the Region of Water. The red time arrow was now nearing its target; they were on schedule.

This was a waterscape more than a landscape, with puddles, pools, ponds, and lakes. They had to bargain to get a small boat so they could continue. Mermaids sported in the water, thrashing their tails to lift their upper torsos well clear of the surface so they could see and be seen. Sherlock managed not to freak out—after all, mermaids had no panties—but the sights did give him pause. Clio stifled her irritation; she couldn't blame mermaids for being what they were, which was splendid halves of women.

As the red arrow connected to its base, they came to an island. There were a nondescript but oddly appealing young man, a pretty young woman of about sixteen, and a child. They seemed to be stranded.

"A boat!" the young woman cried, waving. She looked somehow familiar. "Rescue!"

Clio concentrated, and got it. "Surprise Golem!" and her companion was Umlaut, the formerly nonexistent man; she had written a whole volume about him. The child was unfamiliar; she looked to be about five and would have been cute without a rebellious curl to her lip. No, it wasn't rebellion, it was independence.

The girl looked. "Do I know you?"

"I am Clio, the Muse of History, and this is Sherlock of the Black Wave. We seem to have been directed to come here. How did you get caught on this island?"

"It's embarrassing," Surprise said. "We were boating, when the boatsman abruptly dumped us here and fled. Will you take us to land?"

"Of course. But why did he ground you?"

"That's complicated to explain. We were looking for a nice private place to—to be alone, when—"

"You wanted to $$$$," the child said, smiling.

There was a brief silence as Clio's teeth tried to drop out of their sockets and Surprise's face blushed halfway into her hair. Umlaut looked totally out of sorts, and Sherlock made an effort to blanch. None of them had heard such a word spoken that baldly before, by one so young.

Sherlock was the first to attempt a recovery. "When you encountered this child?" he inquired.

"Yes," Surprise said, her voice strained. "She seemed to be stranded on this isle, and was crying, so we stopped and got off the boat to comfort her and inquire where her mother was. And she said—"

"****," the child said, laughing merrily. It was a thoroughly brutish term, well into the Adult Conspiracy if not somewhat beyond it. There was a little clump of flowers on the island; they keeled over, wilting.

"And the boatsman paddled away," Surprise managed to say though her throat was evidently constricted by the awfulness of the word that had just rammed its way into the dialog.

Now Clio understood why. Anyone caught in the vicinity of such an utterance was in peril of befoulment. There might as well have been ghastlies attacking. The man had fled.

"I think I know this child's talent," Sherlock said. "She is immune to the Adult Conspiracy."

"Her family must have been overwhelmed," Clio said. "So they left her here, hoping never to see her again."

"I don't even know those words," Surprise said. "But they burn my skin." She was two years under the age of induction into the Conspiracy, though obviously that was becoming academic because of her current exposure to the forbidden words.

Sherlock squatted down beside the little girl. "What is your name?"

"Ciriana," she replied cheerfully.

"That's a nice name."

The girl turned shy. She seemed to be normal, except for her vocabulary.

"It's a curse," Clio said. "I understand about them. It's not her fault."

"Obviously she can't live with a normal family," Sherlock said. "Those words she has learned are dangerous around other children, and not very comfortable for most adults."

"But we can't just leave her here," Surprise said.

"It seems we have a problem," Clio said. It was evidently hers to solve, somehow. "Sherlock, do you think reverse wood would reverse her curse?"

"Only while actually touching her," he said. "That's the case with your magic, we found."

"Well, maybe she could keep a chip with her."

A chip appeared in his hand. "Ciriana, hold this."

The girl took it, trustingly.

"Now repeat one of those words you just said."

Her smile became a sneer. "Sweet violets!" Then she burst into tears.

Sherlock nodded. He took back the chip, and the girl's smile returned. "The wood reverses the language, but also her disposition. I think she's better off smiling."

Clio had to agree. "Surprise, it's early for you to be exposed to the

Adult Conspiracy, but I think necessary in this case. You will simply have to learn to tolerate certain ugly words without freaking out."

"I think I can manage," Surprise said.

"%%%%," Ciriana said sweetly.

Umlaut managed to catch Surprise before she hit the ground.

Something needed to be done. "Surprise, you have every talent once and only once," Clio said when the girl recovered.

"Yes. That's why I try not to use them. I may need them later and I don't want to run out."

"This is nonsensical," Sherlock said. "You won't run out."

"But each talent is permanently gone once I use it."

"Consider this: there is an infinite variety of each talent. Suppose you fly: you can do it by floating, or by making yourself light, or by generating a wind to blow you upward, or by invoking antigravity, or by forming an invisible platform to stand on. If you make yourself light, there must be countless ways to do it: by decreasing the mass of your body, or by making your body repel the ground, or be attracted to the sky, or some combination of those. Only your imagination limits your ability to fly. The same is true for other kinds of magic. If you want to be strong, there is giant strength, ogre strength, dragon strength, and so on. You can't run out unless you lose your ability to think of new variants."

As he spoke, Surprise's jaw slowly dropped. So did Umlaut's. And Clio's. Sherlock was right: there would not be time enough in Surprise's life to use up all the possible variants of her talents.

"Oh, you've given me back my talent!" Surprise said, planting a kiss on him. "I don't have to conserve anymore!"

"Just conserve the easiest ways, for emergencies," he said, standing a little unsteady from the kiss. Kisses had that effect; it was inherent in their nature, like panties only less so. "Use the more difficult variants for routine situations."

"I will!"

"Now conjure a bell of partial silence for Ciriana. One that blots out only bad adult words. So we can't hear them."

"Yes!" A translucent hat appeared on Ciriana's head, reaching down around her face."

"——" the child said. It was working.

"That's fine, dear," Clio said. "We'll take care of you." For this was a stopgap measure; they still had to figure out a permanent one.

"What about Lethe Elixir?" Umlaut asked. "So she'll forget the bad words."

"That should help," Clio agreed. "I happen to know where there's a small lethe spring not far distant."

"Then the only problem will be preventing her from hearing them again," Surprise said.

"True. But let's go to the lethe first. Meanwhile we can ponder subsequent measures."

Surprise, Umlaut, and Ciriana got into the boat, and Sherlock and Umlaut paddled them in the direction Clio indicated. They made fair progress physically, but less in finding a permanent solution.

The lethe spring was a small offshoot that had gotten lost from its parent spring some time ago; evidently it had forgotten its home, being what it was, and wandered to the Region of Water. It was on another island that local folk knew better than to visit. The thing about lethe water was that it caused forgetting, and the more of it one was exposed to, the worse the loss of memory. A single drop could make a person forget a single word; a deep drink could make a person forget his own identity.

They reached the island. "This water is dangerous," Clio said. "Therefore only Ciriana and I should go to the spring."

"I insist on accompanying you," Sherlock said. "So you won't forget me." He smiled, but his concern was clearly serious.

"I insist you don't," she said. "So you are in no danger of forgetting *me*."

He spread his hands, yielding. "But if you don't return soon, I will investigate."

"Do," she agreed. She took Ciriana by the hand and led her along the path to the spring. "Now I will sprinkle a drop of water on you and speak a word. You will forget that word. Then I will do it for another word, until all the bad ones are gone. Then you won't have to be concerned about freaking out other children."

"Okay," the girl agreed amicably.

"Now tell me the other bad words you know."

"@@@@. &&&&. \\\\," Ciriana said sweetly.

Clio's vision turned flaming red and the sky seemed to wobble. Grass along the path died. To make it worse, Clio would have to repeat those words to abolish them. She wasn't sure her tongue could manage it without blistering. But she would have to try.

"Where did you learn such words?" she asked when her equilibrium cleared somewhat.

"A nice harpy roosted on a tree behind our house. I used to talk with her. She taught me a lot of great stuff."

That figured. "Please don't talk with harpies anymore."

"Okay."

Then it occurred to her that the harpy might have shared more than words. "Dear, what do you know of stork summoning?"

"I know all about it," Ciriana said proudly. "First the mommy and daddy take off their clothes. Then she lies down on the bed, and he—"

"That will do, dear. I'm sure you do have it straight." Clio was blushing already. They were lucky the little girl hadn't thought to try it herself. Yet.

"Person ahead," Drew reported. "His name is Joe."

She had forgotten the dragon. It was as though the very proximity of the lethe spring was affecting her awareness. "Thank you."

They came to the spring. Joe was there, about to dip out a cup of water.

"Joe!" she called. "Don't drink that water! It will make you forget!"

"But I'm thirsty," Joe called back.

"Any other water will do. Just not *this* water. Please move away from the spring."

"All right," Joe agreed. He started walking away from it, down the path toward her, still holding the cup.

Clio stepped to the side, but Joe stepped the same way. So she stepped the other way, but he did also, at the same time. "Oh, I'm sorry," he said. "It's my talent."

"Your talent?"

"Always being in the way."

"Oh. Then you stand still, and I will go around you."

"Sure." He stood still.

She stepped around him, but though he did not move, she somehow bumped into him. The water in the cup splashed out. She had thought he had been about to dip; it seemed he had already dipped. Before she could react, the water soaked her.

She forgot everything.

Then she remembered. Sherlock was there. "Come away from here," he said, guiding her.

"What happened? I was about to—" She felt her wet shirt. "In fact I—"

"I reversed it," he said.

"Oh, with reverse wood. Thank you. I was in danger of losing my memory!" She gazed somewhat dazedly around. "Drew! Where—?"

"I wasn't splashed," the little dragon said. "I summoned Sherlock, and he came to rescue you."

But she wasn't sure this made complete sense. She had been dosed with lethe water, and should have forgotten everything. So how could she remember? Reverse wood might enable her to remember new things, but the old things should have been permanently obliterated.

"He touched you, and your memories came back," Drew said.

She would have thought that impossible, but obviously she did have her memories back. Maybe the lethe had not been full strength. "That young man, Joe—"

"He reversed too," Drew said. "Now his talent is never getting in the way. In fact he's out of the way now."

"But lethe couldn't do that!"

"It didn't. Sherlock did it."

How could that be? Reverse wood might reverse a single episode, but not a full talent. But now they came up to the others, and her confusion was lost amidst the press of explanations.

Only when they were back in the boat and moving across the water did she remember the main thing: "Ciriana! We never made you forget those words!"

"What words?" the child asked innocently.

"The ones you were saying. The bad ones."

"I don't remember them."

"And the secret of summoning the stork."

Ciriana looked blank. "Storks are summoned?"

"You mean you don't remember?"

"Storks are birds, aren't they? I don't know any more about them."

Clio stared at the child, amazed. She must somehow have been dosed with lethe water after all, and had forgotten all the forbidden knowledge. But how could there have been such selectivity, without guidance?

Then a harpy flew over them. "Get away from my territorial waters, you boatful of ^^^^!" she screeched.

The water around them roiled and bubbled with the force of the bad expression. Sherlock and Umlaut frowned, and Surprise's face froze. The only one unaffected was Ciriana. She had not understood the word at all, or perhaps had not even heard it.

The child had not merely forgotten the words and concepts. Her immunity to the Adult Conspiracy had been nullified.

Something was weird. But Clio couldn't figure out quite how. So she let it be, for now.

15
STORM

They reached the edge of the Region of Water, and solid land. They returned the boat. "This is where we get off," Surprise said. "Thanks so much for rescuing us. But what about Ciriana?"

"We need to take her home," Clio said. "She'll fit in there, now."

Sherlock frowned. "These were the folk who stranded her on an island. Regardless of the provocation, should these be considered fit parents?"

That question required no answer. "Where else?" Clio asked.

"Good adoptive parents," Umlaut said.

"And how do we locate these?" Sherlock asked.

"Surprise can use the talent of pointing the right direction for anything. That should show the way."

"I can do that," Surprise agreed. She closed her eyes, turned around, extended one arm, and oriented roughly south. "That way," she said. "I don't know how far; that seems vague. But there are definitely good parents there."

"Look at your compass," Drew said.

Clio looked. The blue arrow was pointing exactly the direction Surprise was. The red arrow was gone.

"It seems we are going that way," Clio said. "We'll take her."

"That's good," Surprise said. "She'll make some family very happy, now that she's lost her curse."

She surely would. "I'm glad we happened by," Clio said. "It would have been a shame to leave Ciriana on that island."

"Well, we'll be on our way," Surprise said. She turned to Umlaut. "Do you think we can find a private place?"

"Well, uh—"

"This time I'll do the searching."

"Okay."

They kissed and disappeared. Surprise was already using more of her magic.

"That's a remarkable girl," Sherlock said.

"Yes. Remind me to tell you her story, when we have time on our hands."

"Tell *me* her story," Ciriana said.

Clio laughed. "In due course. First we must get started south."

The child started to cloud up. "Maybe just part of it," Sherlock suggested.

That seemed to be a good compromise. "The stork got confused, and by the time it delivered Surprise to her parents, she was five years old—your age. That's why they named her Surprise; she really surprised them."

Ciriana clapped her hands. "My age!" she said, pleased.

"It's a good age," Sherlock said. "They were very glad to have her."

Clio glanced at Sherlock. "I don't want to use the trollway again; for some odd reason I distrust its evening facilities."

Sherlock looked around. "A section of the Water Region is to our south. We may need to borrow the boat again."

"But we don't know how far we are going. We could have trouble returning it."

"Then we may have to walk around the lake."

"Whatever," Clio said, though the notion of an extended walk bothered her. She was getting older every hour, and the daily dangers she faced were getting worse; she needed to get back to Mount Parnassus. But what was there to do except follow the blue arrow?

They started south, and came to a man sitting on a stump. He looked depressed.

"Hello," Clio said.

"Ungh," he replied morosely.

This was not a good sign, but their direction as indicated by the blue arrow seemed to pass right through the man. She doubted it was coincidence. "I am Clio, and these are Sherlock and Ciriana. We are traveling south."

"I am Mister E, and I have no idea where I'm going."

"I can see how that would be depressing. What is your talent?"

"I have no idea."

"So it's a mystery," Sherlock murmured. Ciriana laughed.

Mister E—mystery. It was a pun. But rooted in the man's nature; that was why he didn't know much about himself. "Well, come along with us, and maybe we'll figure it out." She never would have issued such an invitation if it were not for the blue arrow and her need to proceed efficiently.

E stood. He was a tall and moderately homely man. "Might as well."

They walked on south. Before long they came to a fork in the road. It was oddly shaped, and there were strange sounds associated with it. Some were melodic, others discordant. They didn't know what to make of it, or which fork to take; both roads went south, parallel to each other.

There was a man sitting at the side. He looked to be just shy of age thirty. Clio approached him. "Hello, I am Clio." She introduced the other members of her party.

"I am Bill," the man said. "You are surely wondering about the fork."

"Yes we are. We are traveling south, but both roads look the same."

"They aren't. Take the right fork; that's the harmonious one. The other is discordant and will lead you to nothing but trouble. It is infested by discord-ants."

"We'll take the right one. Thank you."

"That's what I'm here for."

"But doesn't it get dull, sitting here all day just to advise travelers?"

"Not at all. My girlfriend Elem stops by frequently."

"Elem?"

"Miss Elem N. Tery. Things are always marvelously clear to her."

Clio recognized another pun: elementary. They came thick and fast on the regular paths of Xanth. "I'm sure she's quite something."

They moved on. Ciriana was getting tired, and Clio knew they would have to stop soon, so as not to wear out the child, but she hoped for some better way to travel.

Soon they found another man. This one was busy carving objects of wood. They weren't very good examples of art, but he seemed satisfied. The blue arrow pointed through him also.

"Hello," Clio said.

The new man turned out to be Darron, the twin brother of Darren, about whom she had once written. Darren made one thing into another; Darron endowed inanimate objects with magical properties.

"What we could really use is something to carry us," Clio said. "But I fear none of your little carvings will suffice."

"But I know what will," Darron said. "Here." He got up and went to a huge plant by the edge of the path. It had a long stalk bearing a single giant pink flower. "This is a car-nation. Watch."

He touched the flower. It lit up in several places and dropped to the ground, purring like a great animal. This way up, the petals manifested as the backs of seats, and some curled-up leaves were wheels. "Ride this," Darron said proudly.

They did. There was room for all of them. Sherlock found a steering wheel and related controls. "This is a car, all right," he said. "Funny in design, but similar to some I used in Mundania. Let's see if I remember how to make it go."

Evidently he did, because the vehicle suddenly lurched forward with a squeal of tires. They waved to Darron as they zoomed on down the trail.

"This is certainly more comfortable," Clio said. "If you see a pie tree, pause there so we can get something to eat." She glanced around. "In fact there is one now."

The car went right on past it.

"Sherlock—"

"I tried to stop. The controls don't respond. It seems I only thought I was driving; it's really driving itself."

Clio was uneasy about this, but did not want to alarm the child. "I'm sure there's some purpose in it."

The road ended abruptly at an arm of the lake. There was a huge boat there, right at the edge. The car-nation chugged right onto it and stopped. Then the boat cast off and moved onto the lake.

"Where is this?" Ciriana asked.

"This is the Fanta Sea," Mr. E replied.

"The Fanta Sea!" Clio repeated. "But this isn't where it is supposed to be."

"It is wherever it chooses to be," E said. "Even in Mundania."

"Mundania!"

He shrugged. "So I'm told."

Certainly it seemed to be here, regardless where it had been when she had written about it before. Like the traveling fields, it went where it wished.

They got out of the car and walked around the boat. "This seems to be a ferry," Sherlock said. "We were the last car to board it."

"And it seems we are going where it is taking us," she said grimly. But the blue arrow pointed exactly the way the ferryboat was going.

The occupants of one of the other cars approached. "We are the Maidens China, Japan, and Mexico," one said.

"Oh! I wrote about—I mean, I happened to know—the Maiden Taiwan. I wonder—"

"She is our sister," China said.

"But she—she's rather older than she looks. I'm not sure how—"

"So are we," Japan said. "But we remain young as long as we remain on the Fanta Sea."

"It's enchanted," Mexico said.

"So you are actually 170 years old," Clio said, doing some quick figuring.

"Yes," China said. "And if we ever leave the Fanta Sea and step into reality, we'll look it."

"So we are on a perpetual cruise," Japan said. "Here on the Acquaintance Ship."

"I thought it was a ferryboat," Sherlock said.

They laughed. "It's a fairy boat," Mexico said. "See, it has a mast and sail."

They looked, and discovered that this was indeed a sailing ship. Clio could have sworn that it had lacked a mast before, but she had been distracted by their manner of boarding it.

"What a sweet child you have," China said. "Would you like some pie, sweetie?"

Ciriana, suddenly shy again, hesitated.

"And eye scream," Japan added.

"And chocolate sauce," Mexico said.

That did it. Ciriana went to their cabin.

"And to think, we could have had pie and eye scream too, if we had just been young enough," Sherlock said.

But Clio was distracted. "Didn't we come here in a car? Where is it now?"

"Why, right here." Then he paused in midglance. "It's another cabin!"

"This really is a magic ship. It changes according to the need. Car to cab." She went to the cabin, which was a cute cottage with a thatched roof and pink flowers growing under its windows. She looked inside, and found a compact kitchen with several pies and fruits on its counter, and a double bed. It was ideal.

"But what of Ciriana?" she asked herself. Then she saw a smaller bed to the side; she must have overlooked it before. "And Mr. E?" At which point she saw another cabin to the side, to which E was going.

Fairy ships were rather special, it seemed. No wonder the Maiden sisters liked cruising.

They fetched pies and fruits and joined E on the deck facing out on the sea. Now Clio saw that the Maidens and Ciriana had similar deck chairs next to theirs. The little girl was having a fine time. There was another child with them, a girl a year or so younger than Ciriana. Her name, it seemed, was Cricket, and her talent was to produce music by rubbing her hands together. It was lovely music.

"Private dialog with Sherlock," Clio said to Drew. Immediately the little dragons connected them so they could talk without being over-heard by others.

"There is something on your appealing mind?" Sherlock inquired. There was something about his phrasing that did indeed appeal to her. He liked her mind and nature, rather than her body. He really did, the dragons had assured her.

"Yes. The three Maidens seem like nice folk. Do you think Ciriana would like to stay with them, and with Cricket, and cruise perpetually on the Fanta Sea?"

"She might," he agreed. "But would she ever grow up?"

Clio hadn't thought of that. "I suspect she would remain a child of five forever."

"She would," Drew said. "Cricket has been four for twenty years."

"Twenty years!"

"Is that her best outcome?" Sherlock asked.

Clio considered. To be always a child, with nice people, on a boat with everything provided. "It may be."

"What is the price?"

That brought her up short. Few things in Xanth were really free, however they might seem at first. The ship or the sea must extract some return. "I think we had better find out."

"We can tell you," Drew said. "We've been into the Maidens' minds."

"It's the soul," Drusie said.

"The soul!"

"One percent per year, until in a century it's all gone," Drew said. "Then the person has either to leave or go to work."

"But what life would there be outside for a person without a soul? She'd soon be very unpopular."

"That's why no one has left," Drusie said. "So they work. They get to keep their youth and cabins."

"The Maidens!" Clio said. "They must have been here well over a century, but they look to be in their twenties. How are they working?"

"To persuade visitors to stay," Drew said. "They get a portion of their souls back for every person they persuade."

"If someone is really good at it," Drusie said, "he can get his whole soul back and keep it. So they are truly motivated."

Clio exchanged a horrified glance with Sherlock. "I don't think we want to leave Ciriana here."

Sherlock nodded. "Mister E, in contrast, may stay if he wishes. He is of age. Perhaps this is what he has been looking for."

Clio saw E in a deck chair the other side of Sherlock. An attractive young woman had joined him. She was quite friendly, and he was quite interested. Probably no young woman had been this friendly to him before. "Nevertheless, we had better make sure he understands the situation."

They stood and approached E and the girl. "Hello," Clio said. "I am Clio, and this is Sherlock. We have the talents of winding back events, and of working with reverse wood. We may have something serious to discuss with you."

"I am Randi," the young woman said, crossing her bare legs in a way that made both E and Sherlock notice, and Clio frown. "I was expected to be a boy, but was delivered as a girl, so my folks never knew quite what to make of me. I had to wear boy's clothes. But here on the Acquaintance Ship I can dress exactly as I prefer, and be accepted without question. I revel in it. It's a wonderful community we have here."

"It sounds great," Mr. E agreed. "I'm really interested in staying."

"But have you mentioned the price?" Clio asked.

"I was still covering the advantages of cruising with us," Randi said, leaning forward earnestly so that the men's eyes clicked from her legs to her loose décolletage. "A person never gets old—"

"The price," Clio repeated firmly.

Randi inhaled, causing four eyeballs to swell. "I was getting to that. There is always plenty of good food, but a person never gains weight, and—"

Clio affixed a stern stare.

"The price," Randi agreed with resignation. "It's really very small, only one tiny percent of the soul."

"The soul!" E exclaimed.

"Just a little bit of it, to keep the ship's magic strong. In return you receive so much—"

"A little bit every how often?" Clio asked.

"Just once a year. It would take a century to use it all up."

"And how long do people live, here on the boat?" Sherlock asked.

"Well, since they don't age—"

"How old are you?" Clio asked.

"Sixteen." Then, reluctantly: "And a hundred. But since I never aged, it's really sixteen."

"So your soul is all gone," Clio said.

"No it isn't. I got some back."

"How?"

"It really doesn't matter." Randi faced E. "I must admit that it can be a bit dull here on occasion, with no work to do. I really could use some fresh male company." Her blouse somehow fell open; perhaps a button had been lost. The men's eyes were locked on its contents.

But Clio's questioning had gotten through to E. "You're a hundred and sixteen?"

"Well, if you want to count external years. But really I am as you see me." She shifted position slightly so that more content accidentally showed. Clio made a mental note: if she ever had curves again, this was a good technique. "And I would be ever so happy to entertain you in my cabin, if you care to look things over more carefully."

"You could be my great-grandmother!" E said.

"Oh, no, I never married! We don't do that here on the boat. We just—" She shrugged.

"Just what?" E asked.

"Just trade around. To alleviate the dullness. But we don't have enough men, really. You would be very popular."

Actually it was a considerable offer for a man who lacked popularity with women. "We'll leave you to your consideration," Clio told E. "You might wish to remain here a few years, then move on to other things."

"Yes, you don't have to stay forever!" Randi said. "You can leave any time you want. And you wouldn't be bored at all, at first."

"Not until you ran out of new women," Sherlock said. "And even old women can have new tricks."

"We do," Randi said, then quickly covered her slip. "Or so I hear."

Clio and Sherlock returned to their own deck chairs. "I presume you had reason to suggest that?" he asked her.

"We don't know where he will be best off. This just might be it, with Randi and the Maidens and whoever else is eager for new blood. Now that he knows the price, and how to escape it. I don't want to be judgmental."

"They may have ways of preventing folk from leaving."

"Then why the effort to persuade them to stay? I think it has to be voluntary."

They looked at Ciriana and the three Maidens. They were getting along famously. Then China focused on Sherlock, and her blouse seemed to fill out somewhat. "You look like a man who hasn't been loved enough," she said.

Clio bit her tongue. This was Sherlock's business, and she had no right to interfere. He could have a dialog (or whatever) with the old Maiden if he wished. She forced her gaze and attention out to sea.

But she couldn't help wondering what the men of this boat were like. Would any be so bored they would find a curveless woman interesting?

A handsome man appeared beside her. "How do you do, fair creature," he said. "I am Tran."

Surprised, she forgot to introduce herself. "Tran?"

He smiled engagingly. "I am not Tran's sister, or Tran's parent, or Tran's Lou Cent, I am merely Tran myself. Completely dull."

She winced at the puns. "I can see that."

"You, in contrast, are interesting. Would you like to see my etchings?"

"Itchings?"

He laughed again. "You have such a quaint sense of humor! I mean, would you like to visit my cabin and pretend we are looking at designs on metal so no one will suspect what we're really doing?"

She had to laugh with him. He was out to persuade her to stay, obviously, but the attention was nevertheless flattering. Why would he bother, if he didn't have some interest? Then she remembered: her soul. That was probably worth a lot more here than her straitlaced body was.

"What's that?" Ciriana asked, pointing out to sea.

They looked. "Oh, that's Wynde Tchill," the Maiden Japan said.

"She's the most recent child of Fracto and Happy Bottom," Mexico said. "She likes to play on the Fanta Sea."

"Oh, goody," Ciriana said, clapping her little hands. "Another child."

"She's coming unusually close," Tran said. "Usually she's shy of this boat."

"Maybe she spied Ciriana and Cricket," Sherlock said. "But I'm not sure quite how they can play together."

"Oh, Wynde can stir up leaves on the deck," China said. "The girls can run through them. That sort of thing."

But Clio felt a chill of alarm. She hadn't encountered her Danger of the Day, and a storm at sea could be bad.

Sherlock picked up on her thought, perhaps with the aid of the little dragons. "Maybe we should discourage such play, this time."

"Oh, Wynde's harmless," Japan said. "She's really not much of a cloud yet."

But now the cloud was looming, and the winds were picking up. A cold gust crossed their bow. Wynde Tchill was making it seem colder than it really was.

"She's grown," Mexico remarked. She caught Cricket's hand and led her away.

"And seems less playful," Tran said. "Maybe we too should repair to our cabins before she wets on us." He glanced sidelong at Clio.

"Sherlock, Ciriana, come inside," Clio said briskly. "Storms at sea aren't fun."

"But I want to play!" the child said. She stood at the rail, raptly gazing into the swirling mists.

"Another time." Clio took her hand.

Then the storm struck. Sleet stung their faces and bounced on the deck. Clio hurried toward the cabin, but slipped on slush and fell, letting go of the child's hand. She quickly wound it back, then stepped more carefully and made it safely to their cabin, where Sherlock was holding the door open. He caught her around the waist and swung her inside, then closed the door when they both were secure. He was a real comfort to have around.

But the storm was just beginning. It slammed at the ship, causing it to wallow in developing troughs. There were surely sailors navigating it, folk whose souls had run out, but this was evidently difficult for them to handle. The floor tilted, causing them to stumble.

"The bed," Sherlock said. "It's anchored."

Now she saw that the bed was bolted to the floor. That was reassuring. The three of them got on it and hung on as the tilt reversed.

"I'm getting sick," Ciriana said.

"No you aren't," Sherlock said, touching her shoulder.

The child looked surprised. "No I'm not," she agreed.

"How did you do that?" Clio asked him.

"Psychology. Illness is mostly in the mind, in Xanth."

She wondered, but was distracted by another heave of the deck. This was worse than the last; the storm was really taking hold.

The next pitch and yaw were worse yet. This was getting out of hand. She was afraid the ship would roll over. Of course that was an exaggeration, but it was brutal experiencing the ponderous rocking of it.

"My curse!" Clio cried. "It's my Danger of the Day!"

"In that case, it won't just blow over," Sherlock said.

"That's right—it won't." An awful decision was coming across her. "I don't want to make everyone suffer on my behalf. I had better go out and face it myself."

He looked at her. "Face it—how?"

"I don't know! I can't wind back the whole storm. Maybe just go out on the deck and let it take me."

"No way!"

"But once it gets me, everyone else will be safe. The curse doesn't care about them, just me."

"But *I* care about you. I won't let you do it."

"You're sweet," she said. She kissed him, then lurched off the bed and stumbled to the door. She jerked it open before he could catch her.

The wind whooped in, caught her, and swept her out. She clung to the door, trying to speak, but the rushing air snatched her breath away.

Sherlock came after her. The wind caught him too, prying him out of the cabin. He slid helplessly across the deck toward the edge. Someone screamed. Clio thought it was Ciriana, then realized it was herself.

Sherlock reached up and caught the guard rail, his legs dangling over the edge of the ship. He had saved himself.

But the ship rolled worse, to one side, back to the other, and then to the first side again. This time a wave caught it and pushed it farther. In fact, the ship really was rolling over!

Clio screamed as she lost her hold on the door and slid across the deck. She passed under the rail and dropped into the heaving sea. The water caught her and hauled her under.

She wound it back. She couldn't help it; she had to make the effort, though she knew it was futile.

She rose back out of the water. The ship righted itself. She slid up under the rail and back up to the door. Then she stopped, clinging. She normally wound back just herself and those in her vicinity. This time she had wound back the entire ship. Her magic was exhausted. She would not be able to do that again.

The ship resumed its motion. It was going to roll over again—and she couldn't stop it. This time everyone would drown, not just herself. Because she had lacked the courage to let the curse take her.

Then something strange happened. The storm remained, but the sound of it was oddly muted. The ship slowly righted itself. The wind died out.

Sherlock let go of the rail, got up, and walked back to the cabin. "It should be all right now."

Clio looked wildly around. The roiling clouds seemed to stop at an invisible barrier just clear of the ship. There was a globe of calmness that surrounded them; beyond it the storm vented its full fury without effect. "What did you do?"

"I conjured reverse wood to coat the hull. It reverses the storm where it touches, so it can't affect the ship."

"But that should affect only the water. What of the air?"

"Maybe the mast is coated too."

The area of quiet air did seem to be as high as the mast, and as broad as the spars radiating from it. The air rushed in, got reversed, and went quiet. But how could he have coated the whole rigging without touching it?

The others came out of their cabins. "Is the storm over?" China asked, looking around.

"It is fended off," Clio said.

"We see it," Japan said. "It changed its mind."

"We're in a bubble of calm," Mexico said.

They walked to the rail. "I wouldn't touch that," Sherlock said.

But China put her hand on it. Suddenly she changed. Her fair young features imploded and her skin turned black. Her hair frizzled. Her eyes stared out of a a gaunt, almost skull-bare face.

"You're looking your age!" Clio cried. "Let go of the rail!"

Japan pried China's skeletal fingers off the rail. Then China returned to her normal appearance. "Oh, that was terrible!" she gasped.

"That's reverse wood," Clio said. "It reversed the magic that keeps you young."

Ciriana had left the cabin and was admiring the storm. Now she touched the rail. "»»»»," she said.

China reeled, Japan sank to her knees, and Mexico fainted. Clio ignored them for the moment and hurried to fetch the child away from the rail. The reverse wood had reversed the reversal, and restored her immunity to the Adult Conspiracy. "Don't touch that," she warned the child. "It's bad for you."

"Okay," Ciriana agreed amicably.

"Do you remember that bad word?"

"What bad word?"

Good: the effect was only while she actually touched the wood. "Never mind. Just stay away from that rail."

Now that the storm had been nullified, they were free to relax. As her emotion settled back into place, Clio realized that she had serious questions for Sherlock. So while Ciriana returned to play with Cricket, and E returned to listen to Randi's reasoning, incidentally keeping a close eye on her outfit, Clio and Sherlock retired to their cabin.

"That was no incidental magic," she informed him firmly. "You did not conjure reverse wood, or shape it; you transformed an entire ship's hull and rigging to reverse wood. How do you account for that?"

"I'm not sure," he said. "You were in danger—the dragons told me you had just rolled the ship back upright, but lacked the magical strength to do it again—and I knew I had to do something. So I made a great effort, as I held on to the rail, and it happened. I think desperation enabled me to do something I could never have done ordinarily."

"But a whole ship! Transformation! This is phenomenal."

"I must have more power over reverse wood than I thought. I'm amazed myself."

That was where it rested. They had no better explanation.

Still, it nagged her. She was glad the danger had somehow been abated, but she didn't like mysteries of this nature.

Once the storm saw that it couldn't get at them, its fury dissipated. The winds died, the swirling fog evaporated, and the sunbeams managed to reach down to the calming sea. The remaining cloud floated innocently away, pretending she had just been passing by.

The Maidens emerged. "Wynde Tchill never threw a tantrum like that before," China said.

"I wonder whatever got into her?" Japan asked.

"My curse," Clio said. "I am cursed to be exposed to danger once a day. This was that danger. I'm sorry it extended to all of you, this time."

Mexico frowned. "In that case, we would prefer that you not remain on the Acquaintance Ship. We're not that immortal."

"I understand," Clio said. "We'll disembark as soon as we can."

The ship seemed to hear that, because almost immediately it arrived at a crude wharf and nudged to a stop. Their cabin reverted to carnation mode, ready to take them off.

"Ciriana, you may remain here with Cricket and the nice Maidens if you wish," Clio said. "But you must understand that you will never grow up."

"They're fun," the child agreed. "But I like you." She scrambled into the car.

Clio was privately flattered, and did think it was the best course, though she remained uncertain where the child might be suitably placed.

"And Mr. E, this seems ideal for you, as long as you know the conditions."

"Yes, do stay," Randi said, clinging to his arm.

"No, I must go," he said, gently disengaging. He got into the car. Randy dissolved into evocative tears and fled to her cabin.

"Are you sure?" Clio asked, feeling vaguely guilty. "She's a pretty girl, and will never be otherwise."

"And I will never be other than I am: homely," E said. "Do you think she'll pay any further attention to me, once I'm safely committed to the ship? She just wants the bonus for my soul."

"Even homely men become attractive to women when there aren't enough men to go around," Sherlock said.

"Oh, I'm sure she would make me extremely happy to be here," he agreed. "And so would the Maidens. For a while. But once my soul ran out, they would be tired of me, and I'd have nowhere to go. I think my destiny is elsewhere. I still want to discover my talent, and with luck, find a woman who needs me for something other than my soul."

"A mature decision," Sherlock agreed.

The car moved forward, driving off the ship and onto the wharf. Clio looked back, and saw the Maidens and handsome Tran waving. That increased her guilt. They were nice people, in a special situation. But for her curse, she would have been severely tempted. But of course she had eternal life at Mount Parnassus, and a job to do, if she could make it safely home before dying young.

The wharf led to a road, and the road led to Castle Zombie. They came to the bridge over the moat, but that was so dilapidated that the car thought the better of it, and halted short of it. They got out, and the car reverted to a big pink flower. Its job was done. "Thank you," Clio told it, and the pink intensified.

"Ooo!" Ciriana exclaimed, admiring the sordid spectacle of the castle.

"Our appointment is at Castle Zombie, it seems," Sherlock said, less enthusiastic.

Clio looked at the compass. "Yes. I hope it is in the living quarters rather than the zombie quarters."

They set themselves, and ventured onto the moldy boards of the drawbridge. It held, barely. Clio kept a tight grip on the child, lest she slip on slime and fall into the gook of the moat. She knew the zombies were merely another culture of Xanth, but this particular castle was rather far from her favorite tourist attraction.

They made it safely to the great warped front door. Clio reminded herself that this was where the blue arrow led her, so she had to follow through. She lifted a quailing knuckle and knocked.

16
SPANCEL

The door creaked open. A zombie stood there, of course. "Whe donz whanz anee," he said.

Taken aback, Clio soon rallied. "We're not here to sell you anything. Please tell the proprietors that Clio, the Muse of History, is here."

"Huh?" the zombie asked. Zombies weren't very smart, because their brains were rotten.

"Fetch the boss," Sherlock said.

That the zombie understood. It turned, dropping a clot of rot, and shambled into the dark depths of the castle.

Soon a dark young woman appeared. "Sherlock!" she exclaimed.

Sherlock was taken aback, not recognizing her. "Tell him it's Breanna of the Black Wave," Clio told Drew. "She was a child when he knew her there."

"Breanna!" Sherlock said, picking right up on it.

"Tell him she and Justin Tree took over here when the Zombie Master and Millie the Ghost retired."

"And how is Justin?" Sherlock inquired.

"He's fine." Breanna glanced at the others. "Who are your friends?"

"This is Clio, the Muse of History. And—"

"The Muse of History!" Breanna repeated, astonished.

"Here on business," Clio said.

"And Mister E," Sherlock continued smoothly. "And Ciriana. We were led here by a magic sign."

"Well come in," Breanna said. "Justin is out at the moment, but I'll try to handle whatever it is. We don't get many live visitors."

Soon they were in the cozy living quarters, which were clean and clear of rot. Clio explained about the compass and its mysterious directions. "So now we're here, and would like to follow the arrow to its destination, somewhere in this castle. Then we'll surely be on our way again."

There was a sound. "Oh, Amber's awake," Breanna said. She went to a crib and lifted out a lovely little amber-colored girl with brown hair like waves of grain. "This is Amber Dawn, my daughter," Breanna said proudly. "Age one."

"Oh, how nice," Clio cooed, taking the child. She couldn't help it; she was a woman. "Do you know her talent yet?"

"Yes. She makes a sticky clear resin that catches bugs and hardens around them, preserving them for future observation. Her father was a tree, you know. She already has a small collection."

Indeed, the child held up a translucent tan pebble. Inside it was a tiny ant, perfectly preserved.

"That's no gi-ant," Clio said, smiling.

"Let me see, let me see," Ciriana clamored.

Clio set Amber down, and she stood a bit unsteadily on her feet. Ciriana took the piece of amber, admiring the insect. Little girls liked pretty pebbles, and this was more than pretty.

"She has more in her box," Breanna said. In half a moment the two were going through the box with enthusiasm. Amber was plainly pleased to show off her accomplishments. "Justin likes to joke that Amber's so active she must be from an embryo I carried for Mare Imbri, and we should call her Embri-Anna."

"Oof," Sherlock muttered.

"Where does your arrow lead?" Breanna asked.

Clio looked. "That way."

Breanna frowned. "That would be Sis. She's new, and doesn't fit in well with the other zombies yet, so we have her in a room by herself. I don't think she really likes being a zombie."

"That would seem to be understandable," Sherlock said dryly.

"What do you mean by that?" Breanna demanded, bridling.

"Only that being a zombie is surely an acquired taste."

"Oh. Yes. Well, Sis is a natural zombie. I mean, the Zombie Master didn't make her; she just formed when she died. We took her in, of course, but she lacks a sense of community with the made zombies, if you see what I mean."

"Perhaps that's why we have been brought to her," Clio said.

"I'll show you to her room. The children will be all right here; no one intrudes, believe me, and the zombies are protective."

Clio, Sherlock, and E followed Breanna through a dark passage and up spongy stone steps. There was no doubt they were going right; the blue arrow kept turning on Clio's wrist, orienting on the zombie's chamber. They came to the door, and Breanna knocked.

"Go waay," a slurred voice answered from within.

"There is someone here to see you, Sis," Breanna said.

"Thee-siss," the zombie said petulantly.

"She always says that," Breanna said. "We don't know why." She raised her voice. "Please let us in."

Finally the zombie relented. She opened the door and stood back, holding what appeared to be a bedraggled circular hank of yarn in her hands. "Waz you wanz?" She was typical, with limp straggly hanks of hair, missing teeth, sunken eyeballs, and a torso best not investigated closely. Zombie maidens did not lose buttons on blouses or cross their legs.

"Please put that away," Breanna said. "Clio wants to talk to you." Then, to Clio: "She came with that zombie snakeskin. She says she needs to give it to someone, but no one wants it."

Clio entered the chamber and moved to the left. Sherlock moved to the right. E entered, tripped on a loose board, and tumbled headfirst through the loop, fetching up against the zombie's decayed legs.

"You idiot!" Sis snapped. "You went right through the spancel! You're lucky you didn't break it." She brought the twisted loop up, making sure it remained unbroken.

E's face was against her calf. "What a lovely leg," he said. "And beautiful foot." He tried to right himself, but lost what little balance he had and slid to the floor between her legs, facing up. "And what phenomenal pan—" He didn't finish; he had frozen in place.

"Cut that out, you faker," Sis said severely. "Zombie panties don't freak out living men; they're too rotten."

"Sis!" Breanna said. "You're talking normally!"

"The-sis," the woman said. "How many times do I have to tell you? My name is Thesis, after my occupation. I'm writing my dissertation on the origin of the magic spancel."

"Thesis," Breanna said. "You're alive again!"

"Ridiculous! I hate being a zombie, but I've never been one to avoid reality. I'll thank you not to tease me further. It's cruel, and I'm hardly in the mood."

"Look at your body," Breanna said. "Your legs."

"Why should I? I hate seeing my wasted limbs." Nevertheless, Thesis glanced down at herself, and froze.

For her legs were full-fleshed and shapely. Above them, her clothing had become fresh and clean, shaped by a torso of nymphly proportions. Farther up, her face had assumed firm beauty, framed by lustrously flowing hair.

"Look in the mirror," Breanna said.

Thesis wadded the spancel into a ball in one fist. She strode lithely across the room to gaze into the mirror hanging on the wall. "That can't be me. It's alive. Is this a magic mirror?"

"No."

Something significant had certainly happened. Clio needed to get to the bottom of it. "You do seem to have been restored to full life, Thesis. What is this about a spancel? In fact, what is a spancel?"

"That is complicated to explain. Suffice to say it is a most remarkable artifact."

E stirred. "What happened? Why am I on the floor?"

Sherlock went to him, helping him up. "You tripped and fell. Right through her—her spancel. You saw up under her skirt and freaked out, as any man would."

"But she's a zombie!"

"Not anymore. She transformed back to her living state."

"How could that be? Zombies are goners. Everyone knows that."

"Especially the zombies," Thesis agreed, turning back toward him. "But it seems I did transform. My flesh is firm." She felt her own arm, verifying. "I apologize for calling you a faker. You did see live panties."

E gazed at her. "I love you!"

"Oh, no! So you do. Darn."

"What are you talking about?" Breanna asked. "Panties freak men, they don't generate love, at least not instantly."

"The spancel," Thesis said. "I see I'd better explain after all. It is made, if I must be graphic, by cutting a narrow band of flesh from a man, all around his body in a continuous loop. If you start at his head, it takes a ribbon of skin and hair, proceeds down past his ear, along his shoulder, down his arm, around every finger lengthwise—"

"His skin?" Sherlock asked incredulously. "That band of skin is gone?"

"Exactly. Then back up the inside of his arm, down his side, down the outside of his leg, around the toes similarly, back up inside the leg, through the crotch—"

"Doesn't it hurt?" Clio asked, appalled.

"Of course. He is screaming all the time. That enhances the magic. It follows down his other leg, then up again, to his arm, and finally back to his head. So you have the complete outline of the man, in one thin band. The spancel."

Appalled, Clio still had to ask. "And what is the purpose of this horrible artifact?"

"It's magical. When passed around any person, it makes that person fall instantly and hopelessly in love with the person holding the spancel. So when this man fell through the loop—" She glanced again at E. "What's your name?"

"Zaven."

"But you said it was E," Clio protested. "Mister E."

"That was because I couldn't remember my real name. Now true love has restored it to me."

"It's not true love," Thesis said. "It's the mischief of the spancel. You passed through it and it made you love me. What's worse, I don't know the antidote. I haven't completed my research on it."

"I don't care what you call it," Zaven said. "I love you utterly and eternally."

"But you have to understand, the feeling is not mutual. I regret your accident, but I have a research project to complete." She returned to the mirror to touch up her hair. "In fax, Iz besser be on my zway now."

"Thesis!" Breanna cried. "You're reverting!

The woman stared at her mirror image. It showed her legs and arms wrinkling and crusting, and her full fresh torso wilting. "Oo, noo!"

"I love you anyway," Zaven said gallantly. He went to put his arm around her shoulders.

Her shoulders lifted. Her body freshened. "I'm beautiful again!"

"Always, in my eyes."

"His talent!" Sherlock exclaimed. "Restoring zombies!"

Thesis and Zaven turned together to look at him. "Can that be so?" Zaven said in sheer or nearly sheer wonder.

"But it's temporary," Sherlock said. "Or at least limited. You have to remain close to your subject or the effect wears off."

Thesis nodded. "So it seems I do need you, Zaven. There is only one thing to do."

"No, don't revert to zombie!" he cried. "Let me stay with you! I promise not to interfere with your research."

"Hold this," she said, handing him the spancel.

"I don't understand."

"You don't need to. Shake it out into a loop."

He obeyed, still protesting. "I just want to be with you and help you do whatever you want to do."

"Now pass it over my body."

He paused, catching on. Then he put the loop carefully over her head and passed it on down her body. When it reached her feet, she stepped out of it. "Now I love you too. We'll do everything together." She embraced him and kissed him passionately. "And I do mean everything."

He seemed about to float away. "How fast can we get married?"

"We have a zombie chaplain," Breanna said. "If you care for that kind of service."

"We do," they said almost together. Because, Clio realized, it was convenient and fast.

Zaven handed the spancel to Clio. "I don't think we'll need this anymore. I now know my destiny."

Clio looked at the compass. The blue arrow pointed right to the spancel. It must always have been that, rather than the zombie woman. That was what she had come for.

"It seems you do," Clio agreed, folding the spancel and fitting it carefully into a free pocket. At this rate she was running out of pockets.

Then she realized that there was still a problem. "Thesis, you are researching the origin of the spancel. Don't you still need it for that?"

"Yes, but I can no longer carry it. It can't remain long in contact with a person it has enchanted; the magic reflection would damage it. So someone else will have to carry it, and I'll come along. If that's all right."

It had to be all right, because the blue arrow said she needed it. The permutations of the directions of the arrow were devious, but had to be followed. "Yes. But I hope your research can be wrapped up soon."

"Very soon," Thesis agreed. "Now that I have my life back, thanks to my beloved." She kissed Zaven again.

Would the spancel do that for her, with Sherlock? Was that why she had been directed to it? The notion was intriguing. But she didn't have to take any hasty action, as long as the spancel remained in her possession. If she used it on herself, she wouldn't be able to carry it anymore, so it was best to wait.

Within the hour there was a brief wedding ceremony attended mostly by zombies. Then Zaven and Thesis returned to her zombie chamber.

"I love a good romance," Breanna said, mopping up a tear.

"So do I," Clio said, mopping her own.

"We'll have to let them be for the night. I remember how it was with Justin. We—" Her eye fell on Ciriana. "Were busy. Tomorrow you can be on your way. I'll assign a room for you." Breanna paused. "You *are* a couple?"

"We can share a room," Sherlock said. "With Ciriana."

"Oh—one of those slow difficult romances?"

"So it seems," Clio agreed.

"It was that way, too, with Justin, at first. He was a tree and I was underage. But once those things changed, we really stirred up the storks." She smiled reminiscently.

They had a nice room for the night. When Ciriana slept, they talked, briefly. "I could use the spancel, once Thesis' research is done."

"No."

"No?"

"I want you to love me, if you do, because it is the natural thing for you to do. That will happen only if it makes practical and emotional sense to you."

"If I don't die first!" she flared.

"I'm sorry," he said, hurt.

"No, I'm sorry. I shouldn't have said that. Of course you're right. It has to be natural. But we do have a time limit, whatever it is."

"We do," he agreed. "It's a gamble. I hate gambling, but it is the way it must be."

"And the way you saved the Acquaintance Ship. I remain unsettled about that."

"So do I," he agreed. "I did what I had to do, but it was beyond what I thought I could do. I worked through reverse wood, but this time I actually converted regular wood to it, at least on a temporary basis."

"Temporary?"

"When the storm abated, the reversal did not continue. The wood reverted to normal. Otherwise there would have been unusual effects as people touched the rail."

He was right. He had done something special, for the time required. "This strikes me as more than mere power over reverse wood."

"Or at least a broader power over it. To conjure it, transform it, limit it—it's all reverse wood."

"What about when I got doused by Lethe Elixir?"

"I must have touched a chip of reverse wood to that, to reverse its effect."

"I suppose." She remained less than satisfied, but what other explanation was there? "Talents vary in strength. Yours still seems to be growing."

"At least when I get desperate."

On that unsettled note, they held hands and slept.

Next day they set off on a new blue arrow direction, with the addition of Thesis to their party. This time they had a new kind of transportation: a huge zombie sphinx. It didn't talk, it just walked, but that seemingly slow amble covered ground at a phenomenal rate.

"Does anyone have any idea where we're going?" Clio asked.

"Surely to Castle Roogna, and Princess Ida," Thesis answered. "Thence to planet Ptero. This is where Morgan le Fay resides."

"Who?"

"She is a nefarious Sorceress with much evil on her atrophied conscience. She made the spancel."

"I am in a position to know of all Magicians and Sorceresses who are or have been active in Xanth," Clio said carefully. "How is it I do not know of her?"

"Well, she's Mundane."

"But there's no magic in Mundania."

"There's very little magic there now. But there was more in the past. Morgan le Fay dates from more than a thousand years in Mundania's past. She was the fairy half-sister of King Arthur, and used the spancel to enchant him so that he summoned his illegitimate son Mordred with her. Both he and Morgan were nothing but trouble for him, and finally succeeded in destroying him. After that there was no mischief remaining for her to do there, and the magic was diminishing, so she departed. She hasn't been active in Xanth. In fact she's been in hiding, and was not pleased when my researches uncovered her presence."

"Inactive," Clio said. "That explains it."

"Does her displeasure have anything to do with your becoming a zombie?" Sherlock inquired shrewdly.

"Everything," Thesis said. "But I was not willing to be balked, so close to the completion of my project."

"What happened? She shouldn't have power in Xanth, if she's just a spirit on Ptero."

"She doesn't. But there are those who owe her favors. One was a demon. He fashioned himself into a pillow on a bush, and placed himself in my way. I harvested him, took him inside, and slept with my head on him. When I was asleep, he turned over and smothered my face. I was caught by surprise, and died before I could free myself." Thesis smiled grimly. "Now I have a long hat pin to use to stab any other pillow demon. But I was already dead, and the best I could do was fight to retain the half-life of a zombie. I lost much of a year, and wandered aimlessly for some time, retaining only the spancel, until Castle Zombie took me in. It was very frustrating to be unable to communicate my situation to them."

"I'll try to help you to never be frustrated again," Zaven said, kissing her.

"That will certainly help," she said, kissing him back. Clio tried not to wince; she wished so much she could have a relationship like that, freed of all reservations.

"So why are you—and we—going to Morgan?" Sherlock asked. "Won't she just try to kill us all?"

"I doubt it. She is devious and subtle. She doesn't like to show her hand directly. She'll more likely try to hide, or to persuade us to desist. But I mean to deliver the spancel to her, and be done with it."

"Why take it to her?" Clio asked.

"Because it is only through the spancel that she can track me or anyone else, beyond Ptero. Once she has it back, she will have no power in Xanth."

"Couldn't you simply throw it away?" Sherlock asked.

"An invaluable magic artifact like that? Never. It must be disposed of properly. Otherwise someone else might find it."

"How did the spancel get into Xanth?" He seemed to have a genius for relevant questions.

"That I don't know. It's one of the last missing pieces of the puzzle of it. She used it on King Arthur, then it disappears from the record. I was able to locate it only by my ability to orient on foreign magic."

"You can locate non-Xanth magic?" Sherlock asked.

"That's my talent, limited as it is. But it does help in my research. I didn't know what the spancel was when I found it; thereafter I researched, and learned a good deal. My best conjecture is that someone else brought it to Xanth, then lost it. It must have been lost for a thousand years. But once I took it, Morgan was able to track me, and knew I was investigating its origin, which meant I would find her. So she stopped me. Until Zaven restored me." She kissed him again.

And now Clio was involved with the spancel and its mystery. This time she didn't need to guess what danger she might encounter; it was Morgan le Fay. But how could this possibly relate to her own mission of finding the Currant, the red berry? Her quest had been remarkably devious and dangerous, and she still had no idea of its ending, except that it might literally be the death of her.

Sherlock took her hand and squeezed it. That made her feel better, illogical as that might be.

By midday they hove into sight of Castle Roogna.

"We've been here before," Clio remarked.

"Perhaps you have," Sherlock said. "I have not, since associating with you."

"And neither have we," Zaven said.

"That's right: I have, but I was alone, then with the dragons."

"Lets hope that there is strength in numbers."

They were going to face a hostile foreign Sorceress. Numbers were unlikely to help much.

The three little Princesses came out to greet them, appearing on the back of the sphinx. "Back again, Muse?" Melody asked brightly.

"Yes, I—"

"With new friends?" Harmony added.

"Yes, Sherlock,—"

"To see Aunt Ida," Rhythm concluded.

"Zaven, Thesis, and Ciriana," Clio finished.

"Oh, a child!" Melody exclaimed, delighted.

"You don't need to take her to Ptero," Harmony said.

"Come with us," Rhythm told Ciriana. "We've got eye scream." She took the child's hand, and the four of them vanished.

"But—" Clio started, in vain.

"She'll be in good hands, I'm sure," Sherlock said. "Did you really want to take her to Ptero?"

"No, actually. In fact, there's surely no need for you to risk yourself there either. We'll just return the spancel to Morgan, and then I'll see where the arrow points."

"Let you face an evil Sorceress alone? I think not."

"As you wish." She really appreciated his loyalty.

"I wouldn't care to risk you either," Thesis told Zaven. "But I can't stand to be apart from you." They kissed.

"And you'd revert to zombie without me," he said. They kissed again.

Something snapped in Clio. She turned to Sherlock, hauled his face in to her, and kissed him soundly.

The three Princesses with Ciriana in tow reappeared. "OoOo, we saw!" Melody cried.

"You kissed!" Harmony agreed.

"You smacked him!" Rhythm said.

"Right on the face," Ciriana concluded.

"Now just a—" Clio began. But they were already gone in a cloud of giggles.

"They aren't taking long about educating Ciriana," Sherlock said. "Sneaking peeks must be a favorite palace occupation."

The sphinx came to a halt and settled down so they could dismount. There was a rope ladder for them to use to reach the ground. The four of them climbed down. Then the sphinx rose and walked back toward Castle Zombie. In barely a moment and a half it was out of sight.

"Do you know the mechanics of going to Ptero?" Clio asked Thesis.

"Oh, yes, I learned that when I researched Morgan le Fay. I have never been there myself, however."

"It's actually just a soul visit," Clio said. "But it will seem quite physical. You can't actually die there, but otherwise your experience will be real."

"Yes, I'm sure. We'll return the spancel and be done with it. I hope, however, that Morgan will condescend to answer a few questions for my dissertation."

"Why would she do that?"

"Evil Magicians and Sorceresses crave attention. I'll give her full credit for making the spancel, and detail where she got it, if she provides the information. She may want that. If not—" Thesis shrugged. "I'll write what I have. It isn't as though my life has no other interests." She kissed Zaven.

Clio had to marvel. The two had spent what had surely been a thorough night fulfilling their love, but still it spilled over into the day. She really was jealous of that surplus emotion. Yet so far she simply hadn't been able to experience it herself.

She pondered that as they walked into the castle. Sherlock was certainly a worthy man, and he loved her. Why couldn't she let herself go and love him similarly?

"Why hello again, Princess," Princess Ida said as they arrived at her door.

Princess: that was it. Despite what she had told Sherlock, she was a princess, and in her secret heart wanted to marry a prince or Magician. Logically she didn't have to, but her early conditioning was a belief system, not a logic system. It would rather see her a spinster, than married to a commoner. "Darn!" she swore, and small blue sparks flew.

Four people stared at her.

Clio felt herself turning medium to bright red. "Oh, I—I'm sorry," she stammered. "I had a chain of thought, and it overcame me. I didn't mean you, Princess Ida."

"Of course not," Ida agreed. She was a very agreeable person. "The dragons told me."

"Told you what?" Clio asked, alarmed.

"I'm a princess too. I suffer the same reservation, and the same annoyance. I don't want to remain single forever, yet I continue to age without marrying."

She really did understand. Clio was overcome. "Oh, it's awful!"

Then they were hugging each other, and crying, while Sherlock looked on bewildered and Zaven and Thesis kissed, oblivious to the rest of the universe.

In due course they untangled. "It's a princess thing," Ida explained to Sherlock. He nodded, but surely remained uneasy.

"Theoretically there is a Magician from long ago, in the Brain

Coral's pool, who is my ideal match," Ida said. "I am told our children will have little moons like mine. But so far that Magician has not emerged, and I don't know when he ever will. It is an unkind wait."

"Oh, yes," Clio agreed.

The three Princesses appeared, with Ciriana in tow. "She needs to stay with you," Melody said, a bit tersely.

"We're sorry," Harmony added.

"But it's necessary," Rhythm concluded.

They vanished, leaving Ciriana looking somewhat unhappy. Clio went to her. "What happened, dear?"

"I said a word," the child confided tearfully.

So the nullification wasn't perfect. It seemed there was only so much a reverse wood chip could do. "That's all right; you can come with us after all." Though Clio wasn't notably easy about that, either.

Ida reviewed the procedure for the others, then let them sniff from her vial of elixir. Soon they were on their way to Ptero. They landed in a wilderness area and took stock as their bits of soul solidified to form replicas of themselves.

"The rules of magic are different here," Clio said. "Colors vary according to direction. Blue is north, red is south, green is west, yellow is east. Also, when you travel east you go into the past, and west takes you into the future. You age accordingly. Sherlock and I can handle several decades, but you young lovers can't. So let's hope that my compass arrow brought us to the time where Morgan le Fay dwells."

It had. The blue arrow pointed south, and there was a path there. It led right into a comic strip.

"One more thing," Clio said grimly. "The comic strips. They are bands separating the various sections of the planet, and they contain the most egregious awful festering puns. Stay out of them if at all possible."

Then a path opened, through the comic strip. The massed puns were squeezed to the sides, groaning in protest. The blue arrow pointed toward it. Was it a trick? Well, there was one way to find out.

Clio took Ciriana's hand and led the way through the strip, following the path. No puns impinged. They strained at the sides, eager to get at the visitors, but were restrained.

Beyond was a neat cottage, similar to those on the Acquaintance Ship. Before its door stood a comely older woman in a royal cloak. That had to be Morgan le Fay.

"Welcome to my abode," she said. "I saw you coming."

"Beware," Drew said privately. "She's a mean person."

"Thank you for providing a way past the comic strip," Clio said, though she was uncertain of the woman's motivation.

"Unfortunately it is a one-way path," Morgan said.

They turned to look. The comic strip had closed in behind them. They were trapped, perhaps.

"She won't let you go," Drew said.

"We'll see about that," Sherlock said.

"We have come to return your spancel to you," Clio said. "We have no other business we know of, though if you care to answer some questions, Thesis would appreciate it." She drew the spancel from her pocket and proffered it to the woman.

"Thank you, Muse," Morgan said, taking the spancel. "It is good to have this back at long last."

"How did you come to lose it?"

The woman sighed. "I got so involved with Arthur that I forgot about it. I conjured myself back home before I remembered. By that time it was too late; I couldn't breach the king's castle defenses a second time. Fortunately I had what I had come for: my baby. Perhaps a servant threw the spancel out, not knowing its nature. Servants tend to be ignorant louts."

That seemed to be enough of an answer. "Thank you," Clio said. "We'll be leaving now."

"Not just yet, I think."

Clio had been afraid of that. "I don't think we have further business here."

"Ah, but you do. Did you think I would summon you here only to send you away, my purpose unfulfilled?"

"Summon?" Clio asked, feeling a chill. "What purpose?"

"I am at present unable to go to Xanth proper, having lost my mortal body. I need a new body." She looked at Thesis. "Yours should do."

"You can't have it," Thesis said.

Morgan's smile was cruel. "And why not?"

"Three reasons: I am not through with it myself. I am a zombie. And I used the spancel on it."

The Sorceress considered. "The first reason is of no account to me. The second I doubt; you look fully alive. But the third—you evidently learned more about the spancel than I thought."

"I did. The spancel will not remain long with a person it has enchanted. You would have to give it up, and with it, much of your power."

Morgan considered. "Of course I could make a new one, once I got a physical body again, and found a suitable man to enchant and operate on. But it would be a hassle, and his screaming might attract attention. So you do seem to have protected yourself rather cunningly, my dear."

"Thank you," Thesis said coldly.

"She's afraid, with reason," Drusie said.

"You're like the Sea Hag!" Clio exclaimed. "You take other people's bodies and degrade them!"

The Sorceress nodded. "Among other things. It is an ancient technique known to a few of the favored. But hardly my only one. A body is not an end in itself, merely a means to power."

"A despicable power!"

The Sorceress's eye fell on Ciriana. "No you don't!" Clio said, holding the child close.

"She is too young for my purpose." Morgan looked at Zaven. "So I may need to utilize a representative to do my business in Xanth, such as locating and securing a suitable young woman's body for me to take over. You should do for that; you are not handsome, but my enchantment can make you so."

"I used the spancel too," Zaven said.

The woman's eyes narrowed. Clio did not need the little dragon's input to know that she was furious. "So you have, I see now. So she protected you too. I underestimated her."

"You sure did," Zaven said. "I love her."

"Of course." Morgan turned to Clio. "So it seems it will have to be you, though it will be a problem to abate your notoriety and your curse."

"You can't have my body either," Clio said more bravely than she felt. Nevertheless, she nudged Ciriana toward Thesis, so that she would be clear of this encounter.

"Oh? Why not?"

"Because I will unwind anything you do to me. You can't control me."

Morgan's hand shot out and caught a hank of Clio's hair. She yanked Clio forward with surprising strength. A stiletto appeared in her other hand, the needle-sharp point orienting on Clio's right eye. "Really?"

Clio wound it back to just before the grab. "Really," she said.

The hand shot out again. This time Clio knocked it aside before it reached her hair. The stiletto appeared in the other hand. Clio's other hand grabbed it and shoved it toward the woman's own flesh.

"Interesting," Morgan remarked, her wrist twisting out of Clio's grasp. "Yet there are other ways."

"We really must go now," Clio said. She did not like the Sorceress at all.

Morgan looked at Sherlock. "Now here is a spectacular prospect. A mild-mannered, unassuming, unprepossessing, decent Magician. Fortune has abruptly smiled on me."

"I'm not a Magician," Sherlock said.

"And modest too. Oh, we shall go far together, you and I. Once I break you in."

"And I'm not going anywhere with you."

"Yet I think you will be amenable to persuasion." The Sorceress's outline shifted subtly, exuding rank sex appeal.

"I doubt it. I love Clio."

"Of course. Love is a marvelously motivating force. But yours is not inspired by the spancel."

"That's right. It's natural. So you won't persuade me to do anything to harm her."

The cruel smile showed again. "We shall see."

"Danger!" the two dragons cried together.

Suddenly the floor around Clio faded out. She was standing on a circular plate barely wider than her feet, with a gulf descending on every side. But she wasn't actually being hurt, so she didn't wind it back. She wanted to learn more of the nature of this ploy, so as not to be caught by it again, whatever it might be.

"Now here is the situation," Morgan said to Sherlock. "Your beloved stands perched above a dreadful abyss. A counterspell blocks her limited talent; she can't wind her way back out of this one. In a moment her support will crumble and she will fall into the horror below. However, I do not wish you to be damaged. If you join her, I shall have to cancel the spell and spare both of you while I ponder my next effort. I advise you to let her go; I can do much more for you than she can." The blatant sex appeal intensified.

This had gone far enough. Clio tried to wind it back—and could not. The Sorceress had cleverly made her demonstrate her talent, then countered it with her own superior magic. Ordinary folk could not compete with Magicians or Sorceresses.

"It's a trick!" Drew said.

The platform crumbled. Clio screamed as she lost her balance and started to fall into the depths. She saw Thesis and Ciriana staring with horror.

Sherlock leaped toward her. Morgan flung a loop out before him. He passed through it and caught hold of Clio as she dropped.

Then they both found themselves on the floor, clinging to each other. The gulf was gone.

Ciriana was crying, and Thesis was trying to comfort her, but lacked enough assurance.

"It was illusion," Drusie said.

"Yes, it was illusion, you little reptile snot," Morgan said. "She was never in physical danger. But her curse is not restricted to that. She has fallen prey to the emotional danger instead."

"What are you talking about?" Sherlock demanded as the two of them got back to their feet.

"Do you recognize this?" the Sorceress asked, holding up the loop.

"The spancel!" Thesis cried.

"He passed through it," Zaven said.

"So he did," Morgan agreed with satisfaction. "I wielded it, he went through it. I trust you understand what that means."

Clio looked at Sherlock, appalled. "It put you in love with her!"

Sherlock didn't answer or look at her. He was plainly ashamed.

"It doesn't mean he hates you, dear," the Sorceress said with thinly veiled cruelty. "Merely that his passion now answers to me. He will serve me loyally, because he can do nothing else, and in time, if he does well, I will reward him in my fashion. I might even marry him, once I have a physical body again."

"Oh, Sherlock," Clio said, sorry for him despite her own numb loss.

"After all, he is worthy. I like him already. Very much, in fact." Morgan's smile was almost tender. "But business before pleasure. Sherlock, take these people back to Xanth. Let the couple go; their usefulness is past. Take Clio and the brat to the next rendezvous her arrow indicates."

"You're letting me continue my mission?" Clio asked, amazed.

"Not exactly, my dear. It is that I don't like to soil my hands with blood. I prefer to leave that sort of thing to Litho. Since your next appointment is with him anyway, it behooves me to let nature take its course, as it were. That will leave me unimplicated, and free Sherlock of any lingering commitment he may feel to you. Then he can attend to my whims without distraction."

The witch had been way ahead of them all along. She had tricked them and won what she needed: Sherlock's commitment to her sadistic interests.

"Can I save her?" Sherlock asked.

"Why how kind of you, Magician. You do not wish to see her die?"

"Yes, I do not. She is a good person."

"Suppose I were to take her body, after all? Would that satisfy you?"

Sherlock considered. "I'm not sure. She doesn't look like you."

"Oh that can be fixed. I will enchant any body I take to look like me in my prime. Have no concern." Then Morgan's voice sharpened. "I will consider the matter. But now, go to Litho. By the time you reach him, I will have decided, and you will of necessity be satisfied with my decision."

"Of course," Sherlock murmured.

The house and Sorceress vanished, leaving them standing in a glade surrounded by comic strip. They were on their own.

17
LITHO

Clio knew they could simply let their soul bodies dissolve and float back to Xanth; return was easier than traveling out, because their souls remained connected and could readily find their bodies. But she remained stunned by the awfulness of the trap they had fallen into. The Danger of the Day had taken Sherlock from her. While she didn't quite love him, she was close, and now that prospect was gone. He remained a decent, worthy man—just not one who was in love with her. That was painful. She needed time to adjust to the ugly new reality.

Also, the blue arrow pointed through the strip. That suggested that her business here on Ptero wasn't finished.

"What's so bad about a comic strip, really?" Zaven asked. "So it's crowded with puns. So are parts of Xanth."

Clio was in no hurry to meet her next engagement. She knew of no Litho, but evidently he was a formidable entity. Morgan thought he would kill her. Well, did she really have much reason left to live? She had fouled up her quest and her prospect for love. Maybe it was time to let her destiny catch up with her. She didn't have to race to it. So she made only a token effort to dissuade the man. "You don't have to face it. The spancel has been returned; you and Thesis are free. Just let yourselves dissolve and you'll be back in Xanth."

"No, I'm curious too," Thesis said. "It would be a shame to come here and not see the sights."

As if it were a honeymoon tour. "It seems to be time for a demonstration," Clio said. "Remember, all you have to do is plow straight ahead, and you'll be out of it soon." She set the example by taking Ciriana's hand and stepping into the comic strip. Let them find out for themselves.

A young woman appeared before her. "Hello. My name is Annie Mae, and I'll be your guide for this tour."

It was starting already. Anime, in an animate strip.

"Thank you," Clio said. "Be sure you introduce yourself to the others."

"They are new to comic strips?"

"Yes. They want to fully appreciate this one." Clio felt almost guilty.

"I'll make sure they do," Annie Mae said with a somewhat predatory smile. She passed Clio by and went to intercept the couple.

There was the sound of bells. A man walked by. The base of his trouser legs was quite wide. It was from them the bells were ringing.

"Bell-bottom trousers," Annie Mae explained.

Clio stifled her groan. Zaven, behind her, didn't quite manage to. He was learning.

She plowed on—and almost banged into another man. Thesis, following close behind her, did crash. It was a full body-to-body collision, face-to-face. Thesis was shapely; this was bound to give the man an idea.

But he backed off. "Sorry, Miss—I have no interest in the stork."

Flustered, Thesis asked, "Who are you?"

"Peter, Miss—Salt Peter."

"That's all right," Thesis said uncomfortably.

"But my sister Afro is very interested," Peter said. "She's something else."

"Who?"

"Afro Disiac. She makes anyone interested."

"Oh." Thesis was learning too.

A weird cylindrical creature in curved metallic plates approached them. "Hello," it said. "My name's Dillo. Armored Dillo." Then it tripped over a rock and dented its armor. "Oh, my rumpled steel skin!" it moaned.

This time Ciriana groaned. She too was learning.

Meanwhile Clio was moving on, still holding Ciriana's hand. The far side couldn't be much farther. But she encountered a swarm of buzzing insects. They formed a cloud around her head, alarming her. "Get away, you bees!"

A big one hovered before her face. It was in a tiny royal robe, and wore a miniature crown: the queen. "We're not B's," she buzzed severely. "We're A's, the superior ancestors of B's."

"Ugh," Sherlock said.

"We're the very best of our kind," the queen continued. "The B's are second-rate descendants, and if you do business with C's or D's or any of the lower grades, you'll really get stung."

"We'll avoid them," Clio said.

Still the A bee hovered before her. "And be sure to mind your own bee's wax hereafter," she admonished.

"By all means," Sherlock said.

The queen, satisfied, flew on to address Zaven and Thesis.

But they weren't through with the letter bugs. A swarm of G's appeared, wearing stringlike clothing. "No thanks," Clio said.

"But you need us," a G protested. "I am Biolo-G."

"And I'm Geolo-G," another said.

Indeed, they were all different: Effi, Ecolo, Chronolo, Proctolo, Apolo, and others. And all wearing their G-strings.

"We certainly do need you," Sherlock said. "Congratulations on a fine job."

Satisfied, they buzzed on. Clio made a mental note: Sherlock had a certain touch with Psycholo-G.

"Groan," Drew told her.

Now there was a sign: SLOW—SCHOOL ZONE. The sign was in the shape of a lightbulb.

Clio paused to let the others catch up. "Do I have to go to school?" Ciriana asked, concerned.

"No, dear. This is just another pun of some sort."

"I don't get it," Sherlock said.

Zaven and Thesis caught up. "We've seen about enough," he said. "We're ready to leave the strip now."

Annie reappeared. "Oh, but you must see this. It's a school for our brightest. This way."

There seemed to be no choice but to follow her. She led them to a tall, thin, round building.

"But that's a lighthouse," Thesis said.

"Yes, it's our school for lightbulbs," Annie said.

Clio suppressed her groan. "But a lighthouse is supposed to be to warn ships in the sea."

"What sea?"

And of course there was no sea.

They came to the lighthouse, and saw the children. They were all lightbulbs. "We have all the best and brightest," Annie said proudly. "They are very enlightened. When they get light enough, they float off into the sky. They are real stars. You can see them twinkling at night."

Sherlock did not quite manage to hold his groan in.

"And of course when you get a bright idea, one of them is there to flash over your head," Annie continued.

"Thank you for that illuminating information," Sherlock said. Clio wanted to kick his ankle, but realized that wasn't the most brilliant idea.

"Oh!" Annie said, flattered. She glanced halfway appraisingly at him.

"Perhaps we'll meet again," Sherlock said.

What was he doing? He had been ensorcelled into love with Morgan le Fay. Was he trying to set up a little something on the side? That hardly seemed like him, but there was no telling how much the spancel had scrambled his feelings. Maybe he was simply trying to charm Annie into getting them out of the strip faster.

They moved wearily on. Clio had the dubious satisfaction of knowing that the others were just as turned off as she was. Of course they weren't lightbulbs.

Clio saw the edge of the comic strip, but there was one more thing in the way. It was a table with a small cake on it, and a sign BITE ME. "No thanks," she said, trying to go around the table. But it extended to bar her way, and the cake slid toward her. It seemed she couldn't avoid it.

Then someone else blundered up, a fat woman, evidently a tourist. "I'm hungry." She took the cake and bit into it.

And turned green. Then red. Then blue. Her clothes went baggy. "I'm dying!" the woman exclaimed.

"No, you're dyeing," Clio said, catching on. "That's a dye-it, turning you different colors."

"And diet," Thesis said. "Making you thin."

"Groan!" the woman said, and blundered on.

Clio finally managed to get around the table and lunged for the edge. But Ciriana tripped and fell, scratching her arm, and causing Clio to fall too. "Owww!"

A little cat ran up. It produced medical instruments, cleaned off the scratch, bandaged it, and put away its equipment. Then it scampered away. The child was satisfied; her arm no longer hurt.

"What was that?" Clio asked, dazed.

"A first-aid kit," Sherlock said, helping her up. "Annie told me."

Evidently he had spent a bit more time with Annie Mae. Clio realized she had no business feeling jealous; his love was no longer hers anyway.

They crossed the border and the puns were gone. So was the bandage on Ciriana's arm; it was mere pun stuff. In another moment Zaven and Thesis emerged, looking disgusted. "Point made," Zaven said. "Stay out of comic strips."

"Dear, let's go home now," Thesis said. "We have seen more than enough here."

"Well, actually—"

She stepped into him and kissed him ardently. Little hearts orbited them. "And there's a child present. Let's get alone." Some of the hearts bore an odd resemblance to storks.

"Oh. Of course."

They embraced and dissolved into vapor. It expanded rapidly, diffusing through the area, and faded out.

All that, simply because each had passed through the spancel. As had Sherlock, unfortunately.

A young man approached. "You folk look as if you got caught in a comic strip," he said.

"We did," Clio said. "We'll recover."

"Do you need to go anywhere? I can guide you."

"But if we wanted to go east, you'd soon get too young," Clio said.

"No, my talent is immunity to the time change. I can go anywhere on Ptero. That's why I'm a guide."

That did make sense. "It was a good idea."

"Yes. Prince Anomie thought of it. His talent is bad ideas, but he got some reverse wood, and now he gets good ideas."

"Anomie," Clio said, remembering. "The one who married Princess Melody, after he stopped being the Dastard?"

"Melody's only eight years old!" Sherlock protested.

"Not here," she told him. "She's any age she wants to be, and surely adult. Remember, time is geography."

"I would like to meet them," Clio said. "But as it happens, I'm on a special mission."

"That's all right. Where are you going?"

Clio looked at the compass. "West."

"That's toward Castle Roogna, about fifteen years."

"Thank you."

The man moved on, and they walked west. But Sherlock paused. "I realize that geography is time, but isn't fifteen years a pretty far distance?"

Clio halted. "Yes, it is. We don't want to have to walk it."

"Maybe I can arrange something." He walked back to the comic strip.

"What are you thinking of?" Clio demanded.

"Annie may be willing to help." He stood at the edge and put his arm across the line. "Annie!"

Annie Mae appeared. "You want me to strip?" She put her hand to her dress. "This is a comic strip, of course, but you'll have to come inside."

"I must be candid," he said. "Much as I might like to see you strip, my love belongs to another. But I'm willing to trade for help."

Her eyes narrowed with calculation. She evidently had a notion how to compete for love. "Trade what for what help?"

"We need to go to Castle Roogna."

"That's fifteen years To."

Clio remembered that To was their way of saying the future; the past was From.

"Yes. So we need help getting there efficiently. If you can tell us how to do it, I'll give you a kiss."

Could this possibly work? Clio wondered if Sherlock's common sense had been altered along with his love.

"Three kisses. There are three of you."

She was going for it!

"A kiss and a hug. One's a child."

"A kiss, a hug, and a caress."

"Done."

They stood at the edge of the comic strip, and he reached inside, she outside, for the hug. Their faces came together for the kiss. Her hand squeezed his rear.

"That's not a caress," Ciriana said. "That's a feel."

Oops—the child's immunity to the Adult Conspiracy was manifesting again. Clio realized that it was like Zaven's zombie-restoring effect: it lasted only in his vicinity. Sherlock had reversed the child's immunity with reverse wood, but when she got too far from him, it came back. This was an unfortunate complication; how were they ever going to find a suitable home for her?

The two completed the hug, kiss, and whatever, and separated. Annie seemed dazed; it seemed she really liked Sherlock's attention. Clio could appreciate that. Then Annie disappeared.

"So what did you accomplish?" Clio asked, trying not to be cutting, as she wasn't that kind of person.

"She's fetching a step ladder."

"A what?"

"It's a pun, of course. A ladder that steps."

"A step ladder," Clio agreed. "What good will that be to us?"

"Puns can have more than one interpretation."

She let it be. Either the thing would help, or it wouldn't. Would Annie Mae really enable Sherlock to go far away with another woman, or had she simply stolen a kiss?

The ladder appeared. It was standing up and walking by twisting so that one side advanced while the other held the ground. It was a highly wavy walk, but it was making progress. It came to the edge of the comic strip and stopped, mostly out of it.

"The ladder will step you to the comic strip closest to Castle Roogna," Annie said. "Just step from this side to that side."

"Thank you," Sherlock said.

"If your true love ever dumps you, you know where to find me," Annie said somewhat wistfully. "Just come to the edge of Sunset Strip and say my name."

"I don't think she'll dump me," he said. "But I will keep you in mind."

"Will this really work?" Clio asked.

"Yes, it will," Drew said. "We read Annie's mind. Sherlock reversed her attitude, so that instead of leading us into mischief she's helping."

"Sherlock is accomplishing a lot," Clio remarked, mostly to herself.

Sherlock stepped onto the ladder on the strip side. He climbed to the top, worked his way over to the other side, and disappeared.

"He's out of range," Drew said. "It stepped him there."

"Your turn, dear," Clio said.

"$$$$," the child replied. Yes, Sherlock was out of range. She climbed and went over, and vanished.

Clio mounted the ladder. It was awkward, but she made it over to the other side. Nothing happened.

She looked around—and there were Sherlock and a mature young woman. Where had *she* come from? "How did you get back here?"

Both laughed. "We didn't. You came here," Sherlock said. "See, there's Castle Roogna." He gestured.

She looked. There was the castle. They were at the edge of a different strip. But she still didn't see Ciriana. "Where's the child?"

"I'm Ciriana," the young woman said. "I'm twenty. We moved west, remember?"

She had aged fifteen years in one step! "I forgot," Clio confessed. "Are you all right? I mean, aging so suddenly must be confusing." Certainly to Clio, if not to Ciriana herself.

"No problem. And now the Adult Conspiracy is irrelevant. I'm Old Enough." She glanced sidelong at Sherlock.

Clio wasn't quite satisfied with this, but thought it best not to argue the case at the moment. "Very well."

"And I do know better, now, than to speak those forbidden words intemperately. I appreciate why they must be kept from children; a person must achieve judgment before power. That is even more true in the case of summoning the stork. Not that I have any immediate plans in that respect. First I shall have to find a good man." Her eyes made half a flick toward Sherlock.

"Let's get on with the mission," Clio said. What was this appeal Sherlock seemed to have for women? The women of the Acquaintance Ship wanted to tempt him there for his soul, but since then other women had been rather obviously attracted to him, including even the Sorceress Morgan le Fay. And of course Clio herself. What had changed?

A dusky young woman approached. "Hello. I'm Kia. My talent is making rain. Does this area need it?"

Clio introduced herself and the others. "It does seem somewhat dry here," she said, looking around. There were bushes and trees, but they were looking thirsty.

"I'll fix that," Kia said. She lifted one hand, and rain began to fall around her. There was no storm, merely a gentle falling from above.

"Perhaps we had better move on before we get wet," Sherlock said.

"Nice meeting you, Kia," Ciriana called as they walked away. The young woman was now standing in a fairly solid, silent shower. The vegetation seemed to appreciate it.

The blue arrow pointed toward the castle, which looked just like the one in Xanth. They walked there, and saw Soufflé the moat monster. He recognized Clio, whose appearance had not changed much, and Sherlock, who now looked to be at the verge of the farther side of middle age, but not Ciriana. But he accepted Clio's vouch for her.

A Princess appeared, full grown at age twenty-three, accompanied by a green man. She had a brown dress, hair, and eyes. "Hello, Clio. Still on your mission to find the red berry?"

"I am, Harmony. I think I have another session with Princess Ida."

"She is expecting you." Harmony looked at Sherlock. "Hello again, Magician."

"I'm not a—"

"And Ciriana. I remember you from when you were five. You were so cute! But that word!"

"I was immune to the Adult Conspiracy. Reverse wood helped stifle it, but it seems I also had to be close to Daddy. His chips seem to lose their power away from him."

Was that really the explanation, Clio wondered? Then what of Getaway and Comealong Golem? They hadn't seemed to be at a disadvantage away from Sherlock.

"We were caught off guard," Harmony said. "We didn't know how to handle it." She glanced sidelong at Sherlock. "I wish you had had the wit to be delivered into my generation."

He laughed. "I never was much of a wit."

Clio was fit to be stifled. Yet another curvy young woman playing up to Sherlock, and this one a princess, yet, in the presence of her evident boyfriend.

"Oh, I am being unprincessly impolite," Harmony said. "This is Borealis. He is destined to be the man for Aurora, the winged mermaid. She was once a blob too."

"A blob?" Clio asked, looking more carefully at the green man.

"I am from a planet made of green goo, some distance up the line," Borealis said. He held up one hand, and it melted into goo. "All creatures there are goo. Fortunately we have the ability to shape ourselves as we wish. When I decided to travel, I assumed the form of a human man. Princess Harmony has been coaching me. When I am manlike enough, I hope to go to Xanth and assume the form of a winged merman, so I can be with Aurora. It seems destined."

Clio remembered how Aurora had come from the world of Cone and occupied a blob in Xanth, shaping it into winged mermaid form.

There were not many of her species. She surely would appreciate a winged merman. "Many dragons have gone from Dragon World to Xanth, animating organic material; you may be able to do the same."

"I am glad to know that," Borealis said.

"But we still need to work on color," Harmony said. "And you'll have to assume the form and practice flying."

"I will, I will," he agreed. They moved off.

They reached Princess Ida's room. There were more amenities. Then they were back on their way along the chain of worlds. The blue arrow facilitated it, so they hardly seemed to stop at individual Idas. They passed a planet-sized blob of green goo; Clio had a notion of its nature now, so wasn't concerned by its Princess Ida's gooey greenness. On they moved.

Until they came to Plane World. This was endlessly wide but shallow, like an infinite pane of glass. They could see through it. On the other side, keeping pace with them, were other people. Beneath Sherlock was a man that resembled him, but seemed somehow arrogant and stupid. Under Ciriana was a woman like her, but looking mean-spirited. And below Clio was a woman like her in outline, but whose bearing was reminiscent of Morgan le Fay.

"This is weird," Ciriana said.

"I don't want to seem paranoid," Sherlock said, "but I don't trust this. Where is this Limbo we're looking for?"

"That's Limo, big Daddy," Ciriana said with half a titter.

He smiled at her. "Limo bean?"

Both of them were joking, getting along well with each other. Clio suppressed yet another wash of unkind jealousy. It was not her business.

Apparently some emotion leaked out, for Ciriana glanced at her. "My heart always belonged to Daddy; you know that. There's no one else like him."

Clio looked at the compass, but the blue arrow had faded out. Apparently they had arrived where they were supposed to be. But what was the point?

"Creature approaching," Drew announced.

It was a huge cat, a virtual panther. Beneath it, on the other side of the glass, ran a young woman. A chip of reverse wood appeared in Sherlock's hand.

"Female and friendly," Drusie said.

The big cat bounded to a halt before them, and transformed into a lithe girl. Simultaneously, the young woman below became a big cat. "Hello. I am Satori, a girl-cat crossbreed. I suspect you're confused about this world."

"We are indeed," Sherlock said. "I am Sherlock, and these are Clio and Ciriana."

Satori nodded. "I see. So I don't suppose you are interested in another of the female purr-suasion." She delivered a feline glance.

Another! Clio could hardly stand it.

"My love is taken," Sherlock agreed. "But we would certainly appreciate learning something about this world."

"Plane World lacks the kind of scenery other worlds may have— mountains, valleys, seas, if you like that type," Satori said. "But it has its compensation. Beneath each person, on the other side of the plane, is his or her polar opposite. A friendly person has an unfriendly opposite, and vice versa. In my case, my girl and cat forms exchange places. Most folk have little or no actual contact with their opposites, so ignore them."

"Thank you," Sherlock said. "That alleviates our confusion."

"You're welcome," Satori said. "Do you plan to stay long? Is there anything I can do for you on an incidental basis?" She turned part way and inhaled.

"We're looking for Litho," Clio said quickly.

A look of horror crossed the girl's face. She transformed back into cat form and bounded rapidly away.

"Something odd here," Sherlock said.

A shadow fell across them. Then a giant stony manlike creature landed on the plane. "Who invokes my name?" he roared. A similar inverted figure appeared below the pane except that it looked benign.

This had to be Litho. Clio was cowed, but did her best to conceal it. "I do. I am Clio, and it seems I have business with you."

"Oh do you!" the mountainous man roared. "I'll crush you like the insignificant mortal worm you are." He took a giant step toward her.

Sherlock stepped faster, getting between them. "I think not, rock head."

Litho halted, staring down at him. "Who the nonsense are you, black mortal?"

"I am Sherlock."

"Eruption!" Litho swore. "Morgan said you were nullified."

"Well, I wasn't. Leave this woman alone."

"What's going on?" Clio asked, baffled.

"As if you don't know, traitorous wench!" Litho said. "You were supposed to be sent to me helpless, not with a Magician to defend you."

"What Magician?"

"I'll be impacted!" Litho said. "She doesn't know."

"I don't know what?"

"That Morgan knew she couldn't keep the Magician if she didn't get rid of you. So she nullified him so I could smash you. But he says—" Litho paused. "Oh, I get it! You're bluffing."

"I am just doing what I have to do," Sherlock said.

"We'll soon make proof of that." Litho swung his huge granite fist down like a pile driver, right at Sherlock's head.

Sherlock did not move. Ciriana screamed.

But when the fist touched Sherlock's head, it shattered. Fragments flew outward. One smacked into Clio's front, stinging her through the cloth. She managed to catch it before it fell. It was just a ragged pebble of no distinction.

But the blue arrow reappeared, pointing to it. This was what she had come for. So she put it in a pocket.

Litho stared at his hand, which was gone. "You weren't bluffing."

"If you are satisfied," Sherlock said, "we'll be satisfied if you simply depart now."

Litho laughed. It sounded like gas hissing from a mountain vent. "You think you have beaten me, you puny excuse for an entity? Know, O foolish one, that I have not yet begun to brawl." His fist reappeared, as stony as before. "Do you know anything about me?" He moved slowly to the side, as if to get around the man.

"We really don't," Sherlock said, moving with similar deliberation to remain between Litho and Clio. "And we're not much interested."

Clio realized that a grim game of maneuvering was occurring. Litho wanted to get at her and destroy her, while Sherlock, amazingly, was preventing it. There was a whole lot more she needed to know about this, especially since this was clearly her Danger of The Day, and her life was at stake. "Yes we are," she said. "What about you?"

"See, even the stupid woman has more wit than you," Litho said, continuing his sneaky march around the circle. "She wants to know."

Sherlock shrugged, continuing his countermovement. It seemed that Litho wanted to distract the man for just an instant, so that he could get at her, but Sherlock was not being fooled.

"Then know, O ignorant hen, that I am the Demon Lithosphere. I was one of the minor Demons of Earth, below the rank of Demon Earth himself, but well above that of the trifling wisps of smoke that call themselves demons today. I was in charge of keeping track of all the rocks and continental plates of the planet. Demon Earth found the lands as seas scattered around the globe, and decreed that some better order should be established. So he set me to pushing all the land together into one big continent called Pangaea. Then he focused on other things, such as the nuisance of pelting rocks from space that pockmarked the surface, and I was left alone to guard the big isle. I got bored and fell asleep, and Pangaea cracked apart and spread back across the globe in ugly fragments. I woke too late to stop it. When Demon Earth discovered this, he was wroth with exceeding wrath, and blasted me into thousands of pieces of D. bris that fell into the neighboring land of Xanth. From these the voles evolved, and maybe other creatures like the goblins; I hardly care. Some of my bones were hurled into the ground of Xanth, where they remain today. But I myself, the essence of me, was cruelly banished to this flat wasteland without tectonic plates, and here I languish until someone helps me to return to the real action."

"Morgan le Fay promised you that!" Clio exclaimed.

"That she did. She has a plan to return to real life herself, and said she would take me with her. But first I had to smash the one who stood in her way. Which I am about to do." Litho suddenly dodged back the other way and shot out his arm toward her. One stone finger touched her.

But Sherlock brought his own hand down as quickly. It brushed the demon's arm, and the arm fragmented. A line of sand fell to the pane. The trick had not worked.

"But she knew I could not do it unless your protection was nullified," Litho continued, his speech and motion coordinating as his arm reformed. "So she said she set out to bind the Magician to her, so that he would not care about you. Evidently she lied, the lady dog."

"She didn't lie," Sherlock said. "She tricked me into jumping through her spancel."

Litho laughed like an avalanche crashing into a hapless river. "Her spancel! I thought she lost that ten centuries ago! How did she get that back?"

"I brought it to her," Clio said.

Now the laugh was like a detonation of boiling smoke from a volcano. "No foolishness in your family, girl! You've got it all! You brought her weapon to her? Ho ho ho!"

Clio saw no point in explaining about the blue arrow. "It was hers."

"So how come you're still balking me?" Litho demanded of Sherlock. "You'll never get close to Morgan unless you do her bidding."

"I don't love her."

"But you said you passed through the spancel. Did someone else hold it?"

"No, she held it. I reversed it."

Litho was so surprised he paused in his stalking. "Is that possible?"

"It is for me. I'm the Magician of Reversal."

Clio began to understand why stray folk had addressed him as Magician, and why women were attracted to him. They had known or sensed his nature, and were drawn to its power. "How did this happen?" she asked, as astonished as Litho.

"It just developed and got stronger with time and practice. I thought it was merely a talent with reverse wood, but then realized that I wasn't conjuring it, I was making it."

"Why didn't you tell me?" Clio demanded.

"Because then Morgan would have known too, and would have found some other way to destroy you. I couldn't risk that."

"Then what's with Morgan?" Litho asked.

"I fear she is now in love with me."

Litho's laugh burst forth like steam from a badly overheated pot the size of a planet. "What a fate!"

Ciriana spoke. "So whom do you love, Sherlock?"

"Why Clio, of course. I never stopped."

Litho pondered. "So Clio isn't my enemy. You are. You are the one I must destroy."

Sherlock shrugged. "I really think you should give this up as a bad job, Litho. I don't want to hurt you. I just want to protect the woman I love."

"Well, *I* want to hurt *you!*" Litho stood tall. A giant boulder appeared in his hands. He hurled it down on Sherlock. Ciriana screamed. So did Clio. Sherlock didn't move.

The boulder exploded. So did Litho, because it was of his substance. Fine sand flew out, forming a dense cloud. But it didn't hurt them. When it cleared, the three of them stood upon the cracked flat surface of Plane World.

"Now I think we can go back," Sherlock said. He spread his arms to take in Clio and Ciriana.

Stunned by the battle and the revelations, Clio agreed.

18
GARDEN

They returned to their physical bodies in Princess Ida's study. Ciriana had reverted to age five. "Mice!" she swore. "I wanted to stay grown-up. I knew so much more then."

"Give it time," Clio said. "Childhood is precious."

Ciriana clearly wasn't convinced, but did not argue.

"Did you accomplish what you went for?" Ida inquired.

"We followed the blue arrow, and learned that Sherlock is the Magician of Reversal," Clio said.

"That's amazing! But he does have the aura now. I had understood he worked with reverse wood."

Aura? It seemed that one person of that level could recognize another. Princess Ida was the Sorceress of the Idea; they had seen only a fraction of her enormous range. That explained why Morgan and Litho had recognized him, and perhaps others too.

"I do," Sherlock said. "But it's not limited to that."

"He reversed the spaniel," Ciriana said. "He made Sorceress Morgan love him instead of him loving her, so he still loves Clio."

That was rather more than Clio would have preferred to share at this time, but she bore with it. "Spancel, dear."

"I had not known of that Sorceress," Ida said.

"She's from Mudania," Ciriana said eagerly. "She can't go to Xanth, but she wants to."

"Mundania," Ida agreed, gently correcting the child's pronunciation as Clio had. "That would explain it." She looked at Sherlock. "When did you conclude you were a Magician?"

"When I had to save Clio. The Sorceress tricked me into leaping through the spancel, and I knew I couldn't afford to be bound to her, so I reversed it. Then I realized I probably couldn't have reversed a Sorceress unless I was a Magician."

"That's not necessarily the case, but is a good general guide," Ida said. "Forgive me for my ignorance, but I don't quite understand how the things you have done relate to reversal. For example, you were conjuring wood chips."

"I do have power over reverse wood," Sherlock said. "That fooled me for some time. I thought conjuration was just part of that. But later I was able to summon other things, and realized that I had not properly understood my developing talent. What I am doing is reversals of place: an object must be either here or there, so I change it from there to here."

Clio was amazed. That was an aspect of reversal she had never thought of. "What of shaping wood?"

"I reverse its nature from rigid to malleable, or if you prefer, hard to soft. But I have to be in contact with it; the moment it leaves my hand, it reverts to its natural condition. The same is true for wood I reverse from normal to reverse wood; it tends to revert when I am no longer in contact with it."

"But the chip you gave Ciriana—that continued to work."

"I thought it did, at first. But I was actually reversing her myself, and when she was out of my range, her curse reappeared."

"I have to stay close to you, Daddy," the child said, satisfied.

Clio kept her face straight. There was another awkward detail: Ciriana considered Sherlock to be her father! Their banter on Ptero had been the easy familiarity of father and grown daughter, rather than any seductive ploy. How would they ever place the child now?

"And the animation of golems?" Ida asked.

"I reversed them from inanimate to animate."

Ida frowned. "And can you similarly render an animate person inanimate? That is to say, can you kill by your touch?"

"Oh, I would never do that!"

But he *could,* Clio saw. This was frightening.

"How about Litho? That was a lesser Demon, equivalent to a Magician."

"I reversed him from solid to fragmented, when he touched me."

"The talent of reversing the characteristics of demons," Ida said. "A remarkable aspect."

"You knew you could do this?" Clio asked.

"I thought I might. I couldn't think of any other way to stop him."

"You weren't sure?"

"I wasn't sure," Sherlock agreed. "But the fragmentation of his hand had worked."

He had stood there unflinching as the monster's boulder crashed down on his head. Was there a better example of raw courage?

"You are certainly a Magician," Princess Ida said.

"Well, I wasn't, until I had to be. When I tried to mold things that weren't reverse wood, early on, I couldn't. My power had not developed enough, then."

"Can you reverse yourself?"

"I doubt it. I think I will have to remain a middle-aged, homely, black man."

"A decent man."

Sherlock shrugged.

"And you reversed the spancel?" Ida asked. "That would be the soul-spancel; what of the physical one?"

Clio dug it out of her physical pocket. "I don't know."

"If that now makes the one who wields it fall in love with the intended victim, it is dangerous to use."

"It certainly is," Clio agreed. "I'll throw it away."

"That would leave it as a danger for anyone who found it. Better to put it away safely."

"I can simply reverse it again," Sherlock said. "Hold it out."

"I don't want to touch it when you change it," Clio said nervously. She set it on the couch she had risen from.

Sherlock touched it. The ribbon of skin twisted, writhed, then expanded into—a naked man.

Clio clapped her hands over Ciriana's eyes before she could freak out. "What is this?"

The man looked at her. "Who are you?"

"I am Clio. Who are you?"

"Stu the stonelayer." He looked around. "This isn't where I was last night. Where's Morgan?"

Clio had a sudden ugly notion. "What was the nature of your business with her?"

"She was going to take me into her bed. The last thing I remember was undressing and walking toward her. She was the sexiest creature I ever did see! Now suddenly I'm here. What happened?"

"Look at your body," Clio said. "There's a mirror on the wall. Check your arms and legs."

Stu did. "I've been flayed!" he exclaimed. "No wonder it smarts."

"A strip of flesh was taken from around your body," Clio said. "Morgan must have drugged you and cut it out while you were unconscious." Actually Morgan had spoken of a man screaming, so it could have been much worse, but he didn't remember that. That was surely just as well.

"Why that bleeping bleep! I should have known she didn't want me for my love!"

"In a manner of speaking. This is some time later, in a different land. You should like it, once you get used to it."

"Well, I'll find out." The man barged through the door and out into the hall. There were assorted eeeks marking his progress through the castle and out.

"The rest of the man the spancel came from," Princess Ida said. "You reversed the dead strip of flesh into the live man."

"Who has probably been dead for over ten centuries," Sherlock said. "He's better off now. Maybe he'll encounter some nymphs. At least the spancel won't be a danger anymore."

Clio agreed. But this was yet another demonstration of Sherlock's power that unsettled her.

They left the castle. The three little Princesses were not in evidence, and Clio was just as glad. She was still assimilating revelations.

A swirl of smoke formed. "So you are astern," it said.

"We are what?" Clio asked before she thought.

"Behind, tardy, posterior, ebb, rear—"

"Back?"

"Whatever," the cloud agreed crossly.

"Hello, Metria. Yes, we are back from Ptero and points beyond."

The demoness formed, every luscious portion overlapping the next. "Then you haven't heard the latest gossip, have you! The Good Magician lost his Book of Answers."

Clio was amazed. "He what?"

"Mislaid, confused, abandoned—hey, I had the right word."

"I mean, how could that happen? He never lets that tome leave his office."

"No one knows. He went to pore over it this morning, as usual, and it wasn't there. In its place was a really raw maple syrup—"

Sherlock extended a finger and touched her.

"A really sappy love story," Metria concluded. Then she looked surprised. "How did I get the right word so fast?"

"Daddy reversed you," Ciriana said.

The demoness rotated to face Sherlock, her clothing shrinking dangerously. But he touched her again, and her clothing expanded to cover all of her more than adequately; she looked like a matron. "Straw!"

She was back to the wrong word. It seemed that only one reversal could occur at a time. "Hey?" Ciriana offered.

"Whatever," the demoness agreed crossly.

"He reversed your outfit," Clio said. "So you wouldn't show Too Much and possibly even flash him with your panties."

"He's dangerous." Metria popped off elsewhere.

"She's fun," Ciriana said.

Clio looked at her wrist. The compass was back, pointing south. The red time hand was well away from the mark. "I think we have a long walk coming up."

"Perhaps I can ameliorate that with a spot reversal," Sherlock said. He reached out to take the child's hand, and Clio's.

"I don't understand—"

Then they stood before Mount Parnassus. "Daddy switched us from Here to There," Ciriana said. "Ooo! Look at the garden!"

Indeed, in the foreground was a lovely garden, on the north slope of the mountain. Clio had been aware of it, over the decades, but never actually visited it. Now it seemed a visit was in order, because the blue arrow pointed into it.

Before they could enter it, a man emerged from a little garden house. "A greeting, Muse," he said. "I am Emell, the guardian of the Garden of Events. I am honored by your visit."

"I don't believe we've met," Clio said, taken aback. For the man had bare shoulders, with markings on his skin. There were pictures of a little fairy on the right, and a tiny green dragon with red wings on the left. She had never before seen body decorations quite like this. How could Emell have been here all this time without her knowing?

"I shall be happy to give you my life history, Muse," the man said.

"That's not really necessary."

But he had already launched. "I'm from Mundania. I was once a fan of Xanth. I avidly read every book smuggled out of the land. They were wonderful."

"Really," Clio said, flattered.

"I even had a map. I hoped this would help me locate a gate or something so I could go there. So one day I simply put my dull Mundane life on hold and set out wearing just shorts, sneakers, a tank top, and a knapsack with a few provisions. My map looked just like Florida, so I figured that was the place to start."

"I'm not sure we need to know this much," Sherlock said.

"Yes we do," Clio said. She remained thrilled by the compliment to her volumes of Xanth history.

"At first my quest was uneventful. I walked through Mundane back-yards, across numerous roads and highways, through fields and forests, all coming to nothing but more Mundania. Days passed, even weeks. I got discouraged: did Xanth really exist? I was trying to make the decision to give up, which I really hated to do. I was taking one more dispirited look at the map, when I heard some rustling in the bushes to my side. I looked—and thought I saw a small naked girl's backside rounding another bush, and then a little man with goat-like legs chasing after her. A nymph and faun! I hardly believed my eyes, but I didn't hesitate; I ran after them. I wasn't paying any attention to where I was going; I just wanted to catch up, and maybe find my way into Xanth. I didn't see the stump ahead of me, and I tripped over it. I fell so quickly I didn't have time to catch my balance, and I bashed my head into a rock. Hurt and dazed, I lifted my head—and looked straight into a hypnogourd."

"This is mischief," Sherlock said.

"It sure was. I was helpless, caught in that haunted house, you know. Actually when I got into it I found a roomful of girls, and every time they flashed their panties I freaked out and had to start over. It was a lot of fun, but meanwhile my body was stuck outside, slowly withering away. But I had friends. My two tattoos, Fern and Dagger, were knocked off my shoulders." Emell glanced fondly at his shoulders, where the little fairy and dragon were. "They gathered their wits, which had been scattered with the impact, and flew off to try to find help. They found the keeper of this garden. 'Please help us,' Fern beseeched him. 'We'll do anything.' Well, the gardener was sort of a lout, but she was too small to do what he might want. So he made them a deal: he'd get me out of the gourd if I'd take over his job guarding the garden, so he could go enjoy himself elsewhere. They had no choice, so they agreed. He came and put his finger between my eye and the gourd's peephole, bringing me out of it. If Fern and Dagger had known it was that easy, they would have blocked it themselves. But they hadn't known, so I was committed. And here I have been, ever since, wearing my loyal friends. Actually it's not a bad deal; it is Xanth, where pies grow on trees, and sometimes one of those sexy maenads comes around pretending she's a regular girl. They get bored sometimes, you know. I play bondage with them, tying them up for an hour or so so they can't hurt me, and we have a really good time."

"A good time with maenads?" Clio asked. "But their passion is blood."

"Not entirely. They are turned on by threats to themselves as well as threats to others; that's why they get along so well with the Python. I threaten them with cellulight until they scream for mercy."

"With what?" Sherlock asked.

"Cellulight. It's a plant that grows near the Faun & Nymph Retreat. I imported some for my garden. It lights up near the river, and it gets on the nymphs, making them fat. They hate that. It turns out that the maenads are like nymphs in that respect. They'll do anything to avoid a touch of cellulight. 'Anything?' I demand in a evil voice, and I force them to pretend they like kissing and stork summoning. They say I torture them almost as bad as the Python does. I take that as a rare compliment. So it's okay, and I take good care of the garden."

Emell paused, his narration completed. "Now what can I do for you?"

"We need to enter this garden," Clio said.

"That's okay, as long as you don't do any harm. I can't let you hurt anything."

"We won't," Clio promised, hoping it was true.

"What section do you want?"

Clio answered based more on hope than expectation. "The currant section."

"Ah, yes, that's a good one. This way."

So the Currant was here! Her quest was almost done—maybe. If so, it was ironic that it was so close to her home all the time. She could have gone right to it, had she known.

Emell showed them into the garden. It was far more capacious than Clio had supposed. In fact a river ran through it. "What river is this?"

"The Currant River. It flows from OgreChobee to the Brain Coral, and thence down to the Currant Sea."

"I do not know of this sea."

"It is deep below ground, in a vault. It is half filled with contemporary coins."

"Currency," Sherlock murmured appreciatively.

"I thought we were out of the comic strip."

"Comic strip," Ciriana said. "Is Annie Mae here?"

Sigh. She shouldn't have mentioned it. "No, dear."

The blue arrow pointed along the river, so they followed it. Here there were currant berries. Clio stopped to pick one, and got a mild shock. She should have known.

"We have some really good currants," Emell said. "See those clusters? Those are highly charged berry bombs. Throw a cluster at something and the berries all explode."

"Goody!" Ciriana said. "I had a friend named Cherrie who could conjure cherries and make plosive pies."

"Explosive," Clio said. She made a mental note to keep the child well away from cherry bombs and pineapples.

"The water here is very good," Emell said. "It's sham pain. That's like boot rear, only more potent. When you drink it, it gives you an imaginary headache and brief loss of memory."

"I want some!" Ciriana said.

"Not at your age," Clio said firmly.

"Awww."

"And here is the powerhouse," Emell said. "Where electric E's and L's are stored. Also M's, or as I prefer to call them, Ems. Em Motive, Em Phasis, Em Pathic—many varieties. You can also see the lightbulbs growing here. They like the currants."

"We have encountered bright bulbs," Clio said a bit tersely.

"They glow when sprinkled," he continued blithely. "Their perfume makes folk light-headed. Related bulbs are incande-scent and flora-scent."

"Thank you for that information." Clio ungritted her teeth and followed the blue arrow. It led her to a rather anemic section of the garden. A single straggly plant grew there.

"That currant hasn't prospered," Emell said. "I have tried all manner of fertilizers, but it just doesn't respond. I wish I knew what it needs."

Sherlock glanced at Clio. "I wonder."

Could it be? She dug in her pockets for the odd things she had been collecting. A piece of stinky fruit. A fragment of a crushed hypno-gourd. A bit of volcanic tuff. A pebble from Demon Litho. She set them down around the languishing plant.

It perked up. She dipped some water from the river and poured it carefully on the nearby ground. The liquid crackled as it sank in, emitting a few little sparks. The plant improved further. In fact it stood tall and flowered, then produced a single large berry.

The blue arrow pointed to the berry. This was the Currant.

She picked the red berry and put it in her pocket. "Thank you," she said to Emell.

"Welcome. I'm glad to see that straggling plant recover. Now it will produce more berries."

But not like this one, she suspected.

They left the garden. "I think I need to take the Currant to my history volume," she said. "This may finally signal the end of my quest." She hesitated. "Do you wish to come along?"

"Sure," Ciriana said.

"We'll see the mission through to the end," Sherlock said.

"We have to," Drew said. "We haven't saved your life yet."

Clio was gratified. "This way. I know a good path up the mountain."

The dragons tried to fly ahead, but both of them dropped to the ground. "Something's wrong!" Drusie cried.

"Oh, I forgot," Clio said. "The Simurgh lives here, the oldest and wisest bird in the universe. She enforces a no-fly zone around Mount Parnassus. No fly is affected, but nothing bigger than an insect can fly. I'm sorry."

"We'll just have to make the best of it," Drew said bravely, accepting Clio's assistance to reach her pocket, while Sherlock picked Drusie up similarly.

She led the way. Several maenads spied them and charged in, but desisted when they recognized Clio. Several did eye Sherlock before going, however. That reminded Clio uncomfortably of what Emell had said about liaisons with them. It seemed the wild women sometimes had more on their minds than sheer mayhem. They could be extremely fetching, with their phenomenal bare curves, if a person liked that type. Men generally did; it was why the maenads were able to lure unwary men to their destruction. Did they really consider stork summoning to be torture, or were they just saying that to preserve their image?

Then the giant Python slithered in, and departed similarly. Clio needed no additional protection here on Mount Parnassus; it was her home. But this time she noticed something disquieting: the Python had eyed her in much the manner the maenads had eyed Sherlock. What could that possibly mean?

They came to her suite halfway up the south peak. Ciriana was delighted; she was promptly bouncing on the bed. Sherlock was more restrained, but he was clearly intrigued. Drew and Drusie scrambled around exploring it.

Clio went to her desk and brought out the *Currant Events* volume. She opened it. And sighed.

The pages remained obscure.

"What do you see?" she asked, showing it to Sherlock.

He squinted at the text. "There seems to be print there, but I can't quite make it out."

"That's my problem. Some enchantment obscured the text of a volume I have obviously already written, so that it can't be read. The Currant was supposed to fix it."

"I think you have to actually use the Currant," Sherlock said. "Merely possessing it isn't enough."

"How do I do that?"

"My best guess is to squeeze it into juice, and use that on the pages."

Clio got a bowl, then took the Currant in both hands and squeezed. It was huge and soft, and quickly squished into juice. Soon she had a fair quantity.

She fetched a small brush and dipped it in the juice. She painted it on part of the obscure text of a page. It made a red smear, but did not clarify the words. So much for that.

Sherlock spread his hands. "I suppose I could try reversing it, but I fear that would merely ruin it for its intended purpose. I am becoming wary of my own advice."

Ciriana tired of exploring the premises with the dragons and came up. "Juice!" she exclaimed. "I want some!"

Clio shrugged and fetched a cup. She poured a little red juice from the bowl, not wanting to risk all of it. "This may be tart," she said.

The girl took the cup and gulped the juice down. She made a face. "Not sweet enough." She glanced at the tome. "What are those words?"

"There are no words," Clio said. "It's just a blur."

"No blur. I can't read them, but those are words."

"She drank the juice," Sherlock said. "She sees the words."

"I'm supposed to drink it!" Clio said, a bulb flashing. She lifted the bowl and sipped from its edge.

The text clarified. She read the words at the top of the last page. "Zyzzyva—Freshly zombied female fighter in very good condition." She looked up, puzzled. "I'm sure I wasn't writing about her in this volume."

"May I have a sip of that juice?" Sherlock asked.

She handed him the bowl. He sipped, then looked at the text. "That's the Good Magician's lost Book of Answers!"

She looked again. So it was: Humfrey's monstrous compendium of magical information, that he had spent a century or so writing, and now used to answer querents' questions. She should have noticed before that this book was much larger than her own. "How did that come to be here?"

"Some rogue demon must have played a prank and switched it with your history volume."

"I'm sure that wasn't the case when I was here before."

"It must have happened while you were out. The prankster figured no one would notice."

"And no one did," she agreed, disgruntled. "What am I to do with this?"

"If I am correct, and the volumes have merely been exchanged, I should be able to reverse that exchange. Let me see." He touched the volume.

It changed. She recognized her familiar text. "That's mine!"

"The real sappy romance?" Ciriana asked.

She saw Sherlock stifling a smile. Just as well. "The Demoness Metria has her own way of seeing things." She turned to the first page. "Chapter 1: Clio. Clio was tidying up her office, as she did every cen-

tury or so even if it didn't really need it." She looked up. "This is definitely it. This is my adventure, my current events."

"Currant events," Sherlock agreed.

She turned to the last page, but it was blank. The next to last page
ended at " 'Let me see.' He touched the volume." "It covers my life up
to a few minutes ago," she said. "But it's unfinished."

"As is your life," he agreed. He looked at the last page. "I see it
does have a message: 'Loose ends not tied.' That seems to cover the
situation."

"But I made it safely back here, and now I can read the volume, not
that I need to," she said. "So my adventure in Xanth is done, fortunately."

"What of the child?"

Clio put her arm around Ciriana. "She can stay here. I like her."

"Will she remain five forever? If so, the Acquaintance Ship would
have sufficed."

"She can wait until she grows up before eating of the Tree of Life.
Then she can remain her maidenly age indefinitely."

"And the dragons?"

"We don't want to stay here," Drew said, surprising them both.
"We're dragons; we need to be out and around, exploring, hunting prey,
toasting the toes of bad folk."

"And we need to fly," Drusie said.

"You are certainly free to go," Clio said, disappointed. "Though I
must say I have enjoyed your company."

"But have you saved her life yet?" Sherlock asked.

"No, and that bugs us," Drew said.

"So we'll have to stick around a little longer," Drusie said.

"But she faces no dangers, here in her home," Sherlock said.

"And that really bugs us," Drew said. "We don't see any chance,
here in this safe place."

"There's really no need," Clio said. "You have been extremely helpful throughout, and have surely earned your freedom."

"It's not the same," Drusie said morosely.

"And it would seem you don't need me further, either," Sherlock said.

"But I thought you were going to stay!" Clio protested. "I thought we had an understanding. That we could be together. That we could marry."

"I believe we do. Can you say the words?"

She opened her mouth—and the words did not come out. "Oh, Sherlock, you're worthy! You're a Magician, and you've done so much for me, and I really would like to have your company. It gets so dull here! But I can't quite say the words."

He nodded soberly. "That's not the basis for marriage. Then I think the kindest thing to do is to consider the adventure concluded. I will go my way. I do thank you for enabling me to discover my full powers."

"Please, Sherlock! Don't leave me! Give me more time. I do want to say the words. I just can't say them insincerely. Maybe in time I'll be able to."

He considered. "I do love you, and do not wish to hurt you. If my absence would cause you distress, I will remain here. But for the moment I will take a walk around the premises."

"As you wish," she agreed, feeling thoroughly clumsy. What was the matter with her? He was such a decent man, and a phenomenal Magician. Any of her sisters would have been glad to marry him.

Sherlock and Drusie went to the door. "Can I come too?" Ciriana asked, running to join him.

"Welcome." He took her hand.

Clio was alone with Drew. "I'm not sure it's my life that needs saving," she said. "I've got a problem, and I don't know what it is."

"You mean if we could solve your problem, it would be like saving your life?"

She smiled. "Yes." But she knew there was nothing the dragons could do. Apparently she had lived alone so long she had lost the ability to love. That was her tragedy.

Drusie appeared, flying in through the window. Drew flew up to meet her, then on out.

"Sherlock has reconsidered," Drusie said. "He wants you to marry him."

Clio was thrilled. "Then we'll do it! I'm so glad."

There was a scream. Clio launched herself out of the suite, horrified by what she might find. It was Ciriana, standing on a knoll, her little hands covering her face. There was no sign of Sherlock. "What happened?" Clio demanded.

"The big snake!" the child cried. "Suddenly it was there. One gulp!"

The Python had ambushed Sherlock! It had gotten him before he could invoke his magic. Now Clio screamed. She ran down the slope, too horrified to think straight. "Sherlock! Sherlock! I love you! I love you! Come back to me!"

The scene changed. There were Sherlock and Ciriana, walking along the path as if nothing had happened. "You said it!" Sherlock exclaimed.

Clio stopped running. "Where's the Python?" she asked stupidly.

"No Python here," Sherlock said.

She must have wound back the scene and saved him, though she hadn't been conscious of that. It hardly mattered. "Yes, I said it. I love you! When I thought you were dead—"

A calculating look crossed his face. "Drew! Drusie!" he said. "Is this your doing?"

The two dragons appeared in the pockets, where they had always been. "Yes," Drew said. "We did it."

"You told me Clio had said the words, and Drusie told Clio I was ready to marry her," Sherlock said. "But what made her scream?"

"We made a scene," Drew said. "So she would think you had died."

"You tricked us!" Clio said indignantly. Now she realized that she should have caught on when she saw them flying: that had to be illusion, not reality, here in the no-fly zone.

"We made you say the words," Drusie said. "So you could marry Sherlock and adopt Ciriana and live happily ever after, and our job would be done."

There was a pause. Then Sherlock nodded. "They did do that. Can you say them now that you know I'm not dead?"

The words came out with no hesitation. "I love you."

He took her in his arms and kissed her. "Then I will marry you, and we'll adopt Ciriana as our daughter."

"Goody!" the child exclaimed, clapping her hands ineffectively. "At last! Now I have a mommy as well as a daddy."

"Our work here is done," Drew said.

"But we don't need to depart if we don't want to," Drusie said.

"But we can't fly here."

"That's right. But we don't really need to if we stay in pockets. Let's remain with these nice people for a while."

They returned to the suite. Clio looked at the end of the volume. "And they lived happily ever after," she read.

Clio thought about it, vaguely unsatisfied. She glanced at her wrist, and saw the compass still there, the blue arrow meandering aimlessly. What was she missing?

She remembered something: the Good Magician had given her the compass, which had sent her on a wild and sometimes dangerous tour of Xanth. He had been evasive about his reason for subjecting her to the indignity of the Challenges, and requiring a Service of her for her Answer. Despite his well-earned reputation for grumpiness, he was not a mean-spirited man, and he did not forget his friends. So why had he done it? He never did anything without reason.

She believed she knew the answer: there was a Demon bet relating to her participation. Probably something like whether she would follow the blue arrow to the end no matter how crazy the route got, or quit in disgust along the way, or get herself killed. That bet had surely been decided by now. The stakes could be as big as worlds; the Demons had no humane limits. Magician Humfrey had had to go along with it, lest calamity befall Xanth. Hence his mysterious behavior.

Demons, she thought. *I need the information for my record. Please, if you care to tell: who won?*

I did, the Demoness Venus replied.

What were the stakes?

One kiss—that I don't have to give.

Clio had gone through all that—for one kiss. So much for worlds at stake! Venus had bet on the woman, and won. *Thank you, Demoness.*

The compass faded out. Its mission was done at last.

Clio took firm hold of the final page and ripped it out of the volume.

Sherlock, Ciriana, and the dragons stared.

"I thought we had an understanding," the little girl said tearfully. "You were going to be my mommy."

"I still am, for a while," Clio said. "Just not the way it is described."

"If you prefer not to marry—" Sherlock began.

"All of you have been catering to me," Clio said. "And I really appreciate it. You helped me get through my very own personal adventure. Now it's done, and you're willing to stay here with me on Mount Parnassus. But think about it: this is really a big garden, supervised by the Simurgh. There's no danger here, not for legitimate residents. Not even the prospect of aging and dying. There's no challenge. There's no flying, and I don't mean just with wings. Before long you'll all be desperate for anything to relieve your overwhelming boredom. You don't have histories to write. You'll be twiddling your thumbs. It will be death in life, eternally. As it was for me, before I went back out into Xanth."

They gazed at her, not arguing. What she said was true.

"And what about me?" she continued. "So now I'll have everything I had before, plus a husband, daughter, and maybe a nice dragon or two. And I'll be almost as bored as the rest of you. What kind of life is that?"

"We thought that was what you wanted," Sherlock said meekly.

"A really sappy romance," Ciriana agreed.

"So did I. But now that I actually face the prospect, I know better. I have had more than a century of this secure, detached, ultimately sterile life. I don't need another century of that scripted existence. When I went out into Xanth, my life resumed, and my curses. I lost my curves, I faced danger every day, and I knew that I was destined to die young. But at least I *lived*. And I found great friends, and a family. And I'll be **damned** if I'll destroy you by locking you into this living coffin." The suite shook with the force of her expletive, which had forced itself through without getting bleeped out despite the presence of the child. This particular child could handle it. "Had that been my object, we might as well have stayed aboard the Acquaintance Ship and let our souls be slowly leeched away."

They watched her, expressionless.

"So you won't be joining me here in the garden," she concluded. "I'll be joining you there in Xanth. I may not live long, but I'll be complete for the time I have left. I regret that I can't promise you a lifetime of me, but I'll give you everything I have in whatever time there is. When I'm gone, maybe Sherlock can reverse a maenad and make her the perfect companion. I hope that's a sufficient bargain. It's all I can offer."

Ciriana ran in and hugged her. Sherlock stepped forward and touched her. "You may have forgotten something."

"Whatever it is, you are welcome to it. There had to be some worthwhile point to this adventure. Not just a stupid Demon wager. You won't have to live for me anymore; I'm going to live for you. Isn't that what love is all about?"

Then she felt odd. Her body was changing. Oh, no! Was she dying already? That hardly seemed fair.

"You forgot my power," Sherlock said. "I can reverse curses too. I have reversed yours. You have your curves back, and you will face some special joy every day of your life, and you will not die young, you will live old. As long as you are with me. I can't guarantee the reversal beyond my immediate sphere of influence."

Clio looked at her body. Indeed, she had curves. She felt the relief of her curses, and knew it was true: he had reversed them all. Only a powerful Magician could do that—but of course, he was one. They would have a long time together, out in Xanth. Suddenly they had it all.

"I'll still have to keep up with my volumes of history," she said. "But I think I can make notes for them as we travel, and return here just briefly every so often to write them up."

"We can bear with brief visits here," Sherlock agreed. Then he kissed her. She floated, as it were.

Clio looked around. "But before we go—Ciriana—my daughter—"

"Oh, I know," the child said. "Come on, dragons. We have to leave them alone while they make with the mushy stuff. Let's go talk with the Simurgh about that no-fly zone."

When they were outside, Ciriana's surprised voice came back. "Look! Storks!" As if she didn't know what was alerting them.

Author's Note

T his is the first novel in the second Xanth magic trilogy,
which of course is three cubed. That is, the twenty-
eighth Xanth volume, as duly recorded by Clio, the
Muse of History. Whether Xanth will reach the fifty-fourth volume,
completing the trilogy, depends on the state of the market and whether
I live to age ninety-four without suffering more than the requisite brain
rot.

Two Xanth novels ago I intended to change from Windows to the
Linux operating system. I didn't make it then; despite what open source
fans may claim, it's not an easy change. But one Xanth novel ago I was
using it. For this one I changed again, to a more advanced Linux system
with parallel hard drives and the next generation of my StarOffice word
processor: OpenOffice. I like it very well, but it still was not easy. You
see, I'm an ornery independent nut—it's the way ogres are—and I
don't use the standard KWERTY keyboard, I use Dvorak. Most computer systems have it, and so does this one—but mine is the original,
not the flawed version the computer folk put on. So I need to change it
to mine, and therein lies the hassle. This system had the wrong Dvorak,
and resisted my modifications. So I started this novel on my old Linux
system and did the first five chapters. Then when I finally got the
keyboard right I changed to StarOffice on this new system, dubbed

MoNsTeR, and did chapter 6. Then I got OpenOffice and did chapters 7–18 in it. OpenOffice is nice; it is file oriented, has beautiful clear font display, and saves files to half the size of MS Word files, effectively doubling my storage space. So if you notice some change of type or quality at these points, that's why, though I suspect it's all in your marvelous imagination.

I try to discourage readers from sending in notions, but they persist, and I try to be selective and use only the best ideas and worst puns. There are about two hundred this time, but I'm really trying to stifle it down to fewer. The dreadful secret is that I have more than enough warped imagination of my own, and it would be easier to write my novels without any ideas from readers. But I don't want to get in any ruts, and figure reader input will help prevent that.

The sheer number of reader notions can be difficult to handle, but there are other problems. Critics claim that Xanth is nothing but egregious puns, but that's because they lack the wit to pick up on the subtler humor. Readers also send in characters, and story ideas. Some are really good, but I can't give all of them full play; there isn't room enough in the novel. So many get only peripheral mention, when they could be significant themes. I feel guilty about that. On occasion a reader is hurt because I haven't made larger use of a notion, or given a larger credit for it; I regret that, but my credits are already voluminous. I prefer that the notions be appreciated in the story, rather than contributed for the sake of credits. Some minor notions get significant play, because they happen to come in when there's room for them to grow. An example is Ciriana, suggested as the name for a child, that I merged with another suggestion; she might have appeared and gone, but remained to become a significant minor character. Was it the best name or the best talent? Not necessarily; she just happened to be in the right place. Some ideas morph when processed, becoming not exactly what the suggestors may have intended. Writing is a creative process, and a story does not necessarily play out as expected. I do the best I can, and hope for the best.

Some reader notions I reserved for future novels, because they fit there better. Several are for *Air Apparent,* and others are for *Stork*

Naked. Naturally the next one scheduled is neither, making the ideas wait a long time; it's *Pet Peeve,* about an irritable bird. There are whole pages of reader puns lying in ambush for that one; they have been festering for two or three novels while I try to get up the gumption to tackle them.

Sometimes there are significant stories behind minor characters. Here, from perhaps imperfect memory, is an example. A correspondent in Thailand told me how he taught a course there on motorcycling. One of his students was a woman in her late twenties, the single mother of two children, small and comely in the manner of women of that area, with black hair to her waist. She joined his class, and made mistakes at first, but persevered until she became his star pupil. But she wanted to get it perfect, and prevailed on him for a practice run just before the final examination. She rode out in traffic, and he followed at a reasonable distance behind, observing. She had it down just right; she handled her motorcycle well, obeyed the traffic rules, and rode in a safe manner. They stopped for a meal, then commenced the return cycle, she leading again. Then a truck barged out from a side road, ran her over, and rolled on without stopping. She was alive but fading, her legs crushed. She expressed her love for her children, and asked for a kiss, and died. I thought about that, and had to do something, though the woman had not been a reader of mine, and probably had never heard of Xanth. I decided to put her into Xanth. Thus came to be the incidental character Noi. Perhaps it's a meaningless gesture. We can rail at the unfairness of fate, when innocent folk die while guilty ones go unpunished, but there's not a lot we can do about it. Except remember, in our fashion. This was my fashion.

Another example is Dragon World. I participated in the story line and geographic details of an online role-playing game, *Dragon Empires.* Some of you may have played it. The first thing I did was work out the dragons—only to learn that those had already been done, and mine weren't needed. So I put them into this novel instead, as you have seen here. So you might say that these dragons migrated from the game to Xanth. I hope they weren't disappointed in the new locale.

My time is always crowded. I'm a workaholic, and there are more things remaining to do than I'm likely to have time for in this life. I'm a Senior Citizen now, and writers my age are booting the KICK ME bucket in the Void with increasing abandon. So I am conscious of priorities; what gets postponed to next decade may not be accomplished. Nevertheless I maintain a healthy correspondence with my readers, who are generally worthy folk. It is currently running a generous hundred paper letters a month, and about four hundred E-mails, and sometimes a given correspondent shifts from one to the other. I refer to a physical address as a snaddy: snail addy. It sounds vaguely obscene, especially when directed at a member of the female persuasion: "Show me your snaddy." But E-mail really is easier, faster, and cheaper. Those who just have to contact me can find me at www.hipiers.com; my E-mail address is there along with my ornery bimonthly column, Xanth database, and ongoing survey of Internet publishers maintained for aspiring writers.

Now for the credits, presented in the approximate order of appearance of the first one a given reader suggested. Some names are partial because that's all that was provided in the E-mails. Clio's blank volume—Chuck Scholz, whose idea got somewhat garbled by the time I completed the novel. Running water, fig mints—Gregory Danner. Cayla—Cayla Tamburello. Baseball diamond—get out—Ray. Talent of knitting anything—Kelly Humphrey. Harold the Handyman—Ori Harish. W who doubles you—Gary Bushman. Gravis, increasing or decreasing gravity—Timothy Bruening. Rorrim—Rhonda Singer, who also wrote the letters in *Up in a Heaval.* How Cynthia Centaur learned lightening—CoolMommyChick. Morphing—Chris Ireland. Bortre the Intimidator—Ulman Smiy. Toney Harper—Tony Harper. Traveler from Xanth's future—Brendan Moore. Nail biting, finger painting, Pebbl Roc, hyperlink—Andrew Hibschman. The agony of D. Feat, Salt Peter, Afro Disiac, Anomie uses reverse wood to get good ideas, Plane World—Gary Henderson. Attention span—Wayne Moore. Psi-clone—William Bradley. Puncheon cask for unruly puns—David Kaplan. Centaur of attention—Richard Van Fossan. Demons are a girl's best friend—Richard Bradley. Gallop poll—Randy Schultz. Eileen—

Mike Mazureke. Squash blossoms—Carole Farrell. Prof. Anity—
Everett Tourjee. Field day, field trip—Britton Centamore. Poop
deck—S. M. Arney. Lemon aid, Mount Pin-a-Fore, Com Pewter's
screen freezes, sewer side—Becky. Cuticle—Michelle Travis. Kwew-
tickle—Natasha Rio. Gulli Bull, bear icade, impro vise—Valli Pata-
balla and Sammy Katta. Gross-ery store—Lev Asimow. Co-bra,
may-pull tree, seed-her tree, Ana Conda—Ray. Dill pickles people—
Robin Dill. Com-post— Michael McCarthy. Search engine—Toby
Hudon. Underpants— Brian Turner. Poe tree—Jessica Barr. Boxing
box—Jared Cole. Sneeze cake—Donna Schutza. Tree frog—Alex
Bowler. Talent of oversight—Deirdre Cooney. Talent of shifting
blame or credit—Michele Rocco. Car-burr-ator—Jake Shearer.
Harang-u-tan—Kyle Kelley. Brown E—Becky and Randi. Retro
specs, two tors, tor mentors, Thesis—Red Plana. Peep show— Robert
Andrews. Couch potato, doorbell—Tanya. Coughee beans—Allison
Moore. Credit onion—Bill Sellers. Loyal tree, royal tree—Jamie Gor-
don. Lon Leigh, Luv Leigh, Re Joyce—Rebekah Joyce Vidal.
Inertia—Jesse Brown. Stephanie—Charlie Mizer. Angel Horse—
Krystle Lawrence. Have a Black Wave Magician—Jeffrey Gordon.
Getaway Golem—Oliver Sudden. Dragondrop—Carol Grubaugh.
Bluebonnet plague—Roger Vazquez. Arch enemy—Diana Gibson.
Bay-o-nets, Bash-ful Ogre, Black Mail, Ann Gina, pun-kin bread, pun-
kin seeds, A's ancestors of B's—Ginger and Richard Kern. The deaf
community—Phil Giles. Steel toad boots—Stuart Funay. D. Zaster—
Mordechai. D. Stroy, D. Viate, D. Mise, D. Mean, twins who manipu-
late bodies or minds—Ray Fleming. D. Lirious—Alexandra Fu. Demon
Waves—Denise Harvey. Nissa Elf—Nissa McCormack. Luna-tick—
Stephen Brisbois. Ice fishing—Tiffany Sille. Iri Sistible—Bill Fitzger-
ald. Mermaids in healing spring—Black Wolph.

Meggie the nymph of a maple tree, Emell, Fern, Dagger—Matthew
Linde. Boarding school—SPC Robert Snow. Bored board—Ann
Marie. Motherboard, fatherboard—James Newman. Princess draws a
blank—Bryan Weber. Elderly person enters Xanth, Russian three-
headed dragon, Russian immigrant—Eugine Lev. Noi, girl with duran
fruit, Fanta Sea exists in Mundania (actually Thailand, near Phu Ket)—

Somchai Chantananad. Tie Land and related puns—George Sanders. Dream man—Jon Zoric. Things break out of the gourd—Katdragon. Panthers and panthis—Kimo. Mare Juana—Stephen English. Wool-gathering—Misty Zaebst. Com Panion—Morrigan, who is half Mundane, half succubus. Anna Sthesia, Auntie Septic—Becky Blair. Yeta Mermaid—Helen Grubb. Mate-Rix—Jason Merchant. Auntie Biotic—Celeste Gregory. Chele Centaur—Chele Furley. Danielle Girl/Unicorn—Danielle von Krebs-Cintorino. Running shoes—Padraig Newman. Arnolde Centaur's aisle explained—Henry Wyckoff. Demon Earth makes deal with David—Michael J. Rohrmeier, Daniel Goldstein. Data Base, clever bug—Jason Jack. Panty hoes—Anna Bryant. Opaque Ogre—Jae de Bird. Parsley, Sage, Rosemary, Thyme—Lori Marateck. Feelup, talent of opposite future, Currant Sea—Kenneth Adams. Digit Alice—Bill Fuller. Demon Construction puns—Janet Yuill. Talent of seeing ourselves as others see us—Crystal Frederickson. Little girl's immunity to Adult Conspiracy—Penny McKeever. Ciriana (the name)—William Clocksin. Unlimited variants for Surprise—Azag. Talent of always being in the way—Kat Eller. Talent of never getting in the way, first-aid kit—Kat Eller, Kevin Eller, Joe Nadeau. Mister E, Miss Elem N. Tery—Meg A. Brinkley. Darron, endowing inanimate objects—Darron Huskey. Tuning fork, Bill, discord-ants—Lahoma Lemanski. Car-nation, the G's—Donald A. Probst.

Maiden Taiwan's sisters China, Japan, Mexico—Cathy Cook. Cricket, music by rubbing hands—Bryan Manning. Randi, girl instead of boy—Randi C. Morris. Tran, Tran's sister, Tran's parent, Tran's Lou Cent—Ray Fleming. Wynde Tchill—Daria Middlebrook. Embri-Anna—Marya Miller. Talent of restoring zombies, Zaven—Karen Rucker, Kia Grooms. Magician in Brain Coral's pool for Princess Ida—Michael J. Rohrmeier. Princess Ida's children will have moons—Michele Rocco. Annie Mae—Herbert Lee. Ringing bell bottom trousers—Ben Lofgren. Armored Dillo, rumpled steel skin—David Seltzer. School for lightbulbs—Marcus Mebes. Dye-it—Lindsay Lovstrom. Talent of age not changing geographically on Ptero—Andrew Hibschman. Step ladder—Spencer Pilz. Talent of making rain—Kia Grooms. Borealis as the man for Aurora—Matthew Boste-

laar. Man from green goo world—Amie Adkins. Satori girl-cat—
Elizabeth Grace Ogletree. Demon Litho, origin of the voles—Jim
Adolf. Talent of reversing the characteristics of demons—Caleb. Book
of Answers lost—Mike Waters. Currant River, currant berries, sham
pain, powerhouse with electric E's and L's, lightbulb puns—Nancy Hill.
Ems—Laura E. Bray. Berry bombs—G & R Kern. Cherrie's explosive
pies—Robin Dill. Cellulight—Courtney.

And that's it, for this time. More is in the pipeline. That's not a
promise, it's a threat.